Shanghai Squeeze

Shanghai Squeeze

A *Nippon Noir* novel

Brian Moeran

Sarsen Press
WINCHESTER

First published in Great Britain in 2025 by the Sarsen Press,
22 Hyde Street, Winchester, Hampshire SO23 7DR, UK

ISBN 978-1-916722-28-6

Let China sleep, for when she wakens,
the world will tremble.

Napoleon Bonaparte

Secrets are difficult to keep in China.
There are too many ears and too many tongues.

Percy Finch

Prologue

18 September 1931

It was only a flash and a thwomp in the night, but it was the beginning of what came to be called the Second World War.

The South Manchurian Railway train was chugging along steadily towards Peking. It was a Japanese train, which meant that I was travelling in an American-style Pullman coach that was clean and comfortable. Staff were plentiful, courteous and efficient, as one had come to expect of the Japanese. The food was more than palatable and the windows of the dining car had been screened to prevent flies, in itself enough to advise passengers that they weren't travelling 'Chinese'.

Feeling in need of some fresh air before turning in, I stuck my head out of the window of my first class compartment, ready to brave the tiny flecks of grit and coal flying from the smokestack of the engine just ahead. Not that I expected to see very much in the dark. That was the nature of night, even one with a bit of a moon. A long straight road, flanked by poplars and a hovel or two, ran parallel to the railway line. In the distance, what seemed like a silvery-grey expanse of water. At the bottom of a slight embankment, the lights from the passing train illuminated the very occasional abandoned vehicle stuck in one of the muddy ruts ploughed up by Chinese ox-carts. If the Japanese really did intend to make use of their well-made roads to invade Manchuria, they could do worse than start by fitting every ox-cart in the province with rubber wheels.

The Harbin-Mukden express began to slow down. Surely we weren't already approaching our destination? I looked at my watch. Ten twenty. No, not yet. A signal, perhaps. I'd been told at Harbin that my carriage was routed directly to the capital and that there'd be no need to change trains. But who knew? The Chinese always had ways of upsetting well-laid Japanese plans. The mice and men syndrome. I'd find out in due course.

It was at this point that there was a flash in the night a few hundred yards ahead and the unmistakable sound of exploding dynamite.

It was almost as if the engine driver knew what was coming. There was a screech of iron on iron and a sudden jolt of carriages as he applied the locomotive's brakes with admirable rapidity. The train then rolled slowly, cautiously forward. There was a large newly-formed crater in the mud-rutted road, extending towards the embankment. Beside it a soldier was waving the train past with a green flag. Half a dozen others were moving hurriedly away towards an armoured vehicle parked in the scrub. Their uniforms were Japanese.

It wasn't until I reached Shanghai four days later that I learned that I had witnessed the Japanese Kwantung Army's excuse to invade Manchuria. That was the trouble with flags these days. Even green ones. They tended to be false.

1.

An early-November evening in Shanghai, a few weeks after I'd arrived in the Paris of the East, the Playground of Asia, the Whore of the Orient, or whatever other sobriquet was being touted around that particular evening. The sun was at least a half dozen degrees over the yardarm. Time for all good men to come to the aid of a party.

A good idea in principle. The trouble was I had only one companion to party with—a rather self-important young customs officer called Freddy Fox. Flap Ears Freddy. Hardly the kind of man to light up a festive gathering.

Anyway, there we were, sitting at a table by the window of a Russian bar on rue de la Soeur-Allegré—better known as the Street of Happy Sisters, because of the prostitutes cruising there at night. Flap Ears was nursing a Manchurian beer. His fingers, I noticed, were like a pianist's, long and slender. They were the only refined thing about him.

"You sure you want to drink that? It's Japanese, you know."

"Is it?" My companion looked up in genuine surprise. "I thought it was Manchurian."

"In case you haven't heard, Freddy, Manchuria has been taken over by the Japanese."

"Has it now? Do the Chinee good, they will."

I let the remark pass and downed my own drink—a generous glass of vodka. Enough to warm whatever humanity I had left in my soul. It needed warming. It was a chilly evening. And a restless one, what with what was going on the other side of the Soochow Creek. Local Chinese were up in arms over Japan's invasion of Manchuria. Mill workers were on strike, consumers were boycotting Japanese goods. I'd heard that a few timid Japanese were already leaving Little Tokyo for the safety of their home country. Clearly, they hadn't heeded the words of Tacitus. Farewell Japanese empire?

That was the trouble with Flap Ears, though. He was too full of himself, a common trait among naïve young men anxious to impress. But he was also British. Not entirely his fault, but all the same. His saving grace, so far as I was concerned, was that he was a useful source of information, if only because he was employed by Chinese Maritime Customs solely to stop smuggling. And smuggling was what Shanghai was all about, especially when it came to opium. If religion was the opium of the people, opium was the Chinese people's religion.

"The waterfront's never quiet, see, Rusty. Somebody somewhere is always smuggling summink. All the time, mate. No question. It's my job to find out who, what and where."

Through the plate-glass window, I could make out the distinctive four-storey tower of the Great World Amusement Palace above the rooftops at the end of the alley opposite. That was where the action was: Chinese hoods and hopeful high rollers at its gaming tables, taipans and socialites pressing flesh on its dance floors, with magicians, jugglers, storytellers, scribes, midwives, barbers, even earwax extractors, adding to the entertainment. Plus, of course, the pickpockets.

There was even a stuffed cetacean to encourage everybody to have a whale of a time—much of it readily dispensed by the sing-song girls. The more stairs you climbed in Shanghai's premier entertainment palace, the higher the slits in the Chinese girls' cheongsam—from knees on the first floor to hips on the third, and armpits on the fifth. The last may have had no pockets to pick, but they offered other recesses to those who could afford them.

Flap Ears was in full flow.

"Unlike most other ports in the world, Rusty, Shanghai's got no lock-up wharves, see."

I had seen. I had been down to the wharves on the Whangpoo River to take a look for myself at the conditions in which he had to work.

"Everythink's wide open, mate. Ships come up-river to the harbour, tie up at a wharf or buoy somewhere midstream and then it's up to us Customs lot to keep both ship and cargo under observation. And that ain't as easy as you might think, given the number of ships that pass through."

He paused to take another sip of his Asian Co-Prosperity beer. I nodded encouragingly.

"Of course, we've learned a lot from experience, haven't we? We know which ships from which countries or ports of call to suspect of carrying narcotics. That means we keep a very close eye on *every* ship coming in from Vladivostok, for example. The same goes for Haiphong. It's a must, 'cos Haiphong's a well-known trans-shipment port for high grade narcotics from places like Istanbul. And, like the French Concession here, all activities to do with dope in Haiphong take place only on the nod of some crooked official with the necessary authority."

"And you get forewarned of shipments?"

"Occasionally. Most of the time, though, it's our personal informants who tell us what's going on, ain't it?"

"Really?" I kept my English accent a notch above his in the sliding scale of class.

"Yeah. Look, Rusty, there are plenty of Chinee ready to tell on their compatriots. Chinks who find it profitable to prowl around the wharves tabulating the stacks of 'excess cargo' waiting ready for the final dash past Customs. Get it? We're talking professionals here, mate. From years of practice, they're able to assess the potential return from any cargo. And with astonishing accuracy, too. But it takes time, right? A ship carrying opium from Vladivostok, for instance, might be in port all of thirty-six hours before any word reaches us ashore concerning the stuff on board."

"Why so long? Surely that's the time it takes to unload and load a ship."

"You got it, Rusty. But those thirty-six hours are also the time spent by the professional informer and his team working out what's going on. They work in relays, see. They hover round the suspected ship—they even go on board—eavesdropping on orders and quick words exchanged, observing all that's going on and then shrewdly piecing everythink together and making their deductions. Then the guy in charge sends word to his favourite official—the one he knows from experience will give him a generous reward for his tip-off."

"Squeeze, you mean?"

Freddy nodded.

"Without several people like that on your unofficial payroll, Rusty, your Customs 'seizure money' wouldn't amount to much, would it? Neither would our salaries. But with a few good contacts I can run up several hundred dollars a month extra with very little effort. And it's all legit, too. That's what I like about this job."

He drank another gulp of Manchurian beer from his glass and his grin was etched with froth. It wasn't that hard to imagine him foaming at the mouth whenever he confronted some poor Chinese coolie.

"The trouble is we don't get a cut with opium seizures, Rusty. Don't ask me why. With anythink else, yes. Ten per cent of whatever the contraband fetches at public auction. But not opium."

"Sounds like a good reason not to report it. Just get your squeeze directly from the smugglers."

Freddy wiggled his ears in the way I noticed he often did when excited.

"Hole in one, Rusty."

He raised his glass in silent toast. Co-prosperity beckoned.

"That's a dangerous game, Freddy."

"I got my bolt hole, mate," he said, eyeing me knowingly. "Know what I mean?"

"Not really. But I'll take your word for it."

He leaned towards me conspiratorially. "Right under where you get your beauty sleep, Rusty."

"What? Not the Astor House?"

"One and the same, mate. Got a lockup in the basement, don't I?"

It had only taken a couple of beers to loosen his tongue. Good for me, perhaps, but not for him.

"You should be careful, Freddy. You don't want to end up as a floater served up to the water rats in the Whangpoo River."

"That'll never happen, Rusty. I've got a dicky ticker, see."

"Dicky ticker?" Sometimes English slang got the better of me.

"Irregular heartbeat. Don't tell my bosses, though. I'd be out of a job if they knew. Anyone tries to beat me up, I'd die of a heart attack, wouldn't I?"

"If you say so, Freddy. Still, I'd hate to lose such a knowledgeable informant."

Freddy grunted. Flattery usually worked.

"Don't you worry about me, mate. I know what I'm doing. Going to make my fortune, ain't I, and get the docs to fix me up. Then I'm outta here. You mark my words."

I marked them and waited. I knew there was more. In my profession, patience was an inviolable rule. Except when it came to drink and women. Which perhaps explained why I was glad to have been assigned to Shanghai. The city was on a roll. Parties every night, many of them decadent and wild. The city didn't know the meaning of depression unless you'd just lost a fortune. In which case you jumped off the roof of a high-rise building or, if you were very brave, placed a pistol under your jaw and put a bullet through your head. Upstanding Japanese, of course, preferred to cut their bellies open with a short samurai sword and leave someone else to clean up the mess.

Freddy took another swig of his beer.

"By the way, Charlie Chaplin's coming to Shanghai, ain't he."

Well, that came out of left field, as an American colleague would have put it. I hadn't heard even a whisper about Chaplin on the hacks' grapevine. Everyone knew he was wandering around Europe, but that was it. The word out was that the Tramp was terrified that silent films were now old-fashioned. That would be my line of questioning if ever I got a chance to meet him. What do you reckon, Charlie? Is it because you don't have a voice that you remain popular? Will your refusal to adopt the new technology of sound turn your audiences away forever? I mean, Greta Garbo survived the transition. Surely you can, too?

I put on my most inscrutable of poker faces and said lightly.

"He is? Wants to see the city's lights for himself, then?"

Freddy didn't get the allusion, but his ears were still wiggling.

"I dunno, Rusty, but he was on the *President Hoover* when it left Singapore yesterday. Must have boarded at Le Havre."

The way he said the name of the French port wasn't all that different from that of the luxury liner. Both denied fair harbour by his jaunty pronunciation.

"Word came in this afternoon. On the ticker tape. I guess the ship'll get here in about a week's time."

"Keep me posted, will you, Freddy? There'll be something in it for you. Not as much as the squeeze you get for overlooking a shipment of opium, maybe, but enough for a couple of drinks at your favourite bar. Just keep the information under your hat."

"Okay, Rusty. Will do." He had to. Once he'd sobered up, he'd realise I had something on him that he didn't want others to know.

Just then a Natasha approached us in the street. She'd spotted the whiteys in the bar and anticipated turning a trick. Or in our case two. I hardly fancied a threesome with Freddy. Like most of the prostitutes who came down from Harbin, she was thin and her skin ivory white. Malnutrition helped her live up to her tag as a White Russian. She certainly wasn't red. Her hair was blond.

The Natasha gave me her best made-up smile, with a coquettish flicker of the gloved fingers of one hand inviting us outside. When I failed to be moved, she pressed her small face up against the window and left an imprint of her lips on the glass.

She was turning away when shots rang out just along the street. She crumpled slowly onto the pavement outside.

I pushed Flap Ears off his chair and joined him on the floor below the window. There was the sound of more gunfire. And screams, of course. Followed by the moans of somebody caught in the cross-fire and glass breaking. A motor vehicle of some sort roared off down the street, its tyres squealing. Thanks to a steady diet of Hollywood films, Shanghai gangsters knew how to play their part.

"Blimey, what was all that?" Freddy was as white as the proverbial sheet and his ears were no longer wiggling. Or flapping.

"Another kidnap, probably." I stood up and dusted the dirt off my trouser knees. "You know how it is here. It doesn't always pay to be rich."

"But who?" Freddy looked nervously around. He was like a deflated balloon.

"Who did it? Or who was it done to?" I shrugged as if I hadn't a care in the world. "Who knows? Probably Tu Yue-sheng's thugs kidnapping a rich Chinese merchant's son. I've heard Chiang Kai-shek needs all the money he can get to buy arms."

"What's that got to do with Big Ears Tu?"

"He and the Generalissimo are blood brothers, Freddy. They go back a long way. Tu helps Chiang who in turn helps Tu. What you might call a lovers' embrace."

"You've lost me there, mate."

"A friendly kind of squeeze, Freddy. One thing we all learn about living in Shanghai, crime is money."

Flap Ears wiggled his ears in appreciation.

"Nice one, Rusty."

It was time to make a move. The bar had suffered no damage. The Russian girl had taken a stray bullet that would otherwise have broken its plate-glass front. Unless, like the vodka, it was bullet proof.

"Sorry, Freddy, but I've got to go." I shook his limp, damp hand. "I need to check this one out. No crime like the present, what!"

A bit unnecessary, that 'what,' but I wanted Flap Ears to remember who was boss.

Outside, the Natasha was dead. Very dead. Her thin body lay like a rag doll on the pavement, her torso twisted and legs akimbo, blood oozing from her neck. I felt sorry for her. Someone would come and clear her away during the night. Shove the corpse onto a cart and chuck it into an unmarked grave up in Bubbling Well Cemetery. Along with the other down-and-outs. Shanghai may have had the glitz, but it was a hard city, full of ghosts.

But she had at least left something behind—the lipstick imprint of two blushing pilgrims on the plate glass of the bar's window. This particular migrant's endless drifting back and forth along the Street of Happy Sisters had come to an end, though. I planted a tender kiss on her youthful forehead to smooth the rough touch of the night.

Then I went out into the road to take a look at the rest of the damage. One of the gangsters had also left something behind under the dashboard of the hijacked car: a bullet casing.

I had another scoop. And, if I had but known it, a clamorous harbinger of blood and death to come.

2.

I found her eventually. She was holding forth in the Elite Bar on Medhurst Road, in the company of three men. A couple of half-empty bottles of champagne stood on the table round which they were clustered. Lily Flohr and her Viennese torch songs didn't give customers that much space to breathe in. That struck me as tempting providence. Kiki was the fiery kind.

"Curtsey first. Then jump into bed. That's how a royal mistress should behave," she finished. "Or so I'm told."

I let the laugher die away. Kiki Montagu-Rose loved an audience. As you would expect with a name like that, she had the polished upper-crust drawl of a British socialite. Her eyes were violet, her shoulder-length hair Mediterranean black, her Cupid lips an alluring shade of crimson red. She was wearing a string of pearls that disappeared between her breasts and a black sequined dress that left little to anyone's imagination. Her companions were almost slobbering at the mouth.

Roger Buckley, seemingly her permanent chaperone, emptied the two bottles into the glasses on the table.

"There you are, Kiki. I was wondering where you'd got to."

"Well, now you know." She puffed lazily at the mouthpiece of her jade cigarette holder before blowing a perfect smoke ring. "Why so glum, Rusty? You're looking Eeyore-ish. Chirp up!"

I wasn't sure I was in the most appropriate company to sound like a chicken. Kiki, though, was in her terribly-terribly element. "You've met Roger Buckley, of course. But how about Major Otto von Holst, Rusty? And Captain Manfred Dobermann?" She indicated her other two companions.

"I don't think I've had the pleasure."

What she was doing with two German army officers in full uniform was anyone's guess, but aristocratic women were known for their kinky ways. The pleasure was probably hers. "*Herr* Hitler has sent them to advise the Generalissimo, you know."

I didn't. The two of them stood to rigid attention and clicked their heels as I said my name—something that Kiki in her enthusiasm for leather boots and shiny black plastic had neglected to do. Dobermann's jaw was as square as the coaster under his glass and his eyes a deep-set and steely Teutonic blue. I supposed they had little choice when they belonged to a young blonde Aryan officer turned out on the production line of the German Reich. I said my name and shook the proffered hand. It, too, seemed made of steel.

Von Holst was older and more human somehow. For a start his hair wasn't blonde and his eyes weren't blue. More like matching shades of national socialist brown. And his batman hadn't used quite so much starch when ironing his shirt. His handshake was firm, but friendly. Instinctively I liked him.

"Rusty's a *journalist*," Kiki said airily. Then to me, "why don't you join us?" She laid a gloved hand on the arm of the chair beside her. "Roger, be a *dar*ling and get us another bottle of bubbly, will you? Our Bloom appears to be *wilting*."

Obedient and silent as always, Roger stood up to do her bidding. I knew there was a story there, if only I could get the Englishman to loosen his stiff upper lip. The trouble was his moustache got in the way.

"I've just witnessed a hold-up," I said as lightly as I could. "Lots of shooting and a dead prostitute caught in the cross-fire."

"How *ghastly* for you!" Kiki seemed intent on making the right impression.

"*Mein Gott!* What is coming to Shanghai?" Dobermann was more forthright. "Every day it is violence. Is nobody safe?"

"Not when they fail to realise that enough is enough, Captain, when it comes to making money."

"I think they have need of a man like Adolf Hitler, no?"

"I'm *sure* you're right, Manfred. Wouldn't you agree, Rusty?"

"I'm afraid I don't know enough about *Herr* Hitler and German politics to form an opinion."

"You should then learn," Dobermann clearly liked to take whatever bit he fancied between his fancy white teeth. "You're a newspaperman, *Herr* Bloom." He pronounced my surname as if it were German—Blum—which was fair enough. I'd been born in Berlin. "The Nazis will be coming to power soon. Mark my words. Then Adolf will teach the world a thing."

If it were only one thing, I could probably live with it. Provided it wasn't extermination, of course. That would be the end. The Major, I noted, hadn't joined in his subordinate's rendering of *Deutschland über alles.* Maybe he preferred a solo champagne flute to the full orchestra of Nazism.

At this point, Roger arrived with a bottle of Pol Roger. Talk about self-absorption.

"Ah! Champers at *last!*" Kiki continued smoothly in her lazy aristocratic manner. "Jolly good *show*, Roger. Our saviour from politics."

He uncorked the bottle, with enough of a pop to attract brief attention, but not enough to make the wine bubble over. Waste not, want not. Who knew when the Depression would come to Shanghai?

After the five of us had clinked our glasses and sipped our fizz, Kiki took over once more.

"So, Rusty darling. *Do* tell us what happened."

"I was minding my own business in a Russian bar, trying to get some information out of a customs officer. A Russian Natasha approached us from out in the street and then gunfire broke out and she slumped to the cobblestones dead as a dodo."

"A dodo? What is this, please?" Dobermann looked confused.

"I'm sorry, Captain. The dodo is a flightless bird that was, so I'm told, eaten into extinction a couple of hundred years ago."

"The dodo is *also*, of course," Kiki was in full lethargic nasal drawl, "a character in an English children's tale, *Alice's Adventures in Wonderland. Surely* you've read it, Captain? it's *awfully* good."

Dobermann was clearly lost so the Major came to his subordinate's rescue. "Ah yes!" he said with a wry smile. "A strange story about a smiling cat from somewhere in England called Cheshire."

"Amongst other things, Otto." Kiki allowed another smoke ring to rise gently above everyone's heads, where it was neatly sliced into a shapeless pale haze by the silently revolving propeller blades of the fan hanging from the ceiling. I had a feeling my story was suffering the same fate.

"You were saying, Rusty?"

"Nothing much more, I'm afraid, Kiki. The usual machine pistol fire, followed by the usual screams. It was too dark to see anything, or anyone, clearly. Figures converging on a car stopped in the middle of the street. A barked command, followed by a pistol shot and another cry. A body, probably a young man's, being dragged by at least two men towards a waiting car. Doors slammed, an engine revved and tyres squealing as the gangsters made their getaway. And then the whimpering cries of the wounded in the returning silence."

"Poetic, Mr Bloom," Roger clapped his hands lightly in appreciation. For once he had found his voice. "For a journalist, at least."

Talk about damning with faint praise. He was better off as a dumb waiter.

"And where was the inspiration for this *poetry*, might I enquire?" Kiki was clearly adept at expressing a socialite's condescension when she deemed it appropriate.

"In the French Concession. One of the bars in Little Moscow on Avenue Joffre. All the thugs left was an empty car with its driver slumped against the steering wheel, his blood splattered all over the upholstery. And, as I said, a few bodies in the street round about. Bodyguards and a couple of innocent bystanders who got caught in the cross-fire."

"Chinese?" Roger Buckley was leaning forward intently.

"The bodyguards? No. Russians."

"And the kidnappers?"

"My impression is they weren't Chinese. Too tall and heavy."

"Russians, too, then?"

"That'd be my first guess."

"Sounds like Tu Yue-sheng's work." Roger was being unusually business-like. "Nobody else would have dared. Big Ears *owns* the French Concession."

Kiki was gazing at me almost mockingly. She put one hand on my arm.

"I say, you *do* have a habit of finding trouble, don't you, Rusty?"

"I guess you could say that. I'd prefer to think it finds me, though. I was just minding my own business."

"You know who it was, don't you?"

"Who what was?"

"Who was kidnapped in the shooting you witnessed."

"Should I know?"

"Depends on who you know, doesn't it?" she said, blowing another smoke ring in my direction.

"I have a feeling you're running rings round me, Kiki."

"You may be right, Rusty *darling*. But I simply *adore* it when you look confused. It makes you even *more* handsome." Kiki was in full phrasal stress mode.

Roger came to my rescue and, by the looks on the faces of our two German companions, theirs, too.

"The bamboo telegraph is saying that Sir Victor Sassoon's one and only nephew was kidnapped earlier this evening. In the French

Concession."

"*Mein Gott!*"

Was this the captain's only expletive?

"You know him, too, Rusty."

"I do?"

"He was playing the piano the other night when we went to the Canidrome."

"Simon Meyer, you mean?"

"You see?" Kiki said enigmatically, blowing yet another smoke ring towards me.

"Very little, actually."

"You just witnessed the kidnapping of the nephew of Shanghai's richest man." She stubbed out her cigarette and stood up. "Come on, darling. Time to pay a visit."

3.

A valet opened the door to Sir Victor Sassoon's luxury penthouse suite on the eleventh floor of the Cathay Hotel.

"Hello, Perkins." Kiki seemed to know the names of everyone in Shanghai. "Is Victor at home?"

"Good evening, Madame." He bowed slightly. "I'm afraid Sir Victor isn't receiving guests right now."

"Of *course*, he isn't. I fully understand. The thing is, my friend here happened to witness his nephew's *abduction* and I thought Victor might wish to hear about it."

"I see," Perkins gave me a slightly superior look, as if nobody of Sir Victor's class would ever witness such a low-down deed. "If you would care to wait, Madame, I will go and enquire." His upper lip seemed as stiff as Roger Buckley's. It explained why the English never moved their mouths when they spoke. Unless it was the other way round. A chicken and egg problem. Chirp up, Bloom.

Perkins allowed us to step through the doorway into a spacious waiting hall, closed the front door noiselessly and, equally as silently, disappeared along a short corridor lined with Art Deco prints. We could hear the murmur of voices, followed by a grunt and the slightly staccato movement of a crippled man heaving himself out of a chair.

"Kiki!" Sir Victor greeted us from the end of the corridor. "This *is* a surprise."

"Victor *darling*," she walked quickly forward and put her arms around his neck, kissing him lightly on the cheek. "How simply *beastly*! You must be feeling *awful*."

"I've been known to feel better," he replied drily. "What can I do for you?"

The hotelier cut an impressive figure—over six feet tall with broad shoulders, jet black hair slicked back from forehead, a longish face with what I suppose could be called a Jewish nose and a pencil-line moustache on his upper lip. There was a monocle in his right eye, though whether it was an affectation or a necessity I had no idea. He was leaning heavily on a couple of walking sticks. One of them had a silver handle.

"Can I introduce you to a friend of mine, Christopher Bloom? I know it's not the *best* of times, darling, but Rusty has something to tell you about your nephew."

"Bloom?" He put out his right hand, looking me up and down in the way that Perkins had done a few minutes earlier. I began to feel like a painting in the Louvre. "Not related to that Irish chappie, are you?"

"Which chappie's that, Sir Victor?" I tried an enigmatic smile as I shook his hand.

"The one in the book. Leopold I think his name was."

"No, sir. No Leopolds in my family, I'm afraid. But my grandmother on my mother's side *was* Irish. A Collins. From Cork."

"Rusty's a *journalist*." Kiki was determined to have her say, even if it meant repeating herself. "He got that scoop on the Mukden Incident."

"Probably not his fault," Sir Victor didn't give me time to say anything as he turned towards me. "I've always thought journalists and businessmen share a deuce of a lot in common, don't you?"

"In what way, Sir Victor?"

"We both have a nose," he tapped one side of his own protruding beak. "Mine is for business; yours for news. I hope you haven't come here under false pretences, Mr Bloom."

The gaze with which he transfixed me behind the monocle in his right eye was penetrating, but also mischievous, and therefore difficult to read. I sensed how he had become such a successful businessman.

"Not at all, sir."

"Good. That's settled then." He gave me a lynx-like look. "But I'm forgetting my manners. Do come in and make yourselves at home." He led us into a large, tastefully furnished—part-Chinese, part-European style—living room, oak-panelled, with door-size sliding windows on two sides, giving onto a terrace that afforded a breathtaking view of the river and the Bund on one side, and on the other, the hustle and bustle of Nanking Road below.

"Have a pew," he indicated a sofa and chairs with one of the two canes he used to propel himself around. "Anyone who can tell me anything about Simon is more than welcome. Drinks?"

Without waiting for an answer the Baronet addressed his valet who was standing attentively by the door. "Perkins, a Suffering Bastard is probably the most appropriate drink for me right now. I'm not sure about my guests, though." He looked at me enquiringly.

"A Suffering Bastard will do me fine, Sir Victor. Thank you."

"Make it three," Kiki said.

"Three Suffering Bastards it is then, Perkins, although I can hardly imagine Mrs Montagu-Rose here being a bastard."

So she was married. Or divorced. I wondered who the lucky man was. Or had been.

"Maybe not, Victor, but that doesn't stop me from suffering like the rest of you bastards."

The valet withdrew in the midst of our polite laughter. Our host arranged one silver-handled stick against the side of his armchair.

"Buggered up my legs in the war, I'm afraid," he explained, looking in my direction. "Hence the props."

"I'm sorry to hear that, sir."

"Don't be, dear boy. It's all in the past." He waved one hand in the air in front of him as if to prove his point. "And while we're at it, can we drop the formalities? I get a bit tired of being reminded I'm the Baronet of Bombay. If anything, I should be the Sheik of Shanghai, but not even British imperialism permits a title like that."

We laughed dutifully. Kiki felt obliged to say something in the silence that followed.

"Rusty's a count, you know."

"Are you now?" He fixed me with another mischievous look. "Of the arithmetical kind? Or one to do with a certain blues jazz pianist?"

"When it comes to jazz, Sir Victor, I must admit to preferring Duke Ellington to Count Basie."

Sir Victor's eyes danced merrily. Twinkle twinkle little stare.

"You've no objection, then, if I call you Christopher?"

"Absolutely none. I've always assumed that's why I was given a first name."

The tycoon laughed again.

"Me, too," he said, his stare still twinkling. Then he was all business.

"So what have you got to tell me about my nephew, Christopher?"

"Not very much, I'm afraid. Only that I happened to witness the kidnapping."

"You did?" Victor sat up straight, alert, his lazy public school demeanour gone. "Pray tell."

I told what little there was to tell. As I finished, Perkins came back into the room with three full cocktail glasses which he set down on the table between us. Victor raised his in a toast.

"To better days!"

"To better days!" we chorused dutifully, although I had my doubts.

The Japanese were getting ready to attack the Chinese part of the city, and the bourbon, gin and ginger beer concoction in my mouth seemed less likely to cure a hangover than to bring one on. Maybe now was the time to pray.

"So, Christopher? They were Chinese, were they, these hoodlums?"

"I don't think so, Victor. Russians, more likely."

"But part of Tu Yue-sheng's outfit? Avenue Joffre is in the French Concession, after all."

"That's true. And nothing happens in the French Concession without Tu's approval, so everything points to his involvement. There's one thing, though, that bothers me."

"There is? What's that, old boy?"

I wasn't sure I liked being reminded of childhood. I guessed it was marginally better, though, than being an old bean. I'd never been fond of gardening.

"While looking around after everyone had disappeared, I found a bullet case under the dashboard."

"So?"

"It was Japanese."

"*Japanese?*" Victor took a second sip of his Suffering Bastard and fixed his lynx-like eyes on me. "What does that tell you, Christopher?"

"One of two things. Either one of Big Ears Tu's mob has somehow got hold of a Japanese pistol and used it to kill the driver. Or…"

"Or what, Rusty?" Kiki moved a fraction closer to me on the sofa. Her voice was soft, coaxing.

"Or there's more to this particular kidnapping than meets the eye."

"And we're being directed to look in the wrong direction?"

"Something like that, yes."

A silent pause. Time for me to lay down my hand.

"Look, Victor. Maybe I can help by asking around the neighbourhood? I speak Russian fluently, and my Chinese isn't so bad."

"You speak both languages?" Victor took another sip of his Suffering Bastard. "Interesting," he mused. Another pause.

Eventually, I filled in the silence. "Might I ask what the French police have to say for themselves? They've been in touch, I assume."

"The Gendarmerie?" Victor came out of his reverie. "Yes, a couple of officers came here, told me what had happened, offered their sympathies in exchange for tea, and answered my questions with splendidly Gallic shrugs. Then they told me to sit tight and wait for a ransom note. There was nothing they could do until then. Or so they insisted. I had a feeling they wanted to get back to the warmth of their mistresses' beds. It's a cold night after all."

"And if Tu Yue-sheng *is* involved, they'll stay put there until their mistresses turf them out and send them back to their nagging wives. What about the SMP? Will they help?"

"Shanghai's Municipal Police? It's hardly likely, is it, Christopher? Their jurisdiction is the International Settlement, not the French Concession."

"But you live in the International Settlement. Surely that counts for something?"

"It should, I suppose, but you know what sticklers the French are when it comes to territorial boundaries. They prefer to do things their way. Which, in this case, probably means doing nothing, as you said."

We seemed to have gone down a blind alley. Hopefully, it wasn't a dead end. But I wasn't all that optimistic. Kidnappings had a habit of ending with a corpse.

Victor wasn't done, though. "How would you like to earn some pocket money, Christopher?"

"Pocket money?" I echoed, a little helplessly. I was supposed to be a hack, not a detective.

"Look! I'll pay you two thousand pounds to look for my nephew. Ten thousand if you find him. You know the lingo and the city. Would you make enquiries on my behalf?"

"Well, I suppose I could, Victor. I'm not sure I'll be of much use, though. And you should keep your money."

"We'll see about that. But you'll give it a go, Christopher? Ask around, I mean? Discreetly, of course."

Like Kiki's hand against my thigh. That's what came of being hired as a dick.

"But of course."

4.

There didn't seem to be much point in lolling around like suffering bastards, so we took our leave of Victor Sassoon sometime after midnight. There had been no ransom note while we were up in his penthouse, and no further contact by the French Gendarmerie. In spite of my protestations, Victor had written out a cheque and filled me in on 'young Simon,' as he called his nephew, who turned out not to be a nephew at all, but some kind of removed cousin. And I'm not referring to his being kidnapped. The property tycoon had no siblings.

Out on the Bund, Kiki expressed a desire to look over my room in the Astor House and, when shown it by way of a last drink in the hotel bar—"One for the stairs," she dubbed it—she was sufficiently impressed to suggest she stay the night. I was wary of the offer for two reasons. I was concerned she'd regard sexual intercourse as emotional surrender on my part—which it wasn't—and use it as leverage at some point—which she well might. There was something about her that roused my suspicions, although of what I wasn't yet sure.

But also, like life, women should never be that easy. Especially a woman like Kiki who oozed class and sensuality. I had never found class that hard to resist. Sensuality, though, was another matter. Against my better judgement, I acquiesced.

I was glad I did. She turned out to be an agile lover, her athletic body ready to adopt one or two positions I had thought impossible. The second time we made love, as night turned to day and the street hawkers and coolies were finding their voice again, she displayed an ability to contract the walls of her vagina to an astonishing degree. As I lay exhausted on my back, I concluded she'd provided a novel interpretation to the meaning of squeeze. That was reason enough to learn more about the woman splayed out on top of my sweating body.

"Where did you learn *that*?" I just had to ask.

"In a brothel, if you *must* know," she replied in a matter-of-fact voice.

"A *brothel*?"

"Yes, my poppet. My husband used to drag me along with him whenever he went whoring."

"Your husband?" I echoed disappointedly.

"Relax, Rusty. My *ex*-husband. A simply *horrid* little man. Long gone now, and good riddance to a violent and abusive drunk. God *knows* why I married him. The folly of youth, I suppose. You know, he actually made me *watch* while he groped the girls in whatever brothel he took me to in different parts of the world."

"Doesn't sound very pleasant."

"It wasn't," she shivered, so I pulled the coverlet over us as we lay there. "Luckily, though, he was usually so drunk he passed out before long. That left me with the whores. They felt sorry for me and over time taught me several tricks of their trade."

"Which you were kind enough to pass on. Thank you, Kiki."

"Not *all* of them, Rusty. Just one or two. Like the Singapore Grip you just experienced," she gave out a deep throaty chuckle. "I keep others to myself. For other men." Then, adding as an afterthought, "and women."

"I'd rename it Shanghai Squeeze, now that you're in this part of the world. But tell me, where did you get your name Kiki from?"

"Kiki? It's short for Kiriakí."

"Kiriakí?"

"Yes. It's Greek for Sunday. My mother was called Friday." She looked at me mischievously, as if that explained everything.

"I've heard of Man Friday," I said, "but not Woman Friday. Could you perhaps enlighten me?"

She sighed theatrically. "If you *insist*, darling. My mother's name is Paraskeví. Which is Greek for Friday. She herself comes from island of Spetses."

"That explains your captivating looks, then."

"And, in case you happen to be wondering, poppet, her surname is Triantáfyllou. Which means *what* in Greek? Come on, Rusty, you're the foreign language wallah."

"Rose?" The light began to dawn. "And you got the Montagu bit from your father. A member of the British aristocracy, if I'm not mistaken?"

"I say, you *are* clever, aren't you. But don't worry, poppet. I'm not about to trump your title of Count. I'm a *bastard*."

"Me, too. Well, almost, my mother claims my father was a Russian count. A Stroganov. Apparently, I'm his only heir."

"No wonder I find you so yummy," Kiki nibbled my ear affectionately. "The trouble with Daddy was he never *could* resist the urge. While I was enjoying life inside Mummy's tummy, he developed a passion for a Greek priest and used to screw him after church on Sunday. An absolute *scandal* on the island. Even the dogs and *donkeys* knew what was going on. But it gave me my first name."

"And there I was thinking the British upper classes were unorthodox," I grinned.

"Not when Greek *priests* are around, I promise. But, tell me, poppet. Why Rusty? And why Bloom, if you're *Swedish*?"

"Simple. When I was a baby my hair was a rusty blonde. Or so my mother told me. As for Bloom, it's my mother's maiden name. There are Blooms with double-o's in Sweden."

"We both have our mothers' names, then. What a coincidence!" she exclaimed. "Actually, though"—it sounded like acksherly—"I have to confess. There *is* somebody else in my life, in case you were wondering. I've known him for simply *ages*. Ever since I was a Bright Young Thing."

"I'm sorry, Kiki. You've lost me there."

"Haven't you heard of the Bright Young Things, Rusty? And I thought you were so *refined*." She laughed and gave me a peck on the cheek to show she forgave me. "We were a bunch of aristos and socialites back in the early twenties and used to get up to all sorts of jolly silly japes. You know, practical jokes, treasure hunts, that sort of thing. And absolutely *super* country house parties and fancy dress balls. They were always *such* fun. Full of high jinks and *masses* of sex." She began to look wistful. "I was only in my late teens then, but imagine what a wonderful introduction to life it all was! We smoked, we drank, we snorted cocaine. We were in and out of virtually every nightclub worth going in and out of. And if you were a young and attractive young woman, which of course I was," she paused, waiting for me to confirm her allure.

"And, of course, still are."

"Thank you, poppet," she acknowledged the compliment as if she had been hearing it all her life. "You could get in anywhere for *free*. The Candlelight, the Gargoyle. Claridge's in Mayfair. The Café Royal. You had to be properly *dressed*, of course, although that wasn't necessarily the case everywhere. And then, of course, there was *Frolics*." She half-closed her eyes and smiled dreamily.

"Frolics?"

"My favourite late night haunt, really." It sounded like ryallai. "You might meet anyone in Frolics. Absolutely *anyone*. I mean, there were the Plunket-Greenes, the Mitfords, the Sitwells. They were all there one night or another. Along with people like Victor Sassoon."

"Sir Victor?"

"Darling, didn't you *know*? Victor was a*wfully* dashing in those days. And a jolly good dancer, too, in spite of his legs. Frolics is where I met *George*, of course."

"George?"

"Yes, George. You know, the King's third son. Or is he the fourth? Not that it really matters. After all, what with David and Bertie around, he's never going to be King, is he? Which means I'll never be Queen."

"But you could be a princess. Or a duchess, or something."

"If I had my way, yes. But, unfortunately, the Palace has other plans for George. They're trying to marry him orf to some Danish princess. And I've been told to make myself scarce. Bloody rude, if you ask me. But that's royalty for you, isn't it?"

"If you say so, Kiki."

"But I *do*. As a matter of fact, it was George who suggested I come and see Victor, before going on to Tokyo and hanging out with Hirohito."

"Hanging out with Hirohito?" My jaw dropped. I couldn't tell if it was because of who Hirohito was, or what she intended to do with him. Did emperors ever hang out? "How on earth do you know the Emperor of Japan, Kiki?"

"Oh, it just happened, poppet. The way things did in those days. I mean, everyone knew *everyone*. *Nothing* came as a surprise to us. Not even when George and David brought the Crown Prince of Japan along to Frolics one night. That's the sort of thing that went on then. Edward was *awfully* naughty, though. Somehow, he managed to get Hirohito away from his minders and showed him what it was like to have a good time. Just for *once* in his life. I mean, poor *chap*. He was going to become Emperor and the only woman he'd ever met was a palace *concubine* or something, old enough to be his mama. So they asked Babe Blanchard-Gough, Dotty ffitch-Hamilton, and me to entertain him and his prince friend, Tada something or other. *Acksherly*, he and George took rather a fancy to each other, I think, although I can't ryallai remember. We'd all been snorting coke off the Blanchard-Gough woman's naked belly. That much I do recall. She'd drenched herself in *Narcisse Noir* and her whole body smelled of orange blossom, jasmine and musk. Mm, *frightfully* yummy!"

"Sounds like quite a party."

"It was, darling. Ask Victor. He took a photo of us, I think. But it may have been someone else who had a camera with him. Cecil, probably."

"Cecil?"

"Cecil Beaton. You know, the *fashion* photographer. Awfully *dapper* little man."

There was silence as I pondered everything Kiki had been telling me. Plenty of food for thought. But then I was a Stroganov.

5.

Later I made my way back to Little Moscow. I started with the bar where I'd been sitting with Flap Ears Freddy at the time of the kidnapping.

"Didn't really notice anything," the bartender admitted a little sheepishly. "Too busy hiding under the counter. Just grateful it was the Natasha who took the bullet, not my plate glass window."

"That would have been a real pane."

He didn't get the joke. The story of my life, really. Always trying to please. It was part of my job description.

I left the bar and traipsed up and down Avenue Joffre looking for witnesses to Simon's kidnapping, but found myself none the wiser. Local inhabitants had been too busy diving for cover to take note of who was involved. "Chinese. Big Chinese," said one; "Russians. Small Russians," said another. Nobody recognised Simon from the photo Victor had provided me with.

On a hunch I tried the Orthodox Church on rue Corneille. There wasn't a soul around, but I found the priest in the vestry sipping tea with a fat, jovial-looking Chinese man, in his mid-fifties. He had sparse greying hair plastered across his pate, the parting not far above his left ear.

I apologised for the interruption and explained in Russian why I was there.

"Well, what a coincidence!" exclaimed Father Nicolas in English as he poured me a glass of scented tea from the samovar on the sideboard. "Inspector Lo here appears to be engaged in the same mission. Unfortunately, as I told him, I cannot be of assistance."

I looked enquiringly at the Chinese detective and put out my hand.

"Rusty Bloom," I introduced himself. "Sir Victor Sassoon asked me to help find his nephew."

"Lo Li-kwei," the other said, shaking my hand. "Chief Chinese Inspector of the International Settlement police. Please call me Lolly. Everyone else does," he laughed loudly and sat down again. "I'm also looking into this unfortunate matter."

"I'm surprised. When did Shanghai's Municipal Police force start taking an interest in crimes that take place in the French Concession?"

"Good question." Lolly sipped his tea and wiped a pudgy hand across his thick wet lips. "But there are—how do you say?—alomanies."

"Anomalies."

"Ah yes, anomalies." Lolly laughed again and slapped a meaty thigh.

"Might I ask what those anomalies might be? You see, I happened to witness the kidnapping."

"Did you now?" Lolly's eyes narrowed very slightly. His joviality could never disguise the fact that he was a policeman. And, who knew, a crook. Most Shanghai policemen were.

"Let's say too many things point to the involvement of Tu Yue-sheng," he continued. "The methods used to effect the kidnap. The fact that it was in the French Concession. The use of Russian thugs."

"So they *were* Russian? Nobody I talked to seemed to know."

"You clearly had your suspicions, though."

"From the size of a couple of the figures in the dark, yes. And by how they moved. They didn't strike me as being Chinese."

"Anything else, Mr Bloom?" For all his apparent flab, the Chinese inspector's look was sharp. Forged with the same steel, no doubt, as Manfred Dobermann's Teutonic eyes.

"We're guessing the kidnappers want a ransom of some kind. And yet there's no demand. As yet."

Lolly chuckled. "Probably too busy arguing about how much to charge Sir Victor Sassoon. Two hundred and fifty thousand Mexican dollars? Five hundred? One whole million?" He sighed. "A difficult decision for people whose actions are determined by greed."

"Unless some other motive's involved. Are you sure it's just greed, Inspector Lo? I mean, Sir Victor calls Simon his nephew, but strictly speaking he's not."

"In what way not?"

"Sir Victor has no siblings."

"A cousin, then?"

"Of some sort, yes. And almost certainly once removed. He's of a different generation."

"Maybe that's what's making it so hard for the kidnappers to agree on a ransom."

"I hardly think fine distinctions in kinship terminology are going to worry them too much. After all, they're just gangsters."

"Are they?"

"Well, I assume so."

"Never assume, Mr Bloom. If there's one thing I've learned in police work, it is never to assume anything. Presumption can be dangerous, too. Even if the kidnappers are gangsters, they're almost certainly obeying someone's command. The question is: whose?"

"That's why I was hoping to talk to Tu Yue-sheng."

The glass Lolly Lo was bringing to his mouth stopped in mid-air.

"Tu Yue-sheng doesn't talk to people he doesn't know."

"Maybe not. But he knows *you*."

Lolly returned his glass to the table, rummaged in one pocket of his uniform trousers and produced a handkerchief with which he wiped his lips and brow.

"So? What if I do?"

"So you can arrange to meet him and take me with you."

"And why should I do that, Mr Bloom?"

"Because I have something from the scene of the crime that might interest him. And you, too, Inspector Lo."

I placed the spent bullet casing I'd picked up the evening before on the table in front of Lolly.

"You realise I could have you arrested, Mr Bloom? Stealing evidence from the scene of a crime is itself a crime, you know."

"Which is why I'm handing it over to you now, Mr Chief Inspector. You weren't around yesterday evening."

Lolly frowned as he examined the casing closely, turning it over this way and that between the fingers of one hand.

"If I'm not mistaken, this is —"

"Japanese, Inspector Lo. Fired from a Namba pistol, I'd say. I found it on the floor of the hijacked car under the dashboard."

"You seem to know your pistols, Mr Bloom." There was a measure of respect, but also of suspicion, in the Chinese inspector's eyes.

"It was a childhood hobby of mine. Also I'm a journalist. I make it my business to know about weapons when they're a flourishing business in China. Second only to opium."

"And what prompted you to pick *this* up?" Lolly pointed a fat finger in the direction of the bullet case he had placed back on the table.

"I don't know, Inspector Lo. A lack of trust in the competence of the French authorities, perhaps? If you were to obtain permission to go through whatever material evidence the Gendarmerie has collected, you'll probably find a couple more casings just like this one. Last night

I wasn't at all sure *La Garde Municipale* would realise its significance in their investigation. As you yourself said, Inspector Lo, there are anomalies."

"Ah yes, alomanies," Lolly gave out another jovial laugh before pocketing the bullet casing I'd given him. "I'll keep this if I may."

He stood up and made to leave.

"I'll see what I can do, Mr Bloom," he said shaking my hand. "Tell me where you live and I'll get in touch."

6.

He was true to his word. Early that evening I got a phone call. I was to meet Lolly at the police station on Foochow Road.

"Tu Yue-sheng's expecting us," he said when I arrived. "And he's not a man you want to keep waiting."

"I'm sure he isn't. So where are we going?"

"Route Doumer. He does his business from the Donghu Hotel there. Come."

I followed Lolly's swaying walk out of the Central Police Station and into a waiting police car parked at the bottom of the steps.

"Tu knows we're coming, of course. But take my advice, Count. Don't speak unless you're spoken to. Big Ears likes to be in control of conversations, as well as crime."

The car soon pulled up at what was obviously a hotel entrance. A quartet of well-built Russian goons was standing on the steps leading up to bulletproof glass doors, eyes alert, flickering here and there up and down the street. One of them held the car door open and nodded at Lolly.

"No Japanese pistols in sight. Not yet at least," the inspector muttered *sotto voce* as we walked up the steps, through the hotel entrance and into a large marbled vestibule. There we were met by another gangster, Chinese this time. He and Lolly exchanged a few words in Shanghainese.

"This is Pan Chan-kee, Tu's right hand man. We call him Chunky."

I bowed politely. Chunky nodded and extended one arm towards a nearby sofa and chairs.

"Mista Broom, sit one piece chair this side," he commanded in pidgin English before disappearing down a corridor at the back of the lobby. An absurdly beautiful Eurasian hostess brought us two cups of jasmine tea, set them down and retired silently. I savoured the tea and the view of her hips undulating lazily across the marble floor.

"There's more where that one came from," Lolly slapped me on the thigh. "If you're a good boy, maybe Tu will make you an offer you can't refuse."

Chunky reappeared a couple of minutes later and beckoned to us. We stood up, crossed the lobby, and followed him down the corridor. At the end, he opened a door and stood aside.

"Lo Li-kwei. Long time, no see, *lo*." A man, above average height for a Shanghainese, with a build that was strong and wiry, greeted Lolly. His face was pitted and mottled by the ravages of opium. A bit like a honeycomb, though hardly as sweet. He had slightly large, protuberant ears, as his nickname suggested, and his thick hair was close-cropped with prominent eyebrows. The eyes themselves were empty and dull, as impenetrable as a taxidermist's bird. A drooping lid over his left eye added to his rather sinister appearance. Not the kind of man you'd want to encounter in an alley on a dark night.

"Yue-sheng, we are indebted to you for your time." Lolly indicated me just behind him. "This is the man I talked about earlier."

Big Ears stared dispassionately at me, weighing me up. Then, abruptly, he let out a rasping grunt and stretched out one long, bony arm to shake my hand. His nails were more than an inch long and stained with opium juice. Somehow they didn't dig into my flesh. A trick the gangster must have learned from Sun Tzu's *Art of War*.

"Thank you for taking the time to see us, sir."

Yue-sheng grunted again and motioned to us to sit down in the armchairs positioned round a low table in the middle of the room.

"So, Li-kwei. How's your family?"

"Thank you, well, Yue-sheng."

"And your children? They must be all grown up by now."

"Thank you, yes. My son Li-chieh has decided to follow in my footsteps and is studying in the police academy."

"Good. Good," the crime boss nodded his head appreciatively. "Shanghai needs good policemen like you Li-kwei." Tu sipped his tea. "And your daughter, Li-ming?"

"Li-ming is married and has a son of her own."

"So you're a grandfather now, Li-kwei? Congratulations. How time flies. And you're still at Central Station on Foochow Road? As busy as ever?"

"As busy as ever, Yue-sheng. Especially with these bombs being detonated all over town. Alas! The Chief of Police there isn't the man you are."

Big Ears gave out a guttural laugh.

"Does that explain your visit, then?"

Lolly smiled. "In a way, Yue-sheng. In a way. I assume you know about the kidnapping last night on Avenue Joffre?"

"Know, Li-kwei? I've *heard* about it, of course. A relative of that Jew man Sassoon, I hear. An unfortunate affair."

"Indeed unfortunate for those concerned," Lolly bowed his head. "It's the reason, though, I'm now taking up your precious time."

"Go on." There was a sharp edge to Tu Yue-sheng's voice. All pleasantries were clearly gone, but Lolly wasn't cowed.

"The thing is, Yue-sheng, the evidence suggests that the kidnapping was carried out, if not on your orders, at least with your knowledge. However —"

"However?" The temperature in the room seemed to drop a couple of degrees as the boss of the famed Green Gang looked coldly at the Chief Chinese Inspector and sipped his tea. I did my best to become invisible.

Lolly was unfazed.

"However Count Bloom here," he indicated me at his side, "happened to witness the kidnapping."

"And?"

"And he found this." Lolly took the bullet casing from his uniform pocket and handed it to Yue-sheng. Big Ears examined it closely, rolling the casing back and forth gently and expertly between his long-nailed fingers. Eventually he handed it back to Lolly.

"None of my men has a Japanese pistol."

"As I thought, Yue-sheng." Lolly bowed his head.

Big Ears turned to me, for the first time acknowledging my presence during the conversation.

"Did you see any dwarf bandits taking part in the kidnapping, Count Bloom?" he asked in English.

"No, sir, I didn't."

"And yet you found a Namba pistol casing afterwards?"

Yue-sheng knew his weapons all right.

"Yes, sir. In the car, under the dashboard."

Yue-sheng nodded to himself. Then he turned back to Lolly.

"You were right to come to me, Li-kwei." He rose. The meeting was at an end. "I will make enquiries."

"Thank you, Yue-sheng. I'm very grateful."

"Maybe it is I who should be grateful to you, Li-kwei." He looked at Rusty again. "And to you, Count. I don't like people who try to blacken my reputation."

"Of course not, sir." Better to be obsequious.

"So thank you for your consideration in this matter. I hope you find Sir Victor's nephew before it's too late. If you need assistance, let me know. In the meantime," he clapped his hands loudly and Tu's right hand man opened the door. "Chan-ki, my car. It's time to let the good times roll. My friends here deserve a break from their onerous duties."

7.

When I awoke next morning I found myself in a strange room. With a strange woman asleep in my bed. Not that I felt the need to complain. She was beautiful, her skin a light brown with the texture of finest silk. The parts of her that mattered were wrapped in a sheet.

It had been quite a night. That much I recalled through the haze of a head-splitting hangover. Lolly and I had hung around the Donghu Hotel, being served cocktails and canapés by classy Eurasian girls while Chunky went about making sure his boss came back alive from his night out on the town. First, he phoned the manager of the Del Monte to advise him of Yue-sheng's intention to patronise his establishment that evening. Then he sent a carload of bodyguards to case the cabaret from kitchen to cloak-rooms and make sure nobody and nothing was hidden anywhere. Even the rats had to move out. Reluctantly.

Eventually, Yue-sheng had appeared all dressed up and off we went across the new part of town in a large bullet-proof sedan, with bodyguards riding the running boards, machine pistols in hand. Behind us was a second carload of goons who surrounded us as we alighted and crossed the few yards to the well-lit entrance of the Del Monte strung with coloured lights. Inside we were met by Al Israel himself, who led us obsequiously to the dance floor where the very best tables were reserved for Yue-sheng and his party. His men were posted at every door and corner and, guns in plain view, they sat at tables beside and behind their boss.

The cabaret was decorated like the Palace of Versailles—extravagantly. Green marble columns were set on gold-painted plinths, their cornices richly decorated in gold. Candle-lit chandeliers hung from the frescoed ceiling. There were mirrors on the walls to create the impression of an infinite space populated by identical twins and quadruplets in their starched white shirts, dinner suits and evening gowns. Two carpeted curved staircases led to an upper floor filled with gaming tables—an extravagance Louis XIV forgot—and wrought-iron balconies from which players could look down on the action below.

Yue-sheng himself was in his element. He may not have been the Sun King, but he appeared to be having the time of his life, even though he danced like a headless green dragon and lost heavily at the roulette tables. There was endless bowing and scraping by all who came near him and I was reminded of Roman Catholics genuflecting at a church altar. Even important foreigners crossed the dance floor to pay their respects to a man known to rule Shanghai's underworld and to control every kind of vice racket behind a façade of philanthropy, as patron of sport and charity organizer, as well as big businessman and banker. As Big Ears' guest, I found myself being handed the calling cards of half a dozen men capable of opening up avenues for me in the future when pursuing a story for one or other of my newspapers. One of them belonged to Otto von Holst. Luckily, perhaps, he was too pissed to recognise me. Unless he was a skilled poker player.

"Majaa maykee pidgin my boss catchee number one piece airplane. Fuckers," Chan-ki jerked his head at the retreating form of the Major. "Fuckers cost too muchee."

I wondered if the same could be said of the Eurasian girl who stirred beside me. I wasn't sure where Maisy had come from. She had appeared out of nowhere and seemed to be a cut above the half dozen Del Monte sing-song girls sitting at our table. Big Ears barked at her to look after my 'interests.' At the time I wasn't quite sure what those interests were, but I soon learned that her 'Del Monte quality' amounted to more than canned fruit and vegetables. Unlike Chunky, she could actually conduct a proper conversation.

Her first question, though, was a bit of a dampener. Maisy's father was from the Philippines, she said, and she was a Catholic. Was I perhaps a Catholic, too?

Definitely not. Why not? I didn't believe in God. Why not? Because, by allowing Shanghai to endure, God owed an apology to Sodom and Gomorrah. How about that for starters? Maybe I had a point, she acknowledged. It probably wasn't my fault, either, that I didn't believe—a comment that was accompanied by a generous smile which, to Maisy's eternal credit, wasn't morally superior. And, she added, there was always time to repent. Were there Catholics in Sweden? Very few. The place was full of Lutherans. A pity. She had thought it might be a country that she'd like to visit. I advised against it. She'd never get used to the cold. How cold? How about minus fifteen degrees for starters? I was right. Too cold. But she'd like to visit France and Spain. They weren't cold because, unlike Sweden, they were Catholic countries. Italy, too. And Columbia. And Brazil. Even Goa and Macau. She'd like to visit them all. In which case, I suggested, she ought to become the Pope's assistant. She doubted His Holiness would employ her. Fair enough. Then why not ask Tu Yue-sheng to buy her a round-the-world ticket on an ocean-going liner?

Mention of Big Ears reduced both the intensity of her smile and the volume of her voice. She was employed two afternoons a week by one of Yue-sheng's wives, she explained, to tutor her children in Christian values. Not the easiest of tasks imposed by God. Every night, however, back in the convent where she was a postulant, she prayed that she might succeed in that task. What did Sir Lusty think?

Sir Lusty wasn't quite sure what a postulant was, but was afraid that she might be wasting her time. Her employer's husband wasn't really the Christian type. True, Maisy was endowed with the most beautiful smile that Sir Lusty himself had ever seen, but it seemed unlikely that God would have noticed it. He had, after all, well over four hundred and fifty million other people under his care in China alone. And, to be frank, God wasn't doing a very good job of that, as you'd readily recognise if you stopped to consider the population's levels of poverty and opium addiction. And look at the many millions of people who had been drowned in the Yangtze River floods last year. This led Sir Lusty to conclude that God had spread himself too thinly on the earth's surface. I mean, just consider all the matters he had to attend to round the world: like completion of the Empire State Building, for example; or Japan's invasion of Manchuria; or even West Bromwich Albion's unexpected victory in the FA Cup.

Maisy had never heard of an FA Cup, nor of a place called West Bromwich, but seemed prepared to be convinced by my argument when I looked deep into her eyes and asked her to dance.

That was definitely the end of the beginning and the beginning of the end, as we shifted from intellectual exchange to physical contact. Maisy had no qualms about pressing her body against mine as we trotted like well-bred foxes among other couples on the dance floor. By the time the music had come to an end, she was holding my hand. By the time we'd sat down, she was resting her head on my shoulder, occasionally looking up at me with that devastatingly attractive and inviting smile.

So far as I could recall, Big Ears had virtually ordered her to accompany the Count to the room he had ready for me in his hotel. Nobody said no to Big Ears. But that didn't mean I had to take advantage of this particular Catholic girl. Anyway, I was more or less beyond it.

Maisy rolled over in her sheet and looked at me with wide open eyes. "Good morning, Sir Lusty."

Her smile was still lovely. It lit up the room again, although how anyone could wake up and smile like that was beyond me. It shouldn't have been legal. In Sweden it wasn't, to judge by the people I knew there.

"And a very good morning to you, too, Maisy."

She looked into my eyes and gave me a chaste peck on the cheek. We lay there for a while—she in her sheet, I in my birthday suit. I didn't ask if she had had to undress me.

I rather liked being given a knighthood, and remembered her telling me that that was the way Filipinos addressed Caucasian men. A hangover from centuries of Spanish colonialism, no doubt. Anyway, I was now Count Sir Lusty Bloom-Stroganov of Petrograd, or wherever it was my father had come from.

Before I left she told me where I could find her. I found it hard to believe it when she said she lodged in a convent of Catholic sisters, right beside Saint Ignatius Cathedral at the end of Avenue Petain. As impregnable a fortress, surely, as Mei-si's own unstained chastity. That was how she wrote her name.

Downstairs I said goodbye and thank you to Chunky and took a
ricksha to the Cathay. Victor met me in the plush Bund Café downstairs
overlooking the river.

"You look like you're in need of some breakfast, Christopher.
Rough night?"

I nodded and gratefully took a sip of the coffee a waiter had
poured for me the moment I sat down. Was my hangover *that* obvious?

"Do you take that with you everywhere?" I asked, indicating his
camera which he had placed now on the table top.

"Everywhere except bed. And even that's not a given. It depends
on who's in it." He thrust a folded sheet of paper across the café table.
"By the way, the ransom note's come."

"That's a start." I unfolded the note. Half a million Mexican
dollars. "This is a lot of money, Victor."

"What did you expect of a kid *pro quo*?"

I admired his ability to keep a sense of humour.

"Half a million quid, perhaps?"

Now it was Victor's turn to laugh. I continued: "It looks like the
kidnappers couldn't decide whether to be realistic or totally fanciful,
doesn't it? Whether to demand two hundred and fifty thousand, or a
million for Simon's release. I met a Chinese detective inspector, Lolly
Lo Li-kwei, yesterday and he reckoned the kidnappers would have
trouble reconciling practicality with greed. It seems he was right."

"Anything else?"

"Do you intend to pay up, Victor?"

A waiter appeared conveniently with scrambled eggs and bacon,
toast, butter and marmalade. Chunky marmalade—the kind I liked,
even if it did now remind me of Yue-sheng's second-in-command. It
was Victor's turn to sip his coffee as he bided his time. Eventually,

"It goes against the grain, doesn't it?" he mused with a downward
turn of his mouth. "Half a million's a lot of money for a distant cousin.
Still, family is family."

"I can't argue with that, Victor. But it's twice as much as Al Ezra
paid a couple of years back. And we're entering a depression. Your
kidnappers strike me as being rather optimistic and possibly foolhardy.
When's the deadline?"

"Tonight at midnight. Did you find out anything about them?"

"Only that Tu Yue-sheng is definitely not involved."

"What makes you say that?"

"Because that's what *he* says. I met him yesterday evening,
together with Lolly Lo. Big Ears was seriously upset at the insinuation
that he might have played a part in Simon's kidnap. He's sent his men
out on the streets to find out more."

"Really? Jolly well done, Christopher. Thank you."

"Don't thank me yet, Victor. We haven't found Simon yet."

Just then there was a deafening explosion on the corner of Nanking Road and the Bund outside the café. This was followed by screams and the moans of a Sikh policeman, lying in the road with half one leg blown off. All around him were scattered a dozen ricksha cushions.

"What on earth —?"

I excused myself and rushed outside. Victor followed as quickly as his sticks allowed. The Sikh was barely conscious, moaning something repeatedly as blood streamed from splintered bone below his right knee. Unless an ambulance arrived very quickly, he would be toast. Without the butter and marmalade. But maybe such niceties didn't matter when you were dead.

I knelt beside him and with the end of his unravelled turban tried to tie a tourniquet as tightly as I could round his thigh. Victor was darting around taking photographs as I wiped the blood from the policeman's face with my handkerchief. The Sikh opened one eye and fixed me with a vacant stare. A bit like Victor's monocle, but without the mischief.

"Pani, Ja!" His voice croaked. "Pani." Blood trickled out of his mouth and his head fell seemingly lifeless to one side. Victor took one last photo and hobbled back inside the café.

The urgent ringing of a bell approached. The rear door was flung open while the police car was still moving and Lolly Lo stepped down onto the road with the kind of graceful elegance of which only ballerinas and overweight men seem capable. He'd been no slouch on the Del Monte's dance floor the night before.

Lolly looked down on the unconscious Sikh policeman and me kneeling beside him surrounded by bomb debris. Then he shook his head as if this was going to be another unsolved Shanghai kidnapping.

"Well, if it isn't our Count," he grinned, "on the scene of another crime."

"Only by chance. I was having a late breakfast with Sir Victor in the Bund Café there." I jerked a thumb over my right shoulder just in case Lolly was unaware of where the latest glitzy contribution to Shanghai's waterfront was located.

"Chance, eh?" Lolly began picking his teeth and pointed with the toe of his foot at the lifeless body beside me. "Is he dead?"

"He will be if an ambulance doesn't get here soon."

Lolly ignored my remark. He had other things on his mind. Like the fact that this was another bomb explosion in the International Settlement, and the police hadn't yet found the culprits.

"You know what they say, don't you Count, when your wife's

found drowned in the bath?"

I stood up, for the second time in two days dusting the knees of my trousers.

"Not sure that I do, Lolly. What do they say?"

"'Dear, dear! What a pity!'" He laughed loudly.

"Fair enough."

"But then there's the second time, isn't there?"

"If you say so, Lolly."

"That's when they give one another knowing looks and exclaim, 'What a coincidence!'"

"And the third time? There has to be one, doesn't there?"

"Of course." For a man standing over what was beginning to look like a corpse, Lolly was in exceptionally jovial mood.

"The third time, Rusty, they hang you." Now that we were more or less on first name terms he laughed louder than usual. "So be careful, my Swedish Count. Things are beginning to add up. Next time, I'll be arresting you on suspicion of murder!"

"But I thought we were friends."

"We are, Count, we are. Which is why you'll pay me to let you off with a caution." He laughed even louder and slapped me heartily on the back.

An ambulance arrived with a splendidly ringing bell. Two attendants got out and attended to the Sikh's body. One of them shook his head silently as he looked up enquiringly at Lolly.

"Take him to the morgue."

They lifted the dead policeman onto a stretcher, which they guided into the back of their vehicle. Then they closed its back doors and drove away, bell silenced.

"OK, Count, what can you tell me?" Lolly was the chief inspector now.

"Nothing, I'm afraid, that I haven't already told you."

"Hm. So you were enjoying breakfast with Sir Victor and a home-made bomb exploded outside your window. Where is His Eminence, by the way? Waiting for me, I hope. And you saw no potential witnesses scampering away up the street? No suspicious-looking bystanders? No last words from our Indian friend?"

"Yes Lolly, as a matter of fact he did say something."

"Ah-ha! So, what was it the Indian gentleman said, Rusty, that he thought might change the world he was on the verge of leaving? Not that last words necessarily mean much. But still. Out with it!"

"Pani."

"Pani?" Lolly's eyes narrowed. His toothpick moved from one side of his mouth to the other.

"Followed by something that sounded like ja."

"As in Japaní, perhaps?"

"Of *course!*" I slapped my forehead. "How stupid of me not to realise!"

"Blame it on your executions with the beautiful Mei-si. I'm sure they were enough to deprive any man of his wits." Lolly was back in jovial form. "But why Japanese? I mean, when did you ever come across a dwarf bandit pulling a ricksha, eh?"

"What do you mean?"

With one shoe, Lolly pushed aside what was left of a ricksha cushion.

"I guess you haven't been here long enough, Count, to know that traffic policemen in the International Settlement—like that dead Sikh who's just been whisked away to the morgue—like to supplement their incomes by seizing cushions from empty rickshas passing close by." The Chief Chinese Inspector shifted into explanatory mode. "Then they charge the ricksha puller with some traffic violation or other. Failure to stop when required, not displaying a permit, that sort of thing. The ricksha puller doesn't like that at all. Without a cushion he can't get customers, can he, and without customers he can't pay his daily rental. Because almost all the rickshas you see on the streets, Count, are rented out. Twelve hours at a time."

"Why not get another cushion then?"

Lolly rubbed the thumb and forefinger of his right hand together as we went into the rotunda of the Sassoon Building.

"Squeeze, Count. Squeeze. Shanghai wouldn't be able to function without squeeze. Surely you've learned that during your time here?"

"You mean, the ricksha puller has to pay the traffic policeman to get his cushion back?"

"Of *course*. As I said, the policeman charges the puller with some minor traffic offence. Which means he has to turn up at the police station the next day and pay a fifty cent fine. But that also means he can't earn any money until then."

"So he pays the traffic policeman half the fine, gets his cushion back, and carries on working."

Lolly laughed and slapped me heartily on the back.

"Well done, my friend. I'll make a policeman out of you yet. But now I'd like a chat with Sir Victor. Do you think he's still around?"

"Sitting at a table in the café right behind you, Lolly, waiting for me to come and finish my eggs and bacon."

"After you, then, Count. It's been a long time since I had an English breakfast."

Victor stood up when we entered the café and I effected the introductions.

"What was that explosion?" The hotelier asked, a little nervously.

"A small bomb placed in a ricksha cushion, Sir Victor. You know how these traffic policemen like to pile them up at junctions and get their tips. Unfortunately one had dynamite in it. Not much, but enough to blow the leg off a Sikh. And make him dead, rather than just," he paused briefly before adding with a smile, "sick."

I'm not sure Victor was amused, but he laughed politely as Lolly sat down on one of the spare chairs at the breakfast table.

A waiter poured him some coffee and asked what he'd like to eat.

"Why not bring me some of what my newly-acquired friends are having?" he responded. Clearly, Lolly could be as commanding as any aristocrat when he felt so inclined. And as well-mannered.

"Sir Victor, let me get down to the reason for my being here. I'm sorry to hear about what has happened to your nephew. Simon, isn't it? I promise you that, with the young Count's help here, I'll do my very best to find him."

"Thank you, Inspector Lo."

"I understand he's a pianist who's been playing at the Canidrome."

"That's right. He's studying at the Royal Academy of Music in London."

Lolly scratched his balding pate in confusion.

"How does a student at the Royal Academy of Music come to be playing *jazz*, Sir Victor? I'm no expert in such matters, but surely jazz isn't on the curriculum of such an august"—Lolly pronounced the word like the month—"institution?"

Victor gave out a loud guffaw.

"Exactly the question I asked him, Inspector Lo, when he arrived in Shanghai."

"And what was his answer?"

"One which, to be frank, I didn't really understand. But it seems he is trying to please his parents by playing classical music, and himself by experimenting with jazz."

Lolly nodded his head and discreetly picked at his teeth with a toothpick thoughtfully provided by the management of the Bund Café for its Chinese patrons.

"And have you by any chance had a ransom note yet?"

"Yes, indeed. It arrived this morning." Victor handed the offending note to Lolly who scanned its contents before putting the sheet of paper down on the table between us.

"Hmm. Half a million dollars strikes me as rather a lot of money. Even for you, Sir Victor. Do you intend to pay it?"

For once the hotelier didn't look his conversant in the eye. Instead, he stared out of the window at a couple of police constables clearing up the bomb debris.

"Do you have any advice about the matter, Inspector Lo?"

"I'm afraid I don't. I've always found that the decision to pay or not to pay a ransom needs to be made by the person concerned. After all, a life is at stake. In this case, your nephew's, or cousin's, or whatever relation Simon is to you. I think you have to ask yourself a couple of prelinimary questions. First, is the sum requested reasonable and, if so, can you afford it?"

Having said which, Lolly took up his knife and fork and started on his eggs and bacon. Neither Victor nor I saw fit to correct his confused consonants.

"Still…" he added, with his mouth full.

"Still what, Inspector?" Victor's monocle gleamed in the early morning sunlight.

Lolly swallowed and wiped his mouth on the napkin that he had tucked into his shirt collar.

"Something strikes me as not quite right." He turned his attention once more to the food on his plate and took another mouthful.

"In what way, might I ask?"

Lolly didn't answer immediately, but raised one hand as he carried on chewing his food, before swallowing demonstrably.

"In my experience, Sir Victor, those who kidnap for money usually follow a fixed itirenary. That is to say, they almost invariably start by demanding what in the context is a little more than a reasonable sum as ransom. In your case, I'd have estimated that amount to be a quarter of a million dollars. More than the average, but still within your financial wherewithal, I think I'm right in saying?"

Victor nodded, the eye behind his monocle closely observing the Chinese detective inspector.

"That becomes the base line for ensuing negotiations. You'd be able to bargain your nephew's price down to one hundred and twenty five thousand dollars and everyone would be happy. Neither side would lose face. In your nephew's case, however, money doesn't seem to be the main objective. Half a million silver dollars is a fairy-tale sum, which doesn't allow for negotiations between you and the kidnappers. In other words, they've kidnapped your nephew for another reason."

"Another reason?" There was a certain caginess in the eye behind Victor's monocle. "But what could that be?"

"That's what I was hoping you might be able to help me with, Sir Victor. A man of your status and wealth must have enemies."

"Enemies!" Victor laughed. "All the Brits in town, I expect. Remember, I'm Jewish. What's more, as you politely pointed out, I'm very rich. What is it they call me and my family? The Rothschilds of the East? I'm sure a lot of people are very jealous of my wealth, Inspector. And of my success."

"Is there anyone in particular you can think of, Sir Victor?"

"Not offhand, no." Victor's attention was transferred to buttering his toast. He could avoid Lolly's penetrating look that way.

"Nobody you've cheated in business?"

Victor looked up sharply and Lolly raised both hands apologetically.

"I'm sorry, Sir Victor. That wasn't well put. What I meant was, is there anybody you've bettered in business who might hold a grudge against you as a result? Anybody who *thinks* you've cheated him in business? A palm you've greased to get a profitable contract ahead of a business rival? A promise you've made and then reneged on? That sort of thing."

Victor furrowed his brow.

"Palms are *always* being greased in my line of business, Inspector. And vague promises made which may or may not be fulfilled, some sooner, some later."

"Hmm." I could see that Lolly wasn't entirely convinced. Every very wealthy man had enemies. But he let the matter go. "As you know, Sir Victor, the young Count here happened to witness the hold-up. And he found a Japanese bullet casing in the car."

"Yes. He told me that. So?"

Lolly's plate was now almost empty. One didn't get fat without an appetite to feed it. Hopefully he wouldn't suffer too soon from a coronary. Or even a cororany.

"The kidnapping itself has all the hallmarks of a job done by Tu Yue-sheng's Green Gang. However, when I confronted him with this fact, Tu became rather angry and confirmed what I already suspected: that none of his gang members owns or uses a Japanese pistol."

"So who *is* responsible? And what do they want?"

"That, Sir Victor, is what I intend to find out. My theory at the moment is that the kidnappers want to make the kidnapping look like the work of Big Ears Tu so that we focus our enquiries in that direction rather than elsewhere. Which is why the Count's discovery was so important. And," he added, "why anything you can tell me would be so helpful."

Lolly laid his knife and fork down together in the English manner and with a grunt of satisfaction again wiped his lips with the napkin that he had untucked from his shirt collar and now folded and lain on the table beside his empty plate.

Then he continued. "It seems likely that the cushion that exploded in the road outside was confiscated from a Japanese ricksha puller."

"A *Japanese* ricksha coolie? But that's —"

"Precisely, Sir Victor. Impossible. Or, at least, extremely unlikely. Which means that we have a lead," Lolly finished his coffee, wiped his mouth again, and dropped the napkin in a heap on the table. "What a breakfast, Sir Victor! If I had one of these every morning, I'd solve all the crimes in Shanghai."

Even Victor laughed.

"As it is, though, I'll confine myself to just this one. Goodbye for now, Sir Victor. And thank you for your hospitality." He laid a visiting card on the table. "Don't forget to let me know at once if you hear anything further from your nephew's kidnappers. In the meantime, I've got work to do. Come on, Count!"

8.

In the hotel's shopping arcade, Lolly made a quick telephone call before joining me in the street.

"Where to now?"

"There's a ricksha wallah we need to talk to near the Hongkew Market on Hanbury Road."

The police car was waiting for us. Lolly barked an order to the driver as we got in the back seat. Another constable was sitting in front.

"My guess was our Japanese was lazy and went to the nearest ricksha wallah in Japan Town to hire a vehicle. My phone call just now confirmed my suspicion. My men have found a ricksha abandoned at the corner of Nanking and Honan Roads, only two blocks from here. Its license told us who the owner is."

"Anyone you know?"

Lolly looked at me sharply.

"The Chief Chinese Inspector of Central Station tends not to socialise with ricksha wallahs," he said, with a twinkle in his eye. "I leave that to my subordinates and informants."

"Of course."

"But since this particular wallah happens to be Russian, Count, I thought you might help me ensure he tells us *everything* he knows."

We crossed Garden Bridge into Hongkew. A couple of minutes later the car slowed down as it approached the market. There were coolies everywhere, carting absurdly overloaded wheelbarrows full of sides of meat, fruit, and sacks of vegetables, or hauling carts laden with squealing pigs and cages stuffed with live chickens. Others carried duck eggs in bamboo panniers on the ends of a pole over their shoulders, or pigs' trotters on blood-stained sheets of newspaper. At one point the car could move no further through this seething mass of bodies and came to a complete stop. Lolly opened the rear door and jumped out.

"Can't hang around here all day," he rasped and started walking briskly through the crowds, occasionally shouting at people to get out of the way. After a couple of minutes we came across a single ricksha, its shafts sticking out from a hole in the market wall.

Lolly nodded to me to go in.

"I'm told the guy's name is Blonsky, but who knows. Ask him if he'll rent you that ricksha now—that one without a cushion that one of my informants brought back a quarter of an hour ago—and see what happens."

"What about you?"

"Me? I'll be back at the Cathay having lunch." Then, seeing my face, Lolly laughed. "I just want to observe things here before I join you."

I crossed the road and stood at the edge of the ricksha wallah's lock-up.

"Anyone at home?" I called out in Russian.

"Who wants to know?" A gigantic bearded man emerged from the gloom. He stood a good head taller than me, held a heavy spanner in one hand, and had a menacing glint in his one blue eye. Someone you definitely wouldn't want to bump into in a dark alley at night.

"Rusty Bloom."

"Blum? What does a Russian-speaking German called Blum want here?"

I thought it better not to get into family matters right now. Blonsky was bigger than me.

"I'm looking to hire a ricksha."

"Everyone is, Mr Blum."

"I'll pay you good money." I held out two silver dollars.

"You won't be the first, my friend." He pocketed the coins. "But I don't rent to strangers."

"What's your name?"

The big man furrowed his brow, a confused look on his face. "Blonsky. Why?"

"Because I've already told you my name. And now you've told me yours, which means we're definitely not strangers. You've admitted as much by calling me 'your friend' just now. So rent me this ricksha, my friend."

"No can do." Surly now that I'd outdone him with my logic.

"Can't? Or won't?"

"Can't."

"Why not?"

"That's my business, inunit?" Blonsky stood towering over me, the grip on his spanner tighter. I leaned back very slightly, enough to alter my balance so that I could overpower him should he decide to attack.

It was at this point that Lolly chose to make his appearance, a three-foot stippled police baton in one hand.

"It's also my business," he said firmly. "Police business. The cushion in this ricksha here," he tapped one shaft of the vehicle beside me with his baton, "was used to blow up one of my colleagues this morning."

I translated what he'd said to Blonsky.

"So?"

"So, that means you're an accessory to murder, Mr Blonsky. You're under arrest." Lolly jerked his head and the other two policemen stepped forward.

"Whaddya mean 'murder'? I don't know nuffink about a murder, right?" Blonsky shuffled his feet, dropped his spanner and wiped his hands on a greasy rag. "All I did was hire out this ricksha to some guy what wanted one for the day."

"Some guy?"

"I dunno. A Chinee wallah."

"He speak Chinese to you?"

"No." Uncomfortable now.

"What then? English?"

Shamefacedly. Like a small boy caught stealing an apple.

"Russian."

"Russian?" Lolly was relentless. "How many Chinee wallahs you know speak Russian, Mr Blonsky?"

"A couple." Defiant now.

"A couple, eh? And Japanese?"

Blonsky froze.

"How much did he pay you, this Chinee wallah?"

"A couple of dollars." Reluctant.

"A couple of dollars? But that's twice as much as you usually charge, isn't it." A statement, not a question. Lolly knew he had his man. "When did you ever hear of a Chinee wallah paying over the odds, Blonsky?"

Silence. Blonsky shuffled his feet, uncomfortable again.

"I don't know what my friend here, Count Bloom, thinks, Blonsky. But I reckon the only people ready to pay more than a dollar to rent a ricksha would be Japanese. Wouldn't you agree, Count?"

"Sounds likely. What do you think, Blonsky?"

The mechanic's voice was so low we both had to stretch forward to hear him.

"Maybe."

"Maybe?" Lolly took over with an explosive laugh and gave Blonsky a whack on the back of one shin with his baton. "There's no maybe about it, *slysh*! It's a dead cert. So, tell me. Where can I find your Japanese friend?"

"I dunno, duz I? He left with my ricksha and never come back."

"But it's here now?"

"Yeah. Some Chinee coolie brought it back, inunit. Said it was abandoned somewhere on the Nanking Road."

"Abandoned, eh? Give him a tip, did you? For bringing it back."

"Sure. Half a dollar."

"Half a dollar?" Lolly pursed his lips and nodded in admiration. "Is that all? Half a dollar for an abandoned cart without a cushion. I'd have thought a ricksha's worth more than that. Didn't the Chinee coolie bargain with you, Blonsky? Or was he too frightened of you? Eh?"

Blonsky shuffled his feet some more, but Lolly was as persistent as a Scottish spider.. "So where's this Japanese guy now?"

"I told you, I dunno, duz I."

Lolly fingered his baton meaningfully.

"What did he look like, then?"

"I dunno, Mista Detective, sir. Never seen him before. I swear to God."

"God? What's he got to do with anything?"

I should remember to recruit Lolly to my side next time Maisy broached the topic of Catholicism.

"All Japs look the same, inunit? Short legs, stocky, crew-cut hair, squashed nose, slant eyes."

Lolly gave Blonsky another whack with his baton. Hard enough for Blonsky to double up in pain.

"Can't you do better than that? I'll ask you again. What did your Japanese friend look like?"

"Short legs, stocky—aagh!"

Another whack. This time on the ribs. I began to feel grateful Lolly was my friend. For now, at least.

"Try again, Blonsky."

"He had a tattoo," the ricksha wallah gasped. "Here." Pointing to the inside of his forearm.

"What kind of tattoo?"

"Looked like a ladder, inunit, with a bit sticking out."

"A ladder with a bit sticking out," Lolly parroted Blonsky perfectly.

"Yeah. Right here," he pointed to the underside of his forearm, "Just above the wrist of his right hand."

Lolly flicked his fingers at the policeman standing just behind him.

"Constable Chang, your notebook and pencil." He handed them to Blonsky, and ordered: "Draw it!"

"Draw what?"

"The tattoo, idiot!" Blonsky got another whack on the back of one thigh. The big Russian crouched down and started to draw.

"Not exactly a Li Ch'eng, are you?" Lolly grinned as he examined Blonsky's artistic work.

"Lee who?"

"What is this anyway?"

"Like I told you—a ladder."

"Funniest ladder I've ever seen."

"What happens," I intervened, turning the notebook in Lolly's hand sideways, "if you look at it like this?"

Lolly looked at the drawing again and then looked up at me.

"You never told me you could read Chinese, Count," he said accusingly in Shanghainese.

"You never asked," I replied in Mandarin.

"Hmm. So you think this is the Chinese character for blood?"

"I think it looks more likely than a ladder, don't you?"

"Maybe." He switched back to English. "I can see your executions with Mei-si last night weren't a total waste of time."

"I think you mean exertions, Lolly."

"That's as may be. As for you, Blonsky, you're coming to the police station with us."

"Police station? But I done nuffink wrong."

"Maybe not. But you've got information we need."

"But I've told you all I know, inunit," Blonsky had lost all his swagger.

"Not quite, Blonsky. You know what this Japanese looks like. And you're going to describe him to a police artist for us. A real artist, who knows the difference between blood and a ladder."

He turned back to me and slapped me on one shoulder. "Not bad, Count. For a *hong mao fan*."

I tried not to snort with disgust. I wasn't a barbarian. Nor was my hair red. Was Lolly colour blind?

9.

Victor was in his penthouse up on the eleventh floor of the Sassoon Building. The view was even more magnificent in daylight, helped by Kiki who was adjusting a bra strap under her cashmere pullover as Perkins ushered me into the living room. After exchanging air kisses on each cheek, she excused herself politely and left. I may have been a *hong mao fan*, but surely I didn't smell *that* bad.

"Ah, Christopher! Just the man I was hoping to see," Victor placed his sticks in their usual position by his chair and sat down heavily. His Leica was still on the sofa beside where Kiki had been sitting or reclining, or whatever she did when posing in front of a camera.

I sat down in the same place. The cushions were still warm and scented with Lanvin's *My Sin*.

"I'm glad you dropped by—if one can call scaling eleven floors to my penthouse 'dropping' by. Would you like a drink?"

"No, thanks. I'm fine for now."

Victor raised an eyebrow archly.

"Well, let's see how you feel after I've finished," he grinned.

I settled back in the sofa and made myself comfortable, displacing the contours of Kiki's body with my own.

"There's something I need to tell you, and only you, Christopher. I realise it's tempting providence for me to confide in a journalist, but I feel like I have no option."

"You always have options, Victor. You of all people should know that."

"I do indeed. I also know there are risks involved, whatever choice one makes."

"Fair enough," I said. "What is it you want to tell me?"

"It may have something to do with Simon's kidnapping and it all began on the night of that terrible typhoon a few weeks ago. I was up here on my own in the penthouse and, to be frank, I was a little scared. I mean, it was the building's first real test since its completion. What if Sassoon House subsided, or if the tower above my head came tumbling down?" he laughed self-consciously. "I know. Hardly the thought of a rational businessman who's made his fortune in real estate, but there you are."

"I can appreciate that. I was out in it, going for a stroll. A wild and windy night—the kind that starts off adventure or detective stories."

"A *stroll?*" he laughed, as if I was mad. "Are all your countrymen as foolhardy, Christopher."

"Most of them, Victor. The trouble is, they don't realise it."

Victor laughed again. "Sounds familiar. Anyway, as I was saying. If you thought it was a wild and windy night down at street level, imagine what it felt like being up here, eleven stories above the ground. The wind *howled*—I kid you not—it howled around the windows, it howled in the structure above me. It was pointless even thinking of going to sleep and anyway it was still only about nine o'clock in the evening. All my so-called friends had disappeared. Locked themselves up at home or in the nearest brothel, or wherever. I was totally alone, apart from the stalwart Perkins, of course.

"The wind and the rain were making so much noise I couldn't even put on the gramophone and listen to music. I couldn't concentrate when I tried to read or even take a turn at sorting all my photographs. Eventually, when I could stand the noise no longer, I decided to go out. Of all things. Mad, eh? I don't know what got into me. Perkins tried to dissuade me, but I ignored his advice and called for a car. Not the Rolls, but one of my less showy ones. I couldn't have an advertising hoarding or bamboo scaffolding crash down on my most expensive limousine, could I?"

"Did you know where you were going to go?"

He eyed me mischievously.

"Oh yes, Christopher. I knew alright. There was a house of dubious repute I'd heard of, called Salon Pink. Run by a Japanese woman, so I'd been told, and offering all kinds of—how should I put it?—'special services' to overcome the loneliness of men like myself with deep pockets. One needed an introduction, but that wasn't a problem. I was, after all, Sir Victor Sassoon, third Baronet of Bombay, reputedly the richest man in Shanghai.

"Anyway, I went to this club called Salon Pink. It's situated on the corner of Kiangse and Ningpo Roads a stone's throw from here, Christopher, in case you feel an urge to try it out. The door was answered by an extremely beautiful Japanese woman in her mid- to late-thirties, I'd say, although it's always very hard to tell, isn't it, with Asian women. She was dressed in informal kimono and spoke almost flawless English. Her name, she told me, was—is—Miyoko.

"The room in which she received me was tastefully decorated in Japanese style, with tatami straw mats on the floor away from the door, and a couple of *sumi-e* brush and ink paintings on the walls. There was an ash-glazed jar with an exquisitely simple flower decoration on top of a cedar and zelkova wood step-*tansu* chest, and a jade statue of what looked like a Hindu goddess in the *tokonoma* raised dais in one corner. In the middle of the room was an open-hearth *irori* fireplace."

"Sounds almost *too* traditional."

"It was. A kettle was steaming on the burning charcoal and Miyoko proceeded to pour me a cup of delicious green tea, which with a deep bow she offered to me. 'From the best young leaves,' she smiled, 'like everything else in this house.' Talk about innuendo.

"After braving the raging storm outside, I gradually felt myself sinking into an oasis of calm, as if I had somehow returned to my mother's womb. Of course, the wind was howling outside and the rain was lashing the windows, but they seemed to be part of another world. Here, sitting inside the Salon Pink on a chair thoughtfully provided by Miyoko, I felt at peace. And that isn't a feeling I've experienced very often, Christopher, I can assure you. The simplicity of my surroundings, the carefully thought out aesthetics of this room, helped me relax completely. Japanese certainly can teach us a thing or two when it comes to interior design."

"True, Victor, but it sounds to me as if the ambience in which you found yourself was carefully contrived to help you forget the fleshly urges underpinning your visit to the Salon Pink."

"Meticulously planned, I'd say. And it worked, Christopher. It worked. Whereas when I entered I had felt unsure of myself, in the presence of Miyoko all my inhibitions miraculously evaporated. She carefully parted the mists of my desires, gently wondering what I might think of this, or how I might I feel about that, until she knew exactly what I wanted without ever having asked me directly about anything."

"The perfect madame."

"The perfect madame, indeed."

"And what *did* you want that she so astutely intuited?"

He didn't answer directly.

"When I'd finished my tea, Miyoko eased herself up from her knees by the *irori* and invited me to accompany her upstairs. She led me to another tastefully furnished room, this time a bedroom, where the bed consisted of two tatami mats on a wooden frame with Japanese bedding laid on top. There was a tall screen in the corner furthest from the window, next to a wash basin. It was decorated with a haiku poem in brush and ink against a background of two cranes leaping up in a mating dance. I followed her instructions and undressed behind the screen and put on the *aizome* indigo-dyed yukata sleeping robe that she handed to me. Miyoko told me to lie down and then gently massaged my shoulders. After a while, when I felt totally relaxed, she invited me to enjoy this feeling to the full and briefly left the room."

"And?'

"And then she came back in with two young Japanese girls, who she introduced as Sakura and Hanako. Two blossoms, Miyoko called them. They could hardly have been more than thirteen or fourteen years old, to judge by how poorly developed their breasts were, but they were, all the same, extremely beautiful. With all the innocent purity of girls who are neither adult nor child. This was what I had come to the Salon Pink in search of."

"So you made love to them?"

"Good lord, no!" Victor was shocked. "Please, Christopher, do not presume. I may be far from perfect. I may have my strange sexual proclivities, but they do not extend to making love to—to having sex with—pre-pubescent virgins."

"Always assuming they *were* virgins."

"As you say, but I wouldn't know, would I?"

"So what *did* you do at the Salon Pink that required a clandestine visit in the midst of a raging typhoon?"

"I took their photographs, of course. I am, after all, a photographer."

"Their photographs? That's all?"

"That's all. I never touched them," he paused. "Until the very end, that is."

"The end?" There was always a catch to sincerity.

"After a couple of hours of having them adopt the kind of poses one doesn't normally see in polite society, I was tired. So I lay down on the bed. The two girls lay down beside me, one on each side. That was when they undid the yukata sash around my waist and laid me bare."

"Completely?"

"Cigar and all. They were clearly far less innocent than I'd imagined."

"But you didn't have sex with them?"

"Absolutely not. Not even when they roused an erection out of me."

"So what did you do?"

"I pushed their hands firmly away, sat up in bed, and readjusted my yukata. Then I got dressed again behind the screen and left the room. Downstairs, I thanked Miyoko for fulfilling my request satisfactorily, and asked her to send me her invoice the following morning. Then I left. With my camera, of course."

"Of course." I let the silence steal back in between us. "And?"

"And?" Victor smiled his lynx-like smile. "And then I received an invoice, didn't I, the following morning? It was a tad more than I'd anticipated, but not exorbitantly so. I arranged payment and thought no more of the matter. I had a roll of film to develop, after all, and was excited to see how the prints would emerge."

"And were they as good as you'd hoped, Victor?"

"Good? They were superb, Christopher, even though I say it myself. Somehow I had managed to capture that in-between state of chaste innocence, on the one hand, and a sort of sensual desire, on the other, that I saw in the two girls."

"But all wasn't well that seemingly ended well?"

"No, it wasn't, alas. Three days later, I think it was, Perkins came into my study to inform me I had a visitor. When I enquired who it was, he replied that it was a Japanese woman and handed me her visiting card. Miyoko Noguchi."

"Noguchi?"

"That's right. I told Perkins to ask my visitor to wait a few moments and to provide her with a cup of Yunnan Pu'erh tea in the meantime. Once I had finished what I was doing in my study I went to meet her. She was standing over there by the window admiring the view, dressed in formal kimono, with wide *obi* belt tied in butterfly style in the small of her back.

"I welcomed my visitor and complimented her on her turn-out. She smiled modestly and told me that the bush clover pattern on her kimono marked the end of summer and the beginning of autumn. It was, therefore, a metaphor for the ephemeral nature of life. A little like the two girls I had encountered a few nights previously, she added, already blossoming into sensual young women."

"Sounds a bit far-fetched for summer into autumn. Spring into summer would have made more sense. Do I sense a bit of squeeze, Victor?"

"You do indeed, Christopher. Although I have to say, it was at first a very gentle squeeze. As she sipped her tea appreciatively, Miyoko complimented me in turn on my taste in Chinese furnishings. She also seemed rather taken by my Georges Barbier prints above the fireplace and in the hallway. The artist, she suggested, had clearly been influenced by Japanese *ukiyoe* woodblock artists. You could see it in the composition of the Flighty Bird and the Judgement of Paris. I responded that while I accepted that Barbier's prints were marked generally by an Orientalist tendency, I wasn't convinced of any specifically Japanese influence.

"And so we chatted rather pleasantly, much as we had done when I had paid my visit to the Salon Pink a few evenings earlier. As I said, Miyoko is the epitome of refined Japanese elegance—well-spoken, cultured and well-informed. Perkins came in to refresh her tea as she told me about Japanese courtesans of the Edo Period, rarefied creatures who not only sang and danced, but who wrote poetry, performed the tea ceremony and created artistic flower arrangements. Some, she said, had children and there are prints by woodblock artists like Utamaro of courtesan mothers bathing their children with their breasts bare. I began to wonder whether I shouldn't study Japanese art more. Perhaps I was too enamoured of Art Deco and Impressionism.

"It was then, after describing one particular print by Utamaro that Miyoko artfully shifted the conversation to the difficulties of being a single mother, although whether she is one or not I have no idea. From there she slipped easily to the plight of orphans, and suddenly she was telling me about an orphanage that she had set up in Hongkew. Wouldn't I like to make a contribution to a good cause?"

Victor paused to relight the cigar that had gone out in the ashtray resting on the arm of his chair.

"This transition from art to orphanage to financial donation was so smooth that at first I didn't quite realise what she had so discreetly asked, and I had to get her to repeat her request. When I asked her how large a donation she had in mind, she replied that it was, of course, up to me and my generosity, but one hundred thousand dollars wouldn't go amiss."

"One hundred *thousand*?"

"My thoughts exactly, Christopher."

'So what did you say?"

"I said what any good businessman would say under such circumstances. I told her I would think about it and let her know. She bowed politely and thanked me, while drawing from the depths of her *obi* a photograph that she placed facing me on the table top between us. It was of me, lying in bed with two naked underage girls, one of whom had her hand on my member."

"No?"

"Alas! Yes. A hidden camera was embedded in the ceiling, perhaps in the light fitting, of the room I'd been in and gave a perfect aerial view of what took place on the bed below. I was now the victim of blackmail."

"So you paid what Miyoko asked?"

Victor gave his lynx-like smile.

"I did nothing of the sort, Christopher. Give in to blackmail once and you're a victim for life. The blackmailer is like an anaconda, wrapping itself around its prey and squeezing the life out of it. I suddenly saw Miyoko for what she was, a deadly snake whose one genuine talent was deception."

"So what did you do?"

"I took the photograph and placed it casually in the inside breast pocket of my jacket. Then I stood up to signal that our meeting was at an end, called for Perkins and informed him that my guest wished to leave. Miyoko bowed wordlessly, smiled in such a way as to intimate that our acquaintanceship had only just begun, and left the room."

"But she came back again later?"

"As a matter of fact, she didn't. Instead, I had a visit in my office the following day by what my secretary described as 'some kind of Japanese army officer'—a certain Kenji Doihara, Colonel of the Kempeitai, Japan's military police."

"Oh my God!"

Precisely my own reaction, Christopher. I don't know if you've come across Colonel Doihara, but, if not, I advise you to try to keep things that way. He's hardly of what you might call a prepossessing appearance. I've always been wary of small men, ever since Napoleon," he laughed grimly. "His eyes are cold and dispassionate, too, a bit like Tu Yue-sheng's—cunning and cruel. In my line of business, Christopher, I learn to judge people by their eyes. It's why I immediately took a liking to you and why I'm confiding in you now."

"Thank you, Victor."

He waved away my gratitude. "In my experience, eyes can invite trust. They can invite fear. They suggest truth and they suggest deception. It often takes just one glance into the eyes of a potential partner for me to know whether I should proceed with a particular business proposition or avoid it.

"Of course, deception can be masked, as I had found out to my cost when encountering Miyoko Noguchi. Miyoko rather cleverly covered with her voice and her overall appearance what a keen observer might have seen in her eyes. I suspect she was able to succeed in this rather better in the presence of a foreign man who was distracted by what was, so far as I was concerned, an exotic beauty and oriental mannerisms.

In Japan, I suspect her wiles may not work quite so successfully. But who knows? When it comes to men's attraction to women, the flesh is eternally weak."

"The story of my life," I laughed.

"And mine, too, I can assure you," he gave me his lynx-like smile. "Anyway, as I was saying, Doihara came to my office without prior appointment, although he seemed to take it for granted that I would see him. I took an immediate dislike to him and realised at once that I didn't want to be on the wrong side of this particular Japanese colonel."

"Understandable. Go on."

"He came straight to the point, I'll give him that. No exchange of pleasantries about the weather or my latest flutter at the Canidrome. Nothing like that. Maybe it was because he felt uncomfortable speaking English. He had come, he said, because it had been brought to his attention that Sir Victor Sassoon—for some reason he kept referring to me in the third person, as if I wasn't right there in front of him— had been involved in a sexual relationship with a Japanese girl who was still a minor. He, Doihara, was tasked with investigating such matters when Japanese citizens were involved. Could Sir Victor please explain himself?

"So Sir Victor did. I told him frankly what had occurred on that fateful night during the typhoon, adding that I was now being blackmailed by the proprietor of the Salon Pink, one Miyoko Noguchi. He didn't bat an eyelid when I mentioned her name and showed him the photo that she had given me. He examined it briefly, then asked how much Miyoko was demanding. When I told him, he gave a supercilious smile and said he thought Sir Victor was lucky to be getting away with so little. If it had been *him* he would have asked for one quarter of a million dollars to make my 'problem' go away. He suggested politely that Sir Victor pay the sum requested to Miyoko's orphanage. It would, after all, be a donation to a good cause and would help numerous other young girls, like the ones who had been my companions at the Salon Pink, by providing them with a home and education. If Sir Victor were, by chance, willing to increase his donation, Doihara was sure that he would be able to convince Miyoko to rename her orphanage as the Sassoon Orphanage for Japanese Children. Think, he said, what that would do for Sir Victor's reputation among the many wealthy Japanese entrepreneurs in Shanghai who were always on the lookout for new business opportunities."

"And who no doubt frequent the Salon Pink in order to consort with the orphans in question."

"Precisely. Once again I assured my Japanese visitor that I would 'favourably consider' his proposition before bidding him a less than fond farewell. That very same evening, before I'd even had time to work out how best to bring this matter to a close, my nephew Simon was kidnapped."

"No coincidence, then?"

"Seems unlikely. Mark you, Doihara or Miyoko Noguchi decided to go the full McCoy when it came to deciding the ransom, didn't they?"

"But we don't know they're involved in the kidnapping, Victor."

"Maybe not. But the numbers suggest they are. I mean, I'd expected to get a ransom note for two hundred and fifty thousand Mexican dollars."

"But instead it was half a million dollars? Twice as much."

"I'm guessing that the extra two hundred and fifty thousand has been added on as insult money. A surcharge for lost face after I refused to agree to Doihara's proposition."

I was glad I wasn't a businessman.

"Are you going to pay up, Victor? Half a million's one hell of a lot of money for a jazz pianist."

"But not for a classical pianist, you mean?" Victor still had a sense of humour.

"That's not what I meant. I was merely questioning the size of the sum. Whether Simon is a Horowitz or a Fats Waller is irrelevant so far as I'm concerned."

"Fair enough, Christopher. But I cannot not pay. Simon's mother would never forgive me if I didn't, and family comes first. Way ahead of money."

"Have you told Lolly Lo that?"

He nodded.

"And what did he say?"

"The same as before. That it was up to me. But he suggested I leave a message instead for the kidnappers, demanding some proof that they were actually holding Simon before I paid up."

"Wise counsel, surely?"

"Inspector Lo also said he has a lead."

"He does indeed. The explosion outside the dining room yesterday morning was carried out by a Japanese and we're pretty certain there's a link with Simon's kidnapping. We've got a description and Lolly's men are all over Hongkew searching for the guy right now. Tu Yue-sheng's men, too. If they don't find the man himself, they'll find another like him. He had a gang tattoo on his arm. It's just a matter of time, Victor."

"Time we don't necessarily have. The ransom drop-off is at 2 am."

"We've got a few hours left then. Don't worry, Victor. Lolly Lo's no slouch when it comes to catching criminals."

10.

On my way out of the building, I ran into a journalist I had met a few weeks back—Joao Sereño. Joao was half-Japanese, half-Portuguese and had been born in Nagasaki to an old trading family there. His great grandfather had changed the family name to Serino in the hope that *os Sereños* would fit into Japanese society better. That, it transpired, had been misplaced optimism. Until fairly recently, they had still been treated as outlanders, *gaijin*, by the local populace.

After being sent to Shanghai by his newspaper, the *Asahi Shimbun*, Joao had decided to become Portuguese, or at least European, rather than Japanese. Which was fair enough, given the current anti-Japanese sentiment among the Chinese. It was still difficult to tell, though, whether he was going to behave like a Japanese or a Portuguese whenever we met, and I tended to feel a bit like the owner of a company who was convinced that half the money he spent on advertising was being wasted. The trouble was he didn't know which half.

"Hello Rusty." Joao was clearly in European mode, dressed like an English country squire in brown Tweed jacket over grey trousers and black brogues. He was wearing a white cotton shirt, knotted by a tie full of red and black stripes that looked like the colours of some Home Counties cricket club. Or not, as the case may be. Joao was hardly the hunting, shooting, fishing type, after all. And definitely not Old School. Maybe he just liked stripes.

We headed up the Nanking Road to a bar where we ordered a couple of beers. Joao got straight down to business. Definitely not in Japanese mode. I could see how he had become such a respected and well-known journalist in Japan.

"Everyone's trying to find out more about the kidnapping of Sir Victor's nephew," he began, "and the French gendarmerie are being tight-lipped."

"I'm not surprised. They're a bunch of incompetents."

"Tell me something new. After all, Tu Yue-sheng's in charge."

"Not this time, Joao."

The beers arrived. Two bottles of Tsingtao and two glasses. What we were going to drink this time wasn't Japanese, or even Manchurian, but German. The Chinese had enemies on every front, including the brewers of beer. All the same, the Tsingtao tasted good.

Joao clearly thought so, too. He licked the froth from his upper lip appreciatively. "It seems like you're the only journalist around who knows anything about Simon Meyer's kidnapping, Rusty."

"Really?" I feigned surprise. What now, though? Like Victor, I had to trust my instinct.

"Look, Joao, the investigation's got nothing to do with Big Ears.

Neither has the kidnapping."

"It doesn't?"

"No, it doesn't. That much I can assure you."

I swore Joao to secrecy and gave him a truncated version of what had happened over the past couple of days.

"You can't go asking Lolly Lo questions, Joao. Not yet. He'll deny everything. But once this whole affair is over you'll know who to talk to. Apart from me, of course."

"And is it going to be over? Soon, I mean."

"With your help, Joao."

"Mine?"

"Do you happen to know anything about a Japanese gang whose members tattoo themselves with the Chinese character for blood?"

Joao mulled over my question for a few seconds. Then,

"Not a gang as such. But there's an association of ultranationalists who call themselves the Ketsumeidan in Japanese. The League of Blood. They may tattoo themselves, I don't know, but they've formed a kind of blood brotherhood whose members come from poor rural backgrounds for the most part, and believe in the unity of the emperor and his people as the basis for Japan's 'spiritual renovation,'" he paused. "There's a rumour going round that they're dissatisfied with Hirohito because he won't agree to the Kwantung Army waging war on the rest of China and Southeast Asia. But I don't see how that ties in with the kidnapping of the nephew of a rich Baghdadi Jew in Shanghai."

"Nor do I," I couldn't tell him the truth yet. "Unless they need financing."

"Always a possibility. To buy arms would be my first suspicion, although half a million Mexican silver dollars seems a bit over the top. For a kidnapping, that is."

"True," I said. "Anything else you can tell me about this League of Blood?"

"Well, their leader's a self-styled Buddhist preacher who believes in the Buddhist principle of *issetsu tashō*—killing one to save many. Goes by the name of Nisshō."

"Nisshō?"

"It means 'Shining One.' Nobody really knows who he is. Some say he spent a decade in Manchuria and China as a *tairiku rōnin*, or 'continental adventurer,' drinking, whoring and living on the knife-edge of danger back in the time of the Revolution in 1911. Others say he even fought for the Nationalists. Whatever, he seems to have taken up religion."

"Always dangerous."

"As you say, always dangerous, especially when zealotry is involved." Joao took another swig of his beer. "But, as I said, nobody really knows. Newspapers haven't bothered to investigate him or his group because this Blood Brotherhood hasn't actually *done* anything, apart from proclaiming loudly that Japan's elites—political parties, *zaibatsu* business conglomerates, liberals, even military factions—are responsible for the country's decline and failure to fulfil the promise of the Meiji Restoration."

"Which was?"

"The welfare of the masses overseen by a benevolent emperor. I don't know how much you've been keeping abreast of affairs, Rusty, but there's plenty of dissatisfaction among ordinary Japanese people. Nisshō has called for the assassination of those he refers to as 'evil' elites."

"Not anyone connected with the Imperial family, surely?"

"Not as far as I know. But there's a rumour going around that somebody close to the Emperor is supporting the brotherhood."

"Who?"

Joao smiled. "You're going to have to give me more than you have done so far for me to impart that information, Rusty. Always assuming I actually know who is involved."

"Touché." He was playing the game. "I'll let you know what happens tonight."

"Do that," Joao gave a very slight burp. "Oops! Sorry."

"I still don't see where all this fits in with the Sassoon kidnapping, though. Maybe it isn't the Blood Brotherhood that's involved? Some other gang, perhaps?"

"Always possible," Joao conceded. "I've heard one of Doihara's spies, a woman called Yoshiko Kawashima, is involved in all sorts of shady stuff."

"A woman?"

"Sometimes." Again the easy laugh. Portuguese, rather than Japanese, mode. "It seems our Yoshiko likes to get dressed up as a man and call himself Yoshio. A bit of a rabble-rouser, by all accounts." He paused to take another sip of his Tsingtsao beer. "And then there's Nisshō's second-in-command, a Lieutenant Fujii, who is also here in Shanghai. Fujii's a real fire-brand, I can assure you. Likes to make use of Russians and Japanese rōnin to stir things up."

"Meaning there's something else going on besides this kidnapping?"

"Could be. I can ask around. Discreetly, of course. But I'm not sure I'll come up with anything useful, Rusty."

"Thanks, Joao. Much appreciated. I owe you."

"You can start with the beers, then."

11.

Half an hour later I took my leave and found Lolly in the Central Police Station on Foochow Road. The fat detective inspector was looking harassed.

"What luck, Lolly?" I sat down beside him at his desk. By way of reply, the Chief Chinese Inspector sucked his teeth and directed a gob of spit into a bucket beside him.

"Nothing yet. But Yue-sheng's got his men out for me, searching every possible den of vice in Hongkew. I live in hope."

"Don't we all? Although I'm not sure about Sir Victor. He seems ready to pay the ransom, even though he's got no proof that whoever's demanding half a million silver dollars is actually holding Simon hostage."

"Not exactly the wisest move of Shanghai's premier tycoon. What's happened to his business sense?"

"Families make morons of us all, Lolly."

"As does blackmail." Lolly was no fool. "Has he asked you to drop off the ransom money in a bag under the bandstand of the Public Gardens?"

"Not yet, but he probably will, if that's where the drop-off point is."

"Seriously stupid if you ask me. Anyone could make off with it and leave us none the wiser."

"I know." A pause. "In the meantime, there's something I'd like to try, Lolly."

"Don't tell me you've got another one of your hunches?"

"Something like that. I've been talking to a Japanese journalist who mentioned something about a League of Blood in Japan. A group of ultranationalists ready to assassinate anyone they don't like."

"Sounds familiar," Lolly directed another gob of spittle into the bucket at his feet. "Do they sport tattoos to remind them how to write 'blood' in Japanese?"

"I don't know, but it'd make sense, wouldn't it?"

"Maybe."

"Something struck me, Lolly, about what this journalist had to say. Its leader, somebody called Nisshō, claims to be a Buddhist priest."

"So?"

"You and Tu Yue-sheng have sent your men out searching for the kidnappers in the dens and alleys all over Hongkew. Right? But what if Simon is being held somewhere else? Somewhere totally different?"

"Like where?"

"Like in a Buddhist temple. There's one in Hongkew, isn't there? It's out of the hustle and bustle of Little Tokyo and very few people go there."

"A perfect place to hide someone, you mean?"

"Why not?"

Lolly closed his eyes as he thought. Then he sighed.

"Sure you're not clutching at straws, Count?"

"No, I'm not at all sure, but it might be worth checking the place out. Come on, Lolly. Humour me."

The detective inspector sighed again.

"OK. OK. I'll try anything to close this case. But after we've come away empty handed, you can buy me dinner at the Cathay Hotel."

"You're on. But no dessert. It's bad for your figure."

"Tell me about it!" Lolly laughed.

"And if I'm right, you owe *me* dinner, Lolly."

"We'll see about that.'

The Nishi Honganji Buddhist temple was on the corner of Chapoo and Quinsan Roads—a dark oasis of trees around a stuccoed building decorated with Buddhist lotuses and Japanese chrysanthemums.

"You're staying here," Lolly said firmly as I made to follow him out of the car. "You're just a newspaper reporter, remember? This is serious police business."

"But —?"

"No buts. Constable Wang, you're in charge of this man. If he tries to follow us arrest him. Shoot him if you must."

"Yessir!" The constable grinned and saluted smartly in the dark. Lolly took a torch from the glove pocket under the dashboard and led the remaining members of his squad up a short flight of stone steps past two stone lions and along a path among the willow trees to the temple building. Soon all I could see were erratic flashes of light from their torches as they probed the darkness. Then they were gone as Lolly and his colleagues disappeared inside the temple building.

I offered Constable Wang a cigarette to help pass the time, but he politely declined.

"Smoking no good for health, sir."

"Probably not."

I lit a cigarette anyway and waited anxiously. I had a bad feeling in my gut and it wasn't just because of the lungful of tobacco smoke I'd inhaled.

Suddenly there was a shout—two shouts—followed by muffled noises that could have been a fight inside the temple. Then there was the sound of a gunshot.

Constable Wang put a firm hand on my arm.

"No worry, sir. Inspector Lolly know what he do, *lo*."

He was right. Half a minute later a couple of torches flashed in the dark. There were half a dozen footfalls along the path and suddenly

Lolly was standing in front of us.

"Good news and bad news, Count. Which do you want first?"

"Good."

"Simon Meyer was definitely being held here in the temple. You were right. The bad news is he's no longer there. Hopefully this gentleman here," he indicated a sorry figure being held firmly by two policemen and oozing blood from one shoulder, "will, as they say, help us with our enquiries. If not," Lolly shrugged, "then he's in deeper shit than can fill the Ward Road Gaol latrine. And that," he couldn't suppress a chuckle, "is a real shitload of shit, Count."

Lolly barked an order and the prisoner was bundled into the second police car, blood and all. Then he turned back to me.

"There's nothing more I can tell you right now, so I'll drop you off at your hotel on the way back."

"And what about our dinner?"

'The starter's on me, Count. You can pay the rest," Lolly was once more his usual jovial self.

"What about the dessert?"

"Only if it's a just one."

12.

"I don't know," Lolly shook his head morosely. "This case just gets curiouser and curiouser."

"As long as you can still see your feet, Lolly, you'll be OK."

That made him even more morose. "I haven't been able to see my feet for years, Count. My stomach gets in the way."

We were drinking coffee on the first floor of the American Club across the road from the police station. Lolly had said he felt more at ease out of sight of his colleagues. He was telling me more than he should. I seemed to have that effect on people.

"Anyway, I interviewed our prisoner—I'm not sure interview is the right word, but you get my drift. I don't know if you realised when you saw him in the dark outside the temple, but he wasn't Japanese at all."

"Don't tell me he was Russian?"

"As Russian as the Natasha you saw gunned down in Avenue Joffre. Lily white, going by the somewhat unusual name, for a Russian, of Ivan," Lolly finally laughed. "He sort of confirmed our theory. The kidnappers were a mixed bag of Russians and Koreans, who were led by somebody calling himself Fujii."

"Fujii? According to my journalist source, a Lieutenant Fujii is second in command of the League of Blood, or Blood Brotherhood, or whatever they call themselves. Did this Ivan have a tattoo just above his wrist?"

"No, he didn't. But he confirmed that Fujii does."

"Well, that's a start anyway."

"Our Ivan claimed the whole thing was Lieutenant Fujii's bright idea and that he was hired to carry out the kidnapping. He described Fujii as small and ruthless. Typical Japanese officer type, he said, who casually used his pistol to shoot the Sassoon driver dead. He then wrote the ransom note demanding half a million silver dollars and told the others that the money was to buy arms."

"Arms? Half a million buys one hell of a lot of weapons."

"Precisely. Our Ivan had a feeling someone else was behind the whole affair. He didn't know who, though, and there was nothing I could do to persuade him."

"Honour among thieves, then."

"That's a charitable way of putting it," Lolly laughed. "Anyway, Fujii sends off the ransom note and they're looking forward to a celebration when, out of nowhere, a dozen Chinese hoodlums come marching into the temple where Simon is being held, knife two of the Japanese rōnin standing guard and make off with Sir Victor's nephew. Our Ivan was lucky. He was having a pee at the time and missed all the fun. But now we've got a new kidnap situation and we've no idea who's responsible."

"No idea at all, Lolly?"

"Well, not much of one. The trouble is I don't really want to admit that I'm pretty sure who's involved."

"Anyone I know?"

"Tu Yue-sheng."

The dull thwomp of dynamite again, this time exploding in my head.

"Big Ears Tu? But how's that possible? I thought he was helping us."

"He *was*, Count. But not now. He's a gangster, remember. He'll play all sides as the mood takes him and, or, as rapidly changing circumstances permit."

"How do you know?"

"I don't. But just like a journalist has a nose for news, and a businessman one for money, a policeman has a nose for suspects. Tu's involvement makes sense. Now that he's got the dwarf bandits out of the way, he can dictate his own terms."

"Terms which are going to be the same as Fujii's."

"Almost certainly. But with Yue-sheng, half a million dollars isn't a fanciful sum plucked out of the fetid air above the Soochow Creek. He's got the back-up to make sure he gets what he wants. I'm afraid Sir

Victor's in serious trouble now."

"Better to pay the ransom then?"

"Yes. Except with Tu there's no guarantee he'll fulfil his part in any bargain. Sir Victor might never see his nephew again." Uncharacteristically, Lolly slammed his empty coffee cup down in its saucer with a crash. "And I'll have failed in my promise to catch the kidnappers. I don't like breaking my promises."

"So, what's our next move?"

"Our? You stay out of it, Count, if you value your life."

"I value *your* life, Lolly. Come on. We're in this together. To the bitter end."

The inspector stared out of the window across the street to where his office was.

"First, I put a watch on Yue-sheng's hotel. See if I can draw any conclusions from his men's comings and goings. I'll have his home watched, too. It's big enough to hide half a dozen hostages. I need to know for certain Big Ears is involved."

"Then?"

"Then, when the ransom note's delivered and the time and place for the drop-off is agreed, I'll have the place swarming with my men. But that's the easy bit. The trouble is, when we catch whoever is sent to pick up the ransom, Big Ears is going to get seriously nasty. He'll probably cut off one of Simon's fingers and send it to Sir Victor as a souvenir, and a warning to the police not to intervene again, or else. At least, that's what *I* would do."

"I hadn't realised you were so bloodthirsty, Lolly."

"I'm not. But Simon's a pianist, remember, and the best way to deprive a pianist of his livelihood is to cut off a finger—or two, or three—to get what you want." Lolly shook his head morosely once more. "This isn't going to end well, Count. Mark my words."

I marked them and secretly prayed for a miracle.

13.

The sister eyed me disapprovingly as she peered through the grille in the convent door.

"And why do you wish to speak with Mei-si?"

"Because a young man has been kidnapped and she may be able to help."

I could have said a couple of Hail Marys in the silence that followed, but eventually she told me to wait, snapped the grille shut, and disappeared.

Ten minutes later, the door opened and Maisy stepped out into the street.

"Sir Lusty," she exclaimed with a happy smile. The stern look of the sister behind her suggested that she was less than pleased to hear my name. Mei-si was going to do penance for the company she kept.

"Maisy, how nice to see you again!" I shook her hand formally. "I'm so happy you remember me."

"How could I not remember you, Sir Lusty? You treated me like a gentleman and I never forget a gentle man." She smiled again. The sister, I noticed, had politely retreated out of immediate earshot. A gentle woman. "But why have you come to see me?"

I explained how a young pianist had been kidnapped by some Japanese, and then kidnapped again—this time by a gang of Chinese thugs who we thought were ordered to do so by Tu Yue-sheng.

"Big Ears?" She shuddered slightly at his name.

"The same. The thing is we don't *know* he's involved. We're just guessing. But we need to find out and I wondered if you might be able to help."

"Me? What makes you think I can help, Sir Lusty? I'm just a sing-song girl. Or I was, until Sister Loretta rescued me."

"Loretta? Is that her name?"

"Yes," she looked back and smiled reassuringly at the nun. "She is very protective, Sir Lusty. But she has my best interests at heart."

"I'm sure she does. Tell me, Maisy. You said you had a job looking after one of Tu's wives' children twice a week."

"Well, ye-es," she admitted uncertainly.

"So I thought, maybe, since you come and go in Big Ears' house, that you might notice if something unusual is going on there." My voice tailed away. She really was extremely beautiful.

"And, by the way, Maisy, my name isn't Lusty."

"It's not?"

"No. It's Rusty."

"Sir *Rusty*!" She exclaimed, putting her arms on my shoulders and kissing my cheek. "A much better name. I'm sure the sisters will be relieved. They always look concerned when I talk about Sir Lusty."

"I'm not surprised, Maisy, but why talk about me?"

"Because you're a good man, Sir Rusty."

"But I'm not a Catholic, Maisy."

"No, but you are the only man who has lain in bed beside me and not tried to make love to me." She entwined the fingers of one hand in mine. Sister Loretta wasn't looking so happy in the background, but she left us alone.

"I hope you haven't told the sisters that."

"Of course not. I talk to them in spiritual terms."

"As only a well brought-up Catholic knows how."

She smiled and, once again, the world lit up around me.

"Of course, I'll help, Sir Rusty."

I squeezed her fingers by way of thanks.

"Why don't you come here the day after tomorrow? I'll be looking after Tu's children again that day, but I should be back here by six o'clock in the evening. I'll warn Sister Loretta you're coming. If you're very well behaved she might even give us tea."

With another kiss on my cheek, she left me for the privacy of her Catholic shelter. As she closed the outer door, Sister Loretta actually gave me a smile through the grille. Sir Rusty clearly had charms that Sir Lusty didn't.

14.

When I got back to the Astor House Hotel, the receptionist handed me a telegram together with my room key. It was from Flap Ears Freddy. *Little tramp steamer admires city lights tomorrow midday.* Charlie Chaplin was coming to town.

On my way to the Customs House the next morning, I dropped by Sir Victor's office. He had received a note with instructions to put—wait for it—half a million dollars in a bag and place it under the bandstand, north side, in the Public Gardens at 2 am that same night.

"Will you do it for me, please, Christopher? I'm not sure I'm capable."

"Nor am I on my own. Half a million silver dollars aren't going to fit into a single bag, are they? You're going to need half the Salvation Army band to carry all that money for you. Anyway, suppose we solve the logistics of that one, what am I supposed to do after the money has been dropped off? Hang around until I hear Simon tinkling on the bandstand piano?"

"Don't be so silly. Simon will be released somewhere else once they've got the money."

"I wouldn't bank on it, Victor. You're dealing with mobsters of the worst kind. They could easily take your money and stagger away, conveniently forgetting to release Simon in the process. What does Lolly Lo have to say? Have you consulted him?"

Victor looked as sheepish as an exceedingly rich Baghdadi jew can look sheepish. More like a camel, really. That's what came of smoking Turkish cigars, I suppose.

"No. Not yet."

"Then I suggest you do so. And do so fast. I'm going to need backup if I'm to act as your delivery boy."

I left Victor to his devices. There was something he wasn't telling me.

Freddy was waiting for me outside the Customs House.

"Got my telegram, then? Come on, matey. This way." He led me round the side of the building, and up a gangplank leading straight into the hold of the giant liner berthed alongside.

"I'm on duty right now, see," he said once we were aboard, "so you'll have to find your film star friend for yourself, mate. He's somewhere up in a state room. Ask the purser. You'll find him on Deck C."

I did as Flap Ears advised. The Purser eyed me with more suspicion than Sister Loretta.

"What name did you say, sir?"

"Chaplin. Charles Chaplin."

The middle-aged Englishman had mutton chop sideburns stopping just short of a meaty chin. I may have been a Stroganov, but they put me off my appetite.

"Chaplin, sir?" He briefly searched the passenger list. It was as if he already knew the answer. "I'm sorry, sir, but we have no passenger on board by that name."

"How about Sydney Chaplin?"

"Sydney, as in the harbour, sir?" He gave me a deadpan look. "That would be Chap-*lin*, wouldn't it, and not Chap-*lain*?"

"It would indeed." Was I talking to another Catholic?

"I thought so." He was enjoying the game he was playing with me. He consulted his list of passengers again, before looking up with a slight glint of a smile. "No. I'm sorry, sir. There is no Sydney Chaplin on board either. Nor a Sydney Chaplain."

"And not Charles Chaplain, either?"

"Definitely not, sir. It wouldn't have suited him at all."

I desperately racked my brain for a pseudonym that the Tramp might have used. He couldn't really call himself 'Kid' or 'Tramp' on board a ship. The Purser waited politely, declining both the cigarette and the hip flask I offered him by way of inducement.

"Thank you, sir, but no thank you. I stopped smoking and drinking when we set sail from Le Havre six weeks ago. My cabin here," he jerked his thumb over his shoulder to the open door behind him, "has therefore become what you might call my 'dry den,' if you know what I mean." His look was meaningful. Was Mutton Chops actually trying to tell me something? If so, what? Teetotaller wasn't a name.

"Ab Stainer?" I tried hopelessly. "Or Steiner, perhaps?"

"Would that be Ab as in Abbott, sir? Or Abner?"

"Either. No!" I stopped him. "Wait a minute! Dryden. Dryden Wheeler."

"Dryden, sir?" Mutton Chops gave me a slightly yellow-toothed smile. "An unusual first name and a greatly-underestimated playwright, if I might say so, sir." We both knew it was also the name of Charlie's half-brother. The purser leafed through the passenger list yet again. "Ah, yes! Here we are, sir. A Mr Dryden Wheeler is indeed on board."

He smiled inscrutably.

"And?"

"And what, sir?"

"Where can I find him?"

"Mr Wheeler, sir? I'm afraid I am not allowed to divulge the whereabouts of the ship's passengers to visitors."

Squeeze again. I slipped him a five dollar bill.

"Except under certain circumstances," Mutton Chops continued smoothly, as he deftly pocketed the note. "Try Cabin 103. It's a stateroom up on the boat deck, sir. Starboard side."

I climbed the sweeping staircase past both Bridge and Promenade decks until I got to the uppermost weather deck. It provided a splendid view of the Bund—a view being enjoyed by Mr Charles Spencer Chaplin himself. Dressed as an English gentleman, rather than as a little man in a shabby suit, with bowler hat and cane, he had beside him a stunningly beautiful young woman, with hair that was almost black, deep-set eyes, magisterial eyebrows, elegantly sculpted nose and full-lipped smile, hanging onto his arm. She looked as if she was hardly more than sixteen years old. Chaplin wasn't known as the Great Charlot for nothing.

"Mr Chaplin, sir," I took off my hat. "My apologies for troubling you, sir, but I heard that you were on board and couldn't resist the opportunity to meet you in person."

The Little Tramp looked at me dispassionately. Spare me another Catholic sister, please.

"And who might you be, sir?"

"My name is Christopher Bloom, sir. My friends call me Rusty. I'm a journalist and I write mainly for a Swedish newspaper."

"Swedish? Then you know Greta?" He straightened up from the deck rail.

"Alas, sir! I haven't had the pleasure. Sweden isn't *that* small a country."

"No, I suppose not," he laughed. "She's *talked* you know. Last year. In *Anna Christie*. What bravery! 'The voice that shook the world,' or so one magazine assured us."

"'Garbo talks!'" I repeated the film's advertising blurb. "The next thing we'll hear is 'Garbo laughs!'"

Chaplin laughed.

"And you, sir? Do you intend to follow her example?"

"What, *me*? Forsake silent films? What kind of voice could I possibly give the Little Tramp? Certainly not Greta's deep husky contralto. If my Tramp *were* to talk on screen, my audiences would laugh at him for all the wrong reasons."

"Maybe it doesn't matter how your voice will record? All you have to do, surely, is speak naturally, as you feel the Tramp's lines should be spoken. Wasn't that Garbo's approach?"

"I don't know," Chaplin shuffled his feet uncertainly and turned to the young woman at his side. "What do you think, Hedy? Is Mr Bloom right?"

"I think you don't know until you try it, *Liebling*." She gave me a less than innocent smile. I could see what Charlie saw in her.

"Tell me, Mr Chaplin, sir, do you intend to go ashore while you're here? I realise you're less than keen on publicity right now, but I know Sir Victor Sassoon would be delighted to entertain you at his new Cathay Hotel. That's it," I pointed in the direction of Sassoon House at the end of the Bund. "A quite remarkable building."

"Sassoon? The property Jew man? I'm not sure I'm ready for Shanghai yet, Mr Bloom. Perhaps another time?"

"I'm sorry to hear that, sir. But would you do me the honour of an interview while you're here?"

Chaplin looked at his watch and smiled.

"Lunch is at one o'clock. You've got thirty-seven minutes until the gong sounds."

So I got my interview. By the time the luncheon gong sounded we were on Christian name terms, exchanging risqué jokes. Hedy seemed to have no other name. She laughed when she thought something funny, but that was it. All I learned was that she had been born in Austria and was all of sixteen years old. More power to Charlie's elbow, or whatever part of his anatomy he was using to seduce her.

As I left the ship, I bumped into Flap Ears. He was overseeing the unloading of half a dozen laundry baskets.

"Hello, mate. Get what you wanted?"

"Yes. Many thanks, Freddy. I owe you. What's that you've got there?" I raised my eyebrows at the laundry baskets.

"Japanese kimono."

"Kimono?"

"Yeah. Jap women reckon no Chinee laundryman can clean their kimono properly. Shanghai water's got too much chemicals in it, dunnit, so their silk kimonos start rotting, see, when they're cleaned. At least, that's what they say. So they send them to Japan to be dry-cleaned. This lot's just come back."

"But the *President Hoover* hasn't come from Japan, has it?"

"No, well… Hey! You! Be careful!" Freddy shouted at one of the coolies unloading a basket. "Can't take your eye off these Chinee buggers, can you? Not for one minute."

Flap Ears was up to something. I knew it. And he knew that I knew it.

"Anything you want to talk about, Freddy?"

"Not really, mate," he tapped the breast pocket of his uniform. "Funny how the world can change in a heartbeat, ain't it."

He grinned and turned away. It was the last I saw of my Customs House informant. Or most of him, at least.

15.

I was late arriving at the convent. Maisy was already back from work.

Sister Loretta brought us tea and took up position on a chair in the corner of the visitors' room. As you'd expect, it was austere. Four hard-back rosewood chairs, a rosewood table, and a large crucifix on one wall. Jesus had bits of red paint daubed on various parts of his more or less naked body.

Maisy brightened up the early evening with her smile. Sir Lusty wanted to kiss her lips, take off her clothes and explore her body, but I knew Sister Loretta would crucify that persona if he tried. Sir Rusty prevailed.

"Well, Maisy?"

"Well, what, Sir Rusty?" She may have decided to become a nun, but she had a long way to go when it came to ridding herself of her flirtatious habits. Mary Magdalene would have been proud of her.

"Did you see or hear anything to do with the kidnapping of Simon Meyer?"

"What did you expect?" Still teasing. Sir Lusty was ready to be true to his name. Sister Loretta coughed demurely in the corner of the room, reminding us of her presence.

"As a matter of fact, I did. Right at the end of the day, as I was getting ready to go home, one of Tu's bodyguards told me to take a tray of food and water to an outhouse at the very back of his property. He's got so much land, you know. His house occupies a whole block near here."

She paused, now a bit frightened.

"And?"

"And so I did as I was told and took the food and drink to where another Russian gangster was sitting by the door of this outhouse with a shotgun cradled in his arms. He stood up, took the tray from me and told me to go away. As I went back to the house I turned round and saw him unlock the door of the outhouse and go inside with the tray. Somebody's being held prisoner there, although I've no idea who."

"It has to be Simon. Thank you *so* much, Maisy. You've helped a lot. I'll tell Sir Victor and the police."

"In that case, please make sure they don't come here, Sir Rusty," She stood up. "I'm frightened. Tu Yue-sheng is a cruel man and I don't want him thinking I'm somehow involved."

"Of course. Take care, Maisy. You know where to find me if you want to get in touch." I put my hands lightly on her shoulders and gave her a chaste kiss on each cheek. It was our last touch.

16.

It didn't take long for word to get out. A large shipment of opium had gone missing and Big Ears Tu was on the rampage. His thugs were out on the streets chasing down all likely suspects. Lolly Lo was having a hard time keeping up with the bodies.

"They're falling like proverbial flies," he said angrily when we met up with Victor in the Horse and Hounds Bar later that evening. "Thirteen bodies at the last count. That means thirteen fewer crooks for me to keep an eye on, so I guess Yue-sheng's doing me a favour," he laughed, joviality restored. "But still…"

"Any idea how much has gone missing?" Sir Victor asked.

"Has to be one hell of a lot. He wouldn't be getting this worked up otherwise. Over one hundred pounds weight, I reckon, at the very least. Maybe two, even three. At thirty thousand dollars a pound, that's a lot of money to lose. Even for Big Ears. No wonder he's pissed off."

"Well, at least he can recoup half a million tonight when I get Christopher here to hand over the ransom money."

"Don't!" Lolly commanded abruptly. "Don't do it, Sir Victor. We don't know for sure yet who the kidnappers are. And we don't know if we can trust whoever's demanding half a million Mexican dollars from you to let your nephew go free. You've got to negotiate."

"Yes, but how, if we don't know who we're negotiating with?"

It was time for me to put in my oar. "Actually, Victor, we do."

Now I had both men's attention. I felt like Kiki. Without the curves, of course, or her inviting voice and violet eyes.

"What do you mean, Christopher?"

I explained how I knew, although I left Maisy's name out of it. A charade, really. Anyone who wanted to find out how the police knew where Simon was would soon learn the source. I should have held my tongue.

"So what do you intend to do, Inspector Lo?" Victor asked.

"Let me think about it," Lolly answered gruffly. "In the meantime, Count, you go to the Public Gardens bandstand and wait for the kidnappers to turn up. Tell whoever it is you must have proof Simon is alive before Sir Victor hands over the ransom. Assure them, though, that he will definitely pay up. Ideally, the money should then be exchanged for the young man himself, but I doubt whether Tu will agree to that. He wants to maintain anominity."

So, at two in the morning, I found myself sitting on an uncomfortable chair in the middle of the bandstand in the Public Gardens. I decided to face the Bund. Tu's men would almost certainly come from that direction.

I wasn't wrong. Soon I spotted three shadows moving among the bushes. I checked the Husqvarna pistol in my pocket. Basically a Browning semi-automatic made in Sweden. Better to be carrying something in case of emergency.

I stayed where I was, sitting by a forgotten music stand, and waited till the shadows materialised into real people. One of them was Pan Chan-ki. If I'd had any doubts before about who was holding Simon, I had none now.

"Hello Chunky," I said, standing up slowly with my hands well clear of my body. "I wondered if it might be you. Thank you for coming."

Chan-ki looked at me hard. Then he gave a kind of smile.

"Mista Broom. You looksee Mei-si again?"

Not the kind of question I wanted to answer. Not even in the dark.

"Sir Victor Sassoon asked me to meet you."

"You hab got dolla?"

"No, I'm afraid not, Chunky. Sir Victor has asked for proof that Simon Meyer is," I paused, "in your care."

Tu's Number One man grunted.

"You come looksee massa, Mista Broom."

He flicked his fingers at the two men with him and they ushered me out of the bandstand, pinioning my arms firmly, and across the gardens to a large black limousine. Chan-ki opened one of the rear doors. Inside was Big Ears himself.

"Well, if it isn't Count Bloom. Are you now an errand boy for Lo Li-kwei?" he rasped. "Get in and join me," he patted the seat beside him, his dead eyes even more frightening in the dark. I was glad Chan-ki hadn't thought of frisking me. I needed protection.

"No, sir. I was sent by Sir Victor. He wants proof that whoever was demanding a ransom actually has his nephew in custody."

"Proof?" His voice was definitely not that of a choirboy. "OK. I'll give you proof."

With a jerk of Tu's head, Chan-ki closed the rear door beside me and got into the passenger seat of the bullet-proof car. The two others who had escorted me stood on the running boards with their machine pistols, the way they always did. At least we weren't going to be kidnapped. This was what people called travelling in style.

As we drew up at the Donghu Hotel, a tall Chinese man in silken robes crossed the street hurriedly in front of the limousine. The driver honked furiously. The jay walker turned, smiled and bowed politely before indicating he was trying to enter the hotel. The car came to a halt, the two Russians riding pillion stepped down onto the road. One of them opened the rear door as Chan-ki got out from the front seat. I stepped out first, with Big Ears behind me. Suddenly he was cursing.

"Bloody kids!" he rasped in Chinese, as he kicked a painted wooden police car out into the street from under one of the front seats. The second bodyguard bent down to pick up the offending toy, while Chan-ki put out a hand to help his master out of the car. It was then that I realised that the tall Chinese man going up the steps into the hotel had turned back towards us and was drawing a pistol from one sleeve of his gown.

"Look out!" I shouted and drew my own weapon. We both fired at the same time, but I was a split second faster on the draw. His bullet grazed my left shoulder, mine went straight into his heart. Tu's would-be assassin slumped dead to the ground. Accuracy always helped. Being a count had taught me that much.

There was pandemonium as Chunky hustled his master past me up the steps and into the hotel lobby, while the Russian thugs backed in after them, letting off a couple of quick bursts of fire into the darkness from their machine pistols. Luckily they missed me, though whether by accident or by design I couldn't tell. It was a don't-fuck-with-me gesture that had the required effect on a couple of dogs copulating across the road, but that was it.

Two other thugs came rushing out of the hotel entrance and unceremoniously dragged me back inside. There was an eerie calm in the lobby. Half a dozen silent men stood around nervously fingering their weapons. Yue-sheng was sitting angrily on a sofa and speaking in a low voice to Chan-ki. One of Tu's beautifully slinky Eurasian hostesses bore him a cup of tea, but was angrily waved away. As she stood uncertainly in the middle of the lobby, I put a friendly hand on her bare arm.

"Do you mind? I could do with a bit of refreshment."

She noticed that my shoulder was bleeding as I took the cup of tea and put one hand to her mouth in consternation.

"I get you doctor, sir."

She quickly disappeared down the corridor that led to Tu's reception room.

"Mista Broom." It was Chan-ki. "My massa wantchee talkee pidgin you."

He indicated an armchair. I went over and prepared to talk business with Big Ears.

"You saved my life, Count Christopher Bloom. Thank you."

"Glad to be of assistance, sir."

"I won't forget." He noticed my shoulder. "You hit? Chunky, get a doctor quick."

"It's OK, Mr Tu, sir. Just a scratch."

The Eurasian girl reappeared with a bottle of vodka. The best kind of doctor. Bowing very slightly in deference towards Tu, she told me to take off my jacket and shirt. Then she poured some of the vodka into a handkerchief and started to wipe the bullet wound with it. I took a swig from the bottle. She smiled and her smile was almost as beautiful as Maisy's. Not quite, but second best in the world so far as I was concerned.

"It's only glaze, Mister Bloom. I will get bandage."

"Thank you, Miss —?"

"Da-nang, sir."

"Thank you, then, Da-nang."

She disappeared again.

"You like her, Count? You have her for as long as you like."

"Thank you, sir, but it's OK. Really," I assured him.

Tu grunted. Then, "You said you want proof I'm holding the Sassoon nephew captive?"

I nodded. The hard part of the night was just starting.

"I give you proof." Tu jerked his head at Chan-ki who in turn jerked his head at one of the Russians standing on guard. The Russian turned on his heel and disappeared down a flight of stairs leading off from one end of the lobby. "Chan-ki will bring you what you need. And when you've given Sir Victor that proof, come back here with the money tomorrow at noon. OK, Count?"

I nodded. "Agreed." There wasn't much else I could do or say. Yet.

"Good." Without another word he stood up to leave the lobby for his limousine. Time to go back home to his wives. Or concubines. Or both. This time his guards were fully attentive, fanning out in front and behind their boss, weapons at the ready. I heard car doors open and close, an engine start and then the sound of the limousine driving away. The dogs across the road breathed a sigh of relief and started to copulate again.

Da-nang came back with some lint and a bandage. After helping me on with my shirt and jacket, she gave me another gorgeous smile. I felt as good as new.

The Russian who had gone downstairs came back up with a small box in his hand. He handed it to Chan-ki, who in turn passed it to me.

"Hap one piece proof, Mista Broom. You go chop chop and talkee pidgin hotel-man Sassoon. One piece car waitee street far-side."

I had a nasty feeling I knew what Chunky's proof consisted of. And it wasn't going to be one of Tu's big ears. That was for sure.

17.

Hesitantly, Victor cut the string and loosened the lid of the box. It was nearly three in the morning and we both looked the worse for wear, although he had the clothes to mask it. A silken cravat, monocle and perfumed hair oil worked wonders for anyone's appearance. Especially if you were born to dress that way.

Victor opened the box. With a cry of dismay he quickly looked away from its contents. As I had feared, it contained a single finger, cut off at the knuckle and bloody. Not too bloody, but bloody enough to upset the tycoon's refined sensitivities.

"How can they be so cruel?" Victor had put aside the box and was holding his knees and rocking back and forth. "Simon is a *pianist*, for God's sake. They've ruined his life, his *raison d'être*. He's lived for music."

I took a closer look at the finger. Long and slender. A pianist's finger.

"I'm sorry, Victor, but I have to ask. Are you sure it's Simon's?"

"Who else's can it possibly be?"

I was pretty sure I knew the answer to that.

"It's just that, according to the information I received late yesterday afternoon, Simon was being held in an outhouse at Tu Yue-sheng's home. When Tu said he had proof that he was holding Simon an hour ago, this box was delivered from the basement of Tu's hotel within a few minutes. Which means that either Simon has been taken from Tu's home to his gang headquarters on Route Doumer, only to have one of his little fingers cut off. Or the contents of this box don't belong to your nephew, but to someone else."

"But who to?"

"Probably to a customs official who was my informant," I said. "In which case, I believe I may have a way to get Simon back unharmed without your forking out a single Mexican dollar."

Victor's monocle nearly dropped out of his eye.

"I don't want to raise your hopes too high, Victor, but listen carefully. Here's what I want you to do."

At precisely twelve noon the following—or was it the same?—day, Sir Victor's Phantom drew up outside the Donghu Hotel. I stepped out with a single bag full of money and passed half a dozen guards until I came face to face with Chan-ki.

"Chin chin, Mista Broom."

"Good afternoon, Chunky."

He eyed the bag in my hand.

"You hap got what thing massa wantchee?"

"But of course. The rest is in the boot of the car outside. Have you got what Sir Victor wants?"

"Maybe."

This time he frisked me before signalling me to follow him down the corridor to Tu's reception room. Lace curtains were drawn across the windows and it was quite dark, but Da-nang's smile lit up the room.

"Count Bloom!" Yue-sheng rose to greet me. Like Lolly, he seemed to be a stickler for titles. "Your shoulder OK?"

"Thank you, yes."

He nodded, looking more than satisfied.

"So you got something for me there?"

"I have indeed, Tu Yue-sheng. And you?"

"Maybe," he said noncommittedly. "I need to count the money first. Half a million dollar, right?"

"I believe that that is what was agreed." I put the bag down on the floor beside me. "But before you start counting, there's something else I'd like to discuss with you."

Big Ears gave me the kind of look that would have turned a skittish man to stone. He had the makings of a Shanghai Gorgon.

"Word is out on the streets that you've lost a large assignment of opium. Is that true, Yue-sheng?"

Big Ears gave me another Gorgon look. I needed a mirrored shield.

"So what, Count?"

"So I've a pretty good idea I know where it is."

"I can find it myself."

"I doubt it, Yue-sheng. You've already killed the one person who knew where it is."

"What do you mean?"

"*Who* do I mean? A customs official called Freddy Fox. You've got him downstairs in your basement. Or what's left of him, at least."

Big Ears indicated the sofa beside his chair. His fingernails rivalled Medusa's hair in length. "Have a seat, Count."

I did as he suggested. Da-nang brought me a cold drink. I needed it if I was to stay cool.

"Go on talkee, Mista Broom." Chunky was looking at me curiously.

"I think you found out pretty quickly who nicked your opium shipment, Yue-sheng, and you brought him here. Your men, though, were a bit over-eager when it came to trying to get information out of Freddy. I don't know what happened, but I'm guessing he had a heart attack. That makee custom walla chop chop die-*lo*," I added for Chunky's benefit.

The silence of the two men in front of me was, to put it mildly, intense.

"Maskee. What fashion you handsome talkee that-same?"

Chunky eventually asked on behalf of his boss.

"Because he had a dicky ticker." Both men frowned. "Sorry. A weak heart. He told me so once."

"What fashion you savvy he die-*lo*, Mista Broom?"

"Because when you sent your Russky friend down to cut off his finger, we heard no shouts, no screams of pain. The fact that there wasn't much blood at the base of the finger when Sir Victor opened the box suggested that its owner had been dead a few hours."

"Maskee." Chunky wasn't giving away anything. The trouble was that I then did.

"It so happens I know that Simon Meyer was alive and well at your home yesterday afternoon, Yue-sheng."

Neither of them said anything, but continued looking at me as expressionlessly as a couple of tigers contemplating their prey.

"Anyway," I continued, "I have a proposal, Tu Yue-sheng, that is for your benefit."

"And what is this proposal, Count Bloom?"

"That I keep this bag of money here on the floor beside me, and the other bags in the car, but tell you where your opium's stored. Then you hand over Sir Victor's nephew. You'll lose half a million dollars ransom, but get at least five million in exchange. Depending on your opium's street value, of course. What do you reckon?"

Big Ears clasped his fingernails together and stared at me intently. As usual what he was thinking was fathomless. Chunky chose this moment to leave the room quietly. Gone to prepare the instruments of torture no doubt.

"You play a dangerous game, Count." Big Ears eventually broke the silence.

"Don't we all?" I acknowledged. "I know what you're going to say. What's to stop you from torturing me to find out where your opium is?"

He nodded. "So what's to stop me from torturing you to get the information I want? Then I don't have to give back the half million dollars."

"Because you're an honourable man, Tu Yue-sheng."

He laughed mirthlessly. "Not many people call me that."

"Not many people save your life from a would-be assassin's bullet."

He nodded slowly, weighing things up. Then,

"OK, Count Christopher Bloom. You have your deal. But you would be wise to remember that now we're quits."

"It's engraved on my liver, as they say. I've got a car outside. Would you like to accompany me?"

"I think I prefer my own limousine. In case one of your friends tries to shoot me." Again his laugh was humourless.

"You'll need a truck, too, for all the laundry baskets."

"Laundry baskets?"

"For your money laundering, Tu Yue-sheng."

This time he really laughed.

"You funny man, Count Bloom. You wanna work for me? I like you."

I wished the feeling were mutual and wondered how long his friendship would last if I was wrong about where Flap Ears Freddy had stacked the opium.

In the event, I got it right. We slipped into the Astor House Hotel by the back entrance and through the kitchen area to a flight of concrete stairs leading down into what seemed like a black hole. One of Tu's men had been prescient enough to bring a torch to light the way. Two more held me firmly by the arms as we all trouped down into the darkness. The basement consisted of a single corridor with four grilles, two on each side, behind which were piled various pieces of furniture—a dining table and chairs, dressers, a couple of wardrobes and gate-leg tables, three upended beds, an ottoman, and a billiard table that had seen better days. At the end was a door locked with a heavy padlock and chain. It provided little resistance to Tu's well-equipped men.

We stepped inside. At least, Tu did. I was pushed roughly through the door. A second torch was lit and to my immense relief I saw it make out first one laundry basket, then another, and then several more.

"You think there are enough baskets here to launder all my money, Count?" Tu asked jovially. For a moment, I thought Lolly Lo had joined us.

"They're a start anyway," I said. "Depending on what's inside them, of course."

Tu barked a sharp order and his men opened the baskets. Sure enough, they were filled with carefully wrapped and sealed blocks of Mesopotamian opium. Flap Ears had made a gigantic haul—enough money to pay for the best heart surgeon in the world twice over.

It was only as I raised my eyes from the baskets on the floor that I realised how Freddy had managed to secrete everything without arousing suspicion. There was a second locked grille and light beyond, seeping down onto the bottom of a flight of steps that led up to ground level. Freddy had had access to his storeroom from the street and never had to enter the hotel itself. I had no idea how he'd found his hidey-hole, but he had. And here were all his ill-gotten gains—Japanese silk kimono, three Japanese swords, half a dozen pistols of one sort or another, and plenty of expensive-looking rings, necklaces and other bits of jewellery. I thought of applying to the Customs House for a job. They were in need of a new officer, after all.

"OK, Count," Big Ears broke in on my thoughts. "You keep your side of our bargain. I keep mine. You go to the corner of Avenue Petain and route de Zikawei at five o'clock this afternoon and you'll find the Sassoon nephew there. We're quits. OK?"

"OK, Tu Yue-sheng. And thank you for your consideration."

He grunted and waved me away. Back in the street, Victor's Phantom Rolls was waiting for me. The chauffeur, Dixon, looked at me enquiringly.

"Back to Sassoon House for now."

"What about the money?"

"Think of it as ballast, Dixon. We're living in unstable times."

Victor was waiting anxiously for me in his penthouse.

"Christopher!" He exclaimed, not daring to ask.

"All's well, Victor. Simon will be released at five o'clock this afternoon."

He let go of his sticks in joy as he placed both hands on my shoulders.

"How can I ever thank you enough?"

"Think nothing of it, Victor. I'm just glad it's all over. Well, almost over."

"Is it really? He won't renege on the deal?"

"It's more than his life's worth," I reassured him, as I bent down to pick up his sticks from the floor. "Oh, and by the way, that finger wasn't Simon's, just as I thought."

"No? Who does it belong to, then?"

"A young British customs official called Freddy Fox. Rather foolishly, he thought he could outwit Big Ears and had a fatal heart attack instead. At least he didn't have to suffer Tu's slings and arrows of outrageous torture. That's what has saved Simon's life."

18.

As the Phantom approached the corner of Avenue Petain and route de Zikawei, I spotted a young man sitting forlornly on a laundry basket outside the convent door. Tu had kept his word.

"Simon?" I got out of the car and went towards him. "My name's Rusty Bloom. I'm a friend of your uncle's and have come to take you home."

The young man almost fell into my arms. There were, I noted, five fingers on each of his hands. He was sobbing with relief, although he had no idea how close his piano-playing days had been to being over.

I ushered him towards the car and helped him in.

"Just a moment, Dixon," I said. "There's something I need to check."

I went back to the laundry basket. When I opened it, Maisy was smiling up at me. Except she was dead. Carelessly, I had given her up to Tu Yue-sheng, and Chunky had carried out her execution. I cursed the over-confidence that had led me to mention how I knew Simon had been alive the previous afternoon.

So now it was Da-nang who owned the most beautiful smile in the world. If I wanted it to stay that way, I'd better make sure I never saw her again.

19.

News of Simon's rescue soon got out. Reporters besieged the Cathay Hotel, hoping to catch a glimpse of Sir Victor and his nephew, but to no avail. Both were locked up in the hotelier's penthouse suite, guarded by the impeccable Perkins who proved to be as snappishly territorial as one of Sir Victor's greyhounds. So they looked elsewhere—in the French Concession where the Gendarmerie could only confirm that Monsieur Meyer was safe, thanks to the diligence and persistence of its Chief of Police, Tu Yue-sheng. One or two brave souls went off to the Hotel Donghu on Route Doumer to find Big Ears himself, only to be told politely by Pan Chan-ki to bugger off. One French journalist made the mistake of trying to waylay one of Tu's kitchen staff, only to find himself being roughly manhandled by Chunky who took obvious pleasure in throwing him into an open sewer. He was in the business of shit, after all. As was the journalist, of course.

A handful of hopeful hacks hung out in the Astor House Hotel Bar, hoping to ensnare me—little knowing that I was by then ensconced in a rather pleasant furnished apartment provided me for free by an overjoyed and ever grateful Victor until such time as I no longer needed it. It came with a cheque for ten thousand pounds and a 'Boy' who went by the name of Fan To-mu, and whom I called Fantom to remind myself of Victor's Rolls Royce. The apartment itself was up on the twelfth floor of Cathay Mansions, on the corner of Rue Cardinal Mercier and Rue Bourgeat in the French Concession. Not far from the Street of Happy Sisters where it had all started.

The convent sisters, however, were far less happy. One of their promising postulants had been found with her throat slit in a laundry basket outside their front door. True, Maisy had been holding an envelope stuffed with enough money not only to cover the cost of her funeral, which took place in a small but pleasantly shady graveyard attached to the convent, but to contribute generously to the sisters' retirement fund. So perhaps in the end they were happy, too, although I somehow doubt whether they would be honest enough to admit it. After all, they were in the business of suffering. As for Tu Yue-sheng, maybe he had for once been moved by remorse and by his children's tears at news of the sudden death of their kind and beautiful tutor. I liked to think that Maisy's lessons in Christian values hadn't been entirely in vain.

The first kidnap story I filed with the China News Agency was soon touted as another scoop for the Swedish Count. It revealed everything. Well, almost everything. With a self-effacement rarely found among newspapermen, I attributed the success of the rescue operation entirely to Lolly Lo, whose sharp observations, smart deductive powers and dogged determination had led the sleuth to an undisclosed location in Little Tokyo where Simon was being held. After an exchange of pistol shots, the culprits had been taken and handed over to the Kempeitai, Japan's feared military police, for interrogation. It was doubtful they would survive.

Or so the story went.

This news led to a minor stampede by Shanghai's journalists to the precinct of the Central Police Station on Foochow Road. There the hacks were met with the disappointing information that Chief Chinese Inspector Lo Li-kwei had been summoned to Nanking by person or persons unknown, for reasons that were also unclear, but which were—so far as *was* known—unconnected with his involvement in the Simon Meyer kidnapping. In hope of collaring Lolly when he returned from wherever he might have been—nobody was really fooled by the 'summoned to Nanking' story—half a dozen newspapermen decided to hang out in the capacious bar on the main floor of the American Club opposite. There they took it in turns to keep watch on the entrance to the police station, while the others played pool in the billiards room next door. One made for the Turkish baths in the basement where a Russian masseur pounded out the kinks in his misshapen ideals. What none of them bothered to consider was the fact that the police station had a back entrance that allowed its occupants to make their way unobserved through the *lilong* neighbourhood alleyways to Hankow Road. Lolly took advantage of their incompetence.

Of course, what I had filed was only half the story. But it had to suffice until I had had a chance to clear things with Lolly. Big Ears needed to be treated with caution and I had to remind myself—as if I needed reminding—that I was a two-finger typist who couldn't afford to lose one of them. I had a living to make.

Which I did by writing and then filing early that same evening a totally unrelated article about Charlie Chaplin's visit to Shanghai. The *President Hoover* had slipped its moorings at high tide early that morning so I felt it opportune to describe the great man's thoughts about sound in film and, for the benefit of my Swedish readers in particular, Chaplin's admiration for Garbo. This had my colleagues reeling from shock and, let's face it, admiration, and they quickly christened me 'Scoop Broom.'

Nobody quite knew how, but Chaplin's presence in a floating stateroom overlooking the Bund for a couple of nights had been the city's best kept secret since Chou En-lai's escape from an interrogation cell back in 1926. In the meantime, I reflected that it was probably lucky for me that Flap Ears had had a heart attack in the basement of Tu Yuesheng's hotel. Otherwise he'd never have kept his mouth shut. I still had Freddy's finger to write about, though.

Over the phone in my new apartment I arranged to have dinner with Lolly Lo in the opulent dining room on the tenth-floor of the Cathay Hotel, where the building's famous tower began. Preferring as much anonymity—Lolly again called it 'anonimity'—as we could get, I chose a table tucked away in a corner, far from the entrance doors flanked by circular panels of Lalique goldfish swimming in an opalescent sea. The colour scheme was jade and gold, relieved in red and black lacquer. Hopefully, the food would be more refined than the interior design.

"We call this place the Chinese Skyrocket," Lolly looked around him appreciatively. "You know what they say, don't you?"

"No, Lolly. What do they say?"

"That the Chinese temple artists who painted this ceiling had to lie on their backs on the scaffolding to carry out their work. Only in Shanghai, eh!"

"Only in Shanghai."

The Chief Chinese Inspector sipped his wine appreciatively.

"So, what are you going to write next, Count? About Simon's rescue, I mean. You can't tell the world Tu Yue-sheng was responsible. You realise that?"

"Of course, Lolly. That's why I wanted to have a chat with you over dinner together this evening. To ask your advice." Diplomacy, diplomacy, there's nothing like diplomacy. Until it all falls apart. "What do you reckon is the best way to present the rest of the Simon Meyer story?"

Lolly tried not to look too pleased by my flattery and kept his expression serious.

"An unknown gang of Chinese thugs kidnaps Sir Victor's nephew from his Japanese kidnappers and then demands ransom."

"Of half a million Mexican silver dollars?"

"Of half a million Mexican silver dollars, once they've given Sir Victor proof that they're holding Simon."

"That proof being a slender finger in the mail?"

"Precisely. But now comes the tricky bit. Somehow you have to make Big Ears seem like the good guy in all this."

"Like he happens to know where this Chinese gang is holding a lot of opium?"

"Something like that, yes. They've been syphoning it off with the aid of a Customs House official. Transferred in laundry baskets to a secret hidey-hole in the basement of the Astor House Hotel."

"On the pretext that the baskets contain Japanese kimono sent back from dry-cleaning in Japan."

"So Tu threatens the gang. Release the hostage or else?"

"Or else lose the opium shipment which is Tu's in the first place."

"But why should Yue-sheng decide to help Sir Victor?"

"Ah!" said Lolly.

"Ah, what?"

"Ah don't know."

Once he'd stopped laughing at his own joke, Lolly did a kind of Gallic shrug. "That's where your imagination comes in, doesn't it, Count? I'm sure you'll work something out."

I wasn't convinced, but at least I had the Chief Chinese Inspector's tacit permission to run the story.

Over the main course of *filet mignon*, Lolly revealed that he himself had been a gangster for a number of years before being converted to police work. Not one of Big Ears' mob, but he'd been sufficiently adept in his role then to earn the big boss's respect. From time to time, therefore, they exchanged information that the other might find useful. And closed down avenues of enquiry when it was mutually beneficial for them to do so.

"Give and take, then?"

"Yes, except in Tu's case, it's give a little, take a lot. There's rarely anything I can do about that. So long as I get given *something*, though, I don't really mind. The little he gives me occasionally ties in with another case I'm dealing with and, suddenly, I find it can be rather a lot."

He wiped his mouth carefully before taking another sip of the excellent Côte-Rôtie I had ordered.

"If only this wine were the same," he laughed. "Maybe your friend Jesus can join us with a few glasses of water?"

"Lolly, if you're in search of a miracle, you're dining with the wrong man. I'm an atheist."

"You sound like a communist, Count. Try Buddhism."

"Thank you. I'll give it some thought."

There was a pause as we both enjoyed another mouthful of excellent *filet mignon*. Then,

"I had an interesting conversation with our friend Ivan," Lolly said, wiping his mouth.

"Oh yes? Did you get anything else out of your Ivan?"

"Only that the money they'd hoped to get out of Sir Victor was, as I told you, intended to buy arms. Something big was going down. He didn't know what, but he was certain it was big."

"Did he indicate when?"

"Probably sometime this month. A lot depends on the anti-Japanese riots going on. Once somebody is killed, then that's it. Or so he said. The Japanese will finally lose patience and start a war."

"The Japanese? Or the Blood Brotherhood? Anyway, they've already started it, haven't they? Up in Manchuria."

"That was just a prelinimary skirmish. At least, that's what our Ivan assured me."

"Did you believe him?"

"Yes and no. In my experience, young men tend to exaggerate the importance of what they're involved in. But, again in my experience, there's often a kernel of truth in their exaggerations."

Lolly put his knife and fork down on his empty plate and wiped his mouth once more with the napkin tucked into his shirt collar. Then he fixed me with a policeman's expressionless look, the kind of look that reveals nothing.

"Tell me, Count, what do you make of the Baronet?"

"Victor? I don't know. Why?"

Still the dispassionate eyes. Another taxidermist's sightless gaze.

"Fortunes are rarely, if ever, made through totally honest business transactions. The Sassoons, the Kadoories, the Jung brothers, Tu Yue-sheng—you name them—they've all got something hidden away at the back of the closet. Or bottom of a laundry basket."

I winced. My secret had been at the bottom of a laundry basket with her throat slit.

"Which makes me wonder," Lolly appeared not to have noticed my reaction, "what has Sir Victor got to hide? Because he *is* hiding something, Count. Something behind that urbane look, that upper-class accent and impeccably smooth appearance. Mark my words."

Yet again I did my best to do as he said.

"I'm a little confused, Lolly. Are you talking generalities? Or something specific, connected with Simon Meyer's abduction?"

"Both, Count. I've had a feeling throughout that there's something Sir Victor isn't telling us. Something that has a bearing on the kidnapping. I also have a feeling that, whatever it is he's holding back, it's very much part of his everyday life. Any idea what that might be? Eh?"

If now wasn't the time, I wondered when *would* be the right time. So I told Lolly about Victor's visit to the Salon Pink and subsequent blackmail attempt by Madame Noguchi and Colonel Doihara.

"Doihara?" Lolly's voice was unusually sharp. "I can see your predicament, Count. But still, you should have told me earlier."

"I'm sorry, Lolly."

"No problem, *lo*."

A waiter arrived to refill our glasses with the remains of the Côte-

Rôtie and took away our empty plates. Lolly raised his glass in toast.

"To the dessert!" He saw my look. "It's alright, Count. I can handle it."

There was no doubt he could, but I was going to be left to foot the bill. Luckily, I had Victor's cheque in my pocket. Lolly would owe me one. And at least another one for my part in negotiating Simon's release with Big Ears. In Shanghai, of course, one and one made three. Maybe four. Lolly owed me big time.

And he knew it. And not just for dinner. As he tucked into a mouth-watering dessert of pineapple upside-down cake topped by Neapolitan ice cream, he waxed eloquent about the way Shanghai's Municipal Police Force functioned. In spite of being now chief among Chinese detectives, Lolly had got as high up the ranks as he was ever going to get as a Chinese policeman. Those above him were reserved for 'whiteys' whose faces were stained permanently pink by alcohol and whose faeces smelled worse than the Soochow Creek.

Just in case I was wondering who he was referring to, he provided me with a list of who was in the pocket of whom, and so what results one could almost invariably anticipate when it came to 'solving' a crime. Payback time. I confined every name, every detail to memory.

"But that's enough for now, Count." He wiped a last crumb from one corner of his mouth. "I can see you've been memorising everything I've told you so that you can write a story about Shanghai crime. But make sure you talk to others, too. Your colleagues probably have plenty of tales to tell. And once you've finished your piece, come back to me with it. I promise I'll make it better."

He stood up and patted his stomach with satisfaction.

"That was almost as good a meal as one gets at the Sun Ya on Nanking Road. Remind me to take you there one day, Count. In the meantime, look after yourself. And," he added as an afterthought, "be careful what you write."

20.

I dropped in at the Horse and Hounds Bar on the ninth floor of the hotel on my way down.

"Christopher! Rusty!" Victor and Kiki chorused together. "We were wondering where you were."

"Just having dinner with Lolly Lo upstairs."

"You didn't pay, I hope?"

"As a matter of fact I did. I signed the usual chit."

"I'll tear it up. Dinner's always on the house for you, Christopher."

Victor was in magnanimous mode. Or possibly, since Lolly was involved, magmanimous.

"Thank you, Victor. And thank you, too, for the wonderful new accommodation. Greatly appreciated. I was getting quite sick of my room at the Astor House."

"Nonsense. It was the least I could do."

"And how's Simon surviving? Playing the piano again?"

"He was," Victor grimaced slightly, "but I've packed him off back home. Put him on a ship this morning."

"A pity," I said. "I'd hoped to hear him play again."

Victor grunted. "I'm holding a fancy dress do on New Year's Eve, Christopher. You must come. Plenty of booze and all that. Bring a woman of your choice."

"That would be a pleasure. How fancily should we dress?"

"Victor's set a theme. He always *does*, you know." Kiki made it sound as if she'd been living in Shanghai for a multitude of years rather than a few weeks.

"Which is?"

"Abandon ship. It's *frightfully* amusing, don't you think? You have to dress as if you were abandoning ship."

"That's going to take some thought. As a rat, perhaps?"

"Ssh! Don't give the game away. The winner gets a prize, you know."

"Hopefully, not of a sinking ship."

"And you simply *must* come to the Christmas party at the German Club on Saturday night, Rusty darling. 9 pm."

"That sounds a little perilous," I tried to look suitably cowed. "Any advice on how I should dress for it, Kiki? In the summer uniform of the League of German Girls, possibly?"

"*Ryallai*, poppet! You're irrepressible." A come-on look.

"I realise that joking about the Germans is no laughing matter," Victor chuckled, "but the mind does boggle, doesn't it, at the idea of Christopher here tarted up as a proper young German girl in Nazi uniform. Ooh! I'd simply *love* to take your photo, ideally with top buttons of your shirt wide open and your toggle fully displayed."

Victor's right eye twinkled merrily behind his monocle. Now that Simon was no longer on his mind, he was back to displaying his customary wit and mockery.

I finished my Manhattan and slid off the bar stool as gracefully as I could manage. It had been a long day.

"I think I'll be getting back to my new lodgings if you don't mind. It's been a long week and I need a proper sleep."

"Me, too," announced Kiki, quickly slipping off her perch and giving Victor a peck on the cheek. "Nighty night, Victor darling. Same time tomorrow?"

"Absolutely, my dear. If you're sure you don't mind."

"I don't at all. In fact, it's been rather fun."

The two of us left the bar and stepped into one of the Cathay's smart new air-conditioned elevators.

"What was that about? Same time tomorrow."

Kiki glanced at me mockingly.

"I *say*, do I detect a hint of jealousy, poppet?" she laughed and kissed me lightly on the cheek.

The lift came to a smooth halt on the ground floor and we stepped out into a grand rotunda with soaring ceiling of leaded glass bolstered by marble reliefs of stylised greyhounds.

"If you *ryallai* want to know, Victor's photographing me."

"Is he now? In provocative poses, no doubt."

She stopped.

"How did you know?"

"*Everyone* knows about Victor and the things he gets up to in his studio. At least, they *think* they know."

"He's a jolly good photographer, Rusty."

"I'm sure he is. I saw how he snapped shots of that Sikh policeman killed by a ricksha cushion bomb the other morning. He framed just the essential details. Street photography at its best. If he didn't have his gammy legs, he'd make an excellent photojournalist."

"He knows how to pose a woman, too, in such a way that she looks her very best."

"A good all-round photographer, then."

Kiki took my arm and leaned into me with her hips as we made our way towards one of the entrances.

"You know he names all his dogs using his initials?" she said, adeptly changing the subject. "Veiled Secret is one of them. Very Soon another."

"Sound like a Very Silly habit to me."

Kiki laughed appreciatively.

"But think how Very Sexy I could be as a greyhound bitch."

"Kiki! Really! You're beginning to sound like you're on heat."

We paused under an awning overhanging Nanking Road. It was raining. A couple of coolies were huddled under the raised back ends of their rickshas, waiting for a fare.

"Why don't you come back home with me, poppet?"

"And where might home be?"

"The Normandie apartments. Where Route Ferguson meets Avenue Joffre. Or I can, of course, check out your new lodgings. I'm sure you're not *that* exhausted. You know how I can make a matchstick feel like a Havana cigar."

"Do I detect the sweet smoke of rhetoric in your words, Kiki?"

"No, poppet. Just another smoke ring."

"Raised with the fume of a lover's sighs." I assented. "If you insist, then."

21.

An evening in the company of Germans struck me as perhaps interesting, but almost certainly less than gay. Still, I wasn't prepared to refuse Kiki's kind offer to accompany her and I had a feeling she might reveal her true colours beyond her socialite's upper-class drawl. Anyway, I was in search of a story.

Dixon picked us up in full livery and drove us across town in Victor's Rolls Royce Phantom, so we arrived in style. Except nobody noticed. Apart from the usual sewer rats, of course. Two of them were wearing uniforms.

Over the front entrance of the German Club hung the German national flag and a giant swastika. Smaller pairs of flags were tied to every lamppost lining the Rue Cardinal Mercier along which guests approached in their black Mercedes-Benz Mannheims and SS seven-litre engine cars. There was, perhaps, a certain *schadenfreude* at work here. Desiré-Félicien-François-Joseph, the Belgian Church dignitary who became Cardinal Mercier, was noted for his staunch resistance to the German occupation of France in 1914. But who cared about the past when the present was being carefully manipulated with an eye to the future?

A young German with slicked-back blonde hair dripping with Henkel's hair pomade opened the rear door of the Rolls and clicked his heels by way of welcome. I stepped out and dutifully offered Kiki my forearm, on which she placed one gloved hand lightly as she, too, left Dixon and the lavish woody smell of soft leather behind her. Together, the two of us glided up a flight of ornate marble steps fitted with a red and black carpet. I enjoyed grinding one heel into the swastika woven into it at the top of the steps.

Inside the entrance, another blonde-haired young man politely requested that the new arrivals sign a Visitors' Book on the table. Kiki wrote her name and, after a fraction of a moment's hesitation, left the space for her Nazi membership number blank. I had no such qualms and filled in my own number. Twenty two thousand two hundred and twenty two. Five 2s were hard to forget.

"I can never remember my membership number. *Awfully* silly of me," Kiki said, slightly embarrassed as she took my arm and walked the walk along a wide corridor towards a ballroom overflowing with guests. "I never realised, though, that you were also a member of the Party, poppet."

"For quite some time actually. Ready for all eventualities."

"So I noticed by your membership number."

"So is yours before or after mine?"

"Oh! *Well* after," she squeezed my arm. "Somewhere around a hundred thousand, I think."

"*Fraulein* Montagu-Rose!" A man in his mid-forties, with a hint of grey in his close-cropped dark hair, bent over Kiki's outstretched gloved hand and gave it an air kiss. He was in army uniform, as he had been when I first encountered him in the Elite Bar. This evening, he also sported a Nazi armband on his sleeve.

"And *Graf* Blum! What a pleasure to meet you again, sir." A click of the heels.

I bowed formally and took his outstretched hand. The grip was firm, but nothing compared with Captain Dobermann's. Or, for that matter, with Kiki's vagina.

"Likewise, Major von Holst."

Noticing the swastika badge in my lapel, he said, "I see you are a member of the Nazi Party, Count Blum. When did you join?"

"Some time ago now, Major."

"His membership number is *very* low," Kiki confided in awe.

"Not as low as the Führer's, surely?" Von Holst laughed. As if anyone could have a lower number than Adolf Hitler's 555. The only 555 in Shanghai belonged to State Express, a brand of cigarettes that wasn't nearly as fiery as our Adolf.

"No, of course not. But still only a *little* above twenty thousand." Kiki was clearly impressed.

"But that means you're a *very* early supporter of the Führer," von Holst said admiringly. "And at such a youthful age, too. My warmest congratulations."

"Thank you. It is an honour. I was greatly impressed by the Führer's oratory when I was young." I had found that modesty tended to be a good substitute for truth. "But please refresh my memory, Major von Holst. What is it that brings you here to Shanghai? I'm afraid I was a little—a little *distraught* when we last met."

"Of course. You had had a traumatish evening to do with a kidnapping, yes? I am an adviser to General Chiang Kai-shek."

"Adviser?"

"To help reorganize his armies."

"*And* to supply them with German weaponry as and when appropriate. You are *far* too modest, Otto."

The Major gave Kiki a sharp look as a waiter circulating with a tray of drinks offered us champagne.

"Ah! Just what I need," I raised my glass. "*Zum wohl!*"

"You speak German, Count Blum?"

"I do indeed, Major."

Von Holst clinked his glass against mine.

"It is a time and occasion to dispense with formalities, I think. Please call me Otto."

"Then I am Christopher, Otto. Or you can call me Rusty. Everyone else does."

My new friend preferred not to take up my offer. "Somebody told me, Kristoffer, that you were born in Berlin. Is that true?"

"My father was Russian Ambassador for the Tsar in Berlin at the time."

"Which means you are a German citizen, yes?"

"By birth, yes indeed. You are well informed, Otto."

"I say, you never told me *that*, Rusty," Kiki put in, very slightly resentful.

"You never asked me, Kiki."

"And an early member of the National Socialist German Workers' Party. But this is wonderful!" exclaimed Otto, taking me by the arm and guiding me gently but firmly into the middle of the crowded room. "You must *meet* people, *important* people who will help you in the future, yes?"

I turned back to mouth an apology to Kiki, but she was already in the steely sights of Captain Dobermann.

"Don't worry about *Fraulein* Kiki." Otto patted me on the arm with his free hand. "She will soon be the centre of attention, as I'm sure you know."

"I must admit, Otto, she does strike me sometimes as a kind of praying mantis, waiting to ambush just the right kind of man."

"And bite off the head of her lover in bed, maybe. This is what makes her so *thrilling*, yes?"

"Possibly, Otto. I wouldn't know."

"Of course not. How can you know such things? You are a German, Kristoffer, not a salon lioness."

He laughed loudly. More champagne arrived, courtesy of another waiter circling the throng. Setting down both our empty glasses, von Holst grabbed two full flutes and thrust one into his new friend's hand.

"To the Führer!" He clicked his heels as he raised his glass and looked me in the eye.

"To the future Chancellor of Germany!" I echoed politely. So long as it wasn't Adolf.

Otto looked at me approvingly.

"Kristoffer, I think we will be friends, yes? We need more champagne." He clicked his fingers in the air above his head. Miraculously yet another waiter appeared beside us. As did two Japanese men. One had taken the tonsure and was wearing the silken robes of a Buddhist priest.

The other was much more like your average Japanese officer—short and stocky, with close-cropped hair and a Hitler-like moustache bristling on his upper lip. The brown eyes glinting under the light of the chandeliers missed nothing.

"Majaa Bon Horusuto? My name is, ah, Fujii. Lieutenant Fujii, nabaru attaché to za Embassy of Japan."

"How do you do, Lieutenant Fujii." Otto was at once the courteous Prussian officer as he shook the Japanese lieutenant's hand. "And have you been in Shanghai long?"

"Shanghai wrong? No, ah, not wrong, Majaa. A few munce onry."

"Really? And how can I be of service, Lieutenant Fujii?"

"Ziss," Fujii indicated his companion standing beside him and smiling broadly, "is za Beneraburu Abbotto."

"Delighted to meet you, Venerable Sir. And welcome to the German Club."

"Za Beneraburu would rike meeting wiz you to discuss weapon."

Otto's face darkened.

"I regret I am not in the business of supplying arms, Lieutenant. I am merely an adviser to General Chiang Kai-shek. Nothing else. You will need, therefore, to approach somebody else. I believe there is a gentleman called Morris Cohen—Two Gun Cohen they call him—who may be able to help you. He lives in Nanking."

"*A sō des'ka?*" Fujii looked annoyed at the way Otto had dismissed him. "No weapon? My aporogies. Maybe anuzza time," he said and with the slightest of bows turned on his heel and made his way through the crowd of guests, followed by his silent but venerable companion.

"Somebody lost a bit of face there," I couldn't help smiling. "To think they might become our allies!"

"Once they turn against the British."

"Or the British turn against them."

Otto laughed loudly and slapped me on the back.

"But we, Kristoffer, *we* are friends, yes? But, tell me. You are a journalist who goes around and hears things. What do you make of these—what is it they are called—these *zwergenbanditen*?" The word was enough to make him switch from English to German. "Will they invade the whole of China?"

"Probably, Otto. In the end," I replied in German. The conversation was turning serious and I knew I was about to be probed for information. Friendship involved give and take and I needed to give before I could take. "But they'll find it a far harder task than annexing Manchuria. Chiang Kai-shek is an able general and, as you know, has several large armies at his disposal."

"Yes, but they are not well-trained, are they? Or well-armed.

Yet, at least. The Japanese are convinced that the Chinese will offer no resistance to their superior power and discipline."

"Well, you're obviously the best judge of that, Otto. As I understand it, a number of German officers are now training Chinese troops. Personally, though, I'm not convinced that the Chinese have yet revealed their true colours when it comes to fighting the Japanese. Remember, Chiang somehow has to overcome the communists in the south if he is to unify the whole country. Until he succeeds in that, he has little option other than to appease the Japanese, rather than fight them."

"But he *will* defeat the Red Army, surely?"

"You would think so, wouldn't you? And yet…"

"Yet what, Kristoffer?" Otto leaned closer towards me. The time had come.

"Stalin has put the squeeze on the Generalissimo."

"Squeeze? How?"

"By holding Chiang Kai-shek's son hostage in Moscow."

"Hostage? But how is this possible? It isn't in the newspapers."

"No, it's a well-kept secret and Chiang would prefer to keep it that way. If the Chinese populace knew that Stalin had the Generalissimo by the balls, if you'll excuse my turn of phrase, they'd lose all faith in him and join the communists. The last thing he wants right now is to be seen to be weak in the face of Japanese threats."

"Especially with all that is going on these days, eh? It seems like the Chinese are on the warpath. Strikes, boycotts, attacks on Japanese businesses and stores. When will it end, Kristoffer?"

"Who knows?" I shrugged. "The good thing about it all is that nobody has lost their life in the riots. Not yet, at least. But if a Japanese *does* get killed, then, I think, Shanghai's going to be in real trouble. Remember, the Japanese Army and Navy are always vying for greater power in Tokyo. The bluejackets are still smarting at the Kwantung Army's success in Manchuria and are looking for an excuse to find glory of their own. Warship Row is filled with Japanese ships right now. You wouldn't know it from the way the city's foreigners go about their daily lives, but we're sitting on a keg of gunpowder, and it could explode at any moment."

"You two gentlemen seem lost in serious conversation." We were interrupted by man of about fifty, with Nazi flag in the buttonhole of his tailored three-piece suit. "And I thought this was a celebration of Hitler's projected rise to power. Anything I should know about?"

"Karl-Heinz! Kristoffer, meet Karl-Heinz Fuchs, Cultural Attaché at the German Embassy. Karl-Heinz, *Graf* Kristoffer Blum is a journalist born in Berlin, but later raised in Sweden. We were discussing China's chances against the Japanese if it came to war."

"Who isn't these days? It seems to be the only topic of conversation in town now that the Sassoon kidnapping has been resolved. If I'm not mistaken, *Graf* Blum, you had a hand in that?" Karl-Heinz smiled and raised a well-arched eyebrow. Clearly the diplomat. As smooth as a Buddhist abbot's silk and as crafty, I suspected, as his surname implied.

"Kristoffer was telling me, among other things, Karl-Heinz, about how Stalin is holding Chiang Kai-shek's son hostage in Moscow. Did you know of this?"

The diplomat was clearly surprised.

"No, Otto, that news has definitely not landed on my office desk in the embassy. Tell me more, Kristoffer. I hope you don't object to the informality?"

"Not at all, Karl-Heinz. As I was telling Otto, three or four years ago Chiang Kai-shek sent his son, Ching-kuo, to Moscow to study. Once the boy had graduated and intended to come back to China, he was denied an exit visa and has been under what amounts to house arrest ever since. Ching-kuo is the Generalissimo's one and only legitimate son and his father loves him as only a Chinese father can love a son. He will, therefore, do anything to secure Ching-kuo's safe return to China."

"Anything?"

"Anything. And that means that Chiang Kai-shek will *never* crush the communists. He will defeat them, yes, but not obliterate them for good. Not until Stalin releases Ching-kuo. It is against his interests."

"That is indeed interesting, Kristoffer. Are you sure you're just a journalist? The journalists I know have so little understanding or knowledge of the intricacies underpinning diplomacy."

"You're too kind, Karl-Heinz."

Karl-Heinz nodded and was silent for a moment or two. Then,

"You seem to have found a very good friend, Otto. Maybe we should all meet again in less public surroundings? With our wives, of course. Are you married, Kristoffer?"

"No, Karl-Heinz. Not yet, at least. I am still of an age when I prefer the company of several different women, rather than of a single wife."

Both men laughed loudly, as men do when not in the company of women.

"But seriously, Karl-Heinz," Otto continued soberly, "as I am fast learning in my employment as adviser to the Generalissimo, things are never quite what they seem."

"Welcome to the world of diplomacy, Otto," Karl-Heinz laughed and arched his right eyebrow again. Then he turned to me. "Do you have anything more for us, Kristoffer?"

"More?" I feigned surprise. "Only that one should never allow oneself to be deceived by Chiang Kai-shek. He is a wily politician who plays all sides to his advantage. The Japanese, the Soviet, even the German Governments will be used by him against one another as the situation dictates."

"For example?"

"For example, Stalin holds Chiang's son hostage, right? This means that the Generalissimo must play his cards carefully. By not eradicating the communists, he can continue to obtain arms and money from the Comintern in Moscow—arms and money that he is in desperate need of."

"As we well know, eh, Otto?"

Chiang's adviser wasn't quite sure how to respond, so he deflected the conversation.

"You may be right, Karl-Heinz, but let's continue this conversation over dinner at my place soon. I have a feeling General Wetzel standing in a group with my wife over there, requires my services. I hope you'll excuse us while I introduce Kristoffer to Ludmila."

Karl-Heinz bowed politely and we crossed the room to join a statuesque Aryan blonde surrounded by several admiring military officers.

"Luda, *mein liebling*, you must meet my new friend, Kristoffer. *Graf* Kristoffer Blum. Kristoffer, this is my wife, Ludmila."

Ludmila turned towards me with a carefully groomed smile. Her blonde hair was swept up to set off a well-chiselled jawline. Her lips were red, her eyes a cool blue, like a flat-calm sea ready to be stirred by the wind.

"Delighted, *Graf* Blum," she said, proffering her hand in such a way that I knew at once that I should bend over it to offer an air kiss. I wondered if she kept count of how many counts had kissed her hand. Perhaps she should wear a Rosary on her wrist instead of a platinum gold bracelet.

"Kristoffer is Swedish, but was born in Berlin, Luda. So he is German, too, and one of us," Otto added with just enough nuance to make it clear that, as a Nazi sympathiser, I was safe to talk to. Not that, as a woman, she had anything of importance to say. I wasn't so sure. There was a deep pool of intelligence in her liquid blue eyes.

"How nice to meet a real Berliner!" Ludmila smiled again, this time a little more warmly. "So many of us in Berlin are just temporary residents."

"As are we all in Shanghai."

"Exactly. *Graf*," she turned to indicate a tall, lean uniformed man in his mid-sixties standing to attention beside her. "Do you know Generaloberst Hans von Seeckt? Formerly Chief of Staff to August von Mackensen and now a member of the Reichstag?"

"I haven't had the honour, *Generaloberst*."

"*Graf*," he bowed stiffly from the waist—not much, but enough to show recognition of what clearly for him was my lesser title.

"The Generaloberst may well be coming to Shanghai on a more permanent basis," Otto continued, "as Chiang Kai-shek's chief adviser."

"Really?" I did my best to sound impressed. "From what I hear, you're sorely needed in Nanking."

Von Seeckt smiled and inclined his head, while touching the moustache on his upper lip with a white gloved hand. He probably wanted to ensure it hadn't been blown away by my breezy words.

"The Generalissimo," he pronounced the word with a very slight tinge of irony at which Prussian officers can be so adept, "may have to wait until I've served my time in the Reichstag."

There was polite laughter from others standing in the circle. Ludmila's was loudest, but then she had no choice. She was the only woman in the group.

"So, *Graf*," she turned back to me with her clear blue gaze, "what brings you to Shanghai?"

"Me? Oh, I'm just a newspaper reporter for the *Frankfurter Zeitung*. What I do isn't nearly as important as the work done by these gentlemen here."

Which was, I thought, a neat way of establishing a link between this attractive *hausfrau* and myself. As I had anticipated, she was smart enough to notice and gave me a discrete but appreciative smile.

"But *Graf* Blum, wasn't it you who solved the Simon Meyer kidnapping case?" one of the young hangers-on put in.

"Well, I wouldn't say *solved* exactly."

"But you *found* him," Ludmila said in admiration. "You are a *hero*, my Count."

At this point, Von Seekt checked his moustache again and drifted silently away from the group. Another officer spoke up to fill the gap he had left behind him.

"Maybe your superiors at the *Frankfurter Zeitung* appreciate your work, *Graf* Blum, better than ours do here?"

"Georg, I'm sure that's not the case. *Every*one appreciates what you've been doing since you arrived here," Ludmila said soothingly, before turning back to me. "General Wetzel is at present Chief Adviser to Chiang Kai-shek in Nanking, as I'm sure you are aware."

I wasn't really surprised if the Generalissimo didn't pay his German adviser as much notice as he felt he deserved. In the short space of a glass or two of champagne I had come across four German officers, all claiming to be advisers of one sort or another. The Generalissimo was in danger of dying of a surfeit of sauerkraut.

"The trouble with the Chinese," Wetzel embarked on what turned out clearly to be one of his set-piece monologues in polite company, "is that they simply don't trust one another. And in any army, as we well know in Germany, there must be trust—a trust generated by the Prussian system of appointments and promotions. But here staff officer appointments are made for political reasons, rather than on the basis of proven expertise. How can that breed trust among the men? And divisional commanders tend to view the troops under their command as their own personal property, to do with as they please, rather than as the military situation demands. Betrayal, then, takes the place of trust." He uttered what sounded like an exasperated expletive, but he may have just been clearing his throat. "I'm obliged to deal with Chinese-style warfare conducted by water-brained military officers who fail to grasp that war is not a matter of politics. It is a matter of *trust*."

I could appreciate why the General wasn't receiving the respect he thought he deserved. He needed to tone down his Prussian self-righteousness and be more conciliatory if he wanted to get along with those he was advising. The Chinese were fed up with being looked down on by Westerners. Not being a military adviser, though, I kept my observation to myself.

At which point, having said all he had to say, the General bowed slightly, turned on his heel and left. Otto hurried after him, casting a quick glance in my direction and shrugging his shoulders very slightly. The remaining two young officers took this as an opportunity to drift away in search of more uplifting company, so I found himself alone with Ludmila.

"General Wetzel is Otto's superior," she sighed, putting a friendly long-gloved hand on my arm, "so my husband has little choice but to follow him about like a lap hound—if you'll excuse my indiscretion."

"If I were Otto," I countered, "I'd greatly prefer to be sitting on your lap, *Frau* von Holst, rather than on the General's." Audacity and foolhardiness made good bedfellows—especially after a few glasses of champagne.

"Oh!" She put her other gloved hand to her mouth to stifle a laugh. "I can see you are a rather naughty Count."

"Not all the time, I assure you. But I like to think I have my moments." I raised my glass in silent toast, relieved that I had judged Ludmila correctly.

"I would like to savour one such moment, if I may," she returned my toast, "but in a less public atmosphere, *Graf* Blum —"

"Kristoffer, please. And can we also please forget that I'm a count."

"Kristoffer," she smiled. "A nice name, I think. As I was saying, perhaps we could meet one evening? Otto has to spend all his time in Nanking, running around after the good *General der Infanterie*. As a result, I have rather a lot of time to pass on my own. I have a daughter, but..." her voice trailed off.

"A daughter? How nice!" I exclaimed with slightly doused enthusiasm. "How old is she, if I might ask?"

"Twelve years old since yesterday. Still young enough to be a child, but old enough to be a woman. We have an *amah* to look after her, of course."

"Of course. But I find it hard to believe."

Ludmila frowned slightly and two rather charming creased lines appeared on her forehead where her brow led onto her strong straight nose.

"Believe what, Kristoffer?"

"That you can have a daughter of such an age and still be so beautiful."

"Oh!" She exclaimed and again a gloved hand went up to cover her mouth as she opened it to laugh. "So you are a flatterer, too, Kristoffer? As well as having—how did you call them—naughty moments."

"Hopefully, though, they are no foe to nobleness."

Ludmila raised herself to full patrician height at my words and looked me in the eye.

"As I was saying, to fill in the time and relieve myself of my own company, I hold a soirée for my friends on the second and fourth Thursdays of every month at the Palace Hotel. I would be delighted, therefore, if you could join us, Kristoffer. January the fourteenth is, I believe, the second Thursday after the New Year."

"That would be an honour, *Frau* von Holst."

"Please," she smiled her full-lipped smile, "if you are to be my Kristoffer, I must be your Ludmila. Or Luda, as my friends call me."

"Then it would be a great pleasure to join you, Luda."

My playgirl in a Nazi world?

"I'm so glad, Kristoffer. The atmosphere is more—how shall I put it?—more *intim* than here. And it would allow us to get to know each other a little better, don't you think?"

The thought had passed my mind. This tall and well-proportioned woman may have been in her mid- to late-thirties, she may have given birth to a daughter who would soon be in her teens, but she had kept her figure and her youth remarkably well. Otto clearly didn't appreciate her enough.

"The soirée usually begins at six in the evening. Why don't you come a little later. Somewhere between seven and eight, say? Room 156 at the Palace."

"Room 156?"

"Yes. I always take that particular suite. The number is the same as that of my birthday. The fifteenth of June."

"I must remember that. And when the time comes, give you an appropriate present."

At which point we were joined by two women, friends of Ludmila's clearly, to judge by the way they shrieked with delight at seeing one another, before dutifully proffering cheeks and planting kisses with pouting red lips. One of them was slightly the worse—or better—for the amount of champagne she had consumed.

"Kristoffer, please meet my friends, Trudi Gassmann and Raina Fuchs." For some reason, Ludmila had spoken in English. I offered my hand to each in turn. Trudi was petite and dark-haired with flashing amber-coloured eyes—clearly vivacious and fun-loving. At least, one of her eyes was amber; the other was blue-grey. A bit disconcerting at first, but they definitely had their charm once you got used to them. Especially when owned by Trudi.

Raina was the opposite—tall, though not as tall as Ludmila, with well-defined curves in places where they mattered. She struck me as serious, perhaps because she had clearly not imbibed as much alcohol as her companion. But she was also a diplomat's wife.

Like Maisy when we had first met, Trudi's opening question was straight to the point.

"Tell me, *Herr* Kristoffer, are you single?"

"Trudi, *liebe!*" Ludmila exclaimed, putting one hand to her mouth in mock horror. "That is not a good question to ask *Graf* Blum," she added, emphasising my title meaningfully. "We are in company, *schatz*, not—how do you call it?—*gemeinschaft*. You are not drinking too much, I hope, yes?"

"But it is a *party*, Luda," Trudi neatly avoided the linguistic conundrum and giggled happily. "Even a straw widow can drown her sorrows, no?"

"I think in English you are a *grass* widow," Raina put in, a little severely. "Isn't that so, *Graf* Blum?"

"A grass widow, yes, but a straw man," I said helpfully. "But do please call me Kristoffer."

"So, Raina, what happens when you light Karl-Heinz's fire?" Trudi's laugh made the chandelier above our heads tinkle with pleasure. "Does he burn with passion-*liche* love? Or —"

"Trudi! *Really!*"

Trudi hiccupped by way of apology. I wondered idly how she had intended to express the alternative to Raina's diplomatic husband's passion, but I wasn't going to find out any time soon.

"Escuse! *Entschuldigung!*" She put one hand to her throat, another to her stomach. "Perhaps I am not feeling so *gut*, Luda. Where do you think I may find the dames' toilet?"

She looked around a little desperately. Maybe that's what heterochromia did to you, but neither coloured eye found what it was looking for, so Ludmila took her by the arm and, with Raina lending her support on the other side of their lurching companion, headed towards the corridor. Luda smiled a little helplessly and mouthed 'sorry' at me as they began to work their way across the crowded reception room.

Left to my own devices, I went in search of another drink. Germans tended to have that effect on me. Unless it was my Russian heritage. While I was replenishing my glass in one corner of the room, I heard behind me a steely male voice saying in an undertone in German. "He wants a Junkers, not a Fokkers."

"Which one?" A voice, though without its usual drawl, that I immediately recognised as belonging to Kiki. "The W34?"

"No. the 87."

"The Stuka? But *why?* The W34 is renowned for the distance it can travel without refuelling, and for the altitude it can fly. *And* it seats six passengers."

My suspicion had always been of her ready tongue. Now in fluent German.

"I know. *And*, as we both know, it is more expensive."

"He's an awful cheapskate, isn't he? After all, what's money to a drug lord like him? Big Ears can afford it."

"True, but he also likes the idea of being able to present a dive bomber to the Generalissimo. A military plane for a military man and all that."

"The Japanese won't be amused."

"No, they won't. Which is why they shouldn't be informed." A change in tone. "Careful! The enemy's within earshot."

I was wondering if they had spotted me, but was distracted by the small voice of a perfectly turned-out Japanese woman in formal kimono. "Excuse me, would you mind terribly passing me a plate of canapés? There is such a crush of people I find it hard to get to the table."

"But of *course!*" I exclaimed, ever the gentleman. Especially in the presence of such a beautiful woman. "Which one would you like?"

"Is there a choice?" She brought one hand up to cover her mouth as she spoke and laughed a little nervously. The sleeve of her kimono followed the movement of her arm, forming a curtain that seemed to shut off the two of us from the rest of the gathering.

I stood on tiptoe and strained my neck to look down at the table between a couple of heads.

"So far as I can see," I turned back to her, "there is smoked herring with creamed horseradish on pumpernickel bread, potato pancakes with salmon, spring cheese and herb pretzels, and some cold cuts. Maybe I should get you a selection?"

"That would be *most* kind." Her smile was encouraging, but her eyes were almost black. Another version of impenetrable. "I am not used to so much alcohol and I need something solid to sustain me," she smiled coquettishly. At least, I assumed she was being coquettish, but who knew. She was Japanese.

I eased my way forward between a couple of burly Bavarians and filled a plate with canapés. Then I turned and made my way back to my new companion who accepted it gratefully.

"Thank you *so* much." She seemed prepared to slip away.

"By the way," I said conversationally, "my name is Bloom. Christopher Bloom."

"How do you do, Mr Broom," she put out a delicate hand to grasp mine lightly. "I am Noguchi. Miyoko Noguchi."

"Pleased to meet you Madame Noguchi. And the name's Bloom. Not Broom. Tell me, what brings you to Shanghai, if you'll excuse my directness? A husband?"

Miyoko nearly choked on her smoked herring and pumpernickel, and waved one hand back and forth rapidly in front of her face.

"No, no, Mr Bloom. I have no husband," she paused, searching for a suitable reply. "But I do look after several young girls." The way she looked up and gave me a knowing smile suggested that she had already tagged me as a potential client in the Salon Pink.

"I run an orphanage."

Maybe not.

"An orphanage? For young girls? But how commendable, Madame Noguchi!"

"Thank you," she said, covering her mouth with her free hand to ensure that no food came out inadvertently.

"Is your work somehow connected with the Church?"

"Church?" she frowned. Maybe the Bavarian Emmentaler didn't agree with her.

"What I mean is, all the orphanages in Shanghai that I know of are run by missionaries of one sort or another. So I was wondering if you yourself were one of them."

"Oh, I *see!*" She laughed in relief. "No, Mr Bloom, I am not a missionary. But tell me, what do *you* do?"

"Me? I'm a journalist. I write for the *Frankfurter Zeitung*."

"How interesting!" She did her best to make it seem so. "And have you been in Shanghai long?"

"A few months now. But do tell me more about your orphanage. How long have you been running it? How many children are there? Are they Japanese? How do you finance it? With donations from Japanese businessmen?"

"You have a lot of questions, Mr Bloom," Miyoko laughed again, giving away nothing.

"I'm a journalist, Madame Noguchi." I changed tack. "But I realise this is not the time or place for an inquisition!" She favoured me with a smile of light relief. "So maybe I could visit your orphanage one day soon and see it for myself. I have a feeling that my readers in Germany would be rather interested to hear about your charitable work. Especially now that our two countries are likely to become allies. What do you think?"

I waited while she mulled over my suggestion. Then, handing me her half-empty plate with an apologetic ducking of her head, she withdrew a stiff cloth wallet from the front of her *obi* waistband, opened it, and handed me her visiting card.

"I am very grateful to you for your sincere interest in my boring work, Mr Bloom. And very glad to have had this opportunity to make your acquaintance. Do please get in touch with me soon. And now if you'll excuse me, a Japanese gentleman is waiting for me." She smiled once more and floated gracefully away with tiny mincing steps, leaving me holding her plate of half-finished canapés. The back of her neck where her hair was swept up and pinned to the top of her head was somehow one of the most erotic sights I'd ever seen. Maybe I should pay a visit to the Salon Pink after all.

"Kristoffer! So we meet again! How are you enjoying the party?" Like Ludmila, Otto had decided to address me in English. To show that he was a cosmopolitan, perhaps?

"It's a great party, Otto. So many interesting people here. Important people, too, but —"

"But what, my friend?"

"*Frankfurter Zeitung* has asked me to write a story about the German community in Shanghai and this Christmas party would seem like a good way to frame it. But I need—how can I phrase it?—I need some sort of *angle* that my readers can relate to."

"Manly interest, you mean, yes? Some gossip, perhaps? This is what you journalists like, I think."

"Some journalists, Otto, but not me. Anyway, *Frankfurter Zeitung* isn't that kind of newspaper. A business deal of some kind, perhaps? Or something to do with Chiang Kai-shek and the German-Japan alliance. Is there anything you've heard that might point me in the right direction?"

Von Holst laughed and gave me a friendly slap on the back.

"Always on the job, eh! Of course, my friend. How about a German aeroplane that the famous Shanghai gangster, Tu Yue-sheng, plans to present to the Generalissimo for his birthday?"

"Now that sounds like a *story*. Tell me more."

Otto looked serious. "But this is the problem, Kristoffer. There is no more—that is, no more that I can say officially. As you know, the German Government is forbidden to sell arms to foreign powers. Everything is done under the hand, yes?"

"And an airplane counts as arms?"

"In this case, yes. Tu wants a Junkers 87."

"What? A Stuka? I see what you mean." I paused to sip my excellent Gewürztraminer. "But Big Ears Tu isn't a foreign *power* as such, is he, Otto?"

"No, this is true."

"In other words, nothing is to stop him buying a German plane as a private citizen."

"This is also correct, but how does he manage to get hold of such a plane? That is the question."

"I assume through you, Otto, or another of Chiang Kai-shek's German advisers."

"Precisely, but you cannot say that."

"Why not?" Knowing the answer.

"Because it contravenes the Treaty of Versailles which prohibits Germany from engaging in arms trade. You see the difficulty, yes?"

"I do, indeed, Otto. But what if Tu Yue-sheng were reported to have bought the plane from the Soviet Union? Hasn't Junkers transferred some of its production there to overcome problems associated with the Treaty?"

"Ah!" Otto smiled. "Now, I think, you have your story, no?" Once more a friendly slap on the back. Once more a juggling act on my part to prevent the white wine in my glass from spilling all over my hand and onto the marble floor.

"But tell me, Kristoffer, have you seen my wife? She seems to have disappeared in this crowd."

"I think, Otto, that you'll find her in the ladies room."

"The ladies room? *I* think, Kristoffer, I will have difficulty to enter such a place."

"Unless you put on a *dirndl*, of course."

Otto slapped one thigh and doubled up with laughter.

"I say, you two seem to be enjoying yourselves. Do you mind if I join you?" It was Kiki. "Something tells me the party in this corner of the room is a jolly sight livelier than elsewhere."

"But of *course*, *Fraulein* Kiki. I was merely wondering whether I should follow Kristoffer's advice and change my outward appearance. I was looking for my wife but, apparently, she is in the ladies room. Kristoffer suggested I put on a *dirndl* in order to go in and find her."

"In that case, Major, might I be allowed to borrow your *lederhosen*? I've always wondered what men get up to as they stand side by side peeing."

"Pissing each other off, perhaps?"

"Better than pissing on each other, anyway. Or on their wives."

"Rusty-*san*! What are you doing here?" It was Joao.

"I could ask the same of you, my friend."

"I'm anticipating an alliance between Germany and Japan."

"In which case might I introduce you to Major Otto von Holst, adviser to Chiang Kai-shek. Otto is German; you are Japanese. Now the alliance between your two countries is cemented."

The two men laughed and shook hands. After a few moments, Otto excused himself. He had a wife to find.

"Kiki you already know, I believe?" Joao was clearly in Portuguese mode. "And I think you've also met Gerda. But maybe not her sister, Irene?"

"Alas! I haven't had the pleasure," I took Irene's hand and kissed it politely. Her hair was as auburn red as her younger sister's, though cut short in a style that was almost masculine. Her face was oval, nose small and up-tilted, and her eyes a startling shade of green. She was as beautiful as I remembered her. "How do you do, Ms Wiedemeyer. My name is Kristoffer Bloom. Or, in present company, Blum. My friends call me Rusty."

"And mine call me Isa, although Rusty might be more appropriate." She touched her hair briefly. Her smile was natural, her teeth even and white, her body still agile and well-toned.

"Rusty wouldn't do you credit, Isa. More like a deep red rose. *Ang mo*, I believe they say in Chinese."

"Not a ginger ninja, then?" She raised her eyebrows beguilingly.

"Not unless you've mastered that particular dark art."

Careful not to let things get out of hand, I stopped flirting. I sensed a certain possessiveness in Kiki, who had put one arm around my waist and was making it clear that, tonight at least, I belonged to her.

"So Joao, what brings you here? Apart from your desire to cement an alliance with Otto von Holst and his friends?"

"I don't know, Rusty. Probably the same as you. Looking for a story."

"As always. And have you found one?"

Joao smiled an inscrutable Japanese smile, then deftly changed the subject.

"Tell me, whatever happened in the Sassoon kidnapping affair? You promised to tell me, remember? But then you went and published your scoop and left me high and dry."

"What? Simon Meyer?" Gerda asked excitedly. "What do you know that the rest of Shanghai doesn't?"

"I'm sorry, Joao. So many of our colleagues were chasing after the story that I felt obliged to write mine quickly. Others could then feed off me, rather than the other way around."

"What *was* the story, Kristoffer?" Isa asked innocently. "I'm afraid that, unlike my flighty sister," this accompanied by a knowing glance at

Joao, "I haven't had time to keep up with Shanghai's gossip recently."

"The trouble is, there are two stories. One I've already published; the other I'll probably never be able to publish if I value my life."

"This is *exciting*, Rusty. Oh, goody! You simply *have* to tell us." Kiki squeezed me more tightly round the waist.

"OK, then. This is for you, Joao, but totally off the record. You never got it from me," I acquiesced reluctantly, knowing that Serino would somehow be able to make use of what I said without having me killed by Tu Yue-sheng or, more likely, Chunky.

I stopped a waiter passing by and asked him to fill all our glasses from the bottle of Gewürztraminer in his white-gloved hands.

"*Prost!*" I raised my glass. "You're going to need this before I'm done."

The other four raised their glasses.

"*Prost!*" They cried in unison, serious now. So I began:

"Here's what *really* happened when Simon Meyer was kidnapped…"

22.

"This is getting to be a habit, poppet."

We were lying in her bed and I had just helped Kiki light her first cigarette of the day. I looked forward to making love to a non-smoker.

"A nice habit, I hope?"

She blew a smoke ring up towards the ceiling of her bedroom by way of answer. Then,

"Like all good things, I'm afraid it's coming to an end."

"Ah! Have people been talking?"

"Don't think you're *that* important," she looked at me sharply. "*Nobody* these days cares what people do in bed or who they do it with, so long as they don't do it in the streets and frighten the *horses*."

That put me in my place all right, although I wasn't sure how the horses felt about it all.

"When?"

"I've booked my passage home on the *Maréchal Joffre*, leaving Shanghai for Marseille and Bremen on January the third."

"Not going to hang out with the Emperor, then? I'll miss you, Kiki."

"Me? Or our love-making?"

"Both."

Another smoke ring.

"Will Roger be accompanying you?"

"Roger? Good God, no. He's a *ghastly* little man. I could imagine *nothing* more taxing than being closeted on a ship with Roger for forty days."

"Is that how long it takes?"

"More or less."

"You could pretend you were Jesus in the wilderness, being tempted by Roger."

"He's certainly a devil," she said drily, "but why should I *fast*, Rusty, when I've paid for *masses* of good food aboard ship?"

A third smoke ring.

"Acksherly, I could imagine being on a cruise with *you*, poppet. Lazy mornings playing deck tennis. Making love in the afternoons. Baccarat in the evenings after dinner. Yes, you'd make a jolly good travelling companion."

"Alas! I don't play baccarat."

"You can *learn*, poppet. We all do, you know. At one stage or another."

"But what about your George back in London? Surely you'd prefer to go on a cruise with him?"

"Maybe. But, unlike you, he's not *here*, is he, Rusty darling? Which means I *can't* be shipwrecked with him, much as though I'd *love* to be."

A fourth smoke ring. I kissed the nape of her neck behind the ear. It wasn't as sexy as Madame Noguchi's, but it was all I had for now.

"Fair enough."

"I'm not sure I really trust Victor. Do you, Rusty?"

I had learned from experience not to be surprised by the *non sequitur*s of pillow talk.

"What makes you say that?"

"I don't know ryallai. He's sent me a box of silk stockings, you know, tied in red ribbon. And *frightfully* risqué lingerie."

"The oldest trick in his book, Kiki dear. That's what he sends to every woman he fancies. Everybody knows that, but somehow the trick always seems to work. Even with Chinese socialites and actresses. Look at Koo Hui-lan."

"All the more reason to know if I can *trust* him. He's told me he'd like to photograph me *déshabillée*."

"He says that to *every* attractive woman he meets."

"Acksherly, I think it would be rather a jape to pose in the nude, don't you?"

"To be honest, it's not something I've ever considered. But you go ahead if it turns you on."

"Thank you, poppet. I mean, if I *were* to do it, I could present the camera with another Kiki, a Kiki Montagu-Rose that *none* of my friends or acquaintances would recognize. Not even Prince George. And probably not you either, Rusty. My nakedness would be my *power*.

That's what makes his proposition so *interesting*. Every woman needs power of *some* sort if she's to survive. Don't you agree?"

"Then do it, Kiki. But remember, it'll be a man who gives you that power. Take off your clothes for Victor's camera, if you feel so inclined. Just make sure Roger isn't around, though. He'd probably die of a heart attack."

"Do him good," she laughed. "But I need to be able to trust Victor completely. Trust him that he won't show my pictures to *any*one outside our close circle of friends My power, you see, would derive from other people's *imagination* of what I might look like without my clothes on. Not from the actual photograph itself."

"Hmm. I see your difficulty." There wasn't much I could add, other than comment on the illogicality of her argument, so I changed the topic. "Tell me, Kiki, what do you make of *Herr* Hitler?"

"That was awfully *sudden*, Christopher. What makes you ask?"

"What you were saying about power." It was the first time she had used my real Christian name, rather than Rusty. A telltale sign. "My impression is that Hitler is well aware of the power of photography, and the image he can project through news photographs."

"Yes, I suppose you're right, now that you come to *mention* it."

"Isn't it a bit dangerous, though? He could come across as a bit of a fraud."

Kiki looked shocked.

"Surely not, Christopher. He's the real thing, isn't he?"

"For Germany, you mean?"

"Yes, of *course*. Germany needs a real leader. And Adolf Hitler is just that. We probably need someone like him in England, ryallai."

"So you think he'll make a good Chancellor?"

"Undoubtedly. You don't agree?"

"I'm sure you're right, Kiki." Her colours were firmly nailed to the *Maréchal Joffre*'s mast. If it had one. Time to change tack again. "By the way, are you going to Victor's New Year's party with anyone in particular? I'm assuming Roger won't be your companion in fancy dress."

She laughed and rolled onto her side to face me.

"Your assumption—or is it *presumption*? I'm never quite sure. Anyway, it's entirely correct, poppet. And your enquiry apposite. The answer is no. Why do you ask?"

"For the simple reason that I myself am—how shall I put it?— unattached. And yet, as I understand Victor's casual invitation, guests are expected to turn up in twos."

"So that Victor's penthouse becomes like Noah's ark, you mean? I should suggest that for his décor. Imagine what would have happened if just one crocodile or cat had fallen overboard."

"Bye-bye species. But you haven't answered my question. Would you like to accompany me to Victor's festivities on New Year's Eve? Or, put another way, would you like me to accompany you?"

There was silence as she paused to consider my offer. I waited for another smoke ring to waft upwards to the ceiling. Eventually, she said, "thank you, poppet, that could be great fun. But how will we dress for the occasion?"

"I've no idea. I must say, though, I don't fancy you as a rat. Your teeth are too even and white. I suspect, too, that they're just as sharp, to judge by your wit." I sat up and slipped my feet onto the floor. "Let me think about it while I have a shower."

I had just finished soaping myself, when the shower curtain was drawn back and Kiki stepped into the bathtub naked.

"I thought I might scrub your back for you, darling."

"How thoughtful of you, but I'm more or less done. Perhaps I should return your offer?" I lathered my flannel and began to rub it gently across her breasts and stomach.

"Mmm," she let out a satisfied sigh.

"Now turn round and I'll soap your back for you."

"I've heard there are bath houses in Japan where masseuses use soap to wank orf a man," she said matter-of-factly as she cast a glance at me over a soapy shoulder.

"Is that another of your whorehouse tales?"

"Possibly. I don't remember." She turned to face me. "Have you had any bright ideas about how we might dress up for Victor's party?"

"Frankly, I've had other things on my mind since you joined me here."

"We can't have that, can we?" She took the shower head and directed a stream of water onto my front and back. Once the last bit of soap had run into the bathtub, she pulled aside the shower curtain. "Out you go, lover. I need some space here."

I stepped out of the tub and began drying myself with a large white towel. When I'd finished, I folded it and put it back on the towel rail, casting a glance at Kiki through the shower curtain as I did so.

"I've got it!" I exclaimed.

"Got what, darling?" Again that lazy upper-class drawl.

"Our fancy dress for the party."

"Oh, *goody*! What?" She poked her head out of the shower curtain.

"The shower curtain."

Her body was pressed against the soft material to reveal both nipples and her mound of Venus.

"You're the perfect picture for Victor's camera."

She followed my gaze for a second. Then, "Oh! *Do* let me see, Rusty." She drew aside the curtain and stepped out of the bath to towel herself dry. "Get in. I simply *must* have a peek."

I did as she asked.

"Absolutely *super!*" she cried excitedly. "Oh, *darling!* This is going to be *awfully* amusing, isn't it. We'll be the talk of the town."

"You realise we'll be like Siamese twins. Inseparable."

"Not *all* night, surely?"

"That depends on you."

"You're forgetting the shower curtain. It might want to have a say in the matter."

"The perfect prophylactic."

23.

We arranged to meet at eleven. It was the last day of the month, as well as of the year, and Kiki had given up her apartment for a room at the Cathay Hotel until she boarded ship.

She was wearing a towel bathrobe and was standing looking out of the window when I pushed open the door of Room 805. Her perfume was Caron's *Narcisse Noir*, mixed with juniper and lime. When she turned away from the window I saw she had a large glass of gin in one hand. She definitely had a head start on me when it came to party mode.

I was wearing what I liked to think of as my Royal Swedish Yacht Club casual gear: a white shirt with neckerchief and bell-bottom trousers. Under one arm I was carrying a more or less see-through shower curtain. We had agreed to change into our joint costume in her room before walking—more likely stumbling—up the three floors to Victor's penthouse.

"Are you sure you want to do this, Kiki?"

"With a little bit of help from this jug of gimlet, I'll doubtless survive."

Her violet eyes were as lethal as her drink. I wasn't certain she was somebody I'd die for, but the gin was another matter.

"I think I'm going to need one of those, too, if I may. Nakedness needs fortification if it is to exert its magical power."

She poured me a generous glass of gin and lime cordial. I downed it in one and held out my glass for a refill.

"I say, that was a bit quick."

"I've got some catching up to do by the look of you."

She refilled my glass first, and then her own.

"One, two, three and down the hatch!"

We emptied the contents of our glasses and looked at each other. Our smiles were seriously wicked.

"Right then?"

"Let's do it, Rusty,"

"As long as we don't end up in the scuppers with a hosepipe on us, all will be well, Kiki dear."

I started to unbutton my shirt. "Come on. Time to make our grand entrance upstairs."

"If you absolutely *insist*."

"I do."

So we took off our clothes, all of them, and wrapped ourselves in the shower curtain.

"We simply *must* take a peek, darling. The bathroom mirror's full length, you know."

I didn't, but we took our peek anyway and were only slightly embarrassed. The fact that we had been lovers helped. So did the gin.

We moved a little awkwardly towards the door of her room. I was reminded of the games we used to play at school. A cross between an obstacle and a three-legged race.

"Have you got your room key?"

"Oh God! No. But where am I going to *put* it, Rusty?"

"Hang it from my willy?"

She collapsed in an uncustomary fit of giggles.

"Are you trying to tell me, my poppet, that you're going to keep up an erection for the next four hours? I'll tell you one thing. If you do, I'll forget about George for a year and a day."

"I was thinking of an elastic band with which to secure the key. Or we can simply hide it in the large flower pot outside your hotel room door."

By mutual consent we opted for the flower pot and, not entirely with the ease of a fashion model's sashaying walk, made our way along the corridor and up the stairs.

Perkins greeted us with his customary inscrutability. He was wearing a Peter Thomson sailor-collared middy blouse and knee-length shorts. On his feet was a pair of ballerina flats with ribbons spiralling up two well-shaven legs.

"Sir Victor will see you in the *sal de bain*," he announced gravely, like a siren singing us to shipwreck. "Hopefully you can make your way unmolested through the not entirely sober throng."

"Did you see that, Rusty?" Kiki laughed as we threaded our way through the other guests. "Perkins actually *winked*."

"Did he?" I smiled through the curtain at two red-headed mermaids who were looking me up and down with a certain knowing admiration. "He must have had a gimlet or two when nobody was looking."

"He needed them to get dressed like that."

We found our way to the bathroom where Victor was sitting in a bubble bath smoking a large fat cigar. He was wearing a bow tie and water wings on his upper arms. His camera was lying on the silver bath rack at his feet. A second bath was empty, apart from a large shark with two large and very naked breasts.

"Welcome! Welcome!" he cried, leaning forward eagerly to admire his latest visitors. "Who have we here? By the way, have you met Amanda? Amanda Arbuthnot? She's only just arrived and is feeling a bit like a fish out of water. I can assure you, though, her nibbles can give one ecstasy."

"Hello, Amanda."

"Hel*lo* darlings! Super bash, what!"

The shark waved a glass of something ecstatically. It definitely wasn't water. Meanwhile Victor was laughing loudly at his own joke, so the shark joined in. She sounded more like a horse than a fish.

Kiki fumbled with the top of the shower curtain to reveal our faces. Victor was visibly surprised, but ready to be amused. It was, after all, New Year's Eve.

"So, dear Miss Montagu-Rose and Count Bloom, *what* have we here? I thought your voice sounded familiar, but tell me, why are you dressed—if that's the appropriate word—in, of all things, a shower curtain?"

"Because, Victor, Rusty and I happened to be having a shower when the alarm went off and the order was given to abandon ship."

Victor laughed so much that the water from his bath began slopping onto the floor. If he carried on too long, he'd be joining us in the shower curtain for a *ménage à trois*. Or maybe *à quatre* if the Arbuthnot woman was agreeable. Ecstasy beckoned.

As it was, Victor suddenly stood up and stepped out of his bathtub. Thankfully, he was wearing a swimming costume.

"Do you like my inflatable armbands?" Victor asked in a queer's kind of saucy voice. "The latest in swimming accoutrements, all the way from California. What do you reckon, you two? Will they save me if I have to abandon ship?"

"Depends on whether your bow tie is mechanical, Victor," I replied. "If it were bigger, it might act as a useful propeller."

"But then it would cut off my chin, wouldn't it? I like the idea, though, Christopher. Maybe I should buck fashion and put bowties on my legs to save me, given that they're a bit useless as they are?" He laughed as he examined us both closely. Not our faces, of course, but the rest of us. He seemed to like what he saw by the way he reached for his camera.

"Before you two join the party I simply *must* take a photo of you both." He pointed the Leica in our direction. "Now then, *pose!*"

We had little choice, but how we posed! It was New Year's Eve after all. A time for frivolity and licentious behaviour, and time for the two of us to enter into the spirit of things. Kiki cuddled close and squeezed my bum while I placed one hand firmly on one of her well-formed breasts and thrust my knee between her thighs. Thus entwined, we gave Victor the benefit of our most winsome smiles. Finally, he had the photo he'd been hoping for ever since he had first met Kiki. All I had to do was persuade the Baronet to give me a print.

24.

The morning after Kiki had left Shanghai aboard the *Maréchal Joffre* I had an unexpected visitor. I was sitting down to breakfast when Fantom showed Roger Buckley in.

"Roger! This is a surprise. To what do I owe the pleasure?"

"I was hoping for a quiet chat, Bloom."

"Rusty please. Are your chats ever other than quiet, Roger?"

Roger's feathers weren't easily ruffled. I suspect Kiki would have referred to him as an odd bird.

"Do you have a few minutes… Rusty?"

"Of course. Why don't you join me for breakfast?"

"I'm afraid I can't. I'm late for work as it is."

"Ah yes. Duty calls. Selling a lot of cigarettes, are we? Hopefully not ones spiked with opium."

He dutifully ignored my tone. Sensibly, too. It was the kind of tone I'd always adopted before breakfast. I was one of those people who woke up after a cup of coffee, not before one.

"What I was going to suggest was that we meet somewhere quiet for dinner this evening. Do you know Gracie Gale's?"

"What man about town doesn't?" Gracie Gale ran a high-class brothel. It was one of a whole string of them, some more reputable than others, making up The Line on Kiangse Road. Not many men about town could afford to spend a night at Gracie's. There was clearly more to Roger's stiff upper lip than met the eye.

"Please don't feel abashed, Rusty. Number 52 is also well-known for its excellent food. I'm simply inviting you to a quiet *tête-à-tête* dinner. That's all. Mark you, other postprandial delights can always be arranged, should you feel so inclined."

He gave me a big smile that ended in a small dimple in each cheek. Trying not to think of Maisy, I managed a demure blush of modesty.

"We can eat dinner in private, without other eyes prying on us, I can assure you. Gracie's totally discrete. She also employs the very best chef in town—Fat Lu. Do you know him? He used to work for the old Imperial Russian Legation in Peking and what he doesn't know about cooking in any one of seven languages isn't worth knowing."

"Well, that sounds like an invitation that's hard to refuse, Roger. Although, from what you say, I suspect it'll take up more than a few minutes."

"I'll take that as an acceptance, then, Rusty," Roger gave me the benefit of another dimpled grin. He should have been selling whiskey, not cigarettes. In triangular bottles.

"Why don't we meet at, say, eight o'clock sharp?"

"I'm looking forward to it."

He marched in slightly military fashion out into the hall where Fantom handed him his trilby, and left without a backward glance. God alone knew where or how he'd picked up such terribly British mannerisms. Some people were like that. Roger could hardly have been more than twenty-six or -seven years old, but the whole of his future seemed to hang dutifully, like his pin-striped suit, from his youthful frame.

My fellow hacks had talked about Gracie Gale's. Most of the gossip was based on hearsay, rather than experience, because none of the journalists I'd met could afford to spend time there. The word was that, in another place and at another time, Gracie Gale might have been a Marie Antoinette or a Catherine the Great. In reality, though, she was from San Francisco—as American as Coca Cola and baked beans—and operated the most exclusive bordello in Shanghai. Which meant, naturally, that it was also the most expensive.

Kiangse Road crosses Nanking Road near the Bund before disappearing northward and ending up in a warren of dark narrow lanes. It was there, at Number 52, that Gracie raised the standard of sin to delectable heights by subtly integrating sex-for-sale with *gourmet* dining, after-dinner coffee and Napoleon brandy. Apparently, some customers enjoyed the ambience so much that they were happy to drop by just for a drink and a chat.

But it was never a cheap drink, even without the charming company of one of the American girls employed there—Singapore Kate, Slinky Sadie, and half a dozen other American beauties. An evening at Gracie Gale's was always worth what it cost. But it cost. So how could a mid-ranking executive in British-American Tobacco afford to take me there?

In the middle of the afternoon, as I was working on yet another article, there was a knock on my study door.

"Massa, sir, letter," Fantom announced solemnly and held out a silver tray. "You catchee one-piece Melican wifey?"

Where he'd found the tray I had no idea.

"What makes you ask that, Fantom?"

"Allo Chinaman savvy Gracie Gale. But no savvy how fashion *fankuei* missy belongey numpa one handsome titty."

Fantom had clearly been influenced by the tarts in rue Palikao where he had lived previously. They liked to advertise their specialities and prices loudly to any male passer-by, but having large breasts definitely wasn't one of their attributes.

"Fan To-mu, you belongey too muchee sassee, galaw."

Fantom smiled and left. Inscrutably. What was it about valets?

I looked at the pristine cream-white envelope in my hands, with my name and address in beautifully executed handwriting. I opened it to find an engraved card on which Madame Gracie Gale requested the pleasure of Count Christopher Bloom's company for cocktails that evening at 52 Kiangse Road. How could one resist such showmanship? I spied entertainment in Gracie. She clearly liked to discourse and, as Shakespeare once wrote, give the leer of invitation.

And so later, as requested, I presented myself at Number 52. Right next door to the Salon Pink of all places. The house had a faded plaster exterior and red louvre shutters that looked as though they were perpetually closed in their rusted frames. Its unpretentious dinginess seemed deliberately to exploit the drab neighbourhood in which it found itself, except for a neat brass plate beside the front door, suggesting that these were the premises of a slightly down-at-heel doctor—or, more appropriately, solicitor—rather than those of a Blood Alley abbess. I knocked.

Gracie herself opened the door, a lit cigarette held between the first two fingers of her right hand. At least, I assumed that the well-built woman with shrewd but fun-loving eyes was Gracie.

"Count Bloom, I presume?" Another encounter between proof and probability. She looked me up and down and seemed satisfied with what she saw. "Do please come in. And welcome."

I stepped into a hall from the end of which rose a splendidly wide, polished oak staircase.

"The bedrooms are upstairs," Gracie said, following my look. "But that's for later, Count. For now, just contain yourself."

She gave a throaty laugh that made her sound like Tallulah Bankhead.

"Why don't we start in here?" she continued, leading me into a drawing room carpeted with Persian rugs and full of Chinese Chippendale furniture. A smiling young blonde materialised out of nowhere to take my hat and coat; another came forward with three glasses of champagne—one for me, one for Gracie, and one for herself.

"This is Annie—Big Annie," Gracie said by way of introduction, although the size of Annie's upholstery said it all. "Roger tells me you're from Sweden," she continued, as she motioned for me to sit down on the davenport beside Annie who, somewhat disconcertingly, took up a shapeless piece of wool and began knitting.

"Yes, I'm yet another journalist."

"But a royal as well." Americans were suckers for aristocracy. "You been in Shanghai long, Count?"

"Christopher, please," I smiled. "Although a lot of people call me Rusty for short. Just a couple of months."

"And are you married, Rusty? Excuse my directness, Hon. But it's always best to know the background of my clients."

"Quite understandable," I replied. "And no, I've been spared the experience of marriage."

"A wise young man," Gracie chuckled and Annie looked up from her knitting. It reminded me of an old adage: when whores thus knit, a brothel ever stands.

"Tried it myself once. No, dammit, twice. It was so goddam *boring*," Gracie laughed loudly. "I keep telling my girls that, but they pay no attention. Why, only last week I lost one of them. Aggie went and married her Frenchman."

"Are you all American here?" I asked somewhat naively.

"As American as pie and ice cream."

"That's sweetie pie and lots of cream," Annie whispered into my left ear.

"And business was good until those damned Russkies started coming here. Number 52 was special, see. The only establishment with pure white girls for pure white men to enjoy at their leisure. No yellow shysters here, like the ones next door at the Salon Pink."

Gracie almost spat out the name. I nodded sagely and sipped my champagne. I preferred not to wonder how much Gracie charged per bottle.

"Those Russian girls have set up shop everywhere in town. And they undercut my business, too. The cheapos!" She exclaimed with a snort of derision. "But you must excuse me, Rusty. I hear you're Russian, too. Or half of you is. Am I right?"

She clearly researched the background of any new client.

"Sort of, Gracie. My father was Russian Ambassador in Berlin. That's where I was born and brought up as a child. Then the Revolution came and he felt it wiser not to go back to Moscow. So we ended up in Uppsala, in Sweden. That's where my mother's from. My father died soon after we got there. Then I had an Irish grandmother. I never met her, but it may explain some of my eccentricities."

"So you're all mixed up, eh?" Gracie laughed again as she stubbed out her cigarette and promptly lit another. I understood why she sounded like Tallulah Bankhead. She was smoking as many cigarettes a night as the actress did in a day.

At that moment there was a burst of laughter out in the hall and Roger appeared in the doorway. He had one girl on each arm and his upper lip had definitely loosened.

"Rusty!" he exclaimed. "You found your way all right, then? Have you met Lotus?" he indicated the stunning and petite blond-haired girl to his right. "And Belle?"

Belle was a raven-haired beauty with deep amber brown eyes, glittering like a pool of water in a forest glade, with an hourglass figure that I could readily spend time with, even though I knew it would cost me.

I stood up to greet the two ladies.

"I haven't had the pleasure." I put out my hand, but the girls were quicker. Before I knew where I was, they'd each planted a kiss on one of my cheeks.

Gracie chuckled her throaty chuckle again.

"Lotus and Belle will be accompanying you two gentlemen to dinner, if you've got no objection."

We had none. At least, I didn't, although I wasn't sure if I was about to dally with a brace of courtesans, or meditate with two deep divines.

"Then why don'tcha follow me into the dining room?"

Gracie led us across the hall to an intimate room that was heavily curtained and flatteringly lit. Only one table was set and the four of us sat down for dinner.

"I've made sure you have the room to yourselves for now, as you asked, Roger. But later will be another matter. The place will be filled with men, young and not so young, seeking food and other tasty delights."

She smiled and produced two menus. Roger shared his with Lotus, while Belle leaned towards me and allowed the scent of Guerlain's *L'Heure Bleue* to waft upwards from the dark cleft between her breasts and envelop my senses. Much better than *My Sin*, although when it came to listing peccadillos I had a feeling Belle would be up there with the best.

"What'll it be, Rusty?" Roger inquired after a couple of minutes as he put down his menu. "And, by the way, this is all on me, in case you were concerned."

"Thank you, Roger. That's most generous of you." I did my best not to show my relief. "I can't decide whether to go nostalgically native and order chicken *à la Kiev*, served in the Tsarist style. Or, in deference to our charming companions here at the table, go native American and order chicken Maryland."

"Why don't we order two of each, then, and share them?"

"An excellent idea. Provided our charming companions don't object, of course."

They didn't, so chickens in two cities—one in the Soviet Union, the other in the United States of America—were prepared by a Chinese chef for consumption by a British businessman-cum-spy and a mongrel Russo-German-Swedish count in the company of two American whores. Roger ordered a bottle of French Clicquot to wash it down and we embarked upon the evening. Conversation was light, sprinkled with laughter and stories that each of us felt fit to tell, one or two of them—with the aid of the champagne—as *risqué* as our environment. A second bottle of Clicquot was ordered, opened and drunk over our desserts—Mille-Feuille for Roger, Mont Blanc for me, and Apple Tarte Tartin for the American girls to remind them of home. And of their figures, no doubt. Their helpings were small.

Once all the bowls had been emptied, Roger politely dismissed Lotus and Belle. Gracie returned to serve coffee and cognac. Then, with the kind of quiet professionalism that made Number 52 the place to go when wanting to be discreetly indiscreet, closed the door to the dining room. We were on our own.

"Rusty," Roger said, stirring a lump of sugar in his coffee cup with one hand and downing a whole glass of cognac in the other. "I'm going to come straight to the point."

"I expect nothing else," I responded. "I've never understood why people spend so much time beating about the bush."

"A man after my own heart, then," Roger smiled, the corners of his mouth creasing into those slight dimples. He refilled his glass and took another large gulp. I had a feeling Gracie's well-aged cognac was being wasted on his palate. He hadn't learned to hold his drink. Which made me wonder how he'd been recruited for the job.

"Look! I'll be frank. I was asked by people back in England to keep track of Kiki Montagu-Rose while she was in Shanghai."

"Well, that was pretty obvious, Roger. I mean, you were sticking to her like a leech, even though you were hardly her type."

"Not a very good leech, though. I found it really hard to keep her in my sights all the while—especially when she was spending a lot of her time with Sir Victor Sassoon. And with you, of course." Another glass of excellent cognac slipped easily down his gullet, without so much as a by-your-leave. "Now that she's left Shanghai, can you tell me: did you spot any funny stuff?"

"What kind of 'funny stuff,' Roger?"

"Did you ever witness her behaving in a manner inappropriate to her standing?"

I began to wonder if he was contesting a court case.

"What standing, Roger? Do you mean her standing as a divorced, or a married, woman? Or as a socialite? Or as a Brit abroad? You need to be more precise, if I'm to answer your question helpfully."

"You know what I mean," he said despondently. "Come on, Rusty. Help me out here. Please."

I took pity on him. Roger knew things that I didn't.

"A couple of things stood out during her stay here, so far as I was concerned. One was that she and Sir Victor seemed to have known each other for quite a long time. I gathered they used to party together."

"Did they now?"

"Yes. Back in the day. Anyway, he seemed determined to photograph her in the nude."

"And did he?" Roger was looking seriously worried.

"Not quite. At least, not so far as I know. If ever I find out something from Sir Victor himself, though, I'll let you know, Roger. All right?"

He nodded. "And the second thing?"

"The second thing strikes me as being a bit more important, so far as the British government is concerned. And I'm assuming that's who you represent. But it's only a suspicion. I have no evidence to prove it."

"Prove what? Go on, Rusty."

"Kiki struck me as being overly friendly with Chiang Kai-shek's German advisers. She admitted to me that she admires Adolf Hitler and claimed that she was a member of the Nazi Party. I've no idea whether that's true or whether she was merely trying to impress me at the time."

"Because you're a member, too."

"Out of necessity, Roger, rather than ideological disposition. As a result, I have excellent credentials that help when writing for German newspapers. They also give me access to German military advisers here in Shanghai. Whether I want to live in Germany or not is another matter."

"Military advisers?"

"Because they *are* military, Roger. Whatever people say to the contrary. You know that. Anyway, as I said, Kiki's connection with German officers based in Nanking strikes me as somehow more than just friendly. She speaks excellent German, too, although that may strike you as a bit far-fetched for an upper-class socialite. What's more, I'm pretty sure she's involved in arms trading, but I don't *know* that for fact. If ever I do find out, Roger, I'll be sure to let you know."

"Thank you, Rusty. Much appreciated." He sat back, nodding his head in such a way that his chin almost disappeared into his neck.

"So what's life like in Intelligence?" I asked casually.

"You know I can't talk about *that*, Rusty. Even if it were true, of course."

"Of course you can't. And I'm not asking you to. I was actually thinking of something completely different."

"Like what?"

"Like what went on in London during the early 1920s. Both Kiki and Victor talked about it. I gather British police spent a lot of their time chasing cocaine dealers, while Special Branch was—probably still is—paranoid about Bolshevism and the Comintern's efforts to fund the British Communist Party."

"So?"

"So did they manage to unearth any undercover spies? British upper class queers who weren't just pink but bright red? Underage girls taking off their clothes for older men? That sort of thing. Come on, Roger. You must know *something* that isn't top secret."

"Maybe," he said coyly.

"Maybe you do? Or maybe you don't?"

Roger paused in reflection.

"Well," he said at length, "there was *one* incident that might interest you. If only because its protagonist ended up here in China."

"And who might that be?" I asked, my curiosity piqued, as Roger intended.

"Mr Brown."

"Mr Brown?"

"I'm never quite sure how much is common knowledge, so I'd be grateful if you could keep this under your hat, Rusty. Just in case."

"Of course."

"After the war, the Secret Intelligence Service shifted its attention from Kaiser Wilhelm to the threat of communism, as you said. They were particularly concerned by the formation of a communist party in Great Britain and the methods Moscow used to fund it. Initially it did so by selling off the Tsar's crown jewels, which they took apart and smuggled into Poland piece by piece, before having them recut and sold in Amsterdam. The money then came into Britain, mainly in the suitcases of members of the Russian trade delegation that arrived once the Anglo-Russian trade treaty was signed in 1921. No customs official was going to threaten a fragile alliance by asking an incoming Russian to open up his suitcases for inspection."

"And it was used to fund the British Communist Party?"

"Not all of it, of course. But some of it, yes."

"Then what?"

"Around then a rather mysterious gentleman going by the name of Mr Brown appeared on the scene. It could have been just before. Or just after. Nobody really knows. He was tall and thickset, with dark hair. Probably in his late thirties, he spoke English with a sort of American accent. He started attending party meetings, usually arriving late and leaving early, but challenging speakers about their commitment to the Marxist cause and their ability to apply revolutionary theories and techniques. He argued that they had failed to capitalise on the potentially revolutionary situation. Unemployment had doubled. There was unrest among workers in the country's heavy industries. The miners had gone on strike, but were then deserted by their 'brother' railwaymen and other transport workers. A golden opportunity for revolution had been missed."

"And?" I was feeling a bit impatient. Roger stayed me with one hand.

"It transpired that this Mr Brown had been sent by the Comintern to reorganise the British Communist Party and make sure it had all its ducks lined up in a row. He was basically an international trouble-shooter."

"Who later came to China, you said?"

"Yes. His name was Mikhail Borodin."

"Good God!"

"Precisely. Although probably not the kind of expletive used by a good communist. Apparently, Borodin had—or has—plenty of charm and wit. But he's also known for being cold and ruthless as occasion demands. The kind of man who'd sacrifice a friend in a minute if he thought it necessary for the cause."

Something to keep in mind.

"So, what happened?"

"Eventually, the intelligence services managed to catch him. At a meeting of communists in Glasgow. He was tried, sentenced to six months imprisonment, and having served his time in a Scottish gaol, ejected from Britain and sent back to Petrograd."

"But how on earth did he get into the country in the first place?"

"Nobody knows for sure. But the assumption is he bribed some Dutch fishermen to bring him across from Holland and drop him off on a secluded beach somewhere on England's east coast. When he was caught and questioned, it was discovered that he had no legal travel documents. Just shows how porous our borders are as an island nation."

Roger finished his cognac. I replenished his glass.

"Have you ever heard of Frolics?"

"What kind of frolics?" I did my best to look confused.

"No, you probably haven't. You aren't British, after all. I was referring to Frolics Nightclub. It was on the corner of Regent's Place and Warwick Street in London and just a short walk from the Russian Social Club where all the ex-pat communists used to gather in rented rooms on Wednesdays and Fridays."

"Ah, the *night*club! But I thought it was closed down *years* ago."

"It was. In 1923. But I'm still talking about 1921, twenty-two, when Borodin was in town. The word I heard was that Frolics was a favourite night haunt of Russian girls who, during the day, worked at the trade delegation offices in Moorgate. It seems Borodin may have supplied them with money so that they could spend their evenings in the company of British army officers and young men of good social background, with a view to converting them to 'the cause.'"

"A bit unlikely, surely?"

"Not on your nelly," Roger spoke sharply. "Don't be deceived by appearances, Rusty. There are a lot of upper crust young men and women who think highly of the Soviet Union and communism."

"But why?"

"Because a lot of things were happening there that weren't happening—at least, by no means as fast—in Britain. The right to vote, for example. And gender equality. Things were moving much more quickly and enthusiastically in Soviet Russia than they were in stodgy old Britain with its entrenched class and gender prejudices. So, the idea of emancipated Soviet women frequenting London night spots like Frolics terrified British Intelligence. And, of course, Special Branch.

"As it turned out, their fear was for the most part just paranoia. Except for one incident that I know of, involving the son of a peer of the realm who was photographed *déshabillé* with a Russian hostess one night at Frolics. The word on the street was that Borodin was responsible for orchestrating the incident. Certainly the young man's father found himself having to fork out a *lot* of money for the return of the revealing photograph's print and negative."

"A lot of money that then went to whom?"

"Ah! That's the million dollar question, isn't it? Special Branch reckoned it went into the coffers of the Comintern, but they could never prove anything."

"So Borodin may not have been involved?"

"Maybe not. After all, his task here in China was very different. Much more a direct unsettling of the Chinese landlord system."

"Did the girl have a name, by any chance?"

"Julia," Roger responded at once. "Pronounced with an initial Y— Yulia."

He pushed back his chair and stood up.

"Well, I think I've probably said enough for one evening and we've covered all we need to cover," he said as he shook me by the hand. "If you'll excuse me, I must be off. But you take your time. I believe Lotus or Belle is waiting for you upstairs. Enjoy yourself, but remember, anything you can tell me about Miss Montagu-Rose could be immensely helpful."

"Of course, Roger. But aren't you going to join me?"

Buckley smiled his dimpled smile and shook his head.

"Another time perhaps."

And with that he crossed the room and opened the door to leave. Gracie was waiting for him in the hall.

"Could you sign this, please, Roger Hon?"

"Of course," he said, taking the piece of paper she proffered him. Then, having done as she requested, he was gone.

Gracie turned to me with a smile and both eyebrows arched up to the stuccoed rose on the ceiling above our heads. She clearly thought Roger was queer.

"Makes you wonder how they ever managed to create an empire, doesn't it?"

"Perhaps by signing for everything and conveniently forgetting to pay?"

"Not on my watch," said Gracie sharply. "I didn't introduce love on chit for nothing."

"You mean, you operate chits even here?" It was my turn to laugh incredulously.

"Of course, Hon. This whole city lives on credit, or haven't you noticed? Only tourists carry round anything more than small change in their pockets."

"But don't you get men refusing to pay what they owe? Skipping town even to avoid their debts?"

"Chisellers? It's been known to happen," Grace admitted, as she led me out of the dining room towards the stairs. "But I didn't graduate from the Barbary Coast for nothing, Rusty."

"I'm sure you didn't. And I bet you got a *summa cum laude*, too," I flattered.

"Yeah, I guess some do come louder. Personally, I can't stand the screamers. They make the hairs on my bush stand on end."

She gave another of her throaty chuckles.

"There was this guy once—a shipping man, and one of the city's civic leaders—who strayed in here unannounced with a gang of fellow revellers. Signed chits left, right, and up his ass before stumbling off home at dawn. When my shroff presented him with his bill a few days later, he refused to pay up."

"So, what did you do?"

"I hate chisellers, Hon, so I took my revenge."

"How?"

"I checked up on him and found out he was a vestryman at Holy Trinity Cathedral. So, far too early for my liking one Sunday morning, I put on a dark dress, as prim as my aunt Eliza's, and went off to morning service."

"I wish I'd seen that, Gracie."

"Now, now, Rusty. You're here to flatter younger dames than me," she said, giving me a quick peck on the cheek. She smelled of roses and tobacco.

"Anyways, the time for collection came round and there was my client, all correct in his morning dress and with an air of unctuous piety. He passed the silver plate along our pew. Everyone placed an offering on it, either cash or chit. And when it reached me, I added the man's unpaid brothel chits. Boy, I could see the old buzzard sweating all the way back up the aisle. He'd darn well have to pay those chits. He couldn't very well tell the Dean where he'd signed them, could he?" she laughed loudly.

"So the Cathedral got his money?"

"It did, indeed. I've always believed in charitable causes." She laughed again and started to move into the hall. Through the doorway to the drawing room Big Annie had put aside her knitting and was sitting on Otto von Holst's knee. He grinned and gave me a mock Nazi salute as I passed.

"So," Gracie continued, "that story got around pretty quick, and now my clients always pay up. They know that I know their innermost secrets and that I can blackmail them all the way to hell. Especially those in respectable positions, with wives and families," she laughed her throaty laugh again as we reached the bottom of the staircase. There she leaned one well-developed arm on the banister and with the other pointed upwards.

"There's a second rule you have to observe here, Rusty dearie. Apart from paying your chits, that is."

"There is?"

"There is, Hon. You have to be sober enough to walk up those stairs without help if you're to enjoy the entertainment awaiting you. And that means no holding onto the banisters. My impression is you're going to make it up with ease this evening, though how you'll fare when you come back down is anyone's guess. Belle's been known to emascoolate many a man. Enjoy yourself, Hon, and let's hope your voice hasn't gone up an octave when you're done."

25.

I decided to pay Miyoko Noguchi a visit in her orphanage.

It was a freezing cold overcast day with occasional flurries of snow. Winter in Shanghai could be like that. Local Chinese shivered and rolled themselves up tightly in balls unless they happened to be rich and could afford a Siberian fur coat, but for a Scandinavian it was like being at home. Bracing air made the more bracing by my riding my Čechie mororbike through the streets of Hongkew, the breath exhaled from my mouth clearly visible as it wafted above the heads of a couple of monks playing their bamboo flutes outside the Japanese Club.

The orphanage was on Darroch Road, out near the border of the International Settlement. It was an old run-down red-brick house, backing onto the Shanghai-Woosung railway line.

"How ever did you find this place?" I asked, as Miyoko poured me tea. She was wearing an informal kimono, bluish-grey with a repeat pattern that looked like a lot of swastikas. A German-Japanese alliance in the offing? Except the swastika was originally a Hindu symbol, adopted by Chinese Buddhists.

"The house is owned by the Japanese government. The Consul, Murai-*san*, kindly arranged for me to take it over. Have you met him?"

"I haven't had the pleasure."

"I will introduce you to him. He is an interesting man."

"Thank you, Miyoko-*san*—is it all right if I call you Miyoko?" I took her smile as a yes, although who knew.

"Tell me, Miyoko-*san*, how many girls are there in the orphanage?"

"At the moment, not too many. Maybe half a dozen. We have only just set it up, you see."

"Yes, of course. And where do the girls come from?"

"One is from a Japanese family in Taiwan. Two others are from Korea. The rest are from Manchuria where life is especially—how can I put it?—especially *fragile* right now."

"I see. And where do you get the money to finance your orphanage? Are you helped by a religious organisation of some kind? Missionaries, perhaps?"

"Goodness me, no." Her hand went up to cover her mouth. "Nothing like that. As a matter of fact, a couple of Japanese textile companies kindly provided me with funds to set up the orphanage. But then we have running costs to be covered." Her voice tailed away. She sipped her tea and looked at me a little sadly. "It isn't easy, Bloom-*san*."

"Rusty, please."

"It's not easy, Rusty-*san*. The girls must be fed and clothed and properly looked after. This requires money."

"Yes, of course. Maybe one or two of my readers in Sweden and Germany will want to help."

"That would, of course, be wonderful." For once there seemed to be real warmth in Miyoko's words. But I realised that she hardly ever blinked her eyes. Like a snake.

"And then there are medical expenses," she was saying. "The girls are becoming young women and need to be examined by a doctor from time to time. To make sure everything is *in order*, if you see what I mean."

I certainly did, and wondered what Victor would make of it all.

"There is the girls' education to consider, too. They must be properly prepared for the outside world once they've grown up."

"You mean, you want the orphanage to be a school as well?"

"Well, there is a Japanese school at the end of the road. But the girls here are still rather fragile emotionally. They have, after all, recently lost their parents. One watched them being killed before her very own eyes. Can you imagine anything more traumatic than that for a twelve-year old girl?"

I couldn't, other than then being forced into prostitution by someone who professed to have her best interests at heart.

"Would you be so kind as to show me round the house?" I asked. "I'd like to meet one or two of your girls, if I may, and talk to them. That would add human interest to my story, as I'm sure you understand."

She did, although she didn't seem too pleased at the prospect. But Miyoko was also too polite to refuse my request.

"Of course," she said, a little unconvincingly, as she stood up. "I'm afraid everything is a little untidy. As I said, we've only just started the orphanage." Her voice tailed away.

"That's all right," I said encouragingly, patting the camera slung from my shoulder. "A photograph will show my readers, much more than words, that you are in desperate need of donations."

That seemed to satisfy her and she led me out of the room into a hallway and along a corridor to a large room at the back of the house.

"This is the girls' common room. A place where they can relax and chat. The Consul has kindly supplied us with a few books for them to read."

"But where are the girls now? It's almost midday. Are they out in the garden, perhaps?"

"They are still in their bedrooms," Miyoko led me out of the drawing room and up the stairs. "We feel it more appropriate that they do not use the common room until after lunch. That way they have time to be alone and face their pasts."

She unlocked and opened the door to one of the rooms.

"One has to be so careful. It would be awful if one of the girls were to have an accident. I do my best to keep them safe, you understand."

Two girls were huddled together asleep in a large double bed.

"Sakura-*chan*, Hana-*chan*!" she called gently. "You have a visitor."

The two girls opened their eyes at the sound of her voice and then sat up, hurriedly wrapping the bed clothes around them when they saw me. One of the girls' feet stuck out, though. There was a small tattoo on her ankle of a cobra uncoiling itself from a basket.

"This gentleman would like to talk to you," Miyoko said soothingly in Japanese, as she sat down on the bed beside them and discreetly rearranged the coverlet to hide the girl's tattoo. "He is a journalist—from Sweden—and is interested in writing about the orphanage."

They nodded, frightened.

"Why don't you ask your questions, Rusty-*san*, and I will translate their answers for you."

So, without telling her I understood a bit of Japanese, I did. I kept my questions simple and to the point. The girls' answers were for the most part monosyllabic, so Miyoko would fill in as she felt appropriate.

After a couple of minutes, I asked permission to take a photo of the two of them, just as they were, on the bed with Miyoko. When I was done I thanked them and turned to leave. As I did so, Sakura suddenly leaped from the bed and ran towards me.

"*Tas'kete*! *Onegaishimasu*," she tugged desperately at my trouser leg as Miyoko tried to restrain her. Then in English, "herupu!"

"The poor girl," Miyoko said, as she pushed Sakura firmly back onto the bed. "She's the one I was telling you about—the one who was forced to watch her parents being killed by Mongolian bandits. Mentally she is very unstable, as I'm sure you can understand." Again the smile. Again the snake's unblinking gaze.

"Of course." What else could I say? But I knew at least that there was something I should do. Get those girls away from Miyoko's deathly squeeze.

26.

In a way I dreaded dinner with Ludmila and Otto on Saturday evening. It wasn't going to be easy to feign dispassionate acquaintanceship with Luda, or ardent friendship with Otto when I had more or less been invited by his wife to fuck her. Mark you, that was before Belle had drained my balls at Gracie Gale's, and before Otto had had his military equipment seen to by Big Annie. We probably should have read our whoroscopes beforehand.

Still, being a newspaperman had taught me to flatter and speak fair, to smile in people's faces, to smooth, deceive and—as they used to say back in the day—to cog. That way I ducked potential traps with French nods and apish courtesy and wasn't yet held a rancorous enemy. Like Lolly's police work and Roger's kind of intelligence, journalism meant studying the science of the everyday.

Punctually at eight o'clock I presented myself at the front door of the large residential villa inhabited by Major and Mrs von Holst at the Kiaochow Road end of Wuting Road. It was so close to where I lived that I could walk there in ten minutes. At least, I wouldn't have to worry about being drunk in charge of a motorbike.

"Kristoffer!" Otto welcomed me, as a Chinese maid ushered me into a large drawing room overlooking a spacious garden. "How nice to see you again!"

"You, too, Otto. Please excuse me for not saying goodbye to you when I left the German Club the other evening. You were nowhere to be seen."

"Think nothing of it. After my visit to the ladies powder room, I found myself arranging for Trudi to be escorted home. Then I had to run around after my boss all evening. *Ach*!" He blew air through his lips with annoyance at the recollection.

"What will you have to drink, Kristoffer?" Ludmila played the charming hostess. "Wine? Schnapps? Champagne? Otto has opened a rather nice bottle of Burgundy if you like red. Or an Alsace white? Whatever you like."

I liked the Burgundy well enough and said so. The three of us were about to settle down to small talk when the door to the drawing room opened and a girl appeared in her nightdress, holding a teddy bear. She was tall and blonde and looked just like her mother.

"Annika!" Ludmila stood up and rushed over to her daughter, "What are you doing here, *schätzchen*?"

"Can you tuck me in, Mama?"

"Of course, my darling," she said reassuringly and ushered her out of the room. Otto raised his glass.

"*Prost*! My daughter can't make up her mind whether she's a grown-up, or still a girl who needs her mother to kiss her goodnight."

"Enjoy her while she's still a girl," I said encouragingly. "Childhood is magical, but it lasts so short a time. Especially for parents."

Otto laughed heartily.

"Kristoffer, you sound like an experienced grandfather."

"I was merely thinking back to my own childhood, Otto."

"Ah, yes." He sipped his wine thoughtfully. "Those were untroubled days."

"Weren't they for us all?" I sympathised, "but not now."

"Not now, alas. Too many drums are being beaten," he sighed, then leant towards me confidentially. "To be honest, Kristoffer, I'm not too happy with what is going on in Germany."

"To be honest, Otto, I'm not too carried away myself."

"But please keep it under your hat. There are eyes and ears everywhere, if you know what I mean."

I did. Just then, Ludmila came back into the room, looking apologetic. "I'm so sorry," she began, but I silenced her apology with one of my more endearing smiles. "We were just saying how wonderful childhood is Ludmila."

"Yes, Kristoffer was suggesting that we enjoy our daughter while we can, *mein liebling*, before she becomes a woman."

"How thoughtful of you, Kristoffer," she raised her glass in toast, just as the maid ushered two more couples into the drawing room.

"Karl-Heinz, Raina! How nice to see you again. And you, too, Trudi, Gunther."

She kissed them all, while Otto did the same with the woman and shook the two men's hands. Then they introduced me, presumably on the assumption that both women had been too drunk at the German Club bash to remember me, although Karl-Heinz smiled his recognition. The air was kissed, a heel or two clicked, and the eternal lightness of polite conversation ensued.

I was determined not to be overwhelmed by Teutonic gravity so, as the seven of us ate and drank, I began to tell stories that were occasionally ludicrous enough to make even the straight-backed Gunther fall about with laughter. At one stage, Ludmila exclaimed, "Oh Kristoffer! You are so *silly*."

"And *naughty*," chimed in Trudi, who when more or less sober had an earthy sense of humour to offset her husband's waxed moustache. She was coquettish, too. Enough to make any man crow.

"I'm told I have my moments," I said modestly and embarked on a joke about a swearing parrot.

Once their laughter had subsided, Karl-Heinz said in a mockingly serious voice, "I'm not sure *Herr* Hitler would like that joke, Kristoffer."

"He wouldn't?" I expressed my surprise. "Why's that, Karl-Heinz?"

"*Herr* Hitler doesn't like people to—how shall I put it?" the diplomat started to laugh at his own joke, "ruffle his feathers."

We all laughed loudly, Otto most of all. Playing the game in front of his fellow countrymen. I turned serious.

"But *will* he become Führer?" I asked.

"Of *course*, Kristoffer. It's only a matter of time," Otto replied, filling my glass with yet another liberal dose of Burgundy.

"How so?

"Look!" Gunther took over. "The economy has been declining for years now. The Communists refuse to take part in parliamentary proceedings. We're the only alternative to the Social Democrats and Zentrum now."

The two other men nodded their heads in agreement, while the women did their best to look interested.

"Most business leaders now realise that the only alternative to this situation where nothing gets done is Hitler," continued Gunther. "And so they've joined the Nazi Party."

More nodding of heads.

"We'll definitely prevail, Kristoffer," Otto reassured me. And his guests. "Just wait."

At which point, Ludmila suggested to Raina and Trudi that they 'withdraw' to the comfort of the living room and leave their men to discuss how to change the world.

"After all," she laughed a little falsely, "they're not going to ask our opinion about what might be best for our children, are they?"

"Definitely not," said Trudi firmly, "although since I don't have any children, maybe it's best I keep quiet!" She laughed infectiously.

The moment the three women had left the dining room and we four men were alone, Karl-Heinz turned to me.

"Kristoffer, I've heard that you are an expert on Sino-Japanese and Russo-Japanese relations. Is that true?"

"Not really, Karl-Heinz. Of course, being here in China as a journalist has helped, thanks to things I hear from colleagues and informants. So I like to think that I'm quite well informed. But I wouldn't claim to be a specialist in the region, by any means."

"What does your being well-informed tell you about East Asia, then, Kristoffer?" It was Gunther's turn to question me.

"Well…" Always be prepared to inform the less-informed. They will in turn inform you. "Nothing that all of you probably don't already know. Stalin has been too busy dealing with internal politics in Moscow to think about Siberia and the Far East. As a result, the Amur River border is porous and the Soviet Union is open to attack from the east."

"Because the Japanese Kwantung Army has taken over Manchuria, you mean?"

"Yes. At the moment, that army is too involved in setting up a new state to turn its attention to Siberia. In other words, both sides are too preoccupied with internal affairs to look beyond their borders. But that will almost certainly change fairly soon."

"And then?" Otto took over.

"And then, who knows? In a year or two, Stalin will probably have started listening to his advisers and begun to strengthen his armies in Siberia. During this same period, Chiang will have had time to strengthen his own armies—with your help, of course—and pose a threat to Japanese troops from the south. If the Chinese and Soviets were to coordinate their armies, they would be able to squeeze the Kwantung Army from both north and south, as well as from the west through Mongolia, in a pincer movement."

"You mean, the Japanese are in a potentially weak situation?" Karl-Heinz's question echoed his role as a diplomat.

"Definitely. Except that the likelihood of Chiang Kai-shek agreeing to ally himself with Soviet troops is virtually zero. The Japanese are banking on the fact that he's a virulent anti-communist. This plays into the Kwantung Army's hands and allows its generals to continue threatening to invade Siberia while mopping up Manchuria."

"But will they?"

"Invade Siberia? In my opinion, not without Tokyo's permission.

They overstepped the line with the Mukden Incident, but they knew that the government in Tokyo was too weak to make a formal objection and order Japanese troops to withdraw to the Korean peninsula. It worked then, but they would be trying their luck to do the same again with an attack on Siberia. At the moment, too, there's no love lost between the Kwantung Army and the Ministry of the Army back in Tokyo. From what I hear, a bitter factional battle is going on."

"So Japan is like China, eh? Full of factional intrigue?"

"Endlessly so. If I were a Russian or Chinese politician, I'd be doing my utmost to fan such intrigues. It would take the pressure off their two countries. Part of the disagreements between different factions stems from how their members see the role of Japan in East Asia. There's an ideological wing consisting of ultranationalists who are convinced that Japan can bring peace and economic growth to the whole of Asia."

"The idea of an Asian Co-Prosperity Sphere?" As a businessman, Gunther clearly approved of the notion.

"Right. So far as they're concerned, it is not the Soviet Union which Japan should be considering, but China. In other words, the Japanese military should be concentrating its efforts on attacking and defeating China, because it can then take over Hong Kong, Singapore, and the whole of southeast Asia, and in so doing deal a deathblow to the trading interests of British and other Western colonial powers."

"Is that what's going to happen, then?"

"I don't know, Otto. You tell me. You have to ask yourself, though, where does Germany come into this equation? I mean, you're helping Chiang Kai-shek, right?"

"Well," Otto said uncertainly, with a glance at Karl-Heinz. "In a manner of speaking."

"Whatever manner that may be, it means that Germany is supporting the Chinese war effort against Japan. As far as I can judge from what I've read, our new Chancellor in waiting, Adolf Hitler, is being quite diplomatic with regard to enunciating a Far East policy, although you, Karl-Heinz, are better qualified to voice an opinion than I am."

Karl-Heinz nodded. "I think you're right, Kristoffer. Hitler doesn't want to offend anyone. Not yet, at least. That is probably because of Germany's relations with the rest of Europe and its current weak position in terms of military might."

"As you say, probably. But it may also be because he's waiting to see which way Japan decides to move, north or south. The thing is, he could actually influence that decision, couldn't he?"

"Influence it? How?"

"By drawing up a mutual non-aggression pact with the Soviet Union."

Karl-Heinz was surprised enough to stop pouring himself another glass of cognac.

"But why should he do that?"

"I'm not saying that he *will* do such a thing," I continued smoothly. "But he might at some stage in the future, if he came to the conclusion that Germany had developed sufficient military might to be able to reclaim territories in Europe that it lost in the Great War. Of course, because of the nature of your business in China, you gentlemen know far better than I the likelihood of such a move. But, as I see it, by signing such a treaty with Stalin, Hitler would protect himself from the East and be able to focus on the rest of Europe. And Stalin would be able to send troops from his European border to Siberia and pose a threat to the Japanese."

"Who would then send its armies south, rather than north."

"Exactly. What we have to remember is that, if Japan were to cross the Amur River now and defeat the few detachments of the Red Army in Siberia, there would be virtually nothing to stop them from attacking Moscow and then—who knows?—Europe. I mean, some ultranationalists are convinced that Japan can conquer the world."

"But that's ridiculous."

"One would think so, but remember, Otto, the Mongolian hoards got to the gates of Budapest quite easily once they moved westwards. What's to stop the Japanese from doing the same? There isn't much between Harbin and Moscow after all."

"My God, Kristoffer!"

"I have a nasty feeling He isn't going to do much about it, one way or the other," I smiled. "But then I'm an atheist."

There was a brief silence as three good Christians sat and pondered an uncertain future. What if God really had forsaken us all? It was Otto who spoke first.

"Maybe we should join our womenfolk in the drawing room?"

Half an hour later, Trudi glanced discreetly at her watch, though not discreetly enough.

"My goodness! Is that the time?" exclaimed Gunther, who had fallen into the trap of looking at his own watch, as had both Raina and Karl-Heinz. Like yawning, it was catching. "It's getting late, my dear. Perhaps we should be going."

"No, no. The night's still as youthful as Kristoffer here," said Ludmila with a pointed look. Room 156 at the Palace Hotel beckoned.

"No, really. We must be going," Gunther insisted as he and Trudi stood up.

"It's been *such* a lovely evening, Luda. You *must* come to us next time." Trudi turned to me, also on my feet, "And you, too, Kristoffer. We won't be satisfied until you accept our invitation, will we, Gunther? It's been a *pleasure* meeting you."

And so they took their leave, quickly followed by Raina and Karl-Heinz who took the hint and said their goodbyes. I, too, was about to bid my hosts farewell, but Otto held me back by the elbow.

"Stay, Kristoffer!" he said in a low voice. "One last nightcap before you go."

"If you insist, Otto."

"I do. Stay here."

He slipped out to bid farewell to his guests. After they were gone, there were brief murmurs in the vestibule before Otto came back.

"Ludmila sends her apologies," he said, "but she's decided to retire gracefully before we two men get out of hand and ply her with too much drink," he laughed. "She can't hold her alcohol these days the way she used to, I'm afraid. Not like," he lowered his voice, "Big Annie. But we men!" he exclaimed, as he filled two shot glasses with *schnapps*. "We men are another matter. Eh, Kristoffer? *Kanpei!*"

"*Kanpei!*" I echoed and downed the clear liquid in my glass as required. Otto refilled it and his own.

"*Prost!*"

"*Prost!*"

"What you had to say earlier was very interesting, Kristoffer. You may claim not to be a specialist in far eastern matters, but you have a lateral vision that many of us lose in our everyday lives. I came to realise that what I had thought was a conflict between two powers—China and Japan—is more like an evening at the Del Monte, where different partners invite one another to tango on the dance floor for a while."

"A pleasing image, Otto, in which China is the taxi girl, each of whose dances is paid for by very masculine powers. I guess what's interesting is what drives each of them to court her."

"Indeed," Otto nodded. "It is Chiang Kai-shek's admiration for German efficiency, you know, that has led to Germany playing a role in China's military modernization."

"Presumably, the fact that Germany has given diplomatic recognition to his Government also helps."

"Certainly it has contributed towards a—how shall I put it?—towards a *benevolent* atmosphere. Of course, the fact that the Weimar Government abandoned all extra-territorial privileges in China ten years ago has also helped. So far as Chiang is concerned, Germany is a relatively safe bet in that it is the only major power unable to resume its pre-war imperialist policies."

"In other words, Germany and China are in more or less the same situation, determined to free themselves from foreign oppression?"

"Exactly. And Hitler has understood that determination. The relationship between Germany and China is based on what one might call reciprocal pragmatism. Both countries have witnessed serious economic decline. Both have suffered revolution and upheaval. And both stand on the periphery of international relations, eager to be accorded Great Power status. That's where military and industrial might become significant."

In spite of the amount of alcohol he had imbibed during the evening, Otto was remarkably lucid. I needed to be careful.

"As Gunther hinted, both countries need a national renewal in terms of their economies. They need vibrant industrial production—production that modern militaries provide. China needs advice on how to strengthen its army by bringing to it German orderliness, discipline and innovation in the use of new weapons and tactics."

"And Germany?"

"Germany needs to cultivate an ally that will be strong in the future," Otto replied, pouring himself another *schnapps*. "It also needs access to raw materials to expedite its rearmament when the time comes. We get almost all our antimony and over half of our tungsten through private trade with China—a trade that we help facilitate, covertly of course, because they are essential ingredients in armour plating, armour-piercing shells, rifle barrels, airplanes. That sort of thing."

"I *see*."

"So you can see how important trade with China is for us, and how important it is that we have something to offer in return."

"A kind of power grid *pro quo*," I tried out a Victor pun. Otto didn't seem that impressed. He was in full *schnapps* flow.

"There is, though, another reason for the current expansion of military ties between our two countries. The post-war Versailles Treaty has severely curtailed the activity of the Reichswehr and so led to a dearth of suitable employment for career officers such as myself. In Germany we have had to lead a shadowy existence. Here, however, we are welcomed and afforded a prestige that we lack back home. But remember, we are economic, not military, advisers."

"That way circumventing the Versailles Treaty?"

"That is the intention, yes, although the press has accused us of serving as soldiers for hire. I hope you don't think that way, Kristoffer."

"Not at all." I did my best to sound reassuring. "It strikes me that, by helping China, Germany is also helping its allies thwart Japanese aggression. Great Britain and the United States should be thanking you, Otto."

"The thing is, Kristoffer," Otto was in full flow, "we can't just impose German institutions and technology on China. Rather, we have to adapt to the foreign environment and fit our advice and reforms into the Chinese context."

"Not all the time, surely? I mean, in order to modernize Chiang's army, you have to reduce its size and follow the European example."

"You *are* well informed, Kristoffer. Yes, large armies like the ones in China tend to get bogged down by lack of funds and resources and become immobile. That's why Chiang wants to reduce the size of his army, yes. To improve the quality of the force and make it more manageable. And Chiang himself would be able to afford the weaponry that Germany could supply him with."

"But how would demobilization and modernization take place? It can't all happen at once, surely?"

"No, of course not. We decided to do it by stages, starting with a single division—a *Lehrtruppe* trained in the use of modern weapons and the conduct of modern warfare. Once proficient, its officers are dispersed to train additional units, so that from last year the Chinese have had a *Lehr* brigade which is now being expanded into a *Lehr* division."

"I can see where Germans get their reputation for orderliness from. And why they have had so many philosophers." I tried to keep the conversation light. "But what about Japan, Otto? Once Hitler gets into power, how long do you think the official German foreign policy of neutrality will continue?"

"A million mark question, Kristoffer. As I see it, a strong Chinese military will deter Japanese aggression and help Hitler formulate a policy. That's why I see our work here as so important."

"Of course. But there's a catch, isn't there, Otto? The stronger you're able to make the Chinese military, the more likely a limited incident—like the one we witnessed in Manchuria in September—will transform itself into full-scale war."

"It's possible, I suppose. But not yet. Surely?"

How wrong he was.

27.

It often pays to make love to a woman. After all, she's been trained to use language from an early age, when she learns that words can trump men's physical strength any time. Especially after a strenuous bout of sex.

On Tuesday, at half past seven, I knocked on the cream-painted door of Room 156 of the Palace Hotel. Ludmila must have been standing behind it waiting because she opened it at once.

"Kristoffer!" She held out a hand demurely for me to kiss. "How good of you to come!"

I allowed my lips to make their salutation. Her hand was firm, her fingers warm, and her diamond ring sparkled at the sight of me. "I'm sorry I'm late, Luda. I was delayed by a hold-up on Sinza Road."

"A hold-up?" she drew me inside. The room was as well-appointed as her low-cut dress. "Anyone we might know?"

"I don't think so. Some rich Chinese businessman or other. The two men in the front of the car were Chinese and well-armed. As were two more standing on its running boards. Two Green Gang brunos were lying dead in the road by the time I turned up behind the police. The other two had run off."

"The police came in time? That's unusual."

"Yes, but whoever it was tried to bop off a Chinese magnate just one block away from the Gordon Road Police Station. A bit short-sighted of them, if you ask me. You'd have thought Tu Yue-sheng would have planned things a bit better."

Luda put one hand to her red-lipped mouth in polite consternation.

"I'm sorry, Kristoffer. I've forgotten my manners in my excitement." Tu and I were clearly rivals for her attention. Were my ears not big enough?

Her suite showed every sign of having hosted half a dozen guests. There were empty glasses on a low table by the sofa and chairs, half-empty bottles of wine on the sideboard, and plates of canapés that looked as if they'd been raided by a couple of starving beggars on the Nanking Road below. The well-off drank and ate more, while the poor had to make do with less. Like the sampans rocking idly in the creeks of the Whampoo River, they ended up lean, rent, and beggared by the strumpet wind.

"I'm sorry," Ludmila apologised again, motioning me with one hand to sit on the sofa. Her apologies were beginning to make her sound like Roger Buckley. "For some inexplicable reason, my guests all left early today."

"What a shame! I'd looked forward to meeting them."

She handed me a glass of slightly tepid champagne.

"Yes," she said, a little dreamily. Or was it nervousness? "But at least now I have you to myself."

"And I you, of course."

She sat down on the sofa beside me and took my free hand in hers. Getting straight to the point in her Berlin style.

"Did you know, Kristoffer, Tu Yue-sheng actually came to see my husband the other day?"

"He did? What for?" I reciprocated her grasp with the slightest of squeezes. "I didn't realise Otto was involved in the opium business."

"Oh, Kristoffer!" Ludmila laughed, "You are *silly*. No, not opium, although I have to say I'd like to try it one day. For fun."

"Don't, Luda. It'll do you an injury. But why did Tu approach your husband? Surely, he doesn't want to join the Nazi Party?"

"Kristoffer!" Another squeeze, harder this time. A few more jokes and her fingers would start rivalling Kiki's vagina.

"Why then?" I persisted.

"He wants to purchase a Junkers 87 from Otto and donate it to Chiang Kai-shek."

"Really? He must be as wealthy as everyone says he is."

"And more, I'm sure. But there's something else."

"There is?"

"There is," Ludmila laughed. "What Tu plans to do with his Junkers is very funny, I think."

"Tell me more."

"He's asked Otto to make sure its fuselage is painted with the Board of Opium Suppression's logo."

I laughed. It was an amusing irony that the gangster who had more or less a monopoly on the Shanghai opium trade also headed the organization set up by the Municipal Council to suppress that very same trade. That was the kind of veneer that made the city's mud flat ugliness and dire poverty look so attractive. Opium may have been introduced to the Chinese by foreign enemies, but it was Chinese who kept people's pipes filled in Shanghai. And Tu, the wicked emperor, shipped it all over the place and nobody in the Shanghai Municipal Police ever piped for justice. Least of all Lolly Lo and his colleagues.

"And how is Otto? Has he recovered from the delightful dinner party you kindly invited me to last Saturday? I have a feeling we both drank too much. I did, at least."

She laughed. "Just about, I think. He went back to Nanking on Sunday night." She drew closer and with one finger dusted an imaginary speck of dust off the lapel of my jacket as she turned her face invitingly towards me. "But let's not talk about him now that I have *you* here."

"And near."

"And dear." And with the hint of a moan, she closed her eyes as her body went limp in a kind of swoon. Then she kissed me, while I, in the very whirlwind of passion, did my best to acquire a temperance that would give it smoothness.

Later, as we lay together naked under a duvet on the double bed in the adjoining room, she started to talk. As I had hoped.

"Life isn't easy for a married woman in Shanghai," she began. "How can one put it?"

"It probably isn't easy anywhere." I kissed her forehead in encouragement.

"No. But in Berlin I had my family and friends. Here I have nobody other than my daughter."

"And Otto."

"So it would seem. But, Kristoffer *mein schatz*, my husband isn't usually with me in Shanghai. Even at weekends. He's always running off to other parts of the country as part of his job. He never takes me with him. I sometimes wonder if maybe he has a mistress I don't know about. Some slender, young, and elegantly turned-out Chinese concubine."

Her description didn't quite match Big Annie, so I confined that well-endowed young woman's knitting to my brows.

"Surely not?" I queried. "You're far too beautiful and smart, Luda, to make a man even think of looking at another woman."

"Flatterer! You never can tell with men, though," she sighed. "The stories you hear in this city. Tu Yue-sheng with his four wives and dozens of concubines, surrounded by White Russian bodyguards in his four-storeyed house on Rue Wagner. Or respectable *taipans* with their sultry Eurasian beauties. Or other pillars of the community who frequent high-class brothels like Gracie Gale's in Kiangse Road."

Ludmila was very well informed.

"You're very well informed, Luda dear," was all I could say.

"That's all we women can do with our time. Inform ourselves."

"About men's infidelities?"

"Not just men's infidelities, Kristoffer. About what they do at work. Take Tu's purchase of a Junkers 87, for example. Otto tells me German airplane manufacturers are desperate to establish a presence in China. So what do they do? Form aviation companies, like Eurasia for example, which then fly German planes around the country, to be examined and purchased by local warlords," she paused. "But I'm boring you?"

"Not at all. Actually, I know someone who is a pilot working for Eurasia."

That seemed to satisfy her.

"But once you start selling aeroplanes to the Chinese, you must have personnel to deliver supplies, mustn't you? You need German pilots to fly the planes, and then German personnel to train Chinese to become pilots themselves. You need German mechanics to repair engines, and to teach Chinese how to repair them. That's all part of Otto's job."

"So lots of Germans are coming into China? But that should make you happy, Luda *liebling*. You'll have more chance of making German friends in Shanghai."

"Kristoffer!" Her voice was reproving. "I have standards, you know. Pilots may be glamorous, but, surely, you wouldn't expect me to associate with mere *mechanics*?"

"Ah!" I said. I didn't want to get bogged down in an argument about the mechanics of her social life. It was time to turn her attention to further lovemaking.

This time we were both more relaxed and explored each other's bodies lovingly at length. I liked the fullness of her breasts, the strength of her legs wrapped about my hips until she rolled me over and sat astride me as she pushed herself forcefully back and forth. She may not have matched Kiki, but there was a lot to be said for the Berlin squeeze. When she came, it was with a shuddering moan before she collapsed onto my chest, her breath coming in short, sharp pants in my ear.

"Ah, Kristoffer!" she whispered. "I needed that." She bit my ear lobe hard.

"Ouch!"

"Ouch?" she looked at me mockingly. "Do you like a little pain, *mein schatz*? I'm sure it can be arranged next time."

"With Otto?"

She slapped my cheek playfully.

"Only if he agrees. And you're not allowed to invite him." She looked at her new lover sternly.

"Of course not. I'll confine my questions to his work."

"He won't tell you anything, of course."

"He won't?" How little she knew.

"Of course not. Most of what he does is very hush-hush. Isn't that what you say?" Then she added, "Like how he's just set up a trading organisation called HARPO."

"That sounds like one of the Marx brothers."

"Marx had a brother?" she looked at me seriously. "I wasn't aware."

My little joke was clearly no laughing matter.

"The Marx brothers made a film called *The Cocoanuts*. They're very funny. One of them is called Harpo."

"Oh! But HARPO isn't an American comedian, Kristoffer. It stands for Handelsgesellschaft zur Verwertung Industrieller Produkte."

"Another of those immensely long and imposing German titles," I laughed and gave her a kiss that was long enough to whet her appetite for more lovemaking, but not quite long enough to arouse her to immediate further physical activity. I knew my limits.

She hugged me tightly.

"Don't you wonder, Kristoffer, why my husband, a German *officer*, is setting up a *trade* organisation?"

"Why is he setting up a trade organisation called HAPRO?" I asked, quietly correcting her, but already knowing the answer.

"Because of the Treaty of Versailles. Officially, Germany isn't allowed to sell military equipment to foreign powers."

"Ah yes, of course. It had slipped my mind."

"Our future Führer doesn't agree with that. Nor do our industrialists who are competing with other nations to supply arms to China. Especially the United States with its Flying Tigers."

I decided to fly a kite.

"Which explains why Kiki is here, doesn't it?"

"Kiki?"

"A Brit who speaks German rather well and has a very high opinion of our future Führer."

"Oh, *him*! Dickie, you mean?" Ludmila raised herself on one elbow and looked down at me. "He is just an errand boy. Otto tells me he brings him orders from Berlin and takes back whatever messages Otto has for his superiors. This Dickie, he has an excellent memory, you know, Kristoffer. Nothing is ever written down. That way, nobody knows."

Tiddly-pom.

28.

A few days later all hell broke loose.

It all started with the monks. Those bloody Japanese monks.

They had been hanging around Boone Road with their tambourines, bells and bamboo flutes chanting and begging for money for well over a week. Not all together, of course. I'd passed a couple standing on the pavement opposite the Japan Club on Chapoo Road, doing their best to make local businessmen feel obliged to empty their pockets of small change. I'd seen two more down by Garden Bridge making enough racket to frighten the nannies with their *gweilo* children in the Public Garden across the creek. The last one hung out by the Hongkew Market and was rewarded with enough scraps of food to keep him and his companions well fed when they retired every evening to the Japanese temple nearby—the same temple in which Simon Meyer had been held hostage.

The grapevine told me that the monks' presence had been duly noted by Colonel Kenji Doihara, head of Shanghai's Kempeitai military intelligence. After putting up with three days of cacophony outside his office window, he sent one of his underlings to have a quiet talk with the monk plying his trade by the market. Why didn't he and his colleagues head off to Boundary Road and cross into Chapei—the Chinese part of the city? A provocative suggestion that was accompanied by a generous contribution to the monks' welfare. They could practice their chanting on the wrong side of the International Settlement and enlighten those ignorant Chinese. Come to think of it—a further handful of coins deposited in the donation box hanging from the monk's neck—they might like to sing the Japanese national anthem while they were at it. Remind those upstart Chinese crows who was in charge of preening their feathers.

The monks, being devout worshippers of both the Sun God Emperor and base Mammon, did as was suggested. In the process they disproved Jesus' theory that one could never serve both at the same time.

Not that they were aware of the eruditeness of their approach. They were, after all, Buddhists, not Christians.

29.

There was more to it than this, of course. Things were never quite what they seemed in Shanghai.

Why the fuss? Basically, because the Chinese had had enough of the invaders of Manchuria. It was *their* country, not the Kwantung Army's. In retaliation, they had initiated a full-scale boycott of Japanese goods all over the country—enough to cause economic chaos and piss off Japanese businessmen and factory owners who complained bitterly to their authorities.

A bit of tit for tat, then, between enemies in a lovers' embrace. You squeeze me and I'll squeeze you in return.

The boycotts had continued all the time I'd been in Shanghai. Japanese textile factories began closing down, their mills rendered inoperative. Hundreds of Japanese ships lay idle up and down the country's river and sea ports. Chinese businessmen stopped buying, stocking and selling Japanese goods. They refused to take on Japanese employees or make use of Japanese banks. Telephone operators discriminated against Japanese subscribers, Post Office employees held up Japanese mail, and tram drivers and bus conductors were openly rude to Japanese women passengers. Tut tut. That was supposed to be a Japanese man's prerogative.

As if this weren't enough, Chinese were also being exhorted to end all contact with Japanese people who were—in an ironic twist on the much-vaunted concept of Japanese imperial purity—now considered to be little short of a polluting race. One Chinese ricksha man expressed his disdain by cleaning the wheels of his vehicle with a Rising Sun flag.

That was really beyond the Manchurian Pale. The time had come to *do* something.

Hence the Buddhist monks.

The day after one of them had had his donation box filled with Kempeitai silver, the five monks gathered up their robes and made a beeline across the International Settlement boundary into Chapei in the Chinese part of the city. I happened to be there at the time and saw it all. Egged on by a female Kempeitai officer dressed as a man—it just had to be the former Manchu princess now called Yoshiko Kawashima—the monks wandered around the streets adjoining Shanghai North Station, making as much noise as possible with their tambourines, bells and flutes. Local Chinese were not amused. There was enough tension in the air to cause a few flashes of lightning, so I hung around. That, after all, is what journalists do most of the time.

It was when the monks played a somewhat discordant rendering of *Kimi ga yo*—Japan's simple, and let's face it, rather beautiful, national anthem—in front of the main entrance of Shanghai North Station that local Chinese patience broke. Perhaps it was unfortunate that the Manchu princess had encouraged the monks to perform their concert just when workers began swarming out of a nearby factory at the end of a day's work. Perhaps she had carefully planned it. Anyway, before the monks knew where they were, they found themselves surrounded by angry Chinese demanding to know what they were doing in *their* part of the city. Unable to answer other than with gestures to signify his incomprehension in the face of spoken Shanghainese, one of the monks further infuriated the crowd, which regarded his sweeping hand movements as overbearing and rude. Typical bloody dwarf bandit.

Although, rather belatedly, the Manchu princess spoke in Chinese to try to calm things down, verbal argument quickly turned into physical assault. The princess made herself scarce, while the monks found themselves being slapped and punched by angry Chinese—one of whom threw a well-aimed cobble stone that felled one of the Japanese brothers. His less-injured companions managed to pick him up in the mêlée and drag him, and themselves, back across Boundary Road to the safety of Japan Town and the International Settlement. Although a doctor was called to the temple where they were staying, the injured monk died later that night.

Even though, or precisely because, this was the first fatality of any Japanese civilian or official in the whole of China, Hongkew's Japan Town inhabitants were not amused. And when Japanese are not amused, anything can happen.

Which, sure enough, it did.

On the following night about fifty rōnin—arch-patriots and ne'er-do-wells who had come to Shanghai to seek their fortune—armed with clubs, pistols, and knives, proceeded to cross into Chapei. Led by a naval lieutenant who had had the foresight to take off his uniform, the rōnin set fire to a near-by Chinese towel factory, on the not entirely false grounds that the monks' assailants had worked there. Still belligerent, they returned to the Hongkew district where they were stopped by Settlement police who had witnessed the incendiarism. The rōnin used their weapons to resist arrest, and ended up killing two Chinese police constables. One of the rōnin also was fatally injured.

Under normal circumstances, these two incidents could probably have been settled amicably by traditional Asian bargaining methods. A bit of give by one side here, accompanied by a bit of take by the other side there, and all would have been well. Alas! That, it appeared, was not what the Japanese wanted this time. At least, not the Imperial Japanese Navy.

"The Navy's smarting over the success of the Kwantung Army in Manchuria," Joao explained. "There are a lot of bluejackets garrisoned in Hongkew. They reckon it's their turn to fight the Chinese now. The Navy's chance of glory."

It seemed like Joao was right. Rear-Admiral Shiozawa's fleet of ten warships lay at anchor in the harbour with guns pointed menacingly toward Chinese territory. Meanwhile, Miyoko's friend, the short, moustached Japanese Consul-General Murai, with familiar flower in the lapel of his morning suit jacket, presented General Wu Teh-chen, Mayor of Shanghai, with a note containing four demands. These called for a formal apology for the attack on the Japanese monks; the arrest of their assailants; the payment of hospital expenses and suitable compensation to the injured; and suppression of all boycott activities and the immediate dissolution of all anti-Japanese associations.

These demands were backed up by a blustering Rear-Admiral who declared that he would "take appropriate steps to protect the rights and interests of the Imperial Japanese Government."

What was clear to Joao, as well as to a number of other experienced 'China hands,' was that it was the fourth demand—the suppression of anti-Japanese boycotts by the Chinese—that had the real punch. The first three were merely a prelude and could be met easily enough. But the fourth? That required interference with, in Mayor Wu's words, "a spontaneous reaction of the people to a series of unfortunate events in the North-East"—in other words, Manchuria. To bring the boycotts to an end would be to force the Chinese people to abandon the only efficient weapon available to them to fight back against their Japanese aggressors. If Mayor Wu yielded to this demand, it was likely public wrath would turn upon China's, still rather fragile, national government—something that was in nobody's interests but Japan's. Talk about being between a rock and a hard place.

29.

The poor Mayor had little choice. The next day, the Japanese Consul's spokesman announced that he had agreed to suppress all boycott activities, dissolve all boycott organizations, and prohibit all anti-Japanese agitation. The Chinese response was considered "fully satisfactory." We all breathed a sigh of relief.

Not Joao, though. "Something's wrong," he said. "Shiozawa's up to something."

"What?"

"I don't know, Rusty, but I expect we'll find out soon enough."

We did. Soon after we got back to the Foreign Correspondents'

Club, the Admiral issued a declaration. I scanned it quickly before reading its conclusion out loud:

> "*The Imperial Navy, feeling extreme anxiety about the situation in Chapei, where Japanese nationals reside in great numbers, has decided to send out troops to this section for the enforcement of law and order in the area. In these circumstances, I earnestly hope that the Chinese authorities will speedily withdraw the Chinese troops now stationed in Chapei and remove all hostile defences in the area.*"

"It's ridiculous, of course," Joao tried to reassure me. He was in Portuguese mode, in spite of everything. "Japanese nationals have already been evacuated from Chapei."

"That man's got enough wind in him to set a whole armada of ships sailing across the Pacific," I shook my head disconsolately. "Still, I'd better sit down and write something. Then cable what I've got to my newspapers in Europe. There's enough time before they go to press."

"And I'd better do the same. If I hurry, I'll be able to submit mine in time for it to appear in this evening's late night edition of the *Asahi*."

The two of us went about our business.

Later, a little after ten o'clock, I found Joao in the library.

"Coming?" I asked.

"Coming where?"

"I thought I'd check things out in Chapei."

Joao shook his head.

"Nothing's going to happen tonight. You go if you like, Rusty, but I think I'll turn in. I've got somebody warming my bed for me." He grinned.

"Lucky you!"

"Let me know if something happens, won't you?"

"Of course. Enjoy yourself, and my regards to Gerda."

"Thanks. Will do."

An hour later the news came in on the ticker tape. Shiozawa intended to attack Chapei. I sent Joao a message via one of the FCC's runners. Then I hurriedly left the building and made my way over to Hongkew. From there I walked past a couple of sentries through the Settlement gate at Honan Road to North Station in Chapei.

It was a cold night and the Chinese didn't seem to be expecting an attack. Only a few gendarmes were standing around idle in the station plaza, where the normal crowd of coolies, farmers and merchants was waiting for the midnight train. In front of the station were two small sandbag redoubts, not even waist high; they were the only defence preparation noticeable. I went in search of the station inspector.

"Aren't you going to warn these people to seek a place of safety?" I indicated the hundreds of passengers waiting to board the train.

The station inspector gave me a puzzled look. "Why?"

"The Japanese have announced that they're going to occupy Chapei. Haven't you heard?"

"That's all off," he grinned. "The trouble has been settled. Mayor Wu has met the Japanese demands." He still wasn't convinced, even when I showed him a copy of Shiozawa's latest declaration. But then a young Chinese military officer hurried up, uttered a few words in a low voice, and moved off rapidly.

"*Ai-ya!*" exclaimed the inspector. "*Ni shuo tui-la.* You're right. That officer just confirmed that the Japanese are preparing to march on Chapei. We can expect an attack at midnight."

I looked at the big clock in the station waiting-room. It was twenty minutes to twelve. I just hoped Joao had got my message. I had only walked a hundred yards along Boundary Road when I heard rifle reports, and then the bark of machine-gun fire. It was too late. The Japanese advance had already begun. I found myself facing a line of Japanese bluejackets, with their conspicuous white leggings, moving at the double-quick towards the station, but halting every fifty feet or so to fire into Chinese territory. Bullets came streaking along at street level. Loiterers scurried frantically for shelter. Two fell; others uttered screams. I didn't bother to wait and watch any more. Dodging down an alley, I ran as fast as I could towards what I hoped was a safer part of Hongkew.

And bumped into Joao. He was with a bunch of other newspapermen at the North Chekiang Road Settlement boundary, watching the Japanese troops enter the Chinese city. Squads of blue-jackets were now running thick and fast. Before them went armoured cars, motorcycles with mounted machine-guns on sidecars, and heavy armoured trucks loaded with light artillery. They took up positions at street crossings, where they set up machine-guns. They also entered houses off Singkiang Road, in Chinese territory, and dragged out Chinese civilians, arresting them, sometimes killing them outright as suspected 'snipers.' By one o'clock, dozens of bodies of dead Chinese lay in the streets beyond the International Settlement border. Firing became continuous, with the rat-a-tat of machine-gunning predominant.

"Thanks, Rusty. I owe you."

"I owed you already, Joao. But I'm sorry I had to ruin your night with Gerda."

He laughed. "I'm sure there'll be another one." A stray bullet thudded into a sandbag nearby. "Provided we're not killed in the meantime."

Still more bluejackets poured into the densely populated district, with bayoneted rifles and machine-gun units. There seemed to be at least a couple of thousand of them. They looked confident and relaxed, almost cheerful some of them, as if they were out on the town on Saturday night leave. Many were smiling at us journalists as they passed. This was better than drunken brawls in Blood Alley. The blood around them now was for real.

What none of them dreamed of was the reception that awaited them. They had all been told the Chinese would run at first shot. Hadn't the Admiral himself said they could blast the Chinese out of Shanghai within forty-eight hours? They clearly believed in the invincibility of the squadrons of the Rising Sun. Little did they know.

At the end of Singkiang Road, a detachment of bluejackets suddenly came running back. Some carried no rifles; some had lost their steel helmets; and three or four had blood gushing from fresh wounds. They all looked badly frightened. Shortly afterwards another squad came hurrying back in disarray from the Chinese part of the city.

We headed off to Navy headquarters to find out what was going on. Things definitely weren't going according to plan. There the officer detailed to smooth over the situation for our benefit was a Captain Baron Samejima. A real one, according to Joao, and not a baronet or count, who came up with the understatement of the night.

"It looks," he said, "as though we are encountering unexpected resistance."

30.

The next three weeks were the nearest to hell I've ever been as Joao and I covered the fighting in Chapei.

The bluejackets may not have been able to occupy Chapei at once, but the rōnin quickly took over and ran amok in Hongkew. Back in feudal times, rōnin were masterless samurai, some of whom are almost deified for their upright behaviour in following the samurai code of conduct. But not now. Shanghai's rōnin were a bunch of ruffians—toughs, hoodlums, thugs and young jingoists who called themselves the League of Blood. And they were being led by Lieutenant Fujii.

The rōnin initiated a reign of terror that wasn't checked effectively for days. We watched them disarm and often arrest International Settlement police constables, challenge every passing pedestrian at street intersections in Hongkew, and capture and abduct Chinese civilians whom they suspected of living under the protection of foreign authorities. Some they took to naval headquarters; others were shoved down back alleys from which they didn't return. I personally saw Fujii put a bullet through the belly of a pregnant woman who later died in my arms.

The worst thing was that we were powerless to do anything about the atrocities we witnessed. One or two Japanese consular officials were embarrassed by what was going on, but were equally incapable of interfering. So, too, were Settlement police who were intimidated by the armed and hate-maddened gangs, protected by bluejackets with bayoneted rifles and machine-guns. During the days that followed, outrage piled upon outrage: looting, banditry, kidnapping, homicide, and brutality of all sorts. And Lieutenant Fujii was at the forefront of it all. I stroked my Husqvarna longingly.

"Now's not the time, Rusty," Joao advised. "Just be patient. Wait till he's less hyped up. Less alert. You'll get your chance."

Neither of us had ever experienced war of any kind, least of all the deadly air raid that Japanese seaplanes unleashed on the densely populated city. Without advance warning of the attack, the Chinese had no chance to escape and scores of them were blown to bits, or incinerated in the rapidly spreading fires. It was terrifying.

Through all this mayhem Joao and I worked together, sharing the pain of death and destruction all around us. We wrote our despatches together. It helped Joao as a Japanese to have a white face beside him whenever we crossed into Chinese territory, although the fact that he spoke Shanghainese fluently tended quickly to dispel any suspicion young Chinese soldiers may have had. It also helped me to have a Japanese journalist by my side whenever we encountered bluejacket patrols. Even though I spoke a bit of Japanese, it wasn't enough to allay their natural distrust of a *gaijin*.

It was strange, though, being able to travel from one side of the conflict to the other, behind enemy lines, and then back again, with Joao perched uncertainly on the back of my Čechie. We were stopped, of course, but usually we were let through. We managed to interview General Tsai Ling-kai, commander of the Chinese Nineteenth Route Army. We talked to his troops—some of them mere lads of fifteen or sixteen years old who looked more like children going on holiday than men going to war. Every soldier, whatever his age, clung onto his broad-brimmed straw hat and over his shoulder carried a coolie's yoke, from the two ends of which hung all his possessions. And we saw all the dead bodies lying in the ditches beside the roads.

"Do you really want to fight the Japanese?" I asked one young man, who was building a machine-gun nest into a hillside graveyard of black-glazed urns filled with the ashes of members of a Chinese lineage.

"Of course, I do," he retorted angrily. Joao stepped back a couple of paces to make sure he wasn't in range of the bayonet on the end of the young soldier's rifle. "The Japanese are murderers and bandits. They've killed our people in Manchuria. They've taken our land. Now they think they'll take over the rest of China, but first they're going to have to kill us."

Their patriotism was unquestionable, and it was supported by the genuine belief that the Japanese intended to enslave the Chinese. "We would rather die than be made subjects of the king of the island monkey-people!"

I wasn't sure how Joao intended to translate that phrase into Japanese, but he assured me he would. In a way he was less shocked than I was by the Chinese hatred of the Japanese.

"It's been a long time coming, Rusty," he mused at the end of another long day. He was in Portuguese mode. "The ultranationalists have been behaving appallingly for years. They think they own the world—if not physically yet, then at least ideologically—and can do what they please. All I can say is, we're not *all* like them. There are plenty of people in Japan who are shocked at the behaviour of our troops abroad. It's my duty as a journalist to report everything we've seen and heard. And with your help, Rusty, that's what I'm going to do."

"I admire your integrity, Joao. It must be really difficult for you to witness all these atrocities by your countrymen."

"They aren't my countrymen right now, Rusty. I'm feeling very Portuguese these days."

But then, as if to contradict his words, he bowed.

31.

In the middle of all this I received a message that Su Bai-li, Chiang Kai-shek's Head of Internal Affairs, wanted to 'have a chat.' That sounded as ominous as the guns on the battleship *Yamato* moored in Warship Row. Like the Chinese, I didn't have much choice. Other than to do as required.

It was said that Su Bai-li never met anyone in his office unless he could help it. It was better for people to think he didn't have an office. He didn't invite anyone to his home either. That would have been the height of impropriety. To himself.

So he arranged to meet me at a café facing the side of Sassoon House on Jinkee Road. I knew it quite well. The Krakow was run by a Polish couple called Bartek who made magnificent pastries and served good coffee. I found the smell of Wanda's apple cake too overpowering to resist. Bai-li went for *faworki* angel's wings.

"Count Bloom, I'm glad I've finally had a chance to make your acquaintance," he began in English. "Your reputation has been percolating throughout the city."

Like Bartek's coffee, I thought, but said nothing. It probably didn't pay to be frivolous in the presence of the Nationalist Government's spy chief.

"So I thought it might be time to have a little chat."

"Thank you." What else was I supposed to say?

Bai-li's glasses gave him a deceptively mild-mannered and owlish appearance. Not unlike Roger Buckley in a way. Birds of a feather.

"You seem to have found yourself very much in the thick of things ever since you came to my country," Bai-li gave me a dimpled smile that could have charmed the socks off a panda. Or more appropriately perhaps, the rear off Admiral Shiozawa. "First the Manchurian incident, witnessed first-hand from a railway carriage, so I understand. Then the Simon Meyer kidnapping. According to Inspector Lo Li-kwei you were instrumental in saving that young man's life."

"Well, I'm not sure—"

"And then, of course," Bai-li cut me off with a wave of one hand, "you managed to interview Charlie Chaplin aboard the *President Hoover* when it docked in Shanghai a few weeks ago. I must say," he reached for a handkerchief in the sleeve of his Chinese gown and began polishing his glasses, "that was quite a scoop. How on earth did you manage *that*?"

"Luck, really, sir. I was given a tip-off by a Customs officer."

"Ah yes. The unfortunate Frederick Fox. What *did* happen to him? I never really understood."

"He had a weak heart, sir, and died suddenly in what was, I understand, a very stressful situation."

"Things like that can happen when Tu Yue-sheng's around, can't they? But I'm sure you're very aware of *that*. I have a feeling that your newspaper articles about the kidnapping skirted the truth," Bai-li smiled his friendly smile. "I've found over the years that self-preservation tends to preside over principles."

"Principles?"

"In the case of a journalist, adherence to accuracy and independence."

"I did the best I could under the circumstances."

"I'm sure you did, Count Bloom. As I said, a matter of self-preservation. And very wise of you, too. We wouldn't want the journalist whose eye-witness account revealed that the Japanese, not Chinese, were responsible for the bomb explosion by the South Manchurian railway line, to meet with an untimely and no doubt grisly death, would we? No. Definitely not." He looked at my empty plate. "Would you like another of these excellent pastries?"

"Thank you, no, Colonel Su. I would, however, be grateful if you could tell me why you have invited me here."

"Yes. Yes, of course." The Head of Internal Affairs took off his glasses and began to polish their lenses with his handkerchief once again. "My apologies. I believe we have a mutual friend, Irene Wiedemeyer.

Some people call her, rather unfairly I think, a ginger ninja. Her hair is definitely *not* ginger, wouldn't you agree?'

"More auburn in my opinion."

"Tell me, Christopher—I hope you don't object to my dispensing with formalities and calling you Christopher? Or would you prefer Rusty?"

"Rusty's fine."

"So, Rusty, where did you first meet Isa?"

There was no point in my trying to deceive Su Bai-li. He was, after all, Director of Internal Affairs.

"At a summer camp somewhere near Helsinki," I said. "It was a long time ago."

"Yes indeed. It must be well over ten years since, if I'm not mistaken, she deprived you of your virginity. And so many conquests since, I understand. Miss Montagu-Rose among them. I'm sorry," he held up his hands, palms facing me, in mock surrender. "That wasn't a very polite way of putting things. But reality, nonetheless, wouldn't you agree?'

"Like your own affair with Madam Sun Yat-sen? Or should I call her Soong Ch'ing-ling?"

"My goodness! How rumours get around! Where did you hear that one?" If I had surprised him, Bai-li didn't show it. The consummate professional.

"From a bird in a tree lining the rue Molière. But you were saying?'

"I mentioned Isa because I think it might be appropriate for you to renew your acquaintanceship with her. Present events are enough to give anyone twentieth century blues, so we need all the help we can get from friends in such perilous times."

I couldn't disagree with him.

"Am I to venture to include you among such friends?"

"Absolutely, Rusty, so please listen carefully. What I am about to say should be of value to you as a journalist. I have persuaded General Chiang Kai-shek to make another 'comeback,' because he commands the respect of the people. But, I can assure you, Chiang isn't interested in 'the people' and has no intention of helping them unless it is to his own advantage to do so. This will become clear during the coming weeks, as the Japanese continue their 'incident' against the Nineteenth Route Army. Chiang will refuse to send reinforcements to help his own Chinese troops, and as a result will aid Rear-Admiral Shiozawa in his quest for victory. And, before you ask, I do not approve and I intend to do something about it."

"So why bring back the Generalissimo?"

"Because he is the only person who can maintain unity among all the political and military factions in China. And unity is essential if China is to defend itself, as it surely must, against the Japanese. But Chiang needs time to train his armies. He is an extremely able general who will never commit himself to battle unless he is sure that he won't lose."

"As opposed to win, you mean?"

The dimples reappeared briefly on Bai-li's cheeks. Like the owl he resembled, he didn't blink behind his spectacles. Maybe the glass was cleaner on the other side.

"You look confused, Rusty. I'm simply advising you not to be deceived by the hoopla that will surround the Generalissimo's return to power. Ask the right questions, please. Reveal him for what he is—a slithery eel. Do I make myself clear?"

I nodded. "But why tell *me* all this?"

Bai-li evaded answering my question.

"There is someone who can help you—someone you've already met, a Japanese journalist called Serino."

"Joao?"

"Yes. Joao Sereño, to give him his other name. As I'm sure you've discovered for yourself by now, Joao's an ethical journalist. He does what he believes to be right and is ready to fight against what he sees as injustice. Unlike Chiang Kai-shek, Joao is on the side of the people. I suggest you continue to work with him as much as you can."

"And Isa?" I asked.

"Keep Isa by your side. She has skills you may need." Bai-li began polishing the lenses of his glasses yet again. "Another thing, Rusty. If I described Chiang Kai-shek as a slithery eel, there's another far more poisonous reptile you must deal with in the form of Miyoko Noguchi. I believe you've come across her?"

"Briefly. She claims to run an orphanage for young girls, but uses them as underage prostitutes in her so-called 'club.'"

"She is also a senior undercover agent for the Kempeitai. Together with a Lieutenant Fujii of the so-called League of Blood. And then there's his sidekick, Yoshiko Kawashima, who also happens to be a Manchu princess, as well as his occasional lover when she's not picking up Russian prostitutes along rue Palikao. I suspect you've come across them both?"

"Only at a distance."

"Then you'll have realised that she's been helping Fujii engineer the war that's about to be declared, thanks to that wretched band of monks. I've disposed of them, by the way. The monks, that is."

"Not her Imperial Highness, then?"

"I have a feeling she might come in useful one day."

"Because she's Chinese?"

"Because she's Manchurian," Bai-li corrected me gently. "Deep down, she resents the Japanese, even though she was brought up in Japan and speaks Japanese fluently. But she also regards Manchuria and the people living there as *hers*. By divine right, so to speak."

"So she may turn against the Japanese in Manchuria, you mean?"

"Not an impossibility, I suspect." He wiped his mouth with the table napkin on his lap. "But to get back to Miyoko Noguchi. Her job is to make sure everything proceeds smoothly from here on, so that Admiral Shiozawa's bluejackets overrun Chapei and defeat the Nineteenth Army. Your job—and Isa's job—is to put a spanner in the works."

"You mean, get rid of her somehow?"

"Fujii, too, if you get the opportunity. Isa knows how to deal with such a situation."

Bai-li put his glasses back on with a certain finality. I sensed our meeting was coming to an end.

"Tell me, Rusty, how did you get on with the world's most famous film star?"

I was glad we weren't in a car being driven by Bai-li. Indicating a change of direction at a crossroads wasn't one of his strong points.

"Chaplin, you mean?"

"Have you been interviewing other film stars without my being aware of it?" He smiled his dimpled smile. It really was reassuring. I wondered how long it had taken him to perfect it. "I assume you were able to build some *rapport* with him to be able to get his views on the use of sound in films in the way that you did? And, of course, his comments on Greta Garbo."

"I think we got on rather well, actually. Both our fathers, we discovered, were alcoholics."

"So you bonded. Is that the word?"

"In a way, yes."

"Good."

"What do you mean 'good'?"

"I'm not sure how to put this because it sounds absurd, but a few days ago I heard from an informant that there is a plot to assassinate Mr Chaplin in Tokyo."

"What!"

"My reaction entirely. But further enquiries suggest that the information may not be as far-fetched as it sounds. If that is the case, you will find that Madame Noguchi is once again involved. Or somebody very close to her. I suggest, therefore, that as soon as matters are resolved here in Shanghai, you proceed to Tokyo, Rusty. And take Isa with you. I'm told that Chaplin is due to arrive in Yokohama during the second week of May. Joao Serino will probably know more about that nearer the date, as well as about Tsuyoshi Inukai's invitation to Chaplin to dine together during his visit."

Was there anything Bai-li didn't know?

"What? The Prime Minister of Japan? That's quite a feather in Chaplin's cap."

"Not if he's going to be killed before he has had time to digest his meal," Bai-li said dryly. "I'm sure the invitation will annoy Mme Chiang. Mei-ling is *dying* to show off her American credentials to all and sundry. To be honest, Rusty, she had a minor tantrum when she discovered that Chaplin had met a Swedish journalist and not *her*. You probably made an enemy for life with that scoop!"

"But who on earth would want to kill Chaplin?"

"The same people who have been behind the present conflict here in Shanghai. Ultranationalists."

"You mean the League of Blood? And Lieutenant Fujii?"

"He's just the ugly face of brute force, Rusty. I suggest you pay more heed to the shadowy figures at Madame Noguchi's side. One of them is a monk going by the name of Nisshō."

"The so-called 'Shining One.' I've heard all about him from Joao. Leader of the Ketsumeidan. As a matter of fact, I may well have met him here in Shanghai back in December."

"Did you now? There's somebody else, though, who you might want to look into. A childhood friend of Madame Noguchi's, according to my information, lurking in the background and orchestrating the League of Blood's activities. Maybe you can dig around and find out more?"

Bai-li pushed back his chair and stood up. "Anyway, please keep an eye on Chaplin when you're in Tokyo. But remember one thing, Rusty. There's more than one way to see stars. So don't let yourself be dazzled by Hollywood royalty."

Bai-li should have invited Kiki for coffee and pastries at the Krakow Café.

32.

In spite of all that was going on, I managed to meet up with Otto von Holst. We had what he called a *Jungennacht* in which we first hopped, then staggered, from one bar to another, in the process pledging eternal friendship. We ended up at Gracie Gale's, where Big Annie and Belle kindly entertained us. The only way Otto and I could get up the stairs without holding onto the bannisters was by holding onto each other. Luckily, Gracie was in forgiving mood and we were allowed to do our thing with the girls. I christened mine Belle of the balls.

My new bond with Otto reminded me of my affair with his wife.

I managed to remember Luda's next soirée—or was it the one after the next one?—but not her room number. It had been that sort of a week. The door of Room 615 in the Palace Hotel was opened by an elderly gentleman in silk underwear, who started slobbering at the mouth the moment he caught sight of me.

"Oh, I *say!*" he lushed. "What a simply *wunderbar* surprise! I hadn't realised the hotel management's hospitality extended to *this*. Come in, *mein lieber junge*, and let me fix you anything you want. Just so long as —"

I beat a hasty retreat—or, rather, fled—along the corridor and down the stairs. It was when I was on the third floor that I recalled that Luda held her gatherings in Room 156.

She was happy to see me. As was Trudi, once she'd stopped flirting with a Chinese poet on the sofa. She seemed more uninhibited than ever.

"Kristoffer!" she exclaimed loudly, "*Lang nicht gesehen.*"

Her kiss was warm and moist, as were her hands around my neck. "How *are* you, my *elfschen?*"

I put on my little elf's voice.

"Well, thank you, my *schmusemaus.*"

"*Schmusemaus?*" queried Luda a little jealously. "How come I'm not your cuddly mouse, Kristoffer?"

"Because you're my *honigbienchen*, Luda," I ad-libbed quickly.

That seemed to satisfy her. At any rate, she made a beeline for the bedroom once all the guests had left.

33.

A few evenings later, I had a visit from Isa.

Fantom answered the doorbell when it rang and took one long appraising look at my visitor before blurting out rather unexpectedly,

"Bossman, you love-pidgin one-piece missee?"

I laughed.

"Olo fren, Fantom."

"Olo fren?" He wasn't convinced. "Numpa one first-chop fren. One man China-side no savvy how fashion *fankuei* missy belong one-piece *ang mo* red hair."

"You cheeky one-piece Chinaman!" Isa laughed and planted a kiss firmly on Fantom's cheek.

"*Aiyaa!*" he exclaimed in astonishment and rubbed his cheek gingerly as if he had somehow become polluted. Isa took off her coat and handed it to Fantom who accepted it only at arm's length. Then she came over to where I was standing and hugged me. Tightly. Just like an old friend.

"Hello, *mein Blümschen*." Neither mouse, nor honey bee, nor even a little elf, I was back to being a little flower.

"Isa!" I hugged her back just as tightly. Her body was as I remembered it, slender and warm. A little more muscular, perhaps, and therefore somehow distant.

Fantom left us in the drawing room, but came back in due course with a couple of Moscow Mules. More appropriate than he might have imagined. Then he diplomatically left us to our own devices.

"It's *so* good to see you, Isa. I never imagined." For once I was at a loss for words. It was true, though, what Fantom had said. Her hair was a magnificent colour. "I meant to get in touch after we met at the German Club party, but the war has been keeping me slightly busy, to put it mildly."

"Is it a war, then? I thought it was just an 'incident.'" Her smile was mischievous, her eyes warm and deeply green. Full of colourless ideas that slept furiously.

"That's what the Japanese call everything—an incident. They don't know what truth is."

"They know very well what truth is, *mein Blümschen*. They simply refuse to say it out loud. Anyway, I heard you'd been caught up in things —"

"From Gerda?"

"Who else? So I thought I'd pay you a surprise visit and hope you were at home."

"Which I was. Thankfully."

"Which you were. And, I'm glad to say, still are." She smiled.

"So…"

"So what?" This time her smile was coquettish.

"So where do we start?"

"Where? Or how, Rusty?"

"Either. It's been so long."

"True, but given that we have strictly speaking already started, why don't I carry on with *this*?" She leaned over and kissed me.

It was a long kiss, a searching kiss that we both enjoyed to judge by its length.

"Bring back memories?" she teased.

"Of course."

"Nice ones, I hope."

"More than just nice, Isa. Memories of a Nordic summer and the taste of blueberries that we'd picked just before we first kissed."

"Ah, yes, the blueberries! I'd forgotten the blueberries." Wistful now. "It all seems so long ago."

"It does, doesn't it! We were young then."

"Young and innocent."

"I was innocent, certainly. I'm not so sure about you, though."

"I suppose that's what being young is all about—losing one's innocence."

"And curiosity."

"And, as you say, curiosity. But not you, surely, Rusty? You're a journalist. You're in the business of asking questions."

"Aren't we all, Isa? In one way or another."

"I suppose so."

A pause. Suddenly she took hold of my right hand and held it up to the light.

"It's still there," she said in a low voice.

"What is?"

"The scar. The one you got when you slipped and fell in the river and cut your hand. Don't you remember?"

"I'd forgotten all about that." I took my hand back and looked at the jagged scar faintly etched in the palm of my right hand. "You tore up your neckerchief, didn't you, to bind the cut and stem the flow of blood."

"My best neckerchief, Rusty," she said reproachfully.

"I thought I gave you one to replace it."

"You did, but I never liked it as much."

"I'm sorry." What else could I say?

She put her arms around my neck.

"Do you remember how we made love there and then on the river bank?"

"Of course, I do, Isa. I remember *all* the times we made love.'

"All two of them, you mean?" She laughed teasingly. "That first time, you were in such a hurry you tore off my underpants with your wounded hand. When it came to my putting them back on afterwards, I found blood all over them. One of the girls back at the camp thought I was having a second period in two weeks." She laughed gaily at the memory.

Her arms were still around my neck. Her lips were close to mine and I could feel her breasts moving very slightly in and out as she breathed.

"And before you ask, *mein Blümschen*, I would never dream of visiting a man I wanted to make love to during my menstruation."

"Have you just finished a job, Isa?"

She laughed.

"Has Gerda been telling tales about me? No, *mein Blümschen*, don't worry. I've been behaving myself. Who knows how long for, though."

I kissed her. She tasted of vodka, ginger beer and lime juice. Fantom should have added blueberries to the Moscow Mules. They'd have given the ginger ninja an added kick.

Not that she needed one. Making love to Isa for the third time took me back more than a decade to a forest outside Helsinki where we spent two months together in a summer camp, doing the things teenagers do at summer camps: sleeping in tents, swimming naked in the lake, following trails, cooking over camp fires, learning boy scout and other tricks of our trade and, in our case, right at the end of our stay making love by a river. It wasn't her first time, but it was mine. I lost my virginity along with quite a lot of blood from the gash in the palm of my hand.

The second time was on a bed of pine needles among a mass of blueberry bushes. The stain of the fruit on her lips matched her auburn hair, as did her deeply suntanned body lit up by a ray of evening sunlight as she rode me to a wild and hungry orgasm. A red squirrel on the branch above us dropped a pine cone as it clapped its paws in quiet applause.

And then, the very next day, summer camp came to an end and she was gone. We sent letters to each other over the next few months, but they became fewer and fewer as we settled in to other, different lives that kept us apart. Until now. Now, it seemed, the gods who ruled our destinies had decided we should be together again. Atheist or not, I wasn't going to object.

34.

It was early evening by the time I got home. I was shattered after all the bombs and bullets whizzing around me all day and decided to have a long soak in the bath. I needed to wash off all the misery of death and destruction if I was to feel whole again.

It was as I was getting dressed that I heard the front doorbell ring. It was a Thursday evening and Fantom had gone out to check on his family in Hongkew, probably wearing my most expensive socks to show off to his mother. I answered the ring myself and nearly had a heart attack when I saw who was standing there.

"Trudi! This *is* a surprise. Come in!" I opened the door wide and let her in. She was wearing a magnificent three-quarter length white fox fur coat and, under it, a long-sleeved black Charleston dress with a plunging neckline that was filled by a string of pearls as well as by the curve of her breasts. Echoes of Kiki. Her perfume matched the allure of her appearance—honeyed tobacco, neroli and vetiver. But I thought I detected a sour note underneath the *Habanita*.

"I hope you don't mind, Kristoffer," she said as she sat down a little nervously on my sofa, smoothing down the hem of her dress demurely. It was well over her knees. I congratulated myself on my choice of cover colours. The blue-grey and amber material matched her two different-coloured eyes perfectly.

"How could I ever mind, my little *schmusermaus*! It's always a pleasure to see you," I replied gallantly. "What can I get you? Wine? Whiskey? Brandy?"

"If you don't mind Kristoffer, I think what I'd like most is a cup of coffee."

"Coffee?" I repeated, a little inanely. "I'll say this for you, Trudi, you tend to be full of surprises."

"Do I?" She seemed distracted.

I made coffee, one cup for her and one for myself. A dry evening might do me good after the day's excitement.

Her hand shook a bit as she picked up the cup and saucer. She definitely wasn't as lively and flirtatious as she had been when we first met at the German Club. Something was up.

"Kristoffer," she began hesitatingly, after sipping her coffee and putting cup and saucer back down on the table with a very slight rattle. "Luda says you're someone I can trust."

"I would hope so," I smiled encouragingly and took a sip of my own coffee.

"I need help, Kristoffer."

"What kind of help, Trudi? You know I'll give you all the help I can, if I can."

"I have a problem."

"Don't we all, my *schmusermaus*?" I joked. Clearly not the best kind of joke because she suddenly burst into tears.

"I'm sorry, Trudi," I put my arms around her and held her as she started sobbing uncontrollably against my shoulder. "What is it?"

It took time for her to recompose herself enough to be able to talk. She took a handkerchief from the sleeve of her dress, wiped her eyes and dabbed her nose. Her voice when eventually she began to speak was without a hint of its normal vivacious tone.

"I don't know where or how to begin, Kristoffer, but Luda said you are somebody who listens, and listens sympathetically, to others. At least, to her. I suppose that's because you're a journalist, I wouldn't know."

I was still holding one of her hands so I gave it an encouraging squeeze. It was a surprisingly lifeless hand.

"I've become addicted to opium, Kristoffer, and I don't know what to do."

"Ah!" was the best I could say by way of response to that sudden confession. Surely I could do better?

"It began innocently enough at one of Luda's salon evenings. There was a Chinese poet there who had just come back from Berlin.

You met him, I think? Lao Shi? I flirted with Shi, the way I usually do with unattached men," she glanced at me and smiled self-deprecatingly before giving my hand a reciprocal squeeze. "He was talking about how wonderful opium could be if taken in small quantities. I asked him a lot about the kinds of dreams he had while smoking. He could see how excited I was at the thought of having, how can I put it, an exotish *oriental* experience, so he suggested that we visit an opium den together a few nights later.

"When we arrived, Shi and I lay down facing each other on two opium couches. Seated between us on a tiny stool was our Chinese hostess who rolled two small balls of opium and heated them over a small flame enclosed by a glass covering with an opening at the top. She showed me how to inhale the smoke slowly through the pipe, but in my excitement I puffed in and out like a toy *Dampfmaschine* and almost choked myself to death," she laughed at the recollection. "But then I got the talent of it and," she closed her eyes dreamily in recollection, "it was *wonderful*, Kristoffer, quite wonderful. I don't know how to describe it, but I found myself casting aside all my cares and inhibitions. I forgot that I was a properly brought up German *hausfrau* with an older husband whom I looked up to. I forgot all the mannerisms and graces that I put on in my everyday life and I became *myself*—somebody who emerged from deep inside me, somebody who was sensitive to beauty, to art, to *love*.

"So I started to have an affair with Shi. Karl-Heinz has been away so much in Nanking and travelling round China that I had all the time in the world to arrange such liaisons. I was mesmerised by Shi—by his looks, his voice, by the way he held himself and dressed. He introduced me to his friends and encouraged me to make love to other men, even to two or three men and women at the same time. It didn't matter who they were. Often I'd never met them before the night in question. But the fact that they were Shi's friends and that we were all together smoking opium was enough to remove all my inhibitions and allow me to *ficken* whatever combination of people and positions I felt like. We all of us felt this way."

She stopped. "I'm sorry, Kristoffer. Do I shock you?"

"Yes," I admitted, wondering what I myself had missed. "And there again, no. These things happen."

She nodded.

"What started as an experiment ended up as an addiction. Not just the opium, but perhaps the sex, too. Karl-Heinz, as you probably noticed when we met that night for dinner at the von Holsts', is considerably older than me. And heavier, too. He makes love like a *missionar*," she laughed. "It is one reason why I'm not fat."

I laughed with her.

"And your addiction needed money?"

"Yes. Of course, I had money from Karl-Heinz, but I didn't want him to notice how much I was spending. My addiction, as I said, also introduced me to all sorts of different people—the kinds of people I had never imagined lived in Shanghai. One of these was a Japanese woman called Miyoko."

"Miyoko Noguchi?"

"Yes. You know her, perhaps? Oh, Kristoffer!" she continued without waiting for my reply, "she was so beautiful. So sensitive. So… so refined and elegant. And when we made love, which we did one afternoon at home when the servants were all having their day off, I was in ecstasy," she paused. "It is all right, Kristoffer, if I tell you such things?"

I nodded again.

"I had never been aroused in such a way by anyone before Miyoko made love to me. She led me to an *orgasmus* which I had only imagined in my opium dreams. I cannot describe how I felt that afternoon. Have you ever had such an experience, Kristoffer?"

"Once. But it was a long time ago now."

"Of course, I wanted to be with Miyoko again. We made love again, this time in a place she called her home, the Salon Pink on Kiangse Road, and when I left she gave me some opium. Just a small amount, but enough to make me go back to her to ask for more when it was finished. We made love once more. She gave me another small ball of opium and, as she did so, she asked whether I wouldn't mind joining her and a friend the following afternoon. She would give me more opium, and money, too. A lot of money.

"I didn't know what to do. I wanted to talk to Luda and seek her advice, but I was afraid because I knew I had become caught up in a situation over which I no longer had any control—especially when having sex with Miyoko. She was so expert in love play that I was like a ball of opium itself, carefully kneaded into the perfect form for her—and my—pleasure.

"The next afternoon I went back to the Salon Pink. Miyoko greeted me and then introduced me to two Japanese men. She couldn't, she said, tell me their names. One of them was quite short, with an effeminate face, full lips, and dark black hair parted almost in the middle of his round head. The other I recognised. He had accompanied Miyoko to the Christmas Party held at the German Club where we first met, Kristoffer, if you remember."

"I do indeed, although I'm surprised you do, Trudi dear. You were *very* drunk that evening."

"Yes, I was rather, wasn't I?" she giggled girlishly. "Anyway, after making the introductions, Miyoko led me to another room where we undressed and began to make love. Of course, the two Japanese men came in to watch. Then they took off their clothes and joined us," she paused.

"Including Miyoko?"

"Only for a few minutes. Then she excused herself and left me on my own. It was then that I realised something was not right," she continued and then suddenly began sobbing again. "It was awful, Kristoffer, so *awful*."

I held her again and she heaved convulsively in my arms.

"It's alright, Trudi. Just take your time."

"This man I'd met at the German Club, his name was Doihara. He undid his trouser buttons and pushed my head down on his penis. It was such a little *schwanz*, I had no trouble taking it in my mouth. But the other man, his was *enormous*. Luckily, he wasn't interested in me. I don't know what would have happened to my *Muschi* if he had decided to put it in there."

She began sobbing again.

"I was all alone with two men, and I was afraid. Of course, I had been with two men before, but that had been different. They were men who were friends or friends of friends—men who I trusted. I wasn't sure I could trust either of these two Japanese men.

"Doihara decided to take me by the… by the *Arsch*," she said ashamedly. "Luckily, he was so excited that he came very quickly. Then he turned his attention to his friend who, I realised, was thrusting his *schwanz* in and out of Doihara's *Arsch*. They were so engrossed in each other that I was able to gather my clothes and leave the room. Once I had dressed, I looked around for Miyoko, but she was nowhere to be found, so I left and went home as quickly as I could."

"And then you were blackmailed?"

"How do you know, Kristoffer?"

"I've heard a similar story from another friend, Trudi," I said gently. "Carry on."

"The next morning, I received an envelope, delivered by hand to my home. I opened it to find a photograph of myself being *gefikt* in the *Hintern* by a man who was himself being *Arsch gefikt* by another man. There was a note, in elegant handwriting, informing me that unless I paid the sum of twenty thousand dollars by the end of this week my husband would receive the same photograph and one or two others.

"I knew I had got myself into a right chaos. The woman who had been my lover had betrayed me and there was nobody I could turn to for help. Karl-Heinz would kill me, literally, if he knew what had happened. Raina was too distanced and bourgeois to even want to help. Luda was my only hope. So I went to Luda and told her everything."

"And what did Luda say?"

"She said she was just a German *hausfrau* like myself and had never experienced anything like this and didn't know what to do. Go to the *Polizei*, she suggested. But before you do, she said, go and talk to Kristoffer. He listens. And he knows people."

Trudi stopped talking, sat back on the sofa and gave out an enormous tearful sigh.

"*Can* you help, Kristoffer?" she asked.

I thought hard for a few moments.

"*Schmusemaus*, as I understand you, there are two things you need help with. One is what to do about the blackmail. The other is how to deal with your opium addiction. Am I right?"

She nodded helplessly.

"I think I may be able to help you with the second problem. Tell me, is Karl-Heinz at home these days?"

"Karl-Heinz?" She trembled at the mention of his name. Clearly she was frightened of him. Maybe she had a third problem—one that only she could resolve.

"He left for Germany a week ago."

"Germany? So he won't be back for a while?"

"At least two months, he told me."

"Good. Then you have time. I know a place which will cure your addiction."

"You do? Where?"

"I'll tell you later. In the meantime, we have to deal with the first problem. Luda was right. You *must* go to the police. But not just any police. I'll go and talk to my friend Lolly Lo Li-kwei. He'll know what to do and how to do it in such a way that you won't have to worry." I looked at my watch. "It's a bit late now for him to be still at work. I'll go and find him at the Central Police Station tomorrow morning."

Trudi looked nervous.

"It's alright. You don't have to go there. The American Club is opposite. You can wait for us there in their ladies' room."

Trudi looked confused. "The *Damentoilette*?" she asked uncertainly.

I had to laugh.

"Sorry, that was a bit confusing, wasn't it! I meant the special room in the club that is reserved for the use of ladies. Normally the American Club is for men only."

"Ah!" Finally she smiled. Then she put her arms round my neck and kissed me firmly on the mouth.

"Oh, Kristoffer!" she exclaimed and her relief was palpable. "*Thank* you. Thank you *so* much."

"And when you've told Inspector Lo everything he needs to know, I'll take you to a convent way out by the Catholic cathedral," I said. "I know a nun there who know how to cure bad habits."

Suddenly she was back to being her mischievous self. "Must I wear their habits, too?"

35.

Lolly seemed pleased to see me although, once I'd explained briefly why I'd come to the police station, he seemed less so. The sight of Trudi, though, sitting demurely in the American Club cheered him up again. Like me, he was a sucker for a well-turned out dame.

Not that he let it show. Rather, he was all business, the professional policeman who knew exactly what questions to ask and in such a way that the woman he was talking to didn't burst into tears and clam up.

"Right," he said with an ominous finality once he had elicited all the information he required. "You leave this with me, *Frau* Gassmann. I would like you to make a statement and sign it if you don't mind. It's alright," he put a reassuring hand on her arm, "you don't have to go across the road to the police station. We can do it right here, once young Christopher finds some paper for you to write on. Otherwise, I have all the evidence I need to search the premises of the Salon Pink and make a few arrests. I'm afraid we're going to have trouble holding this Miyoko Noguchi because she's a Japanese resident and the Japanese police in Hongkew are most particular about dealing with their own citizens. This means that they are almost certain to let her go after a few days, but she won't bother you again with blackmail, I can assure you, and her brothel will be closed down immediately. The Japanese police can't stop that. Kiangse Road is my territory."

"Thank you, Inspector Lo. Is there anything else you are going to want from me? I'm afraid I'm going to be incommunicado for a few weeks."

"Inconnumicado?" Was he secretly an unknown emperor? "That sounds exciting. I hope you're not a spy in your spare time."

"A spy?" Trudi's voice was a little shrill. "*Mein Gott*, no, *Herr Inspektor*. I just need to organise my life."

Lolly was diplomatic enough not to enquire further, although my impression was he knew what was going on.

After Trudi had written, signed and dated her statement, she handed it to Lolly who stood up and made to leave.

"Lolly," I said, "a word or two?"

"Of course, my rusty bloom," he said jokingly. "What can I do for you now?"

I explained. He stopped at the entrance to the American Club and pursed his lips thoughtfully.

"Seems like a fair request, Count. I'm going to have the place watched the rest of today and go in late this evening. You might just happen to be passing by at the time and live up to your name of Scoop Broom. Hopefully, we'll catch Madame Noguchi and her friends in the middle of their blackmail activities."

"What if she's not there?"

"She will be. It's a Friday, after all. Business will be brisk. And if she's not, she'll be there the next day. Or the day after that. I'm a patient man when it comes to waiting, so I'll see you there this evening if you want your story. Ten o'clock OK?"

I went back to where Trudi was waiting in what she had called the '*die Damentoilette.*' She greeted me with a warm hug.

"Kristoffer, what would I do without you?"

"Enjoy more sex and opium, probably. But not anymore, my little mouse. Now comes the hard part. and I'm not sure which will be the harder—curing your opium habit or doing as the Catholic sisters tell you. I can assure you, they're a tough lot, so don't be deceived by appearances. One disapproving glare can be worse than fifty lashes of a barbed whip on your bare back."

Trudi smiled again. When we were outside, she held me tightly. "Oh Kristoffer! How can I thank you properly?"

"Let's worry about that later, my little mouse. First of all, you have to get well again." I kicked the stand of my Čechie and held it vertical for her to get on. "But first, a different kind of thrill. Hop on!"

36.

That evening, I made my way across town to Number 54, Kiangse Road. Trudi was safely locked up in a solitary cell in the sisters' convent and who knew what misery she would be going through once withdrawal symptoms made themselves felt. Sister Loretta had greeted me with a withering stare that made me worry that she'd refuse to help Trudi, but she slowly relaxed as I told her what my poor German friend had been through. She agreed to take *Frau* Gassmann in for a certain 'financial consideration' to be donated to the Convent's well-being. Not being as generous or as wealthy as Tu Yue-sheng, I was uncertain how much to offer, but discovered to my relief that my suggestion of two hundred dollars almost melted Sister Loretta into a proverbial pool of butter. Trudi promised to pay me back later and I had a feeling it wasn't just money she was thinking of.

Lolly Lo was standing on the corner of Kiangse and Ningpo Roads, with his back to the Salon Pink, admiring the view of the Sassoon House tower a couple of blocks away at the end of Jinkee Road. Somewhere up there, Victor was entertaining. Or looking for another young lady to undress for his camera.

I parked my Čechie by the side of the road and took off my helmet.

"Ah! It's you, Rusty. I thought for a moment I was about to be attacked by a Prussian cavalry officer." Lolly laughed, then looked at his watch. "Punctual as usual," he said. "We'll never make a Chinese out of you."

"But you're here, too."

"Yes, but I've been on watch for the past couple of hours. Which means that, unlike you, I've been here a long time. Nothing to do with punctuality."

"If you say so, Lolly."

"I just did, didn't I?" he laughed again. "Anyway, three gentlemen have already gone into the Salon Pink and the door was opened by our friend, Madame Noguchi. So there's nothing to worry about there. She's at home, so to speak, waiting to be arrested." He glanced at two men cross the road on the opposite side of the street and melted back into the shadows. "And here, if I'm not mistaken, come two more of Madame Noguchi's clients. That makes a full house, to judge by the windows back and front. Maybe I should go into this business when I retire."

Across the road, Madame Noguchi answered the doorbell and let two more of her clients into Number 54.

"We'll give them half an hour," Lolly said. "Allow them to settle down and enjoy whatever entertainment is on offer. Then they won't be able to claim they'd gone to have a drink before moving on elsewhere, or whatever other excuse they can come up with. Then we'll go in."

We waited. At one point the door of Number 52 opened for a client and I could see Gracey Gale's full figure silhouetted against the light. The sight of Belle's graceful form behind her made me wonder if that was where I should go later. Anything to rid myself of the pang of desire Trudi's tale had aroused in me.

"Come on, Count! No time to start dreaming now." Lolly slipped across the road quickly and quietly, signalling to half a dozen of his men dotted here and there up and down the street to follow him. We moved up the steps quietly and Lolly pressed the bell. I could hear it ringing gently somewhere inside the house, and then footsteps. The front door was opened by Miyoko Noguchi herself.

"Good evening. Madame Miyoko Noguchi?" Lolly stepped in quickly, thrusting a sheet of paper into her hand, while I stayed out of view outside. "I am Chinese Chief Inspector Lolly Lo Li-kwei of Central Police Station in Foochow Road. And this is a search warrant. I hope you don't mind if my officers and I take a look around."

Miyoko's face was impassive as she read the warrant.

"Are you sure that's a good idea, Chief *Chinese* Inspector?" she asked politely. "I am a citizen of Japan. Any search warrant of my premises should, surely, be issued by the Japanese police in Hongkew and not by Central Police Station?"

"I'm afraid you're under a misapprehension, Madame Noguchi. Kiangse Road—at least this end of Kiangse Road—is under the jurisdiction of the Shanghai Municipal Police's Central Foochow, not Boone Road, station. Later, if we have reason to suspect you of a crime, we will hand you over to the Japanese police, but for the moment I would be grateful if you would cooperate with our endeavours. Tell me. How many clients do you have right now?"

"Five, Inspector."

"Five? And they are upstairs?"

"That is correct."

"Then we will leave them in peace for the moment and allow them to continue to enjoy the pleasures provided by your salon, madame. In the meantime, I'd like to inspect your ground floor rooms and basement."

"Basement?" For the first time, there was a flicker in Miyoko's serpent-like eyes.

"You have a basement, of course. All these houses have one."

"Yes, but it has nothing but old bits of furniture and rubbish in it. Plus a few rats' nests, of course."

"Of course, but we'll be the judge of that, Madame Noguchi. The stairs, I assume, lead down from the cupboard door there?" He pointed to a door under the stairs leading up and then nodded at some of his men. "You three check downstairs."

Three constables did as they were ordered and we could hear their heavy boots clunking down uncarpeted wooden stairs. Suddenly, there were shouts followed by the muffled sounds of a fight and screams.

"You two go down and make sure everything's OK," he ordered two of his men who were looking round what was clearly a reception room. "The rats seem to have grown to human size. Perhaps you have some poison, Madame Noguchi?"

"Boss!" A voice called up from below. "You've got to come down and take a look at this."

"I'm sorry, Madame Noguchi, but it seems like my attention is needed downstairs. In my experience, rats' teeth tend to be sharp. I'm going to have to ask this gentleman here to handcuff you while I check what's going on. Just in case."

"Just in case of what?" Miyoko's eyes were expressionless again. Resigned perhaps.

"Just in case." He turned to the remaining policeman beside him. "Constable, hold Madame Noguchi in the reception room here, and close the door behind you."

Lolly signalled to me to come into the house and follow him as he eased his large frame through the door leading to the stairs down to the basement.

The basement consisted of a single large room. There were four desks in the centre, seemingly occupied by four men now sitting handcuffed on the concrete floor in one corner of the basement. Beside them were three young women, too frightened to do anything other than sob into the sleeves of their nightdresses. They had cobra tattoos on their ankles, like Sakura and Hanako. A fearful sign of ownership.

There were speakers and telephone wires all over the place, all of them leading upstairs, and the desks were littered with notebooks and magnetic tapes, although I couldn't imagine clients saying anything to underage Japanese girls that would be worth recording. One third of the room was partitioned off by sheets of laminated wood to create a separate area. I stepped through a thick curtain and found that I was in a dark room with dim red lighting.

Prints were hanging from clothes pegs along a line above a sink, and on a counter top there were trays with some kind of chemical liquid in them. Along one wall was what looked like a pharmacist's cupboard, with each drawer labelled by nationality—Japanese, British, French and so on—and by date—month and year. I opened a drawer at random and found it filled with carefully labelled reels of exposed film and accompanying prints. Here was a blackmailer's treasure trove.

"Found anything?" Lolly poked his head through the curtain.

"A red light district," I said. "The collected works of a blackmailer, by the looks of it."

"Show me."

I showed him.

"So where are the cameras?" he asked brusquely. "We've turfed all the customers out of their rooms upstairs and put all the girls—and some of them really are just girls—in a Black Maria in the road outside, but we didn't notice any cameras. Better go and have another look."

"There's definitely one in the ceiling of one of the rooms. Mrs Gassmann was filmed from above."

I followed Lolly upstairs to one of the first floor rooms where everything was in disarray. He looked around with a practiced eye,

"Ah! Up there!" he pointed to the ceiling, then grunted and stepped back onto the landing. At the end was a door which he opened, only to find himself caught off balance by somebody hurling himself through from the other side. The man had only one way to run and that was towards me. He put his head down and charged. I put my head down further and tackled him by the legs. Rugby was a game I'd had to play at my somewhat exclusive private school in Lundsberg and this was the first time I'd found it useful in my everyday life. My opponent went down with a heavy thud and was quickly incapacitated when Lolly, having recovered his balance, sat heavily astride the man's back and handcuffed him.

"Well, that was fun," he exclaimed as he stood up. "Everything all right? I must say, I'm impressed, Count. Perhaps you should come and give my constables a bit of training one day."

"I'm sure they have better ways to deal with assailants. I feel as if I've done my collarbone permanent damage."

"Really?"

"No," I grinned. "Not really. But it hurts. Not something I want to do again in a hurry."

"Come on, then, Count. Let's see what goes on the other side of that door."

Again I followed Lolly, to find camera equipment and spyholes looking into the two bedrooms at the back of the house. Film canisters had been carefully labelled, waiting to be developed downstairs.

"Which leaves us with the front rooms. Oy!" He shouted downstairs. "I need a couple of men with handcuffs up here."

Once two constables had joined us, Lolly told them to take a look in the cupboard doors each side of the landing by the front window. "And be careful of flying bodies," he warned. "The Count here doesn't want to bust his shoulder helping you out."

The cupboard space behind the first door was empty, apart from more camera and film equipment. The second door was opened from inside by a Japanese rōnin who was holding his hands up in the air in surrender. My reputation was clearly percolating.

"Now what?" I asked, once the two Japanese had been led downstairs and out of the house into a second Black Maria.

"Now come the interrogations," Lolly said gruffly. "I guess I'll start with the small fry and see what I can learn before turning my attention to Madame Noguchi. She's going to be a tough nut to crack."

"She's got an orphanage on Darroch Road," I said. "There may be more girls—maybe young boys, too—being kept there."

"I'll check it out."

"I guess that's it for now, then?"

"Unless you have plans, Count."

"Plans?" I looked at him as he gave me a Lolly-like inscrutable smile.

"I thought you might like to do some spadework for me."

"What kind of spade have you got in mind, Lolly?"

"The shovelling shit kind. If you've got nothing else to do, you might like to look through all the stuff up here and down in the basement that the rats didn't nibble through. See what you can find that's of interest."

"Surely, *all* of it is of interest?"

"Depends on who you are, doesn't it? I mean, so far as I'm concerned, there's only so much I've got time for."

"Like?"

"Like *any* photographs that have got Chinese in them. And, of course, senior police officers if you happen to recognise them. The rest I couldn't care less about."

"If you'll excuse my saying so, Lolly, that doesn't sound very professional."

"Point taken, Count, But it's not as if I've got the manpower to sift through all these photographs, let alone listen to the tapes."

"Fair enough."

"Anyway, we don't have the space at the station to store all the stuff that's here, so it's going to be thrown away eventually. If you could sift through the material for me, Count, I'd be very grateful. Put whatever you think useful into the saddlebags of that motorbike of yours and ride off towards the horizon, like in the Hollywood films. I don't want to know about it, okay? I'll pick up the rest tomorrow some time. What you do with any photos you take with you is your business, but I'll give you one bit of advice."

"What's that, Lolly?"

"Don't try and blackmail Tu Yue-sheng." He barked out a jolly laugh.

"But how can I, Lolly? You told me to leave all the Chinese stuff alone."

"True, but you never know, do you?"

"Never know what?"

"Never know if you can trust a journalist. Against my policeman's judgement, Count, I've been trusting you all along. And you haven't broken that trust. Yet. But there's always a first time, isn't there?"

"Like with opium," I said remembering Trudi. Every addict had experienced a first time.

"A first time which ends up as the beginning of the end. Break my trust, Count, and I can assure you, it'll be the end of your charmed life here in Shanghai."

I bowed slightly. "Point taken, Lolly."

"Good. Now go downstairs and get to work. You've got until six o'clock tomorrow morning. No longer."

"Thanks a lot. I appreciate it."

"I'm putting a constable on guard outside the front door of the building to keep you safe. I hope you find whatever it is you're looking for."

So did I. But there was one more thing.

"What about the girls?"

"What about them?"

"What are you going to do with them?"

"Hmm." Lolly scratched his balding head. "You've got a point there, Count."

"Miyoko Noguchi told me they are orphans. If so, you need to find them a home. There's a convent I know the far side of Frenchtown. The sisters there might be willing to help."

"For a fee?"

"A fee would help. Maybe Madame Noguchi can be enticed to hand over her blackmail earnings in exchange for her freedom?"

"I'll see what can be done. Now go to work, Count. What is it they say in English? Time flies like an arrow?"

"Yes, and fruit flies like a banana."

That was the one and only time I saw Lolly look puzzled. Maybe he should have joined Archimedes in his bath. He did smell a bit pongy.

37.

I had just over six hours to go through everything. Luckily, I didn't need all that time. I knew that Trudi had been filmed about a week earlier and I quickly found the relevant drawer with a reel of exposed film and more than a dozen prints which I put into the saddlebag that I'd unhooked from my Čechie and brought into the Salon Pink's basement. Photographs of Victor's dalliance with a couple of underage Japanese girls took a little longer to find, at first because I wasn't sure when that evening had occurred. But then I recalled that he'd said it was the night of the big typhoon. More photographs and negatives quickly went into my saddlebag.

I opened drawer after drawer and flipped through a mass of revealing portraits of men and women in various states of sexual arousal. What came across was their sheer monotony. We're all pretty unimaginative when it comes to procreation—none more so than Kenji Doihara whose only position, it seemed, when having sex was to enter, or be entered, from behind. Although, like Victor, he seemed to have a penchant for pre-puberty girls, Doihara wasn't averse to having sex with other men and boys, including the smooth Japanese man Trudi had told me about. The two of them were pictured together, as well as in the company of young boys. They weren't my heterosexual cup of tea, but I slipped them into my saddlebag anyway. Doihara was a full colonel of the Kempeitai, after all. And I wanted to know more about the other man. Whoever he was, he was a real pervert.

Which left Miyoko Noguchi. Except I couldn't find any photographs of her at all. Was she, then, simply a professional Madame running a high-end whorehouse on Kiangse Road, no better and no worse than Gracie Gale next door, except for the fact that she employed underage women? From what Trudi had told me, this wasn't at all likely, so there had to be incriminating evidence somewhere. But it wasn't downstairs in the basement, that was for sure.

I scratched my head. After all, that's what one is supposed to do when puzzled. But scratching didn't produce a eureka moment; just a few flakes of dandruff that I brushed off the shoulders of my jacket. Where could she have hidden her own photographs?

I checked the prints I'd already put in my saddlebag of Trudi, just in case, but Miyoko Noguchi wasn't among them. Where then?

I went upstairs and searched the reception room where she first met clients before introducing them to whoever they desired. Nothing. And nothing on the first floor, either. Not in any of the cupboards housing the secret cameras and recording equipment. I had spent more than an hour searching the Salon Pink and come up with nothing.

But then I remembered the small tattoo of a snake on the ankles of the girls we'd rescued. I slapped the side of my head.

"Idiot!" I muttered and went back downstairs. Against one wall of the reception room was a rather beautiful step *tansu* chest. It was made from cedar and zelkova woods and emitted a very pleasant smell to make visitors to the Salon Pink feel immediately as if they were in Japan itself. On the top step was a tasteful but simple decoration of orchids and bull rushes rising from a shallow bowl, while in the *tokonoma* alcove nearby stood a sandalwood statuette of a black and white krait rising up from a basket, ready to strike and bite its victim with well-sculpted sharp fangs. A frightening contrast to the serenity of the flower arrangement beside it, but a clear indication of the Salon Pink's dual function as a den of aesthetic and sensual pleasure, on the one hand, and blackmail, on the other.

I picked up the statuette. As I had anticipated, the tall base unscrewed itself from the basket from which the snake emerged. Its inside was filled with film negatives. I held them up to the light and, even with black and white reversed, recognized the naked body of Miyoko Noguchi. So far as I could judge, she was always with another woman, never a man. That tallied with what Trudi had described to me. I assumed I would find her, too, among these negatives.

It was time to pack up and leave. I had enough material to blackmail a couple of dozen Shanghai worthies, including a British trading house *taipan*, a manager of the Standard Chartered Bank, a senior executive in British and American Tobacco, Roger Buckley's outfit, and the French Consul General. A shrewder man than I could have made himself rich for life. If truth be told, though, I was afraid of the boredom wealth would bring.

Outside it had begun to rain. The constable on guard looked a bit miserable, but still managed to salute me as I closed the front door. As I reached Ningpo Road, a car came down Kiangse Road from the bridge across the Soochow Creek and screeched to a halt outside Salon Pink. A short stout man with a Hitler-like moustache and wearing the uniform of a Kempeitai colonel jumped out and, pushing aside the constable on guard, leaped up the steps two at a time and banged on the front door. The constable said something, but Doihara brought a key out of his pocket and opened the door. Then he disappeared from view.

It was definitely time for me to get on my bike and beat a hasty retreat. Which is exactly what I did. The question was where should I retreat to? My apartment in Cathay Mansions or somewhere more secure? I needed to get rid of everything in the saddlebag behind me, and offload my haul somewhere I knew Doihara hadn't a hope in hell of finding it—Victor's penthouse at the very top of Sassoon House.

I looked at my watch. 2.40 am. There was a chance that the baronet was still awake, partying even. It was, after all, a Friday—well, now Saturday—night. And Victor wouldn't dream of turning me away when I told him what I had with me. He, too, was one victim among many in Noguchi's blackmailing scheme. He also happened to be a keen amateur photographer who had his own dark room up in his penthouse. I suspected he'd enjoy developing prints of Miyoko Noguchi lying naked in bed with another woman.

I parked my bike by the entrance to the Palace Hotel and walked across Nanking Road to Sassoon House. Taking the elevator as far as the dining room on the tenth floor, I walked up the staircase to Victor's apartment, rang the doorbell and held my breath.

The door was rather promptly opened by Perkins. At least somebody was awake.

"Count Bloom, sir, this is a pleasant surprise." He bowed me in.

"Hello, Perkins. I'm sorry to barge in at such a late hour, but is Sir Victor still up and about?"

"Barely, sir, if you see what I mean. He is in his pyjamas, but you will be relieved to hear that they are for the most part hidden under a dressing gown." He gave me the slightest hint of a dry smile. "Would you like me to announce you, sir? Or would you prefer the informality appropriate to his state of undress?"

Goodness knows how Perkins would have described the undressed state of all the people in the saddlebag under my arm. Unembellished limbs in disarray? I was pretty sure he'd have a euphemistic phrase to describe it. Something to do with birthday suits without a stitch on, probably.

"Good lord! Christopher! What on earth are you doing here at this godawful hour of the night? I was getting ready for bed. Drink?"

"Don't get up, Victor, please. Perkins, if you could make me another of your excellent Suffering Bastards, I'd be most grateful."

"Certainly, sir. And Sir Victor?"

"The same for me, too, Perkins. From the look on Christopher's face, I'm going to need it."

Perkins disappeared in the direction of wherever it was that he mixed his cocktails. A kitchen, I assumed, unless it was a pantry or skulduggery. Or did I mean scullery? It was rather late for thinking clearly.

"Well?" Victor said impatiently, tapping his stick on the table to get my attention. "What's so important that you have to come unannounced at three o'clock in the morning? I *was* on my way to bed, you know."

"Yes, I'm sure you were, Victor, and I apologise. I was myself on my way to bed when I realised that it would probably be of benefit to us both if I dropped by for a nightcap."

"Both of us?"

"Hopefully yes, Victor." I unstrapped the saddlebag that was beside me on the sofa. "I've had a rather eventful evening and I'm going to need quite a lot of your help when you've got the time. Meanwhile, however," I was hurriedly sorting through the prints and negatives I'd taken from Salon Pink and finally found the ones I was looking for. "You may be interested in these." I stood up and handed Victor everything I'd found of him in the company of a couple of underaged girls. It was true what he had told me. Two of the prints showed that he did have a camera with him and that he was indeed photographing his companions. Others focused on his erection. Or what there was of it.

Perkins reappeared with a silver tray and two Suffering Bastards which he set down on the table before retiring diplomatically. Had he seen his lordship in further disarray?

"My God, Christopher!" Victor exclaimed eventually. "Don't tell me you —"

"Yes, I did," I saved him breath. "Everything is here. You have no further fear of blackmail from Miyoko Noguchi."

"I can't thank you enough, Christopher. That woman's a snake alright!" he hissed. "But how did you get hold of these?" He waved one of the prints in the air.

With the measured assistance of, first, my own Suffering Bastard and then, when he realised he no longer needed his, the contents of Victor's glass, I told him everything.

For once he was speechless and sat in silence after I'd finished.

"I'd like to ask you a favour, Victor."

"Of course, dear boy. Of course," he replied absent-mindedly. He was still processing all the details of the story I'd told him.

"In my bag here, I have plenty more prints and negatives that I found in Salon Pink. Some of them are of a friend who came to me for help. Others are of well-known figures in Shanghai. These I'm going to put in a safe place—a bank deposit box or somewhere equally secure. But there is a group of a dozen or so negatives in which Miyoko Noguchi features—so far as I can make out, only in the company of other women, not men. Would you mind making prints of these negatives for me?"

"Prints of Madame Noguchi, one of the most beautiful, sensual and beguiling serpents I've ever come across? How could I possibly refuse, Christopher? You know how much I appreciate beauty in all its forms."

"Thank you, Victor. I was hoping you'd say that."

"Why don't you come round for dinner on Sunday evening? So far as I know, I've got nothing on. And if I have, I'll cancel it. We can have a quiet meal together and afterwards—providing I haven't drunk *too* much, of course—I'll give you a lesson in how to develop film and print it. How does that sound, my boy?"

For a boy I was up way beyond my bedtime. I stood up to leave.

"Perfect, Victor. And thank you."

38.

I found myself back in Sassoon House rather more promptly than I had anticipated. The next morning there was loud knocking on the door of my apartment. Not that I heard it. I was sleeping like a proverbial log until Fantom shook one of my shoulders deferentially.

"Massa, wakey wakey. Just now hab got one-piece Japanman come room inside. He blong muchee smellum wata."

I splashed my own face with water, put a dressing gown on over my pyjamas, and went into the living room where a young Japanese officer was waiting, as Fantom had warned me, smelling strongly of *Eau de Cologne*. He bowed apologetically.

"Kaunto Kuristofa Buroomu? My aporogies, butto Koroneru Doihara wonders wheza you would be kindo enough to join him for burekufasto."

I examined the young man's uniform.

"At Kempeitai headquarters?"

"No, Kaunto Buroomu. Koroneru Doihara is waiting for you at za Bundo Café."

It was probably better not to refuse, however deprived of sleep I felt. I didn't want the 'koroneru' to hold a grudge against me.

"I need to get dressed first."

The young officer bowed and hesitatingly left after I had assured him that I had my own means of transportation and would be at the Bund Café in half an hour's time.

For the second time that day I parked my Čechie in front of the Palace Hotel on Nanking Road. I could see Doihara sitting by the window of the café opposite.

"Colonel Doihara?" I stretched out my hand, the epitome of an affable Swedish count. "My apologies for keeping you waiting. And thank you for your invitation."

Doihara surprised me by speaking Russian—surprisingly good Russian.

"My pleasure, Count Blum. I hope you don't mind my speaking your father's tongue, but I'm afraid my English is far from perfect."

"Not at all, Colonel." We sat down. "It's a pleasure to hear Russian—especially such good Russian as yours—at this time of the morning. Where did you learn it?"

"Thank you. I was stationed in Manchuria for a while and picked it up from all the White Russian émigrés in Harbin. As I'm sure you know, it has been a Russian town for many years."

"So I've heard." It didn't fully explain his Muscovite accent. "But tell me, what is it that prompts you to invite me for breakfast so unexpectedly?"

The waiter took this as a cue to ask for our orders. I went the Lolly route and asked for scrambled eggs and bacon; Doihara continued his Russian pose and ordered blini with sour cream and red caviar as a topping. He had tea in a glass, I had coffee in a cup. And toast and marmalade, of course. Once the food had been served, Doihara got down to business.

"You were asking about my motivation in inviting you to join me here, so I will get straight to the point, Count Blum. I have reason to believe that you witnessed a police raid on an establishment in Kiangse Road last night. Or was it early this morning?"

"A bit of both, I'd say. Yes, I did, indeed Colonel Doihara."

He politely finished his mouthful of blini before asking his next question.

"Might I ask how you happened to be present at the time of the raid? Friday midnight is not the usual time for a newspaper reporter to be on the job, surely?"

"Certainly, it isn't, Colonel. That I witnessed the affair was entirely by chance. You see," I look around conspiratorially and lowered my voice, "I happened to have been visiting the establishment next door. Do you know it? Gracie Gale's?"

"I am not personally in the habit of visiting brothels," Doihara said coldly, his moustache bristling slightly as it probably did whenever he was angry. Or not telling the truth.

"No, of course not, Colonel. But I, you understand, am still a young man. From time to time I need to have my desires placated."

"At Gracie Gale's?"

"I like the atmosphere there," I smiled. "And, of course, the girls. There's one I can recommend if —"

He cut me short.

"So you were going into the brothel next door to the Salon Pink?"

"Not going in, Colonel, coming *out*."

"So early in the night? A bit unusual, surely?"

"Yes, for somebody who goes in at some point after dark. The trouble was I had gone to Gracie's for lunch."

"Lunch?"

"Yes. Didn't you know? She employs the best chef in town, Fat Lu. He used to work for the old Imperial Russian Legation in Peking and what he doesn't know about cooking in any one of seven languages isn't worth knowing." I parroted Roger Buckley.

"*A sō.* So you had lunch at Number 52 Kiangse Road? Then what?"

"Colonel!" I exclaimed in my best ironical mocking voice. "Surely, you don't wish to hear all about what followed. Unless, that is, you have some kind of perverted interest in what I like to do during sex?"

Doihara realised I was joking, but his face paled all the same.

"Suffice it to say, I spent a very pleasant afternoon in the company of an American girl called Belle. Unfortunately, she'd been booked by another client later that evening, so reluctantly we parted company. I went downstairs and spent a couple of pleasant hours in the company of Singapore Kate and Gracie herself. Do you know her? She's quite a character. Smokes like the proverbial chimney, laughs like Tallulah Bankhead, and calls all her clients 'hon.' I guess that would be something like *sakharok* in Russian."

"So you were leaving Gracie Gale's at around midnight?" Doihara prompted me sternly.

"Ah yes. Sorry. As I left Number 52, I noticed a policeman standing outside the house next door. There was quite a commotion going on inside. Men fighting, girls screaming. That sort of thing. Then it got all quiet. Of course, I asked the policeman standing on guard outside what was going on. He said, rather helpfully, that it was a raid. Apparently the Salon Pink was employing underage girls as prostitutes. The constable also said the brothel was run by a Japanese woman—a certain Madame Noguchi. Do you know her by any chance, Colonel Doihara?"

"Anything else?" he asked coldly, ignoring my question. I wasn't sure if he believed my story or not, but it was the best I could come up with at this time in the morning, even though the coffee was beginning to help defog my brain. I had to show that I was a proper newshound.

"Yes. I asked who the detective in charge was and was given a name. Lo Li-kwei. People call him Lolly Lo."

"A man you know from the Simon Meyer kidnapping case."

"Exactly. Which was how I persuaded the constable to call Lolly outside to talk to me. He explained that a complaint had been made by a couple of clients about the Japanese Madame's habit of blackmailing them for money. Apparently, photographs were being taken of clients doing naughty things in bed with young girls. But that's as much as Lolly was prepared to tell me. It was, he said, 'an ongoing investigation.'"

"Anything else?" Doihara asked again. "As you will appreciate, Count Blum, the fact that a Japanese woman is involved means that, as Colonel in charge of the Kempeitai in Hongkew, I, too, am involved. It is my duty to make enquiries and ensure that wrongful arrest hasn't been made."

"Of course, Colonel. Quite right and proper."

"And you didn't go inside this Salon Pink? You didn't observe what had taken place there?"

"No. The Inspector put a constable on guard at the door and wouldn't let me in."

"So that's all you can tell me?"

"I'm afraid it is, Colonel. I was intending to interview Inspector Lo this morning, but your invitation has diverted me. Temporarily, at least."

"Hmmm." Doihara was eyeing me in a slightly pained manner. Perhaps the blinis didn't agree with him for he stood up suddenly and tossed his napkin onto his empty plate. "Please excuse me, Count Blum. I'm not entirely satisfied by your explanation, so let me warn you: I'll be watching you from now on."

"I'm sorry to see you leave so soon, Colonel Doihara." I also stood, but kept my napkin firmly in my hand. There was still the toast and marmalade to be enjoyed. I held out my hand. "But thank you for inviting me to breakfast. Please be assured that I will also be watching you. This is, after all, Shanghai." I gave him the benefit of my most winning smile.

He ignored my hand and bowed stiffly, before turning on his heel and calling for the bill on his way out of the café. A small Datson 10 was waiting for him outside—not quite the shape or size he doubtless felt entitled to as a senior officer in the Kempeitai, but the car—there were only about a dozen of them in the world—was at least Japanese.

39.

I managed to remember my English manners and arrived for dinner at

Victor's ten minutes late. Perkins looked suitably impressed.

"Welcome back, Count Bloom. Might I ask, sir, whether you are still suffering when it comes to drinking a cocktail before dinner?"

"Are you implying, Perkins, that I might be a bastard?"

"Far be it from me, sir, to impugn your parentage. Even if you are not British," he smiled. I guess he needed a sense of humour. It can't have been fun being Victor's lapdog.

"Under the circumstances, Perkins, I think a Stenger will do me fine."

"Very good, sir. I believe you know where to find Sir Victor. He is in his usual chair by the fireplace."

"Thank you, Perkins."

The Stenger, when it arrived, was good, the dinner better—an excellent curried trout, followed by orange pancake. "My recipes, you know," Victor said proudly.

We talked a lot about his family and how he had decided to leave Bombay and transfer the family business to Shanghai.

"In my opinion, Bombay was heading for economic suicide and the outlook for foreigners in India as a whole didn't look too bright," he said, before adding casually, "and then there were the taxes. Totally outrageous."

In my experience, tycoons always did their best to avoid paying taxes. That was how they became tycoons.

Victor also told me about his flying experiences.

"I've always loved flying, you know. The thrill of being in the air, totally free to do as one pleases without being hemmed in by anything other than one's shoulder straps. I got my aviator's certificate from the Royal Aero Club back in January 1911. Number 52, it was. Just imagine. I was the fifty-second person in the whole of Great Britain to learn how to fly," he took a sip of the excellent Louis XIII cognac Perkins had served us with the Stilton. "Not bad, eh?"

"Not bad at all. Mark you, my mother was the third woman in Sweden to get a driver's license."

"Ooh! Do I detect a bit of one-upmanship, Christopher?"

"Of course, Victor. You're a baronet, while I'm a mere count. I can't let you win all the time!"

He laughed loudly.

"Touché. Anyway, when the war came, I started flying an Avro 504. It was early in 1915 and I was a young lieutenant in the Royal Naval Air Service. I still don't know what happened exactly, but I lost control of the plane and crash landed in a field near Dover. I broke my right arm here," he indicated a point just below the elbow, "and dislocated my right hip."

"Doesn't sound pleasant."

"It wasn't. Of course, I'd done it before once."

"Done what? Broken an arm?"

"No, crashed a plane. I was planing in to land without the engine on and got my height above ground wrong. As a result, I 'landed,' if that's the word, about twenty five feet above the ground. Not the cleverest way to show off my skills."

"What happened?"

"What happened? Well, I tried to switch on the engine, but it was too late. The plane pancaked, then bounced up really high in the air before coming down with a crash that broke the landing chassis. The plane then stood on its head, spinning round on the stump of the propeller, with me strapped in as if I were on some kind of very fast miniature Ferris wheel at a funfair."

"No fun, then. But weren't you hurt?"

"Miraculously, no. I suppose that first crash really was tempting providence," he paused. Then, "You must have been too young, Christopher, to be in the Great War?"

"Just about. I suppose I could have joined the German army if I'd felt so inclined. But I didn't. Sweden was neutral and I didn't like what I read about what was happening on the battle front."

"Wise man. Finally, though, we all got peace. And what a time we had of things. I don't know how life was in Sweden, Christopher—it's not a country I'm familiar with—but the 'Roaring Twenties' were quite something. The Great War was behind us, along with Spanish influenza. Both had taken their toll. Between them they'd killed off tens of millions of young men and women—young men mainly. And if they hadn't been killed, then, like me, they'd suffered all sorts of physical mutilations—losing arms, legs, and God knows what else," he laughed uncomfortably before continuing.

"Anyway by 1920, people were tired of wartime austerity. London after the Great War was a strange place to be. To be honest, an interesting place to be if you mixed in the right circles."

"As you did?"

"As I did. Those were crazy times, I can assure you. *Les années folles.* Wild parties, wild young men who embarked on the wildest of deeds, but most of all wild women. Bright Young Things, the newspapers called them, with their bobbed hair, loose clothing, calf-revealing skirts, high heel shoes, and a cigarette dangling from one hand or painted lips. They'd learned from Hollywood films how to tart themselves up, you know; how to make their mouths alluring with lipstick, and eyes mysterious thanks to a touch of mascara and kohl. They varnished their nails, dressed in *the* most revealing clothes, and frequented all the trendy night spots in town. They wanted to be *seen*, you understand, to make a splash and they'd do anything to attract a man's attention. That sort of thing was quite new."

Victor refilled his tulip glass from the square-shaped decanter of cognac on its silver platter, before holding it up in my direction with a querying raised eyebrow. I leaned forward to have my own glass topped up. We raised our glasses in silent toast.

"It's hard to imagine the things we'd get up to, or why we got up to them, but we did. Partying all night in fancy dress. Dancing the Charleston, the cake walk, the flea hop, or whatever the latest craze from New York was. Going on treasure hunts throughout the city on public transport, drinking alcohol, snorting cocaine, taking off our clothes in public, even swapping married partners," he sighed, almost nostalgic. "You name it, Christopher, we did it."

He paused to light a cigar, then sat back puffing contentedly, eyes distant.

"Some of the young women were *very* young—too young, really. Like our mutual friend, Kiki. But you know how we men are. Always eager to be flattered and praised, and these youthful flappers knew how to flatter. They used to hang around all the clubs that the high and mighty frequented—the Kit-Kat, the Embassy, Frolics, the Trocadero— waiting for the chance to join a drunken crowd of highfalutin frolickers and later take off their clothes for the man they decided to fancy that particular evening."

Victor paused and puffed. He seemed to be weighing something up. Then he began again.

"As I said, the looseness of these young women's fashions was accompanied by a loosening of morals. They started drinking and smoking in public. They danced and socialised happily with whoever they met. Romances were formed and almost as quickly broken off. Both men and women seemed intent on experimenting with relationships of all kinds."

Like Trudi, I reflected. Maybe Shanghai was going to experience its own Roaring Thirties.

"Meanwhile, they were content to lose a virginity that had, before the Great War, been prized as an essential attribute to marriage. Remember, they could now get instructions in birth control and had learned how to avoid unwanted pregnancies by not having sex during certain days of the month.

"And it was the same for men. For a certain kind of man, that is. Suddenly, it seemed no longer necessary for queers to hide in the cupboard. Homosexuality was—still is, of course—a crime, but somehow it didn't seem to matter quite so much. All sorts of liaisons were formed. Mark you, I'm talking about the upper classes, Christopher, not the ordinary working men and women of the country. They just carried on in their conservative ways, even if they did vote Labour."

Another pause, another puff. I sensed we had come to the crux of Victor's story.

"I'm not sure how good your knowledge of recent history is, old boy, but in 1921 the Crown Prince of Japan paid a state visit to Europe. He'd never been abroad before, you know. In fact, no member of the Japanese Imperial Household had ever been on a state visit abroad. So there was quite a palaver and all the stops were pulled out to make sure young Hirohito had a good time while he was in England, which was in fact most of the time he was travelling. The palace did its utmost to accommodate the shy young man. On the very first morning after the Crown Prince's arrival, King George wandered into his bedroom in his dressing gown and suspenders and began to explain to his Japanese visitor the meaning and practice of a constitutional monarchy."

"Didn't seem to have had that much an effect."

"No, maybe not. Meanwhile, as Prince of Wales, Edward was charged with accompanying Hirohito to state banquets and less formal occasions. This made sense for they were, after all, equals in terms of succession to their respective thrones. Actually, Edward took quite a shine to the young Japanese and tried to teach him how to play golf. I know, I was there. There's a photograph I took of the two princes together in their tweed caps and jackets, plus fours, woollen stockings and brogues, each with driver in one hand and arm on the other's shoulder. Quite touching really."

"How come you managed to take a photo like that?"

"It was thanks to my cousin Philip. He was in with Edward so he invited me along, together with two or three other members of his set. After the golf, we all had tea, because that is what *one did*. And then we had drinks. And then Edward suggested we all go to Claridge's for dinner. Which, of course, we did and a jolly good time was had by all. There were a couple of terribly, terribly young ladies who took Hirohito in hand. One of them you've met, Christopher."

"You mean, Kiki?"

Victor gave me the benefit of one of his enigmatic lynx-like smiles. "They taught him how to dance the fox trot and something one of them had just encountered in New York called the Charleston. Goodness! That was quite something, Christopher. Everybody went simply *wild*. Even Hirohito took off his rimless spectacles and began to let his hair down."

"Didn't his entourage get a bit nervous about that? I mean, he was heir to the Chrysanthemum Throne, after all."

"They probably would have, but Edward rather cunningly had got Hirohito to dismiss them all, except for one young man from the Imperial Household. I think he was a minor prince, son of one of the Emperor's courtesans, although *which* emperor I've no idea. Maybe it wasn't one of the emperors at all. I really don't know. All I know is he was *there*, together with Hirohito, dancing wildly with Kiki and a couple of other girls with double-barrelled surnames. Even with Prince George at one point. Just as flushed and excited. Just as determined to have the time of his life. Which is what he did, I suppose."

"And then, in need of some sleep, you all went your separate ways and the imperial visitor accompanied the Prince of Wales back to Buckingham Palace."

"The palace? Good God, no. True, some of the party did in fact head off home, but not our Hirohito."

"So what happened, then?"

"About eight of us went on to Frolics. Do you know it?"

"Frolics?" Roger's hideout, "can't say that I do," I lied.

"No, probably not. It's closed down now. It was a nightclub located just off Regent Street and was popular because it provided people like us with somewhere to drink and dance after the pubs had closed." Victor sighed theatrically. "That's what I like most about Shanghai. There are none of these ridiculously restrictive licensing laws of the kind you find in England."

"So what happened after you got to Frolics?"

Victor grew sombre and pursed his lips.

"I suppose you could say things got a bit out of hand."

"How much out of hand?"

"Totally. The management decided to get rid of all its other guests soon after we arrived. I mean, it's not often that the Prince of Wales turns up for a dance, is it? So they shooed everyone out, apart from a couple of rather gorgeous, young blondes whom Edward—or David as we all called him—had taken an immediate fancy to. I've no idea who they were and I don't think anyone else did, either. But they were, as I said, rather attractive. They certainly put the shotguns to shame."

"The shotguns?"

"The women with double-barrelled names. Blanchard-Gough, ffitch-Hamilton, and our friend Kiki, who had been instructing young Hirohito in the latest dance crazes."

"And the other two women?"

"The blondes you mean? They had quite exotic names, too, I seem to remember. Elena. Or was it Katerina? And Julia, pronounced with a Y. Swedish, I think, unless they were Estonians. At any rate, they were continentals of some sort from your part of the world," he sighed wistfully. "Definitely not your average English woman."

"But they spoke English?"

"Better than you or I, old boy. And properly brought up, too. They didn't know the Charleston or turkey trot, but they could waltz and tango and certainly knew how to press their shapely forms against the two men they were dancing with. Lucky devils!"

"You mean Edward and Hirohito?"

"Spot on. Edward was his usual suave self, of course, but Hirohito was clearly over-excited. He'd definitely had too much to drink during the course of the evening. He started shouting loudly and grew very red in the face. And then, at one point, he suddenly took off his tie and started unbuttoning his shirt, laughing loudly and exclaiming 'Too hot! Too hot!' Edward, of course, was the perfect host so he did the same. Prince George and the Crown Prince's companion went a bit further and took their shirts off completely. It was clear they'd taken a fancy to each other. The girls joined in. Babe Blanchard-Gough got up on the table at which we were sitting and did a striptease, laughing shrilly all the while until she was in nothing but her high heels, stockings, silk panties, and suspender belt. Elena and Yulia were rather more modest. Maybe things weren't done that way in Sweden or wherever.

"As you can imagine, the booze we'd been drinking more or less since teatime, when we'd each downed a glass of splendid Armagnac, was having its effect. George exclaimed he simply had to 'powder his nose,' so Babe suggested he sprinkle some 'talcum powder' on her naked body. This seemed like a simply *divine* idea, although Hirohito was a bit lost as to what was going on. His English teachers in the Imperial Palace had obviously failed to tutor him in conversations involving cocaine."

"But he got the gist?"

"And not just the gist, old boy. Blanchard-Gough proceeded to lie down on the table. George sprinkled the powder liberally onto her body and we all took it in turns to sniff our way around her belly button and nipples."

"All of you?"

"*All* of us. Yes, even our Hirohito. We were soon all as high as kites, of course. Maybe that's why I took it into my head to use my camera to record what was going on."

"You didn't?"

"I did. Of course, I had to ask his Royal Highness' permission. But he was as high as the rest of us and said it was OK by him. Hirohito was still dancing round the room half-naked shouting God knows what in Japanese and laughing his silly falsetto laugh. George and the others thought it'd be a jolly good show if I were to provide both Japanese chappies with a souvenir of their night out on the town. Probably the only night out they'd ever get in their lives, to judge by the way the Imperial Household stooges normally marshalled their inhibitions."

"So you took photos of them all?"

"The whole lot. The Blanchard-Gough woman spread out on the table with her head lolling over the edge, looking at me with what I can only politely call a lascivious smile. My cousin Philip with our Kiki sitting on his knee in a state of *déshabillé* with her arms draped around his neck, and the red smudge of her lips on his cheek. Not something, really, that he would want to show his wife. Or, for that matter, his constituents in Hythe."

"And the Crown Prince?"

"Ah! Now we come to the crux of it all, don't we?" Once again he puffed on his Havana. I definitely preferred Trudi's *Habanita*.

"Meaning?"

"Our Japanese Crown Prince had by now divested himself of his shirt, so I snapped a portrait of him looking straight at the camera— his eyes, it's true, slightly glazed over, but clearly aware of the fact that he was being photographed. It's a half portrait of him from the waist up, with one arm thrown carelessly round the waist of a young woman, the mysterious Yulia, who is cuddling up against his naked torso. The shoulder strap of her dress has somehow slipped down to reveal a perfectly formed breast, while her left arm extends diagonally downwards towards—if the portrait were full length—the Crown Prince's crotch. Of course, he's wearing trousers, but you don't know that from the photo. Hirohito's normally shy appearance has disappeared, along with his rimless glasses, and his expression, thanks to the wine and the coke, is one of complete abandonment. It has the triumphant look of a man who is certain he's on the brink of losing his imperial virginity."

"A pose not quite befitting the future Emperor of Heaven, then?"

Victor laughed. "Definitely not."

"And what about his companion, the Japanese princeling? Did you snap him, too?"

"Did I snap him!" It wasn't a query so much as a triumphant exclamation. "The princeling and George were in total disarray. Each was fondling the other's cock while their tongues explored each other's mouths. To judge by the size of their respective appendages, George may have realised he'd bitten off more than he could chew."

"In a manner of speaking."

"In a manner of speaking. And, of course, doing."

"And did they? Do it, I mean."

"Possibly later. Who knows? But not then."

"Why not?"

"Because suddenly, with no warning at all, the nightclub was overrun by plain clothes police. "

"A liquor raid, then?"

"No, Special Branch. Somebody, somewhere had tipped them off. Not surprising really. After all, two future heads of realms were carousing gaily without their customary court chaperones. That wasn't *on*. The Special Branch officers *knew* who they were going to find inside

Frolics and they already had a Rolls Royce outside the door waiting to usher their royal highnesses home. The rest of us were questioned briefly, then ordered to leave and keep mum on pain of death. So I got in a taxi with this Japanese princeling chappy and dropped him off at the Savoy where he was staying with the rest of his bunch, before hieing back to my flat in Belgravia."

"A bit of a come-down, that ending, after all the earlier excitement. What happened to the two Swedish girls?"

"God alone knows. Maybe languishing in Wormwood Scrubs for improper use of a royal cock? Or deported as Bolshies, more likely. The Soviet Union is Special Branch's *bête noir*, after all, and they probably thought that Sweden or Estonia was part of Russia. Really, though, I've no idea, Christopher. Never set eyes on them again."

"So everything was hushed up? No scandal in the newspapers? Nothing like that?"

"As one would expect. Special Branch is very protective of our royal family."

"And of Japan's, too, it seems."

"But of course. The Crown Prince was on a state visit, after all. The last thing anyone wanted was a diplomatic incident."

"A scandal, you mean?"

"A scandal," Victor acknowledged. "The funny thing about it all, though, was that the police never searched my bag."

"What bag?"

"Ah! Maybe you haven't noticed? I often carry a small satchel over my shoulder when I go out. It's because of my pegs. I sometimes need medicines to relieve the pain and I can hardly carry them around in the pockets of my dinner jacket, can I? The satchel's useful, too, because it allows me take my camera with me as well."

"And you had your satchel with you that night?"

"I did, indeed. The first thing I did when the police came into the room was put my camera into it and hang the satchel across my body from one shoulder. I also made my war wounds look rather more obvious than usual as I hobbled around on my sticks." He smiled at the recollection. "Maybe that was why they didn't search me. But still. They should have known I was in the habit of going around town with a camera. And yet they never wondered out loud if I'd happened to take a photograph or two of what they clearly thought of as 'debaucheries.' It seemed like, once they'd got their royal personages in hand, the rest of us didn't matter one jot. I've always thought that a bit odd, frankly."

"As you say, they were probably relieved just to have found Edward, Hirohito and the other two princes."

"Probably."

"Still, it reeks of scandal, doesn't it? I mean, there you've got the

Prince of Wales *in flagrante delicto* with some possibly Swedish, possibly something else bird; the Crown Prince of Japan naked to the waist with another Swedish, or whatever, blonde bombshell clutching his crotch as they pose for a snapshot; a Japanese princeling standing half naked with one arm thrown round the equally naked torso of Prince George, each grabbing the other's royal penis. At least one double-barrelled aristocrat stark naked on the dining table. It's not just newspapermen but spies, too, who'd have a field day if they knew what had gone on and were able to get hold of those photos."

"Precisely."

I sat very still and waited for more.

"And now, Christopher, I think there's something a bit different you should see." He stood up from the table and grabbed his sticks. "Come."

I followed Victor out of the dining room and along a corridor towards the back of the penthouse. The walls were lined with framed photographs of young women—both Caucasian and Chinese, many of them well-known actresses and socialites—in various states of undress.

Victor stopped, took a key out of his dinner jacket pocket and inserted it in the keyhole of a door half-way down the corridor.

"One can never be too careful," he said as he unlocked the door and showed me into a large well-appointed room. One half of it contained camera equipment and dozens of pharmacists' chests like the ones I'd looked through in the Salon Pink. These, too, were carefully labelled with names of photographic subjects, I assumed, in alphabetical order under each year.

"Sit yourself down, Christopher, while I get you your prints."

He hobbled into the other half of the room—the dark room—and came back with a pile of prints and negatives.

"These are what you gave me on Friday night, the photographs of Miyoko Noguchi that you found and asked me to develop for you." He began to lay out one print after another neatly aligned on a large rosewood table set under a strong lamp in the middle of the room. Each showed Miyoko Noguchi, lying on her back naked, facing up towards the camera.

Beside her were a dozen or so different women, one of whom was Trudi who, I had to admit, looked gorgeous. The photo must have been taken early on before her decline into opium usage. Another print, which made my heart beat a little quicker, was of Isa. The other women were of all kinds—Asian, Caucasian, Eurasian, even one black. Miyoko was clearly catholic in her tastes. But most of them, the black woman was one exception, were well-known Shanghai figures. The other exception brought back memories and almost had me crying. Maisy. How the two women had come to know each other I had no idea, but it was a joy to be gazing at Mei-si's beautiful smile once more.

I pushed the print towards Victor.

"Victor, this woman helped me find Simon for you and lost her life as a result. Could you enlarge the print for me? I'd like to frame it and hang it on the wall above my bed. For old times' sake."

"But of course, dear boy," he looked at the photo. "What a beautiful smile!"

"That's what I thought. The most beautiful smile in the world. She deserves immortality."

"I'll do it straight from the negative. The print will come out much better that way," he paused for a fraction of a second before continuing. "There is, however, another print that you might like to see."

He turned over the last remaining photograph on the table. Miyoko was lying face up again with the kind of distant, satisfied smile that suggested she had just attained an orgasm. Beside her, with one hand firmly between her thighs just below her tuft of pubic hairs, lay Kiki Montagu-Rose.

For a few seconds I was too dumbfounded to say anything. Then, "Good lord, Victor. Had you any idea?"

"That she was bisexual? None whatsoever. Although now that I've seen the evidence, I'm not surprised. Kiki is nothing if not enigmatic. I have a favour, though, to ask."

"I think I know what it is. You'd like to keep a print?"

Victor fixed me with his mischievous lynx-like gaze.

"If you have no objection."

"None whatsoever. But I have a favour to ask of you in return."

"And what might that be?" Cautious now.

"Would you be prepared to give me a print of the photographs you were describing earlier? The ones at Frolics."

He pursed his lips and frowned.

"I'm not really sure I should do that."

"No. I appreciate your hesitation. The thing is, I believe there's a photo of the Japanese princeling you mentioned among the prints I took from the Salon Pink on Friday night. I need to go through them all to find out and then show both to a Japanese journalist whom I trust completely. For purposes of identification and advice, you understand."

It was a flimsy excuse and we both knew it. But Victor also knew he was deeply in my debt.

He put his stinking cigar once more into his mouth. Maybe the lungful of smoke helped him come to a decision. After what seemed like an age, he said.

"Christopher, you've helped me twice during the past couple of months, first with Simon and now with some unfortunate photographs taken in the midst of a typhoon. To put it bluntly, I owe you. And if there's one thing I've learned as a businessman, it is always to repay one's debts. So, yes. I will give you prints of the photographs I was talking about earlier. But I beg of you, do not publish them. Ever. Do we have a deal?"

"We have a deal, Victor. And you've got one, too, that you probably decided you'd never get."

"I have? What's that?"

"A photograph of Kiki without any clothes on."

He laughed. "And not a shower curtain in sight, either."

40.

For once I missed all the fun. Other hacks had got the scoop. But only because they happened to be at their customary watering hole—the Horse and Hounds Bar on the ninth floor of Sassoon House—exchanging gossip about what was being called the Battle of Chapei. Anything to avoid going into the danger zone.

Isa and I had arranged to meet each other in the bar. By chance we arrived downstairs at exactly the same time. In the street outside half a dozen rōnin toughs were threatening a couple of policemen standing by the entrance to the rotunda, but they quickly ran off at the sound of a police car bell approaching.

"Bloody rōnin!"

"Yes, but what are they doing outside the Cathay Hotel?"

We soon found out. On stepping out of the lift at the ninth floor we were surrounded by chaos. The bar was in total disarray, chairs and tables turned over, glasses and bottles broken. One barman, whom I'd heard Victor address as Chappell, was nursing a deep cut in his forehead. Another was helping a couple of waiters to clear up the mess.

"What's been going on here?"

"Had a visit from some Japanese rōnin, didn't we?" Chappell muttered angrily. "After as much drink as they could get while their bosses were upstairs."

"Upstairs?"

"Yes, Count Bloom," one of the waiters had recognized me. "Two men and a woman, I think it was, went up to Sir Victor's penthouse. He happens to be out this evening, at the Canidrome races I believe. They must have known that because they were up there at least fifteen, maybe twenty, minutes before they came back down again. That was the signal for the half dozen monkey men here to leave. But they decided to cause a bit of damage first by throwing the furniture around and breaking as many bottles and glasses as they could lay their hands on. That got rid of our customers, of course."

"The woman," I asked. "Was she wearing a kimono, John?"

"Yes, sir. Tasty item, she was. Unlike her companions. One of the men was in naval uniform. Nasty piece of work, if you ask me. Real dwarf of a man. Ordered everyone around as if he was God or something. The way small people often do."

Lieutenant Fujii. Unless Napoleon had come back to life.

"And the other man?"

"He was some kind of army officer by the looks of him. Short, stocky, with a little moustache."

"Wearing an armband with Chinese characters in red?"

"That's it, Count. And a red band round his cap. Had long boots up to his knees, he did."

The Kempeitai uniform. Doihara.

"Thanks a lot, John. You've been most helpful." I jerked my head up to Victor's penthouse. "Is anyone up there now?"

"Yes, sir. The police. A Chinese detective is in charge."

Together with Isa, I mounted the last two floors to Victor's penthouse. A police constable was standing at the door. I remembered him from our failed attempt to find Simon Meyer at the Japanese temple in Hongkew.

"Constable Wang, how are you?"

Wang came to attention.

"Mr Broom, sir. Chief Inspector Lo is inside, inspecting the damage. You'll find him in Sir Victor's photography studio."

We stepped inside. One of the Art Deco prints on the wall was slightly askew, but otherwise the penthouse and its rooms seemed as usual. Victor's studio, however, was another matter. The door had been broken open and Lolly was standing in the midst of a mass of film and prints that had been scattered all over the floor and trampled on. The intruders had clearly been in a hurry to find what they were looking for.

"Well if it isn't my young detective," exclaimed Lolly with a smile that became more welcoming the moment he spotted Isa behind me. "What brings you up here?"

"The same that has brought you here, Lolly. A break-in. Know who it was?"

"Japanese, that's for sure. And a Japanese who controls the gang of rōnin who created such a mess downstairs in the bar. I wonder who that might be."

"To judge by one of the waiters' description, Colonel Doihara, Lieutenant Fujii, and the ever present Madame Noguchi."

"The usual suspects, then? But what are they doing ransacking Sir Victor's studio while he's out? They clearly knew it was the valet's day off. Parkin, I think his name is."

"Perkins, Lolly."

"Parkin, Perkins, the point is, the one evening he isn't here, the rōnin break in. I'm suspicious of coincidences like that."

"Perkins is absolutely straight, Lolly. Believe me."

"Hmm." Lolly didn't look convinced.

"Remember what you told me about the man whose wife was found drowned in the bath."

"Maybe you're right. But tell me, Count, why does Sir Victor have *two* baths in his bathroom?"

"Ah! So you've been exploring, eh?" I laughed. "Apparently, while he's happy to share his bed with any woman, he refuses to allow her to share his bath. Don't ask me why."

"Hmm. Since you know so many of the baronet's secrets, young man, perhaps you can enlighten me on what the intruders were looking for in this studio? I assume it has something to do with his hobby of taking compromising photographs of famous people."

"Almost certainly, Lolly. Victor had some of the photos I took from the Salon Pink the other night."

"He did? Do you think they're still here?"

"Somehow I doubt it. They were of Madame Noguchi."

"So that's what they were after?"

"Amongst other things, yes."

"What other things, Count?" Lolly asked sharply.

I thought it advisable to come clean. The last thing I wanted was to spend hours or days being 'interviewed' by Lolly and his subordinates. So I told him what I knew. Which was what Victor had told me about photographs he'd taken of the Emperor Hirohito during his state visit to England ten years previously. Isa's look of open-mouthed astonishment made me improvise and place the Blanchard-Gough woman at the Crown Prince's side, but I described accurately Prince George's mutual fondling of a Japanese princeling.

"Well, well," Lolly shook his head admiringly, "The things members of royalty get up to in their spare time."

"Which is virtually all their time."

"True. Idle bastards. Thank Buddha we got rid of our own imperial dynasty. But imagine, Count, what someone like Tu Yue-sheng would do if he managed to get his hands on a print like that."

"Or even the Nationalist government."

"*Any* government, come to that. British, Japanese, Russian, Chinese—you name it."

"Maybe the Japanese have now got hold of it. That's what Madame Noguchi and her friends were here for."

"Makes sense," Lolly pushed away an upturned box of negatives on the floor with one foot. "Still, that's not my problem, is it? I'm here to investigate the break-in itself, and if it's Japanese who are involved—

especially if one of those Japanese is Colonel Doihara himself—all I can do is take a statement from the waiter downstairs, file a report and move on. There's no way I'm going to be allowed to make an arrest, especially in the current climate. Admiral Shiozawa will be screaming for my blood and claiming I've insulted the Chrysanthemum Throne, or something equally pretosperous. No. I'm done here for now, Count." He turned towards the corridor. "What about you two?"

"I guess we should stick around till Perkins comes back."

"He should be here soon. He's been at the Canidrome betting on Sir Victor's greyhounds at the races."

"Hopefully they won?"

"Not by the look on his face, I'm told. It hasn't been Sir Victor's evening really, has it?" He stopped in the drawing room and looked out of the window. "Not a bad view, eh? Frankly, I think he'd be better off eating those dogs. Except greyhounds are far too thin to make a proper meal. Have you ever eaten dog, Missy?" He turned to Isa.

"Not knowingly," she smiled.

"No, I suppose not. You don't know what you're missing, though. Take it from me, I know plenty about gastromony," he patted his stomach lovingly. "There's nothing like a good dog for dinner. A real delicacy if properly prepared."

We were saved further gastronomic discussion by the sudden arrival of Perkins.

"Count Bloom, sir, and Madam," was all he could exclaim. For once he really had lost his composure.

"Perkins! We've just been assessing the damage with Inspector Lo here. I'm afraid Sir Victor's studio is in rather a mess."

"That's alright, sir. Just leave everything with me."

We did just that and headed back to the hallway, where a porthole-like window afforded us a view of the river and Admiral Shiozawa's battle fleet at anchor in Warship Row. I was about to comment on what I'd like to do to that gentleman when Victor appeared, a little out of breath after hauling himself up a couple of flights of stairs with his sticks.

"Christopher! And, if I'm not mistaken, Irene Wiedemeyer. This *is* a surprise. A very pleasant one given the circumstances. I've only just heard the news."

He came towards us down the hallway and pointed one of his sticks in the direction of the drawing room as Perkins emerged from the study, ready as always to serve his lord and master's visitors.

"Why don't we all sit down while you tell me about what happened in my absence. I'm sure Perkins here will be able to attend to our needs. This evening, I suspect, a Corpse Reviver might be the most appropriate cocktail."

"Not a Greyhound, Sir Victor?" Lolly laughed jollily.

"Not if it's anything like the one which ran at the Canidrome this evening. It looked more like a Brass Monkey by the time it got to the finishing post." Victor smiled wryly, before fixing Lolly with his lynx-like stare. "So tell me, Inspector Lo, what happened?"

"It seems as if Colonel Doihara, Madame Noguchi and a certain Lieutenant Fujii, to judge by the description we have of them, broke into your penthouse and did a thorough search of your studio along the corridor there," Lolly pointed towards the drawing room door. "In the meantime, their gang of thugs made a mess of the bar downstairs, Sir Victor, and roughed up a couple of members of your staff.

"And?" The lynx-like stare bore into Lolly who, as usual, seemed unperturbed.

"And what they did or did not find, I have no idea, Sir Victor. To judge by the mess, I suspect that they didn't find whatever it was they were looking for. At least, not all of it. The studio is covered with upturned boxes and drawers and negatives and prints all over the floor. But you, Sir Victor, are the only person here, I think, who knows why they broke in. Any thoughts you might like to share with me?"

Perkins chose this moment to deliver four Corpse Revivers. I wasn't sure that the gin and Cointreau did more than dull my senses, but the hint of absinthe made my heart grow fonder. I gave Isa's hand a discreet squeeze.

After returning his glass to the table beside him, Victor took hold of one of his sticks and placed it firmly between his legs. Carefully, he twisted its silver handle until it separated from the stick.

"This, Inspector Lo, was what they were almost certainly looking for." He turned the silver handle upside down in his hand and tapped it gently. Out popped a small black canister—the kind that held film. "I'm not going to tell you what this film contains, Inspector, but I can assure you it's scandalous enough to bring down a government or two, including the Japanese government. That's why Doihara wants to get his hands on it."

Victor slipped the canister back inside the silver handle, which he then carefully screwed back onto his stick.

"Do you want me to put that in my report, Sir Victor?"

"I'd prefer it if you didn't, Inspector Lo. What the thieves were looking for isn't relevant, is it? Especially since they didn't in fact steal anything. Or did they?"

"Possibly. I don't know. But what about the identities of the thieves?"

"What about them? It's not as if you're going to arrest a colonel in the Kempeitai, a naval lieutenant, and whatever role Madame Noguchi is playing other than that of procuress."

"A gang of rōnin, then?"

Lolly stood up to take his leave. Unusually, he seemed in a bit of a hurry.

"A gang of rōnin it is," Victor drawled. "And in the meantime, life must go on."

"Until it doesn't."

Isa had her killer look. Woe betide anyone who stood in her way.

41.

"There are things I think you should know, *mein Blümchen*."

We were back in my apartment, where Fantom had served us *char siu pao* meat buns and *jiaozi* dumplings to go with a bottle of chilled Côtes de Provence rosé. A strange combination, perhaps, but it suited our mood. 'Little flower' had always been her pet name for me. I preferred it to *Zuckerschnute* or any of the endearments I'd exchanged with Luda and Trudi.

"What things, Isa?"

"I hope you won't be too shocked, Rusty, when I tell you that I know Madame Noguchi."

"Know Miyoko?"

"In the Biblical sense."

"Ah." Isa was, in baseball terms, a switch-hitter. But I already knew that. "How did that come about?"

"The way most relationships between people 'come about,' as you put it. A bit of serendipity, followed by lots of chemistry. Then you need opportunity, and Miyoko's Salon provided the perfect opportunity."

"Why don't we start with the serendipity?"

"A lesbian bar in rue Palikao that I happened to drop by, although I didn't realise it at first. That was where I met Miyoko."

"Both of you on the prowl, then?"

"Yes, except I hadn't thought I'd be attracted by a woman on that particular night. Others, yes, but not that night."

"So what happened?"

"What usually happens, *mein Blümchen*. I bought a drink; she struck up a conversation with me and chemistry took over. So we went back to my place and made love."

"You realise you're making me horny, Isa."

"I know," she ruffled my hair. "I can see them coming out from the top of your head. They look almost as fearsome as the fangs on Miyoko's back."

"What fangs?"

"She has this giant snake tattoo on her back, uncoiling itself from between her legs until its head reaches between her shoulder blades with fangs bared."

"Ugh! That sounds a bit off-putting."

"Not if you like snakes. Or close your eyes," Isa laughed and gave me a kiss. She had always been unpredictable. Great fun but totally unpredictable. I think that's what attracted me to her most.

"Anyway," she continued soothingly, "after we'd made love, Miyoko told me one or two things that I thought might interest you."

"Like what?"

"Like whom."

"Like whom, then?" I wanted to ask more questions, but she stayed me with one hand on my arm.

"It's quite a long story, Rusty, so why not keep your questions till after I've finished?"

I nodded agreement and refilled our glasses.

"Miyoko was born on the last day of the Year of the Snake. February the fifth, 1894."

"Which makes her thirty-eight years old, if my arithmetic is correct."

"It is," Isa said drily. "She seems to have had quite an unusual life. Apparently her father sold kimono at an exclusive store in the Gion district of Kyoto, where all the *geisha* live and work. Miyoko could have expected to be betrothed to the son of another *kimono* merchant or even to the young man apprenticed in the family business, but her father died suddenly in mysterious circumstances and Miyoko was taken to Tokyo to live in the household of her mother's sister. She was married to a high-ranking bureaucrat called Doihara. One of her sons goes by the name of Kenji."

"Ah!"

"You probably don't know it, but the current head of the Kempeitai in Shanghai shares a hobby with Sir Victor. Photography."

"I can imagine where this story might be heading."

Isa ignored me.

"One day, young Doihara asked Miyoko to pose for him. She was still a young teenage girl and was flattered that her male cousin should want to photograph her. All went well until he suggested she take off her clothes. He wanted to photograph her in the nude."

"This sounds familiar."

"Miyoko refused. After all, she was only fifteen years old and nobody had ever seen her naked body, apart from her mother when they bathed together. Young Kenji persisted and eventually she gave in, but only on condition that he give her a valuable jade figurine in his possession of Saraswati, the Hindu goddess of knowledge, music and art. Kenji got his photographs."

"Wait a minute! Saraswati is depicted as a snake, isn't she?"

"I've no idea." She shrugged before continuing. "As you might expect of a man who is now chief of military intelligence, Doihara had an ulterior motive: to ingratiate himself with an imperial prince called Tadamaro, whom somehow he had got to know, and be recommended for a senior army post abroad—something his family background didn't otherwise permit. At least, that's what Miyoko told me."

"She seems to have told you a lot. You must have been quite a lover for her to reveal so much, just like that."

"I am, as you well know," she pecked me on the cheek. "But I'm summarising a number of post-coital conversations that we had."

"You mean —?"

"Yes, *mein Blümchen*," she patted my hand like a mother does that of a small child. "Su Bai-li ordered me to get closer to Miyoko."

"So you did?"

"So I did. Anyway, as I was saying, young Doihara showed the prints of his young cousin to Prince Tadamaro who immediately insisted that Miyoko become his concubine. Her uncle initially refused even to consider the idea. It was his duty as Miyoko's guardian to protect the young teenage girl and find a suitable husband for her. But his son pointed out the indisputable advantages to the Doihara family were Miyoko to be accepted into the Imperial Household."

"And so the father eventually agreed, and a pubescent teenager became an imperial prince's concubine."

"How perceptive you are, Rusty, in spite of your name!"

I ignored her irony.

"And Kenji Doihara got his commission abroad?"

"First, in Peking. Then in Manchuria, where he engineered the assassination of the warlord, Chang Tso-lin, and then, a couple of years later, the incident that you yourself witnessed by chance on the train to Mukden."

"Miyoko told you this?"

"Not all of it, no, but Su Bai-li has since confirmed what I suspected. But I haven't finished yet. Be patient, *mein Blümchen*."

The story of every flower's life. And then, before you knew it, bees like Luda came along and sucked the life out of you.

"When Miyoko was just twenty years old, Prince Tadamaro died. Quite suddenly, according to her. Of a snake bite. So now she was no longer a concubine. Or rather, she was, but she had nobody with whom to practice her concubinage. And so she was politely 'let go,' as they say in such circles of Japanese society."

"Pensioned off, in other words."

"Pensioned off. I gathered Japan's Imperial Household takes good care of those who have served it well."

"So then what happened?"

"Then Miyoko followed her cousin to Harbin before coming down to Shanghai as a Kempeitai agent."

"How do you know that?"

"Again, Bai-li told me. Doihara instructed her to set up the Salon Pink with the sole purpose of blackmailing clients."

"Sounds like a cross between a honey wagon and a honey pot."

A German honey bee seemed much more preferable.

42.

Meanwhile the war was continuing. Relentlessly. Rear Admiral Shiozawa had brought in ten thousand more bluejackets to add to his original five thousand. Sheer numbers, together with superior ground and air fire power, were beginning to tell. Contrary to all expectations, the Nineteenth Army was still putting up fierce resistance, but we all sensed that it was just a matter of time now before it was forced to withdraw completely from the area round Shanghai.

Chiang Kai-shek behaved exactly as Su Bai-li had predicted. He did nothing to help the soldiers fighting for his country, preferring instead to play a waiting game. He only engaged in battles that he knew he could win and if there was one thing he knew in these confused times it was that his troops wouldn't be able to resist a full-scale Japanese invasion.

It was at this point that Joao told me that he'd received his marching orders.

"Marching orders? Are you joining the bluejackets?" I asked frivolously. Fear did that to you. And the war had made both of us jittery.

"Don't be silly, Rusty. My editor has ordered me back to Tokyo. It seems I'm required there."

"Required? Required by whom?"

"By the Prime Minister among others."

"What? The Old Fox Tsuyoshi Inukai? You *are* going up in the world, Joao."

He looked a little embarrassed.

"His son, Ken, is a good friend of mine. I've been asked to join an advisory group to the Prime Minister."

"Congratulations, then. Unless it's commiserations. When do you leave?"

"Tuesday week. On the *Sasebo-maru* to Nagasaki."

"That's your home town, isn't it?"

"Yes. I'm going to get married there."

"Married?" Talk about dropping bombshells. Joao should be

promoted to rear admiral. "Who to? Surely not Gerda?"

"No, of course not. Someone called Fusa."

"Fusa? Who on earth is Fusa?"

"A young woman I was introduced to when I was in Tokyo a couple of years ago. It was arranged that we should get married once I was recalled from Shanghai."

"You mean, it's an arranged marriage?"

"Yes. To the granddaughter of the last clan lord of Hirado in Nagasaki Prefecture."

"You're *seriously* going up in the world, then."

"If you say so. I'm sorry, Rusty. Maybe I should have told you."

"Of course, you should have, Joao. We're supposed to be friends," I said sullenly.

"Hopefully, we still are. I'd like you to come to our wedding."

"But what about Gerda?" I wasn't going to be appeased that easily. "What's Gerda going to do without you?"

"I don't know. I'll miss her, of course, but I'm sure I'll learn to love Fusa. She's Japanese."

That seemed an odd way of talking about the woman he was going to marry. But then Joao was clearly in Japanese mode.

"Nagasaki's your home town, isn't it?"

"That's right."

"And Gerda?" I persisted. "Are you inviting her, too?"

"Of course."

"Does Fusa know about the two of you?"

"And I'm inviting Isa, too," he said, avoiding my question.

I relented. "In that case, Joao, I'll accept your invitation. I'd like to meet your Fusa and find out what she sees in you."

Joao laughed and switched into Portuguese mode as he punched me playfully on my upper arm.

"Maybe you can marry Isa while you're in Tokyo."

"What?"

"Come on, Rusty. Gerda's told me all about your first love. I saw the way you two looked at each other when I introduced you at that do at the German Club before Christmas and I thought 'ah hah!'"

"Ah hah, what?"

"You know."

"No, I don't know, Joao. A week ago, I would have told you I hadn't seen Isa since then, and that I doubted very much whether any ah-hahing was on offer."

"Ah! But that was a week ago, wasn't it? That's the thing about 'ah hah.' You never can tell what's going to happen next, can you?"

Joao's expression was beginning to look as cryptic as one of Kiki's smoke rings. I changed the subject.

"What am I going to do now that you're leaving? I've got no-one to work together with."

"Yes, you have. Isa."

"But she's not a journalist."

"Maybe not," he agreed, "but she's fearless."

"You mean you're not?"

"Me?" Joao snorted. "I was petrified every time we ventured behind enemy lines. That is why I clung onto you the whole time."

"No, Joao. I was clinging onto *you*."

He laughed his easy laugh. I couldn't imagine him being so relaxed back in Japan.

I decided to follow his suggestion, though, and the day after he left Shanghai, I took Isa with me on one final sortie behind Chinese lines. I told her I wanted to get a feel for the soldiers' mood and she seemed quite content to accompany me on the back of my Čechie.

The roads and tracks were littered with the bodies of the dead. The Nineteenth Army had suffered heavy casualties. The Japanese spokesman at Navy headquarters had been insisting that its own losses were few and far between, but that day we saw for ourselves just how many bluejackets had also died in the fighting. The Japanese may have more or less won their 'incident,' but at what a cost. We both felt by the end of our trip that we had witnessed a colossal waste of human life.

For all her fearlessness—and she *was* fearless—Isa was as upset as I was. On our way back, we went into the Chinese part of the city. Despite the rat-a-tat of machine-guns not far away, coolies trundled their barrows along the streets and rickshas moved between shops still open for business. Chinese police kept order and there was no panic behind the lines. Everyone seemed quite calm—certainly much calmer than people within the Settlement.

Nobody stopped us until we were within rifle-shot of yet another conflagration near the station.

"Where do you think you're going?" a soldier asked us politely in Shanghainese. I think he was just curious at seeing a red-haired woman on the back of a motor bike because, once I'd explained that we were trying to get back into the International Settlement, he suggested we take a roundabout route.

"The North Honan Gate is under fire at the moment," he explained. "The Britisher in charge is doing his best to hold back the monkeys, but it isn't safe. Anything could happen. Go west and then south to North Thibet Road. Things should be quieter there."

I thanked the young soldier and did as he suggested, only to find ourselves caught in the midst of a shooting match between a squad of bluejackets on the far side of the gate and several snipers holed up in redoubts on the second and third floors of Chinese houses this side.

Bullets were flying all over the place, so we abandoned the bike and took refuge in a doorway. The door wasn't locked and we stepped cautiously inside.

The occupants of the house seemed to have fled, but we could hear shots being fired above our heads by one of the snipers. Maybe there was a story here.

I went up the stairs, with Isa behind me, calling out as I did so that I was a Swedish journalist and, please, refrain from shooting us.

It was dark at the top of the stairs and I couldn't see the face of the sniper by the window because the light was behind him.

"Well, well, Mista Broom. Wrong time, no see *lo*."

The unmistakable voice of Pan Chan-ki, Tu Yue-sheng's henchman.

"Chunky! What are you doing here?"

"Shoot monkey, *lo*. Wha-ting else?"

"Any luck?"

"Four piece dead monkey say Chunky hab skill, galaw, not luck."

"Not bad, Chunky. Did Yue-sheng send you to help out, then?'

"So fashion true, but no send. We come Chapei side on our own."

"We?"

Chunky waved one hand at a row of windows across the street.

"Three piece fren in houso that side. Two piece more houso this side," he tapped the partition wall beside him. It was then that he noticed Isa standing behind me.

"*Haiyaa*, lookee! My see one piece *ang mo* Missy. My no sabee Mista Broom hab catchee wifoo."

"My no hab wifoo, Chunky. Olo fren."

"Olo fren soon got wifoo, Mista Broom. Chunky know."

There was a sudden burst of fire from the street below and the sound of glass breaking across the street.

Chunky peered cautiously between some curtains out into the street.

"Hmm. No good, *lo*. Monkey bandit hide allo place. We go topside, okay?"

We followed him up a flight of stairs and then up a ladder into a well-lit attic.

"Lookee here! Monkey hide but Chan-ki seek," he grinned.

Keeping his head well down, he slowly pushed his rifle barrel out of the window. From where I was standing in the shadow of a wall, I could see several bluejackets lying behind their sandbags and at their back an officer exhorting them to do something the marines didn't seem to be entirely happy about. The officer was none other than Lieutenant Fujii.

"Chunky, you got how muchee good that rifle?"

Chunky looked at me disdainfully.

"What you sabee, Mista Broom?"

"Come look see, Chunky," I beckoned him over to where I was standing. "My watchee one piece monkey man down side ma-loo, Japan officer."

Chunky crawled away from his position by the window. Cautiously he stood up beside us and peered down into the street at where I was pointing.

"Wha side?" he asked.

"Thisee side. He stand up talkee belong sailor man. My wantchee Chan-ki shoot him. Can do?"

Then he nodded.

"Can do, can do. Whafo no can. No fear! Hab number wun popa rifle. You my same side now," he grinned happily before crawling back to his rifle. Slowly he raised his head above the window sill. Fujii was gesticulating wildly. Suddenly he pointed his pistol at one of the bluejackets and fired. Just as he did so, Chunky fired his own rifle.

And missed.

"Monkey move wrong time. My wanchee finis chopchop," he muttered.

"*Man-man*," I said. "Slowly-slowly. Take your time, Chunky."

He took aim again. Fujii had realised that a bullet had passed by too close for comfort, but seemed to think it might be one of his own men who was responsible because he turned to shout at three bluejackets behind sandbags on the other side of the street. He didn't finish whatever it was he was he was saying, though. Chunky's second bullet blew the right side of his face away and Fujii sank to the ground and lay there in a pool of blood and fragments of bone.

"Monkey man loosee facey," Chunky laughed loudly at his own joke.

Without an officer to give them orders, the bluejackets rose as one from the sandbags protecting them and began to turn back down North Thibet Road. As they did so, Chunky's friends opened fire from their positions. Soon Fujii was joined by six more dead bodies.

"Thank you, Chunky," I shook him by the hand. "I owe you one."

"No. We allo same. You go catchee wifoo now, Mista Broom."

"Good wind! Good water, Chunky!" I bid him God speed.

Once we were back on the Čechie and speeding across the Soochow Creek into the International Settlement, Isa spoke into my ear.

"Well, that's one less assignment to complete, isn't it, *mein Blümchen*? But don't worry. I'll still make love to you tonight."

"Passionately?" I shouted back over my shoulder.

"Like an Amur tiger." She bit the back of my neck hard.

"That's why they call you *ang mo*," I laughed. "An *ang mo* tiger."

43.

And then, a few days later, Victor was mugged.

It was in all the newspapers, but when you yourself are writing for newspapers, you don't always bother to read what your fellow hacks are writing. At least, I don't. I've never wanted to get caught up in that small world of news and gossip. I was afraid I'd end up taking it all too seriously.

It was Luda of all people who told me about Victor's mugging. It was a Thursday evening—that time of the month, so to speak—and I was at her usual soirée in the Palace Hotel. I'd even got the room number right. It must be getting to be a habit.

A habit I'd decided I should quietly break. After our first tryst—unlike Otto who was far more forthcoming—Luda had told me little of interest during post-coital conversations. She seemed to be caught up in a German *hausfrau*'s tight-knit social world of food, shopping, and teenage children. I began to yearn for Otto's company, but he seemed to be endlessly busy in Nanking. Unless, of course, he was holed up with Big Annie at Gracie Gale's, where she probably dropped a few stitches in her underwear while he spun her a yarn. Joao's wedding, I reflected, offered a good way out of what was becoming a sticky situation. What else could I expect of my *honigbiene*?

The next morning, I bumped into Roger Buckley. Literally. I was backing out of a bakery. My hands were filled with Viennese goodies so I had to push the door open with my behind. Which worked well enough until suddenly there was no door and I almost stumbled over backwards.

"Sorry, old chap," Roger steadied me with a strong arm. "I thought you might need a hand."

"Roger! Thank you. Long time, no see."

"Yes. I've been out of town a while. You know how it is. Here today, gone tomorrow. How are things with you?"

"You know, same old, same old. This war's been keeping me busy."

"Yes, I've been reading the despatches that you've been writing with Joao Sereño from the front lines. Riveting stuff. You wouldn't have thought the Chinese had it in them, would you? To resist the Japs, I mean."

"Yes, they've been pretty heroic. Unlike the bluejackets, the Nineteenth Army soldiers have been prepared to take risks as they lay down their lives for their country."

There was a pause as we both looked at each other. Roger was, as always, in a suit and tie, his shoes polished so brightly I could see my face reflected in their toecaps. I was wearing an open neck shirt and baggy trousers, and my shoes hadn't been cleaned for at least a week. So far as I was concerned, it was still early. The day hadn't yet begun. And it would stay that way until I'd had a couple of cups of coffee and a slice of *schwartzbrot* with cheese.

"Got a moment, have you, Rusty?" Roger was still holding the door open and raised one eyebrow in the direction of one of the two tables and chairs by the window. "Let me buy you a coffee. You look as if you need one."

"I do," I said, taking up his offer and planting myself down on the Thonet chair nearest the door. My pastries spilled onto the marble table top. "A *Mélange* will do me fine, if you don't mind."

A couple of minutes later Roger was back with my *Mélange* and an *Einspänner* for him. He'd always struck me as a potential horseman of the apocalypse.

"I've been wanting to have a chat," he took a sip of his coffee with thick cream topping and licked his upper lip. Some of the froth clung in tiny droplets to the hairs of his moustache and sparkled in the morning sunlight. I was envious. Of the sparkle, rather than the froth.

"Yes, I'm sorry, Roger. The war has been taking its toll on me, I'm afraid. These past couple of months have been sheer hell."

"Yes. Yes, I can imagine." A pause, as he took another sip of his coffee. I offered him one of my apple strudels, but he shook his head politely.

"Thank you, Rusty, but no thank you. I've already breakfasted."

"An early bird, then, in search of its worm."

"Which in this case happens to be Kiki Montagu-Rose. Did you happen to find out anything more about her, Rusty?"

"I did, indeed, Roger. I should have let you know. I do apologise. This war —"

"Quite understandable, old boy," he paused, waiting expectantly.

"I learned two things after she left. First, she is working as a courier for the German armaments industry. She memorises orders here and conveys them back to her contact in Berlin so that there's no written trace of what's going on. The Versailles Treaty, I suppose."

"No harm in that, really, is there?" he said lazily, his grey eyes unfocused.

"If you say not, Roger."

"And the second thing?"

"She's a lesbian. Or rather, she's bisexual."

That woke him up. He jerked out of his reverie.

"What!" he exclaimed loud enough to turn the head of a man reading his newspaper at the table next to us. "How on earth did you find that out? Are you sure?"

"Absolutely positive." I told him the story of Madame Noguchi's Salon Pink, her blackmailing activities, and the photographs the police had found there.

"Where are these photographs now?" he asked anxiously.

"No idea," I lied. "Scattered around on the floor of the Salon Pink's basement the last time I saw them. The police didn't seem that bothered, to be honest. They were more concerned about the underage girls being forced into prostitution by the Kempeitai. I expect the photographs—prints, negatives and all—have been incinerated by now."

He nodded to himself. Then, "You heard about Sir Victor, of course?"

"Heard what?"

Hear something once, and you hear it again and again. One of the laws of conversation.

"He was mugged a couple of nights ago. Coming out of the Columbia Country Club. Luckily a couple of other guests came to his rescue, but he was still quite badly beaten up."

"Poor Victor!" I sympathised, wondering whether Roger's smooth transfer from talking about the Salon Pink to mention of Sir Victor was more than mere chance.

"Yes indeed, although what seemed to worry him most was the loss of one of his sticks."

"Sticks?"

"Yes, you know, those walking sticks he always uses to prop himself up with ever since his plane accident. Apparently, one of the muggers walked off with one of them. I've heard it said she was a woman, too. Really! What is Shanghai coming to these days when women start robbing upright citizens like Sir Victor Sassoon?"

What indeed?

44.

That evening I paid Victor a visit. It was six o'clock—the hour when his courtiers paid their courtesy calls. Unsurprisingly, Perkins opened the door to the penthouse suite.

"Count Bloom," he smiled. "We were wondering when you might honour us with a visit. Please, do come in. Sir Victor has been waiting for you for—what?" he glanced at his fob watch. "Forty-five hours now. He will be relieved to know that you are alive and, if I may say so, sir, looking very well."

That was quite a speech. For a valet.

"Thank you, Perkins. And where do I find our invalid?"

"Where it is customary to find invalids, Count Bloom. In his bed."

"With a host of pretty nurses attending to his needs?"

"If only, sir. My life would then be much more manageable."

"Is he that bad?"

"Goodness me, no," Perkins chuckled. "But don't tell him I said so. He is—how might I put it?—keeping up appearances."

He took my coat and hung it on a clothes stand in the hall.

"Now, if you'd care to follow me," he swished off, leading the way.

Victor's bedroom was opposite his studio. It was almost as dark, too, lit by a single lampstand by the bed where Victor was reading. The invalid was wearing fancy silk pyjamas with two dragons breathing fire across his buttoned-up chest, and a silk Chinese nightcap. One stick was propped against the bedside table—the one without a silver handle.

"Christopher!" he exclaimed, putting his book face down on the coverlet and swinging his legs to the floor. "What a relief to see you! I was worried, you know. I thought maybe you'd been shot and killed by one of those ugly Jap sailors."

"Maybe it would have been better if I had been." Was the lightness of my conversation bordering on the unbearable? "I only heard about what happened to you this morning when I ran into Roger Buckley. He told me all about it. A bad business, I gather."

"To put it mildly," he reached for his lone stick propped against the wall. "Madame bloody Noguchi walked off with my other stick."

"The reason she had you mugged, of course. *This* is what it's all about, isn't it?" I was pissed off, at my own obtuseness more than at Victor's deception.

"What *what* is all about, old boy?" His lynx-like eyes were as merry as they always were when he knew he'd won whatever game he was playing.

"Simon's kidnapping, naughty photos of you in the Salon Pink, a break-in in your apartment, and you getting mugged on your way out of the Columbia Country Club. They're all part and parcel of a single event, aren't they? That evening of debauchery at Frolics ten years ago and the commemorative photos you took at the time."

"Except they weren't properly commemorative, were they, dear boy? I mean, it's not as if I've broadcast their existence and had them printed on postage stamps, is it? I've simply kept them to myself."

"Yes, but *someone* knew about them. And that someone has made sure to spread the word around. Hence Miyoko Noguchi's interest in you."

"Yes, but who told her?"

"Lolly Lo, of course." I wasn't prepared to beat about any conversational bushes. "Unless there's someone else, besides you, Isa and

I, who knew about that photograph and where you kept it. Perkins, maybe?"

"Perkins? Please, don't impugn my valet's honour. Perkins is as loyal as they come."

"Then it has to be Lolly."

"But *why*, Christopher? Why?"

"Squeeze, Victor. Squeeze. Madame Noguchi owed him one when he let her go after her arrest, so he decided to add to her debt. And get paid for it, of course."

"Is nobody straight in this wretched town?"

"Only the whiskey. And that rarely."

"Talking of which, how about a drink?" Victor heaved himself off the bed and began hobbling towards the door. I lent him an arm.

"Thank you. Ah, Perkins!" He spotted his valet hovering in the corridor. "Bring us something to drink, will you? What will you have, Christopher?"

"Perhaps a Ginger Ninja, for a change."

"Sounds sexy. I'll have one, too, if I may."

"Very good, sir."

Perkins turned on a well-polished heel and went his way down the corridor, while we went ours to the drawing room.

"Bloody nuisance, this mugging business!" Victor exclaimed as he sat down heavily in his usual chair by the fireplace. "What on earth am I going to do now?"

"Get the negative back, of course. And buy yourself a new stick."

"Get it back? But how?"

"I may have my ways," I said, trying to look as cryptic as a smoke ring.

"You do?" His eyes lit up expectantly. "I'll pay you, you know. Whatever you ask, Christopher. Plus expenses."

"You may regret that offer, Victor. I will almost certainly need to go to Tokyo."

"Go wherever you like. Stay at the best hotels. Just tell me how they compare with the Cathay," he grinned slyly. "Seriously, though, how about a down payment of five thousand dollars? With another fifty thousand if you get hold of the negative and bring it back to me? Does that sound fair?"

"More than fair, but I'm not sure I share your optimism."

"That's because you're a pessimist, Christopher. You're really a Russian at heart."

At which point, Perkins came into the room with our cocktails. After he'd set the two glasses down in front of us, Victor asked him to take the framed print above the fireplace off its hook and hand it to him. Victor turned it over, unclipped the board backing and extracted three picture postcard-size photographs.

"These should cheer you up, old chap. The prints I promised you." He handed me the photographs. One was of Hirohito with Yulia. Another of the two princes. A third encompassed the full scene of royal and imperial debauchery at Frolics that he had described to me— Hirohito, Yulia, Prince Edward with Katerina on one arm and Kiki on the other, and George and 'the princeling.' Hirohito was clumsily kissing the cheek of the girl by his side.

"Thank you, Victor," I said, as I examined the prints in my hand. In the background of the last one a waiter was walking by with a tray held high above his shoulder. His face was half hidden by the tray, but he had a shock of neatly coiffed, long and slightly wavy, dark brown hair brushed back from a high, wide forehead. Whoever it was cut an impressive figure for a waiter.

"You realise, don't you, Victor, that it's not just the Japanese who are interested in these commemorative photographs."

"The British Secret Service, you mean?"

"It's fairly obvious, isn't it? I suspect that's the real reason for Roger Buckley's presence in Shanghai, however much he claims it's to do with Kiki Montagu-Rose. If the Kempeitai is concerned about Japanese royalty being depicted in compromising positions, the Secret Service must be equally as concerned about the two British princes— especially George."

"And that other chappie with him. Who *is* he anyhow?"

"I don't know, Victor," I lied. "But I have a feeling I may have bumped into him somewhere. Is it alright by you if I keep these?"

"Of course, old boy. Be my guest."

It seemed like I had been ever since I'd arrived in Shanghai.

45.

"Being a naughty boy again, Lolly?"

I had waylaid the Chief Chinese Inspector in a *lilong* alley behind the Central Police Station. He was on his way to his weekly rendezvous with a young and extremely beautiful Chinese woman, the wife of a colleague whom Lolly kept out of harm's way by assigning him to one task after another in far-off parts of the city. What Suyin saw in an older man like Lolly, other than a large amount of flesh lying on top of her in bed, was hard to fathom. But, like Trudi with Gunther, his weight probably helped keep her trim.

I knew all this because I had been watching Lolly ever since the evening at Victor's. I was angry at having been cheated by a man I'd grown to like and respect and, in an intemperate moment, was all for

Isa's despatching him down a dark alley like the one I was in now. Sanity prevailed. As Isa had wisely pointed out, it would be unwise to kill the Chief Chinese Inspector of the Shanghai Municipal Police—especially if I intended to continue living here.

"Count!" Lolly was surprised to see me. His expression was one of a naughty boy caught in the act of stealing an apple from a neighbour's tree. "What are you doing in this wreck of the hoods?"

"Nicely put, Lolly. I just wanted a word."

Lolly looked at the watch on his wrist—a new and expensive watch.

"I'm in a bit of a hurry right now, Count. Can we talk later?"

He made to move on, but I stepped in front of him to bar his way.

"I'm sorry, Lolly, but no. Your girlfriend probably won't mind waiting a few minutes. And if you don't have much time when you do get to see her, I'm sure you can come a little quicker than usual. Or do you 'go' when speaking Chinese? I've never managed to discover."

"What do you want, Count?"

"Want?" I echoed disdainfully. "I *want* to know why you betrayed my trust, Chief Chinese Inspector Lo."

"Betrayed? How so?" Playing for time.

"You know perfectly well, Lo Li-kwei. You revealed the whereabouts of a photograph to Madame Noguchi."

"What makes you say that?"

"Because you were the only person, other than Sir Victor, Miss Wiedemeyer and myself, who knew he secreted it in the silver handle of one of his walking sticks. That's what makes me say what I said. My only question is, how much did Madame Noguchi give you for it? I assume a substantial amount."

"Of course."

"How much? Half a million Mexican silver dollars?"

"Let's say, enough for my retirement."

"I heard somebody else say that only a few weeks ago. And look what happened to *him*. Be careful!"

"Are you threatening me, Count?"

"Not at all. Just giving you a word of advice. But you haven't answered my question, have you? I seem to remember your saying you'd drop me like a ton of hot bricks if ever I dared betray your trust."

"That was then," Lolly said cryptically. Spare me another smoke ring.

"What do you mean?"

"Circumstances change, Count. Surely you understand that?" He patted his stomach. I could sense his jovial self was coming back. "When we were working together on the kidnap case, I learned to trust your judgement, and so to trust you. But then you told me something you'd learned from Sir Victor that you were keeping from me. That made me pause for thought. And I asked myself, why am I trusting a red-haired barbarian? Trust is like that."

"Like what?"

"Trust deceives you, doesn't it? It makes you believe one thing when something else might well be true. Like all those photographs in the Salon Pink. So many men and women trusting that their sexual frailties were private affairs, only to discover that they were potentially very public. It was the same with Sir Victor's photograph of the future Emperor of Japan. I never saw it, but Madame Noguchi convinced me that nothing good would come of its being made public."

"But Sir Victor had no intention of making it public. He's kept it a secret for over ten years."

"Maybe not. Not now, at least. But who knows what he might have decided to do with it later. After all, it's not often one gets a chance to blackmail both the future King of England and the Emperor of Japan at the same time."

"I'm surprised you care about either."

"I don't, but the policeman in me tells me that it's dangerous for a photograph like that to exist."

"Why not burn it, then?"

"Who says I haven't?" Lolly grinned.

"That watch on your wrist for a start," I retorted. "And the fact that Madame Noguchi was seen walking away with Sir Victor's silver-handled stick in her grasp."

"Ah!" he said.

"Ah what?"

"Ah couldn't resist the bribe, could I?"

"For a man who's in love with Shanghai squeeze, Lolly, I'm surprised you're so overweight."

"You've got it all wrong, Rusty. The fattest are those who've squeezed the most out of everyone else. And now, if you'll excuse me," he pushed me roughly out of his way, "my squeeze is waiting. See you around."

So much for friendship and trust.

46.

It was a pleasant time to be visiting Japan. The weather was warm without being too hot and humid. The cherry blossoms were long gone, but purple wisteria covering the walls of the Catholic church in Nagasaki where Joao and Fusa's wedding ceremony was to take place were in full bloom. It was May 5th—Boys' Day—and colourful carp flew from the flag masts of houses where boys had been born.

Gerda had decided at the last minute not to accompany us on our trip. In spite of Joao's protestations to the contrary, she felt that Fusa would feel uncomfortable in her presence, so Isa and I travelled alone together. We only just made the wedding ceremony in time, though, after our ship from Shanghai had been delayed in a storm. As a result, we turned up at the church in a taxi full of suitcases.

Not that it was their proper wedding. That had already taken place in private in a Shinto ceremony at the local shrine. But the Portuguese side of Joao's family was Catholic and Fusa had apparently dabbled in Christianity, so they got married before God as well. Covering all the bases. But then Joao had always struck me as the careful type. Japanese mode.

Ken Inukai, son of the Prime Minister and Joao's best friend, was best man and I, of all people, was asked to give away the bride whom I had been introduced to literally five minutes earlier. Joao explained that Fusa's parents had both died recently and that she had no close family. She'd had a brother, but he'd died of smallpox a few years earlier, so now she was a grown-up orphan. To my mind that meant that she couldn't really be 'given away,' but I wasn't going to spend precious minutes arguing the minutiae of semantics when I needed to get dressed for the occasion. Since the vestry was already occupied by Isa changing into a formal dress, I stepped behind a cluster of tombstones and put on my best dinner jacket and trousers, over a starched white shirt and—wait for it—gold bow tie. That was the trouble with living in Shanghai. You became as lurid as the decorations in the night clubs and casinos.

"At least your dinner jacket and trousers are black. I think they set off the gold rather nicely," Isa purred. Ever the Amur tigress.

As for Fusa, all I can say is that she struck me as delicate, graceful, and demure—reflecting the personification of the kind of Japanese woman people like me tend to idealise because of her difference from what we are used to when it comes to appreciation of the opposite sex. She had the same aristocratic poise as Miyoko Noguchi, but Fusa's prim and restrained elegance suggested that passion might not be her *forte*. I also suspected that beneath her willow-like soft and pliant beauty was an inner strength and determination that would keep Joao firmly in place when it mattered. I wondered if his Portuguese self knew what he was getting himself into. Not that it was my business. Still, how he'd kept quiet about her all those years in Shanghai, I had no idea.

It transpired that, being the properly brought up granddaughter of a feudal lord, Fusa spoke enough English to make polite conversation to Joao's foreign friends. This had one hilarious moment, when at the wedding supper she deftly picked up a piece of grilled octopus with her chopsticks, put it in her mouth, and announced gravely as she dabbed her lips with a linen napkin,

"I rike octopus berry much. It has eight testicles."

Although I doubted whether those involved in bringing Joao and Fusa together had anticipated such a startling revelation from the bride's prim lips, especially since they had yet to consummate their marriage, Isa and I couldn't help roaring with laughter. For a moment or two, the bridegroom couldn't make up his mind whether to be in Portuguese or Japanese mode—to join our amusement or look suitably shocked. Fortunately, Portuguese mode prevailed. Perhaps there was hope for their love life, after all.

47.

In Tokyo we stayed at the Imperial Hotel, Frank Lloyd Wright's minor masterpiece which, on its very opening day, had somehow survived the Great Kanto Earthquake that had destroyed the city and killed one hundred and forty thousand of its inhabitants. A miracle, said the survivors. Proper planning and construction, said the architect.

The sheer size of Tokyo had us wondering how on earth we were going to find Miyoko Noguchi and, once found, how we were going to get back the film she had stolen from Victor. We belatedly realised what an alien environment we now found ourselves in. We were two foreigners, each easily distinguished by the colour of our hair, although Isa had now dyed hers black, not to mention our European facial features, and we were being followed everywhere by agents of Japan's secret police force, known as Tokkō. We hadn't a hope in hell of extracting information out of Miyoko; she was, after all, former concubine to an imperial prince and probably under surveillance herself. Our only hope of achieving our aim, we concluded, was to seek Joao's help, although, if there was one thing that was obvious now that he was back in Japan, it was that he was Japanese, not Portuguese. Luckily, he was also in love.

One evening Joao came by our hotel and invited us out.

"Come on, you two! It's time to educate you both in traditional Japanese ways."

"What do you mean?"

"Wait and see." Kiki's smoke rings seem to have been blown across the China Sea to Tokyo.

A limousine was waiting for us at the hotel entrance and a white-gloved chauffeur stood with its doors open.

"Rusty, this is Kobayashi-*san*, the Inukai family chauffeur. He's been of great help to me in the past and he's a real *Edokko*, child of Tokyo."

"*Hajimemashite!*" I bowed in greeting. "*Burūmu to iimasu. Yoroshiku o-negai shimasu.*"

"*Ara!*" Kobayashi exclaimed in surprise. "You speak Japanese? You have very strange foreign friends, *Sensei*," he laughed, turning to Joao.

"I know, Kobayashi-*san*, but he saved my life once during the fighting in Shanghai."

"He did?" The chauffeur turned back to me. "Then, thank you, Mister Burūmu. Japan can't afford to lose good men like Serino-*sensei*."

We got into the car and Kobayashi started the engine.

"Kagurazaka, *Sensei*?"

"Yes, please. The Sakura tea house."

"Kagurazaka? That sounds like you're taking us to a geisha house."

"Possibly." There was a twinkle in Joao's eye. Portuguese mode.

"So *that's* what you meant by traditional Japanese ways?" Isa said excitedly. "A geisha party."

"Something like that."

After ten minutes or so, Kobayashi brought the car to a smooth stop outside a wooden gated building facing onto a narrow alley. There was a clump of bamboo to one side with a single dim light with the word '*Sakura*' written in tasteful calligraphy on its glass shade. On the other, a large rock set in small white stones and, against the dried mud and straw wall of a shingle-roofed tea house, climbing wisteria in full flower.

We alighted from the car and Joao pushed open the wooden gate and stepped inside. Isa and I followed him across half a dozen stone slabs laid haphazardly on the ground. On one side was a *kara sansui* miniature Zen garden, consisting of three asymmetrically placed rocks in a raked sea of small white stones; on the other, a large clump of bamboo and a maple tree that concealed the entrance to the tea house. The path was bordered by a carpet of thick moss. There was the sound of trickling water somewhere close by and the sudden echo of a *shishi-odoshi* bamboo clapper. As Joao had said, echoes of old Japan.

He slid open the wooden door to the tea house and entered.

"*Gomen kudasai*," he called in a voice just loud enough to be heard. Japanese mode again.

There was a quick shuffle of *tabi* stockinged feet on the wooden floor of the house and a middle-aged woman in kimono appeared.

"*Okoshiyasu*," she greeted her guests. Surprised at seeing who it was, she continued: "*Ara, Serino-sensei. O-hisashiburi de gozaimasu ne.*" She then bowed silently and a little uncertainly towards us.

"Thank you, *Okāsan*. Rusty and Isa are two friends of mine from Shanghai."

"*Uerucamu!*" The Okāsan said in English, bowing low. "Please follow me."

She turned and led the way along a narrow passageway, first one way, then another, and then another until finally we found ourselves looking out onto a beautiful Japanese garden.

"The irises are so pretty at this time of the year, don't you think?"

The Okāsan led us into a small tatami-matted room, then knelt and slid open the *shōji* papered screens so that we could sit and view the garden. There was the sound of *tabi* stockinged feet along the corridor and two geisha appeared, wearing formal kimonos, *shimada* wigs with *kanzashi* ornaments, white face make-up and blobs of rouge in the very centre of their lips. They bowed and introduced themselves as Chiyotsuru and Asakichi, before preparing saké and putting dried squid, boiled *edamame* beans, braised *renkon* lotus root, and other refreshments in bowls on the low table. Then one of them placed herself beside Joao, while the other knelt down between Isa and myself .

"My name Asakichi," she said in halting English. "*Yoroshū otano-mōshimasu.*" She then held a small bottle of saké, ready to pour. We got the hint and picked up our cups. "*Dōzo. Purīzu. Otsukareyasu.*"

"You never pour a drink for yourself in Japan," Joao explained, as Chiyotsuru filled his cup. "Which means that one of you now has to fill Asakichi's cup for her. Like this." He poured some of the sake into the cup Chiyotsuru was holding towards him. Then he raised his own cup. "*Kampai!* And welcome to the real Japan."

"*Kampai!*" we chorused dutifully and drained the slightly sweet rice wine in our cups, which Asakichi immediately refilled. After the third cup, she offered me her own cup and filled it. Once I had emptied it, Joao said I had to return her favour. I realised that we were racing down a slippery slope to drunkenness and that a *geisha's* stomach had to be as strong as an ox. So much for soft and pliant beauty!

It was clear that this wasn't the first time Joao had encountered Chiyotsuru. There was an intimacy between them that suggested I had a lot to learn about the Japanese side of my Portuguese friend, but I felt it wiser not to intrude by asking questions that he'd probably regard as a crass invasion of their privacy. He'd tell me whatever there was to say, once he felt comfortable enough to do so. Portuguese, rather than Japanese, mode.

But not yet. Asakichi took up a *shamisen* stringed instrument and began strumming it as she sang what we were assured was a classical Japanese song about warring warrior clans, the frailty of life, and the beauty of transience. Not being Japanese, I thought her song probably appealed more to the neighbourhood cats on the garden wall than to two foreigners who weren't well versed in geisha arts.

Next it was Chiyotsuru's turn to show off her skills—this time in dance—as Asakichi strummed her *shamisen*. She certainly had a mesmerising way with her fan, which she used with consummate skill to narrate a story that revealed a willowy and graceful body under her kimono. Even foreigners as uninitiated in the geisha world as Isa and I could more or less work out the tale of love told by Chiyotsuru's sinuous moves. Lucky Joao! The Amur tigress purred at my side.

And so the evening continued with, so far as I could make out, fairly inane conversation—at least, what Joao translated for our benefit seemed pretty inane—and plenty of flattery. Yet somehow Chiyotsuru and Asakichi managed to make everything they said seem natural, not false. Even in my cups, I marvelled at their skills honed by years and years of training. I also recognised that such an ability to dissimulate would make great spies of these women. Perhaps one of them already was. After all, what other profession had access to such an exclusive clientele? Politicians, senior bureaucrats, and managerial executives in Japan's largest and most important companies. Plus, of course, the occasional underworld figure. A yakuza here; an ultranationalist conspirator there.

As if she was reading my thoughts, Chiyotsuru suddenly became serious. "*Sensei*, two or three weeks ago, we had some clients here you should know about." It sounded like Joao had already recruited her as an informant. No doubt, he'd tell me in due course. Or not, as the case might be.

"You did?" Joao was immediately sober. "Who?"

"General Araki, the Minister of War. Together with half a dozen junior officers and a smooth, sleek-haired man they all seemed to look up to as their leader. One of them mentioned that they were members of some kind of blood brotherhood."

Joao translated what Chiyotsuru had said.

"Ah! The *Ketsumeidan*," I exclaimed. "Did their leader have a name?"

"No. They just called him '*Kakka*,' as if he was a cabinet minister or something."

"What did he look like? He wasn't by any chance a small man, with an effeminate face and hair parted in the middle of his head, was he?"

Chiyotsuru looked surprised. "How did you know?"

"It's a long story, but he's the reason why Isa and I are here in Tokyo."

"And there I was thinking you'd come here for my wedding," Joao laughed. I was surprised and impressed at how he could shed his drunken behaviour like a snake its skin.

"We did, Joao." Isa took over. "But your wedding was in Nagasaki, remember? Now we're in Tokyo, and we came to Tokyo because we're in search of two people who have been causing a lot of trouble back in

Shanghai. One of them is Nisshō, the man you told us about. The other is Miyoko Noguchi."

"Noguchi?" Joao was surprised. "Prince Tadamaro's former concubine?"

"The one and the same. And then there's this mysterious third man who seems somehow to be involved with the League of Blood," I added. "I'm sorry. Perhaps you should explain to Chiyotsuru, Joao."

Joao did so. The geisha listened and nodded thoughtfully from time to time. When he had finished, she started telling us about General Araki's visit to the Sakura teahouse.

Like many men of his age who had reached positions of power, she said, Araki had an exaggerated sense of his own attractiveness to women—this despite his flabby neck, balding head and generally unprepossessing facial features—and he certainly didn't know how to keep his hands to himself. He seemed convinced that no woman could possibly resist him. Chiyotsuru, however, was experienced enough to be able to deflect his attentions without upsetting his pride. Fortunately, the younger men present lacked the bravado of their senior officer and confined their flirtation with the young women present to sexual innuendo. These kind of men were the least dangerous when it came to molesting the geisha who were there to entertain them.

"What about the sleek-haired gentleman addressed as 'Your Excellency?'" I asked.

"He didn't join in at all, but kept himself to himself for the most part. From time to time he exchanged a few quiet words with General Araki, but otherwise he just sat there drinking quietly. I had a feeling —" she stopped.

"What kind of feeling?"

"I don't know. That perhaps he didn't really like women. I began to wonder whether he wasn't a monk or something."

"Most monks I've come across are pretty lecherous," Joao laughed.

"As I said, it was just a feeling."

Chiyotsuru continued with her story. Araki had never visited the Sakura before, but had been introduced by Ken's father, Tsuyoshi Inukai, who was an old customer of the teahouse. As a result, she had had no alternative but to agree to the War Minister's visit, even though she had heard 'on the wind' that he could be a difficult customer who wouldn't take no for an answer when it came to requests concerning his physical desires.

Luckily, however, just when she was beginning to wonder how best to fend off his groping hands, he suddenly sobered up and dismissed all the women from the room. This was unusual. A customer usually retained the services of the *okāsan* of a teahouse, however confidential the discussion taking place. Discretion was key in the geisha world.

But this particular geisha had been indiscrete. "I decided to hide in a small cupboard within earshot of General Araki and his party," she continued. "As a result, I overheard things that I would have been better off not hearing at all."

"Like what, Yuki—Chiyotsuru?" Joao had given himself away. There *was* something between them. He knew the geisha's real name.

Chiyotsuru continued as if she hadn't noticed her lover's gaff. "Once we had all left the room, His Excellency began to speak. He had an aristocratic voice and occasionally used old forms of the Japanese language that I hadn't ever heard. He started off by saying that, although a Lieutenant Fujii had unfortunately lost his life to a sniper's bullet, the Brotherhood's activities in Shanghai had worked really well. There had been full-scale war between Japanese bluejackets and Chinese troops and Japan had won. The Western Powers had had no idea how to respond. As a result, Japan had no need to fear Great Britain or America, or even both together, any longer. It was time for those in the room to initiate the second stage of the League of Blood's plan."

"Which is?"

"To carry out a series of assassinations on the fifteenth of May. The Brotherhood—or whatever they call themselves—is planning to place General Araki in charge of Government and '*Kakka*', His Excellency, as the country's 'Supreme Leader.' In his words, 'appointed by Heaven.' Araki claimed to have the support of all army troops stationed in and around the capital."

"A *coup d'état*, then. Who do they plan to assassinate?"

"A couple of businessmen, three politicians—including Ken's father—and Charlie Chaplin."

"The Prime Minister!"

"Charlie Chaplin!"

Joao's and Isa's exclamations revealed their priorities.

"My God! This has to be stopped."

"Yes, but how?"

"I don't know, Joao. It's your country. Tell Ken Inukai for a start. He's your friend, isn't he? He has to warn his father."

"Yes, of course. But Tsuyoshi's as stubborn as a mule. He won't listen to anything Ken tells him, even though he believes in dialogue above all else when it comes to disagreements."

"There's something I don't understand, Joao. How can this guy referred to as 'His Excellency' be 'appointed by heaven'? Is the Ketsumeidan planning to assassinate the Emperor?"

"It seems unlikely, Rusty. But we need more information. Who exactly are they planning to assassinate? And when and where. We've only got three days until the fifteenth."

"As a matter of fact, Araki has booked the Sakura tomorrow

evening," Chiyotsuru put in. "And he's told Okāsan not to accept any other clients. He wants the place to himself."

"And his friends."

"Chiyotsuru, is there anywhere one of us can hide and listen to what they say? A secret room or something?"

"We-ell, now that you mention it, there *is*."

"Where?"

"Right here," she stood up and opened a *fusuma* sliding cupboard door. Beyond it was a deep cupboard, an *oshi-ire*, with cushions stacked neatly on a shelf in the middle and some bedding at the bottom. Behind it was a blank wooden wall. Chiyotsuru reached in behind the bedding. There was the click of a catch and suddenly one half of the back wall opened into a hidden recess.

"There isn't much space here," she said, looking back at us enquiringly. "But it should fit one of you, and you'll be able to hear everything that's said in this room."

"Are you sure, Yuki-*chan*?" This time Joao's use of her name wasn't unintentional. He turned to me. "Perhaps I should explain something, Rusty." Portuguese mode.

"Not unless you really want to, Joao. After all, your private life is your affair."

"True. But still. Yukiko—Chiyotsuru—and I became lovers when I was in Tokyo a few years ago. Fusa, of course, knows nothing of this and I hope it's going to stay that way." He looked at me nervously.

"Why shouldn't it, Joao? Anyway, Fusa is in Nagasaki. And, as I understand it, will continue to stay there until you find suitable accommodation for the two of you here in Tokyo. Don't worry," I glanced at Isa. "Your secret's safe with us."

"Thank you," he put both hands on the *tatami* matting and bowed. Japanese mode again. Then, "Why not try this cupboard space and see for yourself if there's room, Rusty? You're the biggest of us all. I'll close the door after you and we'll have a chat here in this room. See if you can hear us or not."

I did as he suggested and climbed into the space behind the cupboard. It was roomier than I'd imagined and I could sit up quite comfortably against the back wall with my knees up.

Chiyotsuru slid the *oshi-ire* cupboard door closed and started talking with Isa and Joao. I could hear them perfectly. I felt a bit like a ninja hiding out in a samurai lord's house, waiting to kill my prey. The only trouble was I wasn't ginger. Twentieth century blues?

48.

Trying to get hold of Victor's film was proving to be a pretty hopeless endeavour—like looking for the proverbial needle in a haystack—but then the fates intervened. And for once they chose to lend a helping hand.

We were having a late breakfast on the mezzanine floor overlooking the lobby when none other than Miyoko Noguchi walked in through the hotel entrance. It was then that I noticed a man with sleek black hair rising from a settee to greet her.

"No prize for guessing who that gentleman is," Isa said in a low voice.

After the two of them had sat down and exchanged a few words, 'His Excellency' beckoned to a waiter hovering nearby and ordered what turned out to be coffee and pastries. Were we about to kill two birds with one scone?

We could hear the sound of their voices, but neither of us was close enough to follow their conversation. Not that it mattered. My Japanese was little more than rudimentary. After a couple of minutes, however, Miyoko unwrapped a *furoshiki* cloth that she had brought with her and presented her companion with a bamboo *shakuhachi* flute. He smiled and examined it carefully, before putting the mouthpiece to his lips. Miyoko stayed him with one hand and pointed to a middle section of the flute between the finger holes. 'His Excellency' looked at it closer, said "Ah!" loudly enough for us to hear, and began gingerly to unscrew the bamboo pipe.

Once separated, he peered into both parts of the *shakuhachi*. Then he bowed. Miyoko bowed back. After a few more minutes of conversation, she stood up, bowed deeply and left. Her companion screwed the two parts of the *shakuhachi* back together before wrapping the musical instrument carefully in the *furoshiki* cloth that Miyoko had left behind. Unhurriedly, he finished his coffee, wiped his lips, stood up and left the hotel.

"What now?" I asked. "We can't follow him."

"Not unless we want to be arrested!" Isa laughed. "Why don't we ask the hotel doorman who he is and where he went?"

"Isa, you're a genius."

"I prefer to be a tiger, but if you insist. Let me deal with this, *mein Blümchen*. I think this is going to need a woman's subtle conversational skills."

She got up and went down the staircase to the lobby, leaving me to my toast and marmalade. One thing I could tell Victor that would please him—the Japanese had no idea how to make proper marmalade.

Isa soon rejoined me.

"The doorman didn't know His Excellency's name," she said, a little breathlessly, "but thought he was staying with a priest at the Yasukuni Shrine. Apparently, it was built to honour the souls of those who have died fighting for Japan. The doorman seemed very proud of this and suggested I go there right now. He would call a taxi for me. I declined on the grounds that the Prime Minister was waiting to have lunch with us."

"He isn't, is he?"

"No, of course not, silly. But it means you're going to have to take me out to lunch."

Always one step—or was it a tiger's leap?—ahead of me.

We took a taxi to the Ginza and walked around Mitsukoshi, Japan's premier department store. It boasted an excellent café, a rooftop playground for the children of women visiting the store, an art gallery, and on the fifth floor a theatre where an all-girls troupe was playing. All this in addition to the usual things a department store sells.

We decided to go to a theatre play and bought tickets for what seemed at first to be a pretty run-of-the-mill melodramatic revue, except that all the parts were played by women and the period costumes, set designs and lighting were lavish. Quite impressive, really. And definitely entertaining enough to take our minds off 'His Excellency' and Miyoko for a couple of hours. Well, that was the theory anyway.

In practice, a man sitting beside Isa began to explain to her in passable English what was going on. When the interval came, we went out into the foyer where, together with our new found friend, we found ourselves quickly surrounded by half a dozen American tourists who had heard our Japanese informant speaking English and wanted to know more about what was going on. He dutifully obliged by explaining that the show was called the Takarazuka Revue, after the name of a small town near Osaka where the first theatre had been built about fifteen years previously. The actors were trained for two years before being assigned to either masculine or feminine roles and placed in one of five different troupes. They called themselves Takarasiennes.

When I said I was a journalist, he immediately offered to take me backstage after the performance. His sister was one of the actresses playing a feminine role on stage.

"Not resbian," he said, waving the palm of his hand in front of his face to signify 'no.' "Bi-you-chi-furu, desho?"

I agreed to everything, saying that I'd like to go backstage to do an interview after the performance, that his sister was indeed beautiful, and that, so far as I knew, she wasn't a lesbian.

The Americans with me laughed loudly, as Americans tend to do. Isa had slipped away, presumably to 'powder her nose,' but I should have learned by now never to presume. Nor to assume.

I was heading back into the theatre when she came up from behind me and said in a low voice.

"Keep walking and don't look at me, *mein Blümschen*. Just glance at your watch and have a sudden urge to go to the Gents toilet. I'll meet you there."

I did as she suggested. While I was inside, a bell rang to indicate one minute before the curtain went up. I washed my hands unhurriedly and left the Gents to find her waiting just outside the door. The foyer was already almost empty, the last stragglers hurrying into the theatre past an usherette waiting by the double doors. Like their soldiers in Manchuria, Japanese audiences were clearly used to obeying commands. Even discreet ones.

"Miyoko's here," Isa said quickly.

"What!"

"She suggested we meet after the performance. The last thing either of us wants is for her to notice you."

"I'd better leave, then."

"Yes. Go back to the hotel now. I'll come and find you later."

So I forewent the opportunity to interview a beautiful Takarasienne who wasn't a lesbian and made my way back to the Imperial, only to encounter none other than Charlie Chaplin outside the hotel entrance. He was getting out of a black limousine driven by Tsuyoshi Inukai's chauffeur, Kobayashi.

"*Ara! Kanshaku*!" Kobayashi exclaimed and bowed. Where he'd learned I was a count, I'd no idea. "This is a coincidence."

"Indeed, Kobayashi-*san*. And thank you for your services the other evening."

"My pleasure, *Kanshaku*." He bowed again.

A bell-hop started taking the film star's luggage out of the car's capacious boot.

"Why! If it isn't my good friend Rusty Bloom," Charlie beamed and slapped me on the back. Not only had he recognised me; he seemed genuinely pleased to see me. "You're the last person I expected to meet here in Tokyo."

"And you're the last person I expected to bump into outside the Imperial Hotel," I replied. "Mark you, now that I stop to think about it, I can't imagine where else you'd stay in this city. How's everything? No Hedi with you?"

Charlie laughed. "No. She escaped my clutches in Hong Kong for the bear hug of Hollywood. I'm on my own. Unless, of course, one of the delightful young Japanese women I've seen in the streets can be persuaded to join me while I'm here."

"I'm sure the Prime Minister would be happy to help."

"Ah! So you know about that, Rusty? You really *are* a newshound, aren't you?"

"I'm paid to write what my public expects."

"While I'm paid to entertain the public in the manner it expects."

"Birds of a feather, then. Your dinner with Prime Minister Inukai is on Sunday evening, isn't it?"

"Yes. Five o'clock. I've got a lot on tomorrow, but am free all day Sunday. Any suggestions about how to fill in my time?"

By now we were inside, and a receptionist was hovering nearby, waiting to usher Chapurin-*san* to the front desk for check-in. He probably had the most luxurious of suites somewhere near the top of the building with a view of the palace and its gardens. Lucky him.

"There's a *sumō* wrestling tournament going on, I believe. You might find that interesting."

"*Sumō*?"

"The largest and fattest men you'll ever see in Japan wrestling more or less naked in a sand ring."

"Sounds different. What would the Little Tramp make of it, I wonder?"

"Probably not much. But it might well give him some ideas about how to entertain his public in the future. I gather Sunday is the last day of the tournament. It should be fun."

Charlie stood there thinking, while the receptionist hovered ever more uncertainly.

"Why don't we go together?" he said eventually. "If you're not busy, that is. Can you get tickets?"

"Of course," I said, not having the faintest idea how or where to buy them. Joao would help. He'd have to if he wanted to tag along, too. With his Yuki-*chan* in tow, no doubt.

"Why don't we have lunch together in the hotel and then go on to the tournament? How about twelve noon here in the lobby? If what you say is true, it should be a lot of fun."

Little did he know.

49.

Joao had promised he would come to the hotel the moment *Kakka* and his blood brothers had left the Sakura teahouse. He was earlier than I'd expected and Isa wasn't yet back. I had a feeling, though, that she'd be otherwise engaged throughout the night, if past meetings with Miyoko were anything to go by.

Joao arrived with Ken, and Yukiko still dressed up as Chiyotsuru. In order not to attract attention in the lobby, they came up to the room Isa and I were sharing.

"Where's Isa?"

"Not here," I said, impatient to hear their news. "She came across Miyoko Noguchi at the Takarazuka Theatre in Mitsukoshi Department Store earlier this afternoon."

"And left you on your own, Rusty? I should have asked Asakichi to come and keep you company."

"Never mind that," I said brusquely. "What did you learn at the Sakura?"

"Something rather shocking, I'm afraid," Ken took over, the consummate politician. "*Kakka* and his friends plan to assassinate not only my father and Charlie Chaplin, but the Emperor as well."

So Bai-li had been very well informed about Chaplin, though not about the emperor.

"What? Hirohito himself? But how?"

"His Excellency, it seems, has access to and knows his way around the Imperial Palace. At least, so he claimed."

"What's the plan then?"

"Whose plan? Ours? Or theirs?"

"Both, of course."

"There's not much we can do about theirs," Ken said authoritatively, "other than warn those concerned, especially the Imperial Household."

"Will they listen?"

"Almost certainly. If only because they can't afford not to. Imagine the scandal if something *were* to happen to the Emperor. The real difficulty will be persuading my father to cancel dinner with Charlie Chaplin and to stay at home in our house on Mejiro Hill. He's as obstinate as a mule."

"Talking of Chaplin, I've just met him."

"You have? Where?"

"Downstairs in the lobby. He's staying here."

"Well that simplifies things a bit."

"And the two of us have a date to go and watch the *sumō* tournament on Sunday afternoon," I added. "If one of you gentlemen can find us tickets."

Ken was first to recover from his surprise.

"Whatever gave you that idea, Rusty? It's brilliant. Nobody's going to try to assassinate Chaplin during a *sumō* tournament. The arena is hallowed ground. Leave the tickets to me. I'll buy half a dozen so that we can all go. I assume Isa will be back from her tryst with Madame Noguchi by then?"

"One would imagine so. If she isn't, it means she's been done away with by the Tokkō. Or the Kempeitai. I'm due to have lunch with Chaplin here at the hotel. We're meeting in the lobby at twelve noon."

"Right. We'll all join you, just to make sure nothing goes wrong.

I'll book a table and we can take it from there. Chiyotsuru, why don't you bring Asakichi along, too, to entertain Chaplin. Is that a plan?"

"Sounds like it. Time for bed, then?"

"Seems like a good idea."

"What have you got on tomorrow, Rusty?"

"Nothing. Should I have?"

"How about a day in the countryside, then? The forecast is good, so you should be able to get a good view of Mount Fuji. I'll arrange for Kobayashi to drive you and Isa to Lake Kawaguchi. And Yukiko and you, too, Joao, if you'd like to go."

"That sounds wonderful. Many thanks, Ken."

"My pleasure. And Kobayashi's, too. He was very excited to learn you're a count, Rusty."

"Yes. He kept calling me *kanshaku* when I met him with Chaplin downstairs."

"It makes a change from his usual '*sensei*,' or teacher. In Japan they say that if you throw a pebble off the top of a mountain invariably you'll hit a *sensei* in Japan. There are so many of them. But not a *kanshaku*. Counts are a rare breed."

"Hopefully not about to become extinct."

50.

It was five thirty in the morning when Isa finally came back. She looked exhausted.

"Long night?" I asked, as I rubbed my eyes sleepily. Kobayashi was due to pick us up at eight.

"Very," she collapsed on the bed beside me and put an arm across my chest. "Miyoko was all hyped up and spent the whole night either making love or talking. I don't think I got a wink of sleep."

"You can sleep in the car, then," I said encouragingly. "We've got a long drive ahead of us."

"What do you mean?"

I explained.

"Oh!" was all she said.

"So what did Miyoko talk about? Anything interesting?"

"Apart from scolding me for dying my hair black, yes, although she was happy I'd kept my red tufts down below. You may want to cancel our excursion when you hear what she told me, though."

"Try me."

So she did.

"Do you remember how I told you all about Miyoko's past—her first encounter with Kenji Doihara leading to her becoming a concubine to an imperial prince?"

"Prince Tadamaro?"

Isa put her lips firmly together and gave me a look that showed she was impressed.

"So you *do* listen to me occasionally."

"Occasionally, yes. Carry on."

"What I learned last night was that Prince Tadamaro had a son. The Prince was, of course, older than Miyoko—much older—although she professed to have grown to love him during their time together. But he was married, as is the case with princes, and had a son by his wife. That son was, or rather is, more or less the same age as Miyoko."

"So she had a companion when living in the imperial villa in Hayama?"

"Yes. He was also born in the Year of the Snake. She said they used to spend hours playing music together. She on the *biwa* lute, he on the *shakuhachi* bamboo flute. They became very close."

"Too close?"

Isa ignored my query.

"You will remember that Prince Tadamaro died rather suddenly when Miyoko was twenty years old."

"Of a snake bite."

"My goodness, Rusty! You *were* paying attention." She gave me a kiss on the cheek as a reward. "Well, because Miyoko was no longer officially a concubine, it was briefly mooted by those concerned that she be transferred to Tadamaro's son. The Imperial Chamberlain quashed that idea, however. The young prince should get formally married first, before taking a concubine. Moreover, having already been a concubine, Miyoko wasn't entitled to become a prince's wife."

"Does this prince have a name, by any chance?"

"Tadahito."

"Sounds a bit like Hirohito. Any connection?"

"Only that Tadamaro was apparently quite close to Hirohito's father, sort of cousin to the Emperor Taishō, and wanted to please him by giving his new-born baby a name similar to the Emperor's one year-old son. Hirohito and Tadahito played together a lot when they were children."

The light was beginning to dawn inside the room, as well as outside.

"You mean—"

"Let me finish, Rusty," she put one finger to my lips. "I'm not done yet. After Miyoko had left her teenager friend behind in the Imperial Household, Tadahito found himself being advised by those around him to get married. He was, it seemed, next in line to the throne until Hirohito produced a male heir. So various eligible young ladies were introduced, but all were found wanting, mainly because Tadahito preferred men—something he discovered, according to Miyoko, when he accompanied his cousin Hirohito on a state visit to England in 1921."

"Victor's photograph! The one he took at Frolics."

"Yes. It was there that Tadahito took a shine to Prince George."

"The same Prince George that Kiki seems to have fallen for."

"Hardly surprising. By all accounts, he's an extremely handsome and charming young man. According to Miyoko, Tadahito fell head over heels in love with the English prince. But there was nothing he could do about it on such a short trip and he reportedly pined for the object of his passion all the way back to Japan. When the Imperial Chamberlain introduced yet another well-brought up eligible young lady to him, Tadahito refused point blank to get married, told the Chamberlain he was a homosexual, and demanded permission to retire from the Imperial Household."

"That must have created quite a stir."

"It did indeed, although it was never made public, of course. There was a flurry of inconclusive meetings among various members of the Imperial Household. Eventually Hirohito himself intervened on behalf of his childhood friend and told the Imperial Chamberlain to let Tadahito go—again with a generous pension."

"So the young prince went out into the big wide world."

"Where he started talking to people, real people. Before long, he had gathered round him a group of like-minded young army and navy officers —'

"'Like-minded' in terms of political ideology? Or sexual orientation?"

"For the most part, both. Tadahito claims to have had some kind of mystical experience soon after leaving the imperial household and convinced his coterie that what Japan needed was a 'spiritual rebirth.' Meanwhile, he changed his name to Chikubu."

"Chikubu? What kind of Japanese name is that?"

"I've no idea, *mein Blümschen*. Apparently it is some obscure reference to his flute playing."

"So where does Miyoko fit into all this?"

"She's a fervent believer in Chikubu and has been convinced by him that what is needed is an imperial restoration. Party politics must be eliminated, the bureaucracy revamped, corrupt political and financial elites erased."

"In other words, she's in favour of a *coup d'état*."

"Which returns the Japanese people to the 'right' way of thinking. Japan's sacred mission is to conquer the world."

"Making Yamato great again, in other words."

"That's about the sum of it."

"Which explains what Ken Inukai told me last night. While hiding in Chiyotsuru's geisha house cupboard, he overheard Chikubu outlining a plan to assassinate the Emperor on Sunday, along with the Prime Minister and various other political and financial leaders."

"What! The Emperor? But he and Chikubu are childhood friends."

"It seems that General Araki has persuaded Prince Chikubu—yes, prince once more—that the Emperor is standing in the way of Japan's glorious destiny by refusing to sanction the Kwantung Army's march north into Siberia and southwards into China. By removing Hirohito from the Chrysanthemum Throne, as Minister of War, Araki can proclaim martial law in Japan and proclaim Chikubu Emperor. He is, after all, next in line and his 'retirement' from the Imperial Household has never been made public."

"And what about Charlie Chaplin?"

"He's one of the League of Blood's targets. Apparently, they're convinced that by assassinating Chaplin, they'll be able to instigate war with the United States."

"But Chaplin's British, not American."

"Precisely. Shows you what misguided crackpots they are, doesn't it!"

"So Su Bai-li was right."

"Seems like it. He's here, you know?"

"Who? Bai-li?"

"No. Chaplin. Here in this hotel. Holed up above us in some luxury suite. I bumped into him after I got back from the theatre and we arranged to have lunch together tomorrow, before going to a *sumō* wrestling tournament. Ken, Joao and a couple of our geisha friends are going to join us. Hopefully, you will, too."

"I wouldn't miss it for anything."

"Not even Miyoko?" I teased.

"I said 'anything,' *mein Blümchen*. Not 'anyone.'" She laughed and gave me another kiss—this time firmly on the mouth to allay any pangs of jealousy I may have had.

"It's all falling into place, isn't it?" I said, once we drew apart. "Simon Meyer's kidnapping, Victor's photograph, the Blood Brotherhood. Now we have to put a stop to it all."

"As usual, easier said than done."

"As usual."

51.

We never got to see Mount Fuji. Not that Saturday, at least. Once

Kobayashi had driven up to the hotel entrance with Joao and Yukiko in the back seat, we told them everything Isa had learned. Joao was on the telephone to Ken for a good twenty minutes, while Yukiko, Isa and I had coffee together in the lobby. In halting English, she told us a little about herself—her background, how she had met Joao, that sort of thing— before expressing her fascination at hearing that Isa's hair was really dark red, not black. She wished she could have seen it. Whereupon Isa whispered something in her ear and the two of them giggled girlishly before standing up.

"We need to powder our noses," Isa said and the two women went off arm in arm laughing. It was only much later that Isa told me she had shown Yukiko the red hair under her arms. The geisha had learned a new English phrase—'ginger ninja'—and almost died laughing. Isa had made her first Japanese friend.

Joao was all business once he'd finished his phone call.

"I'm sorry," he said, "but our planned excursion is off for today. There's too much to do. Can you look after yourselves? We've got to warn the palace. Chikubu, or Tadahito, is still a prince of the realm, even if he has chosen to step away from his royal duties. This is a matter which, even as Prime Minister, Ken's father isn't allowed to deal with. Only the Imperial Household can intervene."

"Do you have any contacts in the Imperial Household?"

"Very much so. Don't worry. Ken has already alerted Prince Saionji to what the League of Blood is planning. The three of us are to meet in the palace across the road. Actually, four of us. Prince Saionji has a special affection for Chiyotsuru and asked her to come, too."

"Just when we begin happy relationship," Yukiko smiled, gently squeezing Isa's hand.

"Never mind, Yuki-*chan*. There will be another day." Isa kissed her on the cheek, the way German women often do when saying goodbye. Yukiko blushed, then smiled.

"Yes, I hope."

Beware the *ang mo* tigress.

52.

Left on our own, Isa and I were discussing how best to spend the day when who should walk past us but Kiki.

"Kiki?"

"Rusty, *darling*! And Irene Wiedemeyer. What on *earth* are you two doing here?"

"I might ask the same of you. Attending a wedding, actually."

"*Ryallai*? Anyone I know?"

"Joao Serino."

"Ah yes. That Japanese newspaper chappie who dresses like an Englishman in flannel suits."

"That's him. Anyway, what brings to you to Tokyo?"

"I'm with *George*," she said, indicating a handsome man talking to a couple of Japanese military-looking types near the concierge's desk. "You *know*, the prince."

"But what are you doing in Tokyo, Kiki?" It was Isa's turn to ask.

"Oh, just tagging along, you know."

We didn't.

"Tagging along?"

"Yes, there's a German airplane designer chappie who wants to sell one of his designs to the Japanese. George said he'd be happy to fly it here for him, so the two of us came over in it to show how far the plane can fly. Kind of *advertising*, I suppose."

"But surely, you didn't fly all the way from London, did you?"

"Berlin, *acksherly*. Not all at once, of course. We did the trips in hops—kangaroo style—although, to be *frightfully* honest, I'm not sure I'll do it again in a hurry. It was *freezing* coming over Siberia, I can tell you. I thought I'd join the choir invisible. Luckily, George had loaded plenty of vodka on board. I'd *never* have survived otherwise."

I had by now taken a long look at our George across the lobby. He was definitely the English prince in Victor's photo. The question was: would he be meeting the Japanese princeling? And if so, when?

The answer to that came soon enough. Kiki was in the process of introducing her simply *fabulous* friends from Shanghai to Prince George, when we were suddenly joined by a short Japanese with an effeminate face and hair parted in the middle.

He was also holding a *shakuhachi* which, in order to shake hands with us, he placed on the concierge's desk beside him. Nobody offered me a prize for guessing who he was.

The two men almost, but not quite, melted into each other's arms as they greeted each other longingly. But both had been properly brought up in their respective royal households and knew how to behave in public. So we made polite conversation about the delights of Tokyo versus those of Shanghai. For a prince, Tadahito—or Chikubu, or whatever it was he called himself in the privacy of George's bedroom—knew a lot about the seamier side of life in Tokyo and happily advised us to try a certain Turkish bath in Shibuya, one or two Kagurazaka geisha houses, which didn't include Chiyotsuru's Sakura, and several bars of more and less dubious reputation in Shinjuku.

After a while, George made some flimsy excuse about needing to change before lunch and Tadahito took the opportunity to ask whether he might see George's room. He had never actually stayed at the Imperial

Hotel and wanted to know if it might be a place to recommend to his friends. So off they went up the central staircase from the lobby, almost hand in hand. In his excitement, Tadahito left his *shakuhachi* behind on the concierge's desk.

Kiki sighed.

"George likes women, *too*, you know. It's just that he's bisexual."

"That can't make life easy for you, Kiki."

"No. Still, I feel *awfully* sorry for his future wife, don't you?." She sighed again. "But enough of that! I must be orf. I've got a *frightful* lot to do, you know. Will you be here long?"

"A few more days," Isa answered for me.

"Oh goody. We simply *must* meet."

"Absolutely!"

"Jolly good. Toodle pip, then."

And many toodles of her pip, too, I thought uncharitably. Or should that be pips of her toodle? If only I had the Encyclopaedia Britannica to hand.

But what we did have to hand was the princeling's flute and, if we were lucky, Victor's original negatives inside it. The concierge was dealing with a guest on the other side of the foyer so, as casually as I could manage, I picked up the *shakuhachi* and slipped it under my unbuttoned jacket. Then I put my arm around Isa and escorted her up the sweeping staircase to an indoor balcony where there were a few tables affording a view of the Imperial Palace across the road. Nobody else was around, so we sat down quickly on two of the hotel's famed peacock chairs with the *shakuhachi* between us.

"You do it, Isa. I think my hands are trembling too much."

"No, Rusty. *You* do it. I don't trust my fingers. I've had a long night, remember?"

So I picked up the flute, examined it, and slowly and carefully began to unscrew one section of it between the four finger holes. The top section came off and, holding my breath, I turned it upside down.

Nothing came out.

I turned the bottom section down towards the table and gently shook the *shakuhachi*. Again nothing. Desperately, I looked inside. If the film wasn't here, where on earth was it?

But it was inside the hollowed-out bamboo. The negative had been removed from its canister, probably because the canister was too big to fit, and the film had naturally unrolled itself against the inside of the bottom half of the bamboo pipe.

"Here," I handed Isa the *shakuhachi*. "Your little finger's smaller than mine. You get it out."

Which she did.

I looked around nervously. There was still nobody near us.

"Is it what we're looking for?"

Isa held the negative up to the light by the window.

"Yes."

Bingo.

It was all the rage in Shanghai.

53.

The following morning, the hotel receptionist handed Isa a handwritten letter.

"It's from Miyoko. She wants to meet me this evening," she said after reading it.

"Where?"

"A bar called Indigo, somewhere in Harajuku."

"A place to meet a duke, perhaps, and give you the blues? You'll end up like Kiki, Isa."

"I doubt it. Miyoko says she wants to celebrate."

"No prizes for guessing why."

"None whatsoever."

"So you're going? What time do you have to be there?"

"Nine o'clock. Of course I'm going. We both know I have no choice."

"True. Looks like another long night ahead, Isa dear. You'd better get some rest before we go to watch the *sumō*."

"I will."

She got up in time for what turned out to be a lazy drawn-out lunch. Chaplin was in good form and seemed to enjoy our company. But then Yukiko was sitting opposite him and he could hardly take his eyes off her. I had a feeling he would have been all over her if Joao hadn't made it clear that she was his. For now, at least. He had also brought Asakichi along in all her finery. Now was the opportunity for the Little Tramp to charm the wig off a geisha.

Eventually we headed off in two of Ken's father's cars to the Ryōgoku Arena, known affectionately by locals as the 'big iron umbrella' because of its dome-shaped roof. Ken had purchased what turned out to be a kind of box in which we could all sit on comfortable cushions and watch the action only a few rows in front of us. He and Joao found themselves spending a lot of time explaining the different kinds of winning throws, who was who, and what the different *sumō* wrestler ranks were. There was great excitement because the tournament champion would only emerge in the last bout of the afternoon when two undefeated wrestlers with seven wins each were due to fight each other.

At one point towards the end of the bouts, Charlie said he needed an extra cushion to sit on. Unused to sitting cross-legged on tatami mats, his legs had become numb. There was a cushion seller just behind us—apparently an ardent fan of the Little Tramp because, having handed a thick cushion to the object of his admiration, he asked him for his autograph.

"Purīzu, Chapurin-*san*, name sign *onegaishimasu*."

Chaplin duly obliged by scribbling on a postcard the attendant held out to him, before putting his new cushion on top of the old one.

"Takanofuji is the one to watch," Ken said, as excitement built up for the last fight. It was already past five o'clock, the time Charlie was supposed to be joining Ken's father, Tsuyoshi, for dinner at the Prime Minister's residence. Ken himself was clearly worried about what might be about to happen to his father, but the Little Tramp was fascinated by everything going on in the ring and refused to leave.

"Which of the two is Taka-whatever his name is?"

"The thin, wiry one on the left."

"Him?" Charlie expressed his doubt. "But the other guy's a giant. He'll steam-roller Taka-whatsit, surely?"

"You'd think so, wouldn't you? Asanishiki's got an enormous weight advantage, so the longer the fight drags on, the more likely he is to win. But Takanofuji's lightning quick and he knows he's at a disadvantage when it comes to a head-on attack. He'll probably step aside to avoid Asanishiki's initial charge and slap the big man down from behind."

"And there's a lot at stake for both of them. Asanishiki has just been promoted to the rank of *yokozuna* and will want to prove his worth, while Takanofuji has never been a champion, so they'll really go for it."

The two wrestlers stalked out of the centre of the ring to their respective corners where they rinsed their mouths, grasped a handful of salt, turned and stood impassively facing us, waiting for each other.

"What's the salt for? You told me earlier, but I've forgotten in my excitement."

"Purification. The *dohyō* ring has to be purified before every fight."

"Ah yes, of course!"

The two wrestlers strode into the centre of the ring and squatted down on their haunches facing each other.

"They're going to fight now?"

"Not yet, Chaplin-*san*. They're still checking each other out. The *gyōji* referee is the one who judges when wrestlers are ready to fight and he hasn't given the signal yet."

Eventually, though, he did and the gigantic Asanishiki squared off against the much smaller Takanofuji. They crouched down in the middle of the ring, eyeing each other fiercely. Then Asanishiki tapped one fist on the sand and launched himself forward. As Ken had predicted, Takanofuji stepped quickly to one side, stuck out one leg to trip his opponent, and used the other's speed to dump him unceremoniously onto the sand in the middle of the ring.

The crowd erupted. The underdog had beaten a Grand Champion. People began throwing their cushions up in the air towards the ring where the crestfallen Asanishiki dropped his head in submission to the new champion. Takanofuji himself crouched down on his haunches to receive a dozen envelopes filled with prize money.

The cushions kept flying. In his excitement Charlie suddenly stood up and hurled his own cushions towards the ring. A moment later there was a loud thwomp as one of them exploded in mid-air. For a few seconds there was total silence in the vast arena. It was as if the frame of a film had been frozen. But only for a few seconds. Then there were screams and the mass panic of hundreds of people, including ourselves, trying to get out of the arena as fast as we could.

And that was how the League of Blood nearly, but not quite, managed to assassinate Charlie Chaplin.

54.

Reuters Stop Press, **Prime Minister of Japan Assassinated**. Sunday May 15, 1932

The Prime Minister of Japan, Tsuyoshi Inukai, was assassinated at 5 o'clock this afternoon (Japan time) in his official residence opposite the Diet building in downtown Tokyo.

It is at the moment unclear who the assassins are. It was rumoured that they might be disaffected army and navy officers, but a police spokesman described them only as 'men wearing uniforms.'

Updates to follow.

Asahi Shimbun, **Charlie Chaplin and the *Sumō* Championships**, by Joao Serino. Monday May 16, 1932

Extraordinary scenes took place on the final day of sumō's *summer championship at the Ryōgoku Arena in Tokyo yesterday afternoon.*

This year's tournament has been marked by a wrestlers' strike, which meant that a number of well-known sumō rikishi *did not participate. This, perhaps, enabled the meteoric success of a lower-ranked* makunouchi *wrestler,*

Takanofuji, who came into the last day of the tournament undefeated with seven wins to his credit.

He was not the only one, however. His opponent yesterday was the mighty Asanishiki, yokozuna grand champion, also with an unblemished record of seven wins. Would the small and wiry Takanofuji be able to overcome the gigantic Asanishiki who was at least half again his weight? This was a match of almost Biblical proportions, with the Kagoshima-born David pitted against the Tōhoku Goliath.

Both wrestlers are extremely popular with sumō aficionados and Ryōgoku's 'Large Umbrella' was soon filled with the noise of the crowd's vociferous support for one wrestler or the other.

One of those lending their support to the 'little man' was none other than Mr Charles Chaplin, who is visiting Tokyo for a few days and was due to be entertained at dinner yesterday evening by the Prime Minister, Mr Tsuyoshi Inukai. Chaplin was accompanied by the Prime Minister's son, Ken Inukai, as well as by Count Christopher Bloom, a Swedish journalist, and his charming companion, Miss Irene Wiedemeyer. Two geisha from a Kagurazaka teahouse were also present in their party.

Eventually the time came for the much anticipated bout. After going through the customary preparations, the two undefeated wrestlers faced off against each other. Asanishiki charged; Takanofuji nimbly stepped aside, and the bigger man quickly found himself face down in the sand. The low-ranking maegashira *wrestler had defeated the* yokozuna *and won this year's May tournament. The last day was indeed a* senshūraku, *'the pleasure of a thousand autumns.'*

The crowd went absolutely wild with delight. Many threw the cushions on which they had been sitting all afternoon into the ring to show their appreciation for Takanofuji's remarkable victory.

However, one cushion contained a bomb and exploded in mid-air above the dohyō *ring. Fortunately, nobody was injured, but the explosion quickly gave rise to panic among many of those attending. This led to a mass exit from the arena. As a result, the prize-winning ceremony was sparsely attended—something which Takanofuji surely did not deserve on the occasion of this, his very first, championship.*

It later emerged that the bomb which exploded had been placed in Mr Chaplin's cushion by one of the perpetrators of yesterday's attempted assassinations, in which the Prime Minister himself was killed. However, we are glad to report that Mr Chaplin and his entourage escaped unharmed. It is to be hoped that members of this so-called League of Blood will soon be brought to justice and sentenced for their crimes in the manner that they deserve.

The Japan Times, **News in Brief***, Monday May 16, 1932*

A spokesman for the Imperial Household this morning announced the sudden death yesterday evening of Prince Tadahito, son of the former Prince Tadamaro, cousin of the Emperor Taishō, and childhood friend of Hirohito, the current Emperor Shōwa. Prince Tadahito was 38 years old.

Details are as yet unclear, but the spokesman attributed Prince Tadahito's death to a snake bite—the manner in which his father died some years ago. Although the Imperial Palace grounds with their thick shrubbery and numerous ponds provide an untroubled refuge for snakes, it is rare for one of them to be poisonous. A thorough search of the palace grounds is now being conducted to ensure that no other member of the Imperial Household suffers such a tragic inconvenience.

The Emperor Shōwa, we are delighted to inform our readers, is in the best of health. He spent the weekend at the imperial pavilion in Hayama pursuing his scholarly interest in marine biology.

The Shanghai Times / Frankfurter Zeitung, **An Intriguing Death in Tokyo***,* by Christopher Bloom. Wednesday May 18, 1932

The recent discovery of a dead body in an unfrequented part of a Tokyo park has given rise to all kind of rumour and scandal involving both the Imperial Household and a popular all-female theatre troupe known as the Takarazuka Revue.

At around midday on May 16, the body of a Japanese woman was discovered in Yoyogi Park. According to a police report, she was 38 years of age, five foot five inches tall, and elegantly dressed in expensive kimono, footwear, and hair trappings. Contents of the purse in her hand revealed that her name was Miyoko Noguchi, once concubine to Prince Tadamaro, former cousin of the Emperor Taishō.

Shibuya Police Station, which has been tasked with investigating Madame Noguchi's death, first let it be known that the victim had died of poison—in all probability the venom of a cobra. An empty phial of this venom was found by the victim's side, suggesting suicide.

Detectives, however, were not convinced and suspected foul play. This may have been because Prince Tadahito, son of Prince Tadamaro, was also found dead of a snake bite in the Imperial Palace last Sunday evening. He and Madame Noguchi were childhood friends who enjoyed playing traditional Japanese music together. Both were devotees of Saraswati, or Benzaiten, the 'goddess of eloquence.'

Investigations have revealed that, a few afternoons prior to her death, Madame Noguchi attended a special performance by the Takarazuka

Revue of the play, The Snake Goddess, *held in the theatre of Mitsukoshi Department Store theatre at the northern end of the Ginza in Tokyo.*

The Takarazuka Revue is an all-female musical theatre troupe which puts on Western-style song and dance shows, in which both male and female roles are played by women. The Revue is extremely popular in Japan and every year stages a number of successful Broadway-style shows, with lavish costumes and opulent sets. They attract large audiences, primarily of Japanese women.

Actors are auditioned among fierce competition and, if selected, undergo training for at least two years. They are only then assigned to masculine or feminine roles, in which they specialise during the entirety of their careers. Once a man, always a man. On stage, at least.

But maybe—as the death of Madame Noguchi has suggested to some— they retain their feminine masculinity in the outside world as well.

The plot of The Snake Goddess *attended by Madame Noguchi revolves around a young woman who believes that she is the reincarnation of Benzaiten, Japan's 'Madame White Snake' goddess.*

Benzaiten owes her origin to Saraswati, the Hindu river goddess of knowledge, music, arts, speech, wisdom, and learning, and was imported into Japan through China sometime around the seventh century AD. She is now included among the Seven Gods of Fortune in Japan, and is honoured as a river goddess of fertility and abundance, as the mistress of serpents, as guardian of the sacred wish-granting jewel, and as defender of Japan itself. She is sometimes represented with the head of a snake.

The goddess is believed to reside on Chikubushima, a small island at the northern end of Lake Biwa, Japan's largest lake whose name comes from the fact that its shape resembles that of a Japanese lute, or biwa. *According to police, a* biwa *was found at the side of Madame Noguchi's corpse.*

The tale of The Snake Goddess, *as performed by the 'Takarasiennes,' is typically romantic and improbable. It takes place in the tenth century on the shores of Lake Biwa. Its hero is a handsome young prince with green eyes, who overhears a beautiful young woman playing her* biwa *lute one evening as he sits admiring the full moon rising over the lake. Entranced by the skill and emotion that she puts into her music, he approaches her and asks politely if he might sit together with her to admire the moon.*

She makes a place for him on the matting on which she is kneeling. Her name, she says, is Miyoko, meaning 'child born of a snake'—the name, we should note, of the deceased, Madame Noguchi. They talk deep into the night of literature, poetry and music, and he accompanies her on his shakuhachi *flute, before inviting her to accompany him back to his imperial pavilion built on wooden stilts out over the lake. There they lie down and make love. In the heat of her passion she leaves two tiny bite marks at the base of his neck.*

When he awakes the next morning, Miyoko is gone. But that night he hears her again playing her lute nearby. He joins her and once again they play music together before making love. Again, she leaves before first light after leaving two tiny fang-like marks on his neck.

And so the tale goes on for a full two hours, during which time the prince slowly becomes emaciated and loses his life force. The audience realises that Miyoko is in fact not a beautiful young woman, but a venomous snake whose intention is to kill the handsome prince. Although his friends and courtiers wonder why he never sees his lover in broad daylight, the prince is too entranced by Miyoko's beauty and accomplishments to pay heed to their warnings. And so he wastes away and eventually dies one night in her arms.

Police investigations have revealed that Madame Noguchi was particularly fond of The Snake Goddess *and frequently attended performances of the play. Witnesses came forward to attest that she had been seen in the company of a beautiful woman with green eyes on the day of her death.*

One eyewitness suggested that this woman was in fact the Takarazuka actor who played the masculine role of the prince in the play. Although the actor in question had a fool-proof alibi, the story quickly gave rise to all kinds of lurid—and, surely, unfounded—speculation in the Japanese press about lesbian activities in Imperial Japan.

Another eyewitness attested to the fact that the woman seen in the company of Madame Noguchi was not Japanese, but Caucasian. This seemed unlikely, given that all foreigners living in Japan are subject to extremely competent police surveillance. Nevertheless, popular newspapers quickly began discussing whether it was 'right and proper' for Japanese women to have love affairs with foreigners—men or women.

In an obvious attempt to quell such improper discussions, the police have now accepted—perhaps slightly reluctantly—that Madame Noguchi indeed took her own life. At the inquest held at Shibuya Police Station yesterday afternoon, a coroner pronounced Madame Noguchi's suicide as death by misadventure.

Japanese people's attention can now be focused on more serious topics worthy of the nation's Heavenly Mandate—in particular, bringing to justice the perpetrators of last Sunday's heinous assassinations of leading figures in Japan's political and financial world.

The New York Times, **Government by Assassination**, by Hugh Byas. Special Correspondent. Sunday May 22, 1932

It is now a week since we heard the shocking, and disturbing, news that the Prime Minister of Japan, Tsuyoshi Inukai, had been assassinated in his official residence in Tokyo by a group of young naval officers calling themselves the League of Blood. Precisely why they chose to shoot their Prime Minister is still not known. What has since become clear, however, is the sequence of events that led to Mr Inukai's demise.

May 15 was a Sunday—a day, it transpires, when the Prime Minister's residence is more or less unmanned. As a result, there was nobody in reception when the assassins turned up in two taxis and, pistols in hand, asked a police sergeant to show them to the Prime Minister's apartment. To his credit the policeman refused, so the young officers split into two groups and set out to find their target by themselves.

What they probably were not aware of was the fact that the Prime Minister of Japan's official residence is marked by the general bizarrerie characteristic of the Imperial Hotel, designed by Frank Lloyd Wright. As a result, they were soon lost among seemingly endless passages and staircases going nowhere in particular. One group went upstairs and found the cabinet room. It was empty, but one of their number heard a key turning in a lock nearby and shouted: "This must be the way to the private apartment." They knocked and a voice called: "Who is there?" One of the naval lieutenants burst open the flimsy door with his shoulder and found himself face to face with Prime Minister Tsuyoshi, or Ki, Inukai.

The Emperor's first minister led the officers into a Japanese room, where he asked them to take off their shoes and sit down, so that they might talk matters over. His daughter-in-law, carrying a baby, was with him. One of the officers, fearing what might be about to take place, ordered her to go away, but she remained by her father-in-law's side. The old man himself had a cigarette in his hand and lit it. The young men were both confused and impressed by the Prime Minister's demeanour, and the most senior among them seemed ready to talk with him.

However, just at that moment, the second group of officers broke open a back door and came bursting into the room. They were headed by a man of action, Lieutenant Masayoshi Yamagishi, who immediately shouted: "Words never get us anywhere. Fire!" The others immediately did as ordered. One bullet hit the Prime Minister in the neck; another lodged in his stomach. Mr Inukai sank silently to the tatami-matted floor and never spoke again.

Their task accomplished, both groups of officers left, shooting a policeman who challenged them on their way out. Nobody else tried to detain them. Outside, their taxi-drivers, who had been told to wait, had decamped, so the assassins walked down the hill and picked up two other taxis near the American Embassy, from where they drove to Metropolitan Police headquarters. There they found nobody, so they drove on to the headquarters of the military police, commonly called the Kempeitai or Gendarmerie, where they surrendered.

A third group of officers had been detailed to destroy the offices of the Seiyukai, the Prime Minister's political party. They threw two bombs, neither of which exploded. They then went on to a nearby Metropolitan Police station where they threw three more bombs, one of which struck an electric-light pole and shattered a window. A naval cadet went to the Mitsubishi Bank and threw another bomb which exploded in the yard. Another conspirator went to the house of the Lord Keeper of the Imperial Seals, Count Makino, and flung a grenade at a man who happened to be standing outside the front door. It missed him.

Messages sent to newspapers abroad that night—and published in last Sunday's edition of The New York Times*—said that the Prime Minister had been shot by 'men wearing officers' uniforms.' It has since come to light that the group consists of maybe as many as two dozen disaffected young officers in both the army and the navy. They are led, apparently, by a mysterious figure going by the name of Chikubu, but he has disappeared. His real identity is at present unknown.*

Correspondents and the public were unwilling to believe that officers of the army and navy could have taken to political murder. The whole affair seemed like a murderous prank by a troupe of bloody-minded boy scouts carrying pistols and grenades instead of clasp knives and whistles. Its amateurishness seemed to prove that the movement was confined to a few young fanatics. The public soon recovered its confidence in the discipline and loyalty of the army as a whole.

In fact, however, the actions of the League of Blood have made it clear that the army is honeycombed with political agitation and that the conspirators were ready to bring about martial law by bombing the House of Representatives. In other words, their aim has been nothing short of government by assassination. It remains to be seen what will now happen to Japanese plans for democracy.

Epilogue

It was the nicest time of the year to be in Moscow and it felt good to be back. The lime trees filling the streets and squares of the Sadovaya were in full fresh green leaf. Young women had shed their heavy, dour winter clothes and boots for flowery dresses and fine shoes that showed off the curves of their bodies and the shape of their legs. Young men displayed their biceps in open collared shirts with rolled-up sleeves and ogled the girls as they passed. In the evening, young couples strolled arm in arm along the Gorky Prospekt. Even in the midst of Soviet austerity it was a time for love.

"Comrade Ruskin, the General will see you now."

I was in the first floor gallery overlooking the courtyard at the centre of an Italianate mansion, situated on a quiet side street behind the Pushkin Museum of Fine Arts. This was the headquarters of— to give the place its full title—the Fourth Directorate of the General Staff of the Workers' and Peasants' Red Army. Better known as the Fourth Department, it was one of six Soviet spy agencies operating abroad. Under the leadership of General Jan Berzin, however, it had quickly established itself as at least the equal of, if not better than, the Comintern's OMS spy network, as well as the GPU which was more concerned with hunting down enemies at home and abroad than with systematically gathering economic and political information in the way we did.

Berzin, I already knew from experience, was a ruthless professional. A Latvian by birth, he had, among other deeds, pursued, arrested, and 'liquidated' Russian sailors at the Kronstadt naval base who had mutinied against Bolshevik authority. Not a man to cross. A true disciple of Count Felix Dzerzhinsky, founder of the first Soviet secret police force, he sought to create a puritan and steely high-priesthood, devout in its atheism. Those of us whom he had selected were the avengers of all ancient evils—a far cry from the bickering dreamers employed by the Comintern. We were, in Stalin's words, the decisive weapon against the countless plots and attempts to destroy Soviet power. I was proud to have been selected by Berzin as one of his agents.

Mark you, I had been given a grilling two days earlier at my debriefing. Three impassive intelligence officers in mufti—only one identified himself, as Moskvin—had sifted through my reports and proceeded to question me relentlessly about virtually every move I'd made, every drink I'd had, where, when and with whom, and every man and woman I had met in Shanghai and Tokyo. What was a Chief Chinese Inspector of the Shanghai Municipal Police doing in the vestry of an Orthodox church when I happened to go there? Had I considered the possibility that I might have been compromised? Had it been wise to reveal that I could read and speak Chinese? Why did Mrs Montagu-Rose make a move on me so soon after first meeting me? Why bother to save the life of Shanghai's premier gangster when, by all accounts, he would be better off dead? Had I considered the potential unravelling of a carefully cultivated German asset when Major von Holst discovered, as he surely would discover, that I had seduced his wife? And so on, and so forth.

They wanted to know everything about Simon Meyer's kidnapping and, of course, Victor's photographs, and kept circling back to these two topics, searching for inconsistencies in my account. They elicited in detail my methods, as if I had any, of forming friendships and of seduction when in pursuit of intelligence. And so it went on, for the best part of five hours. Their faces gave nothing away. I had no idea if they approved, or disapproved, of what I told them. My only consolation during the next couple of days was knowing that I was one of Berzin's favourites. So far, at least.

"Comrade Ruskin," the General exclaimed with a welcoming smile as he came from behind his desk to greet me. "Or should I be calling you Rusty and making some allusion to Noel Coward's twentieth century blues?" he laughed. "Anyway, it's good to see you again, and looking so well, too."

He indicated one of two armchairs with chintz-covered cushions facing his desk and I sat down. A relic of pre-revolutionary days by the look and comfortable feel of it. Berzin returned to where he had been sitting behind a polished mahogany desk consisting of two pedestals with drawers and overhanging top inlaid with gilt-lined deep green leather hide. It was massive—strong and tough enough to protect him against all threats and intimidation. The consummate tactician.

"Thank you, Comrade General."

Berzin waved away my formality.

"Rusty, we know each other well enough for you to dispense with my rank."

"Thank you, Jan Antonovich."

"So, let's get down to business." The General was in uniform as always. He crossed his legs to reveal between the two pedestals of his desk a rather snazzy pair of tartan socks. Not quite what one might expect of the Director of the Fourth Department, but the tartan was at least predominantly red. He needed to be careful if ever he came across Fantom, though. Like an agent when burned, the socks would likely 'disappear.'

"We have, of course, received and read with great interest your reports from Shanghai and Tokyo," Berzin interrupted my daydreaming. "I also have here an assessment of your time in the field based on judgements formed during what I gather was quite a lengthy interview earlier this week." He tapped a file on the desk in front of him. "We have no reason to be in any way displeased," he looked at me reassuringly. "All the same, I thought it best that we have this little chat while you're here in Moscow. I hope it doesn't inconvenience you in any way."

"Not at all, Comrade."

"Let's start by going over basics, then. Would I be right in saying that your mission in Shanghai was not tied to any specific aim or purpose?"

"That is correct."

"Instead, you were asked to send us general information on the social and political policies of the new Nationalist Government in Nanking, as well as its opposing factions. I think it fair to say, upon reflection, that this ended up being the weakest aspect of your reports to us."

I made to speak, but Berzin held up his hand.

"I am merely stating a fact, Rusty, not formulating a criticism. Relax!" He smiled. "You were also asked to assess the military strength, deployment, weaponry and morale of Chiang Kai-shek's armies. In this you far exceeded our expectations. Not only did you go deep behind Japanese and Chinese lines, you also developed an extremely promising relationship with a German military attaché who isn't a military attaché, Major Otto von Holst. Not to mention his, surely charming, wife Ludmila."

"She had her moments, Jan Antonovich," was all I could respond. I'd forgotten how oppressive bureaucracy could be in the Union of Soviet Socialist Republics.

"I should hope so, Rusty. Otherwise your blushes would be wasted," Berzin laughed loudly. "On Irene Wiedemeyer, too, I understand." He was enjoying my discomfort. A good sign.

"But let's not get waylaid by your modesty. During your assignment in Shanghai, you were also encouraged to study Chinese agriculture and industry, which you did with a useful analysis of tensions arising from the landlord-peasant system of land tenure."

"If I may offer an opinion, Jan Antonovich?"

"Of course, go ahead."

"I left it out of my report because I regard the observation as bordering on the heretical in terms of communist dogma."

"Tell me more, Rusty." He was no longer quite so relaxed, but I ploughed on anyway.

"The tensions you mentioned suggest that the communist

movement in China will probably be achieved through the rural peasantry rather than through the activities of an industrial proletariat as in the Soviet Union."

"But there *is* an urban proletariat in China."

"Yes, Comrade General, but only in cities like Shanghai and Canton."

"Anyway, all the peasant does is follow. Either the worker or the bourgeois. But he *follows*, Comrade Ruskin."

The way Berzin addressed me revealed that I was in dangerous territory again. Like going behind Japanese and Chinese lines with Joao.

"True, Comrade General. The question then becomes: *who* does he follow? More than ninety per cent of the population of China consists of rural peasants. This makes me tend to agree with the Chinese communist leader, Mao Tse-tung, that the revolution will be born and prosper in the countryside."

"So long as it is led from the countryside, you mean, and not from the city?"

"Precisely. This is Mao's intention, I believe."

"So what you're suggesting, Rusty," the General indicated a way back from the minefield into which I'd strayed, "Is that we should support Mao Tse-tung, and not Chiang Kai-shek?"

"It makes sense, Comrade General."

"Hmm. I see what you mean about holding potentially heretical views," Berzin looked at me hard. "But what you say is certainly of interest. We will need to discuss it further at a later date."

There was a good half minute during which neither of us said anything. A fly buzzed ineffectively against a window pane behind me, as the General tapped his fingers on the desk top.

"Now then, where were we?" he asked finally. "Ah, yes! Your assignment. If you failed to carry out one part or another of your far-reaching—and, let's face it, somewhat vaguely formulated—mission, Rusty, you have more than compensated for this in other ways. I am referring, of course, to your endeavours regarding the kidnapping of the nephew of Sir Victor Sassoon and to your extremely useful information regarding the supply of German armaments to Chiang Kai-shek. All this in addition to your first-hand involvement in the recent hostilities between the Japanese Navy and the Chinese 19th Route Army, at what was, I am sure, great personal risk to yourself."

"And to my journalist colleague, Joao Sereño or Serino."

"Whom you managed to cultivate as a Japanese ally in turbulent times," the General paused, as if mulling over whether he should continue. Then, "I think you should be aware, Rusty, that Serino is already one of our assets."

"What!" I exclaimed, although not entirely surprised as the tone of my voice suggested. Joao had always seemed too good an ally to be true. "When did that happen?"

"About three and a half years ago now."

"Who recruited him?"

"Let's just say that Serino played a major part in the Tokyo Protocol affair, an extremely successful false flag operation that I assume you know all about."

"You discussed it at some length, Jan Antonovich, during my orientation prior to my being assigned to Shanghai," I reminded him gently. "You never told me who ran that operation, however."

"No? Well, it's what we call 'ears only,' isn't it? Anyway, the relationship that you've developed with Serino is most impressive. My congratulations."

Berzin leant back in his chair, his look one of satisfaction that a man he had personally recruited as an agent had performed his task in such a manner as to reflect creditably on himself as Director of the Fourth Department.

"And then, of course, there are those photographs that you brought back with you from Tokyo. What can I say other than 'absolutely phenomenal'? You cannot imagine how happy you've made one or two comrades around me. Let's face it. To provide evidence that enables us to blackmail one national government is hard enough. But two? That, in my experience, is unheard of."

"Thank you, Jan Antonovich."

"What I have said so far, Rusty, hopefully informs you of the result of the deliberations of the three gentlemen who interviewed you three days ago." He smiled, before leaning forward, putting his head in his hands and gazing at me intently. "And now to the future," he continued. "In spite of these successes, here in Moscow we recognize that the work that you have been doing in Shanghai remains unfinished. We are of the opinion that it is there that the Japanese will strike next and we need to have people on the ground to advise and warn us as necessary. For this reason, we think it best if you return to Shanghai for the time being."

"It will be my pleasure, Comrade General. And an honour."

"Good. We have established that, in spite of everything in which you were involved during the May 15th Incident in Tokyo, there is no *kompromat*. Your cover has not been blown or compromised in any way. People still believe that you are a Swedish journalist with a nose for a scoop who writes for the prestigious *Frankfurter Zeitung*. Some are in awe of your inherited title; others impressed by your membership of the National Socialist German Workers' Party; yet others envious of your ability to attract members of the opposite sex. So, go back to the life you were leading in Shanghai. Get closer to Major von Holst while he is posted there, and maybe to his wife. Or, better, to one of her charming *hausfrau* friends whose husband is involved in German business opportunities with the Chinese. Understood?"

Trudi beckoned.

"Understood Comrade General."

"One person who will no longer be with you, though, is Irene Wiedemeyer. The Department has decided to reassign her and her sister to Berlin."

"Berlin?"

"We think it makes sense. They are German nationals, remember, and we need people on the ground to cultivate informants among the Nazis and relay what they learn back to us. Both sisters are eminently suited to such a task," Berzin smiled. "In their different ways, of course."

"Of course, Comrade General."

Always the interests of the state before those of the individual. I would probably never see Isa again. A part of me felt empty over losing her.

"And don't forget to cultivate Sir Victor Sassoon and his friends. His network could prove useful."

It was time for me to answer as expected of a junior agent in the presence of his superior officer.

"I will endeavour to complete whatever mission the Comrade General assigns me to the full satisfaction of both yourself and the Fourth Department."

"Good. I'm glad that's settled." Berzin pressed a buzzer under his desk and the door to the office was opened by the general's aide. I rose to go.

"No, Rusty. Not yet. Sit yourself down. There's still one matter remaining to be discussed and for this I have requested that we be joined by a colleague, Comrade Borodin."

Right on cue, a man in his late forties, with high forehead, wavy dark brown hair and high-bridged nose came into the room. I recognized him at once even though I'd seen only half his face in the photograph Victor had taken eleven years previously. Mikhail Borodin had aged well.

"Comrade Ruskin," he extended a welcoming hand as I rose to greet the newcomer. "It is a pleasure, a great pleasure to meet you."

He sat down in the other chair diagonally facing Berzin's massive desk.

"I believe, Ruskin, that you have already made the acquaintance of Mikhail Markovich in a certain photograph?" the general enquired with a sly smile, as always keeping my identity secret.

"Indeed, Jan Antonovich. Comrade Borodin was that evening employed as a waiter in a London night club, if I'm not mistaken."

Borodin chuckled.

"A job for which I wasn't particularly qualified, but which I was obliged to do under the circumstances. As you have discovered for yourself in recent months, Comrade Ruskin, an agent gets called upon to be a Jack of all trades in the expectation that he or she can master them all."

"A weighty expectation in my own experience."

"Indeed. Unfortunately I was still relatively inexperienced back in 1921 and made an unfortunate mistake—one that threatened an otherwise brilliant operation devised by Comrade General Berzin when he was Deputy Head of the Diplomatic Mission in the UK. I am here to thank you for helping erase that mistake from history."

"I would like to say 'I see' at this point," I replied, "but I'm afraid I don't. Perhaps you would be kind enough to clarify things for me, Comrades?"

"Of course, Ruskin," Berzin said smoothly. "That is why I asked Mikhail Markovich to join us. We thought you should be made aware of certain details underlying the events that led to your successful acquisition of what here in Moscow we have called the 'Court Jester photos.'"

"Allow me to take you back, Comrade Ruskin," Borodin took over, "to an evening that you spent with an informant in a Russian bar on the Avenue Joffre."

"You are referring to the evening when Sir Victor Sassoon's nephew, Simon Meyer, was kidnapped?"

"Precisely," Borodin affirmed. "Now that you have come back to Moscow, you are probably able to disengage from the minutiae of everyday life in Shanghai, and so have occasion to reflect on the events that took place there. I've always found that time and distance help clarify confusions. Wouldn't you agree?"

"Yes, certainly, Comrade Borodin."

"During the course of your ruminations during this pleasant Russian summer, therefore, you might have asked yourself whether it was luck or coincidence that led you to witness the kidnapping of Sir Victor Sassoon's nephew."

"Ah!" was the best I could respond. I had a sickening feeling deep down inside that I had been played. Every agent's nightmare.

Borodin was sensitive enough to overlook my discomfort.

"Let's face it, Comrade Ruskin, you were, so far as is known, the one and only foreign witness to the incident that led to Japan's invasion of Manchuria. For your report regarding this, Josef Vissarionovich and the Soviet Union are, of course, extremely grateful. But it does suggest that Lady Luck was on your side. Agreed?"

"Most certainly, Comrade Borodin."

"It would be logical to conclude, therefore, that she was once more at your side when you happened to witness Simon Meyer being kidnapped in the French Concession. Quite a coincidence, if you stop to consider it."

I recalled Lolly Lo's story about the man whose wife was found drowned in the bath and hoped I wasn't heading for execution. One never knew these days.

Berzin took over.

"The harsh reality, Ruskin, is that it was neither luck nor coincidence."

"Meaning?" My voice was far from steady as I began to discern a totally new take on everything that had happened while I was in Shanghai.

"Meaning that young Meyer's kidnapping was engineered."

"Engineered? By whom?"

Borodin looked at Berzin enquiringly.

"By Chiang Kai-shek's Director of Internal Affairs, Su Bai-li. Assisted by us, of course."

"You mean, Bai-li *is* a member of the Chinese Communist Party? I must say, I wondered. He intimated as much when we met."

"And a very committed member, too," the General said. "I think I can safely say he is one of the Comintern's more successful operatives, planted many years ago in the early days of the Chinese Communist Party here in Moscow. His close relationship with Chiang Kai-shek during their student days has been most—how shall I put it?—most productive."

"And the kidnappers? Were they really Russian?"

"All except their leader, who was a Korean ne'er do well." It was Borodin's turn to fill in the gaps. "As you know, Comrade Ruskin, westerners tend to have trouble telling the difference between Koreans and Japanese. This worked in our favour. Bai-li gave him the name of Fujii and made sure he was armed with a Japanese pistol."

"Leading me to think the kidnappers were in fact Japanese."

"Not just any old Japanese, Ruskin, but a group of ultranationalists called the League of Blood."

"Blonsky!" I blurted out.

Borodin and Berzin looked at me nonplussed.

"Blonsky was a Russian ricksha wallah who said that one of the kidnappers had a tattoo of a Chinese character signifying 'blood.' That's what got us looking into the so-called Blood Brotherhood."

Borodin smiled. "Whatever you say, Comrade Ruskin. We weren't made privy to all the detail, you understand? Our interest was in the bigger picture."

He crossed one leg over the other. His socks were regulation brown.

"Unfortunately, however, Bai-li hadn't taken Tu Yue-sheng into account. He had his gang members searching all over Japan Town, as you know, and one of them learned that young Meyer was being held in a Japanese temple nearby. Tu couldn't resist the chance to make a bit more money —"

"So he re-kidnapped Victor's nephew and held him to ransom."

"Which upset Bai-li's plan to have you find Sir Victor's nephew and so ingratiate yourself with the property tycoon. Fortunately, though, you had your own solution to that difficulty and in the end all turned out well."

Apart from Maisy. Mei-si, the Queen of Smiles.

"But what was the point of his rousing my interest in the rōnin when they weren't involved at all in the kidnapping?"

"Bai-li had learned from a well-placed informant that their leader was also interested in Sir Victor Sassoon. He just didn't know who or why. He hoped that somehow you might find out."

"Which you did."

"It's reassuring at least to know that Comrade Su was as perplexed as I was," I smiled and had to ask the next question, even though I already knew the answer. "But why the subterfuge, Comrade General?"

"Because of the Frolics photos."

"You mean, you planned everything in such a way that I would meet Sir Victor Sassoon and find out about the photographs' existence? And then get hold of them somehow?"

"Precisely. Which is what, as journalist and well-trained agent, you did. For this, once again, the Soviet Union is most grateful to you." Berzin gave me an almost fatherly smile. "Of course, there's always an element of chance in such activities—unexpected chance that can facilitate or impede their outcome. In this respect, you were—dare I say it?—lucky."

"You're referring to Kiki Montagu-Rose?"

"Exactly. We had no idea that Mrs Montagu-Rose would be heading for Shanghai when we devised our plan. Nor did we dare to imagine that you would come across her so soon after your arrival or, indeed, that she would take to you in the way that she did. Without her you would never have managed to meet Sir Victor so promptly. Moreover, because of his infatuation for her, Sir Victor was prepared to take you into his confidence rather more speedily than might otherwise have been the case."

Borodin took over again.

"In his report following a conversation with you over dinner in what I gather is a rather exclusive and high-class Shanghai brothel, Roger Buckley wrote how pleased he was with—how shall I put it?—

developments that were taking place between you and Mrs Montagu-Rose."

Another bombshell. Maybe I should check the cushion I was sitting on.

"So, what you're saying is —"

More 'need to know'?

"Buckley works for us, as well as for the British. And what we're also saying, Comrade Ruskin, is that General Berzin and I engineered that evening of debauchery involving Crown Prince Hirohito of Japan, together with the Prince of Wales and his younger homosexual brother, Prince George, at the Frolics Club off Regent Street in London. We supplied the two 'Scandinavian' women, one of whom—Comrade Yulia—you have since recognised as Gerda Wiedemeyer, complete with blonde wig, and instructed them to supply Hirohito with enough alcohol to get rid of all his inhibitions and accept the advances of a foreign woman."

"But didn't you arrange for your own photographs of the event to be taken?"

"Ah!" Borodin smiled wryly. "We now come back to my comment about being a Jack of all trades."

"And, unfortunately, not master of one particular trade in this instance," Berzin added with a laugh. "At least, not then."

"Now we can all laugh," Borodin said sheepishly, "but we couldn't before you managed to get hold of the one visual record of that raucous evening. Of course, we knew that Sir Victor Sassoon would be present at the gathering and that he always carried a camera with him. We were also aware of his fondness for photographing women in various states of undress. So we were fairly certain that he would record what went on."

"As you have surmised, Comrade Ruskin, we also had our own agent, a certain Mikhail Markovich Borodin, posing as a waiter. He was supposed to take pictures himself of what went on with his mini-camera. Alas! His inexperience meant that the film, once developed, was useless."

"Fortunately, Sir Victor's photos were of much better quality. The only trouble was that, just when the amateur photographer took his snap, a waiter—namely myself—happened to walk into the frame. At least, I was fairly certain my face could be seen behind the Prince of Wales and his girlfriend."

"Only half of it," I said. "The tray you were holding provided quite good camouflage."

"Yes, but not enough. The whole point of our getting hold of the photograph has been to enable us to blur the waiter's face so that it would be unrecognizable."

"Thereby enabling you to blackmail both British and Japanese governments without fear of their realising that the Soviet Union is somehow involved."

Soviet squeeze.

"Hopefully, an embarrassment to both countries that will be to our advantage when the time comes."

"An embarrassment compounded for the British by the fact that, as we now know through your good offices, the almost totally undressed woman who has been the constant companion of a British prince of the realm is an asset for Nazi Germany."

"But couldn't you have found a way to get hold of the image earlier? I mean, it's been more than ten years since the photos were taken."

"And don't we know it, Ruskin." It was Berzin's turn to give me the benefit of a wry smile.

"The trouble was," Borodin took over, "I myself was very soon after apprehended by the British police for aiding and abetting communist gatherings in Glasgow, and deported after serving a year in one of His Majesty's prisons. As you probably know, Sir Victor's father died a year or two later and the new baronet moved to Bombay. Then, just as we thought we had found a way of getting hold of the photograph in Bombay, Sir Victor decided to move himself and his business lock, stock and barrel to Shanghai. That's where you came in."

"You have done us all a great service, Ruskin," Berzin was reassuring. "And I am recommending to Stalin that you be awarded the Order of Lenin, although whether Joseph Vissarionovich will agree is another matter entirely. Much will depend on his mood that particular day."

I mumbled my thanks. Borodin stood up.

"I think, Comrade General, that I have now fulfilled the purpose of my visit. I will, therefore, respectfully take my leave." He turned to me. "It was a pleasure meeting you Comrade Ruskin. I look forward to hearing about your further exploits on behalf of our country. In the meantime, give my regards to Madame Sun Yat-sen when you meet her."

He shook my hand firmly.

"Am I likely to?"

"Almost certainly," Borodin smiled behind his bushy moustache. "Su Bai-li will make sure of that."

After he had left the room, Berzin looked at me hard.

"I'm sorry if you feel we deluded you, Rusty. But your mission—your real mission—had to be kept secret. Only Mikhail Markovich and I knew about it, apart from Su Bai-li, of course."

I bowed my head in deference. Berzin continued.

"You should get to know Bai-li when you return to Shanghai.

An unassuming but quite remarkable and devoted comrade. He will be there to help when help is needed. Remember that."

"Thank you, Jan Antonovich."

"As I said, we've decided you should return to Shanghai for now. That will be your base. But we'd also like you to spend time in Manchuria. Our Siberian border is threatened and Stalin needs to know how best to counter this threat. You should probably pay a visit, therefore, before winter sets in."

"Yes, Comrade General."

"In that regard, you may wish to approach Yoshiko Kawashima for assistance."

"Yoshiko Kawashima?" I repeated, a little non-plussed. "The Manchu princess, you mean?"

"Also known as Aisin-Gioro Hsien-yü. Our information suggests that she may be playing a double game with the Japanese when it comes to affairs in Manchuria."

"I will keep that in mind, Comrade General."

"Do that, Rusty," Berzin allowed himself a chuckle. "By the way, I understand that prostitution in Harbin has given rise to venereal diseases of epidemic proportions. I wouldn't want my most able agent to fall foul of the White Russian women there. So be careful when you start screwing around. Even if it is with a Manchu princess."

"I will indeed, Comrade General."

"And then there's Mr Sereño, or Serino, or whatever *his* name is."

"I think of him as Serino now that he has returned to Tokyo."

"Serino it is, then. Keep in touch with him as best you can. We believe he will continue to be a useful asset," Berzin paused. Then, "By the way, how did you like Tokyo?"

That came out of the summer blue.

"It wasn't bad," I said honestly, as I thought about our stay in the Imperial Hotel. Isa and I had enjoyed ourselves, in spite of the stress involved in getting hold of the Frolics photos.

"So you wouldn't mind being assigned there?"

"To Tokyo?" I was incredulous. "But, surely, it's impossible to work there. I'm comparatively tall, my hair is fair, my eyes blue. I'd stick out like a sore thumb among the Japanese."

"A weakness that can be turned into a strength, perhaps?"

"I'm not sure how, Jan Antonovich."

"No. Well, it's early days yet." Berzin patted his pockets and brought out a pack of cigarettes—a sign that our talk was at an end. Although he enjoyed smoking, he rarely did so in the company of others. At least, not in his office.

"Anyway cultivate your German friends, Rusty. They tend to get transferred from Shanghai to Tokyo in our experience. In which case, it may make sense for you to be assigned there, too. Just imagine! You could become the undercover agent of the century."

Except nobody would know who I was. Such was the nature of espionage.

Incognito ergo sum.

Author's Note

This work of fiction makes use of a number of facts to achieve its ends—notably the so-called 'Shanghai Incident,' when Japanese naval troops attacked the Chinese part of Shanghai in January 1932, and the planned assassination of the Prime Minister of Japan, Tsuyoshi Inukai, and his celebrity dinner guest, Mr Charles Spenser Chaplin, on May 15, 1932.

I have relied heavily on the work of two journalists when writing about these events. In *Far Eastern Front* (Jarrolds Publishers, 1934), Edgar Snow recounts his experiences in Shanghai in the weeks leading up to and during the Japanese attack on the Chinese. Hugh Byas, a British journalist working as foreign correspondent in Tokyo, gives a detailed account in *Government by Assassination* (Routledge, 1943) of a group of young ultranationalist officers entering the Prime Minister's residence in Tokyo one Sunday afternoon, then searching for, finding, and shooting Tsuyoshi Inukai, who was 75 years-old at the time. Extracts from this account I have quoted virtually *verbatim* under his name at the end of the penultimate chapter of this novel.

Other books I found very useful were Percy Finch's *Shanghai and Beyond* (Charles Scribner's Sons, 1953) and *Shanghai: The Rise and Fall of a Decadent City*, by Stella Dong (William Morrow, 2000). In *Shanghai Saga* (Earnshaw Books, 2022; first published in 1963), John Pal—the pen name used by Alan Palamountain describes in detail his life as a customs officer and the goings-on in Shanghai's river docks in the 1920s. He unwittingly provided me with the inspiration for Freddy Fox.

Several websites about old Shanghai have also proved to be helpful sources of information. First and foremost is Andrew David Field's *Shanghai Sojourns* (https://shanghaisojourns.net/). Others include *that's China* (https://www.thatsmags.com/china) and *History of Shanghai: Foreigners, Concessions and Decadence* (https://factsanddetails.com/china/cat15/sub95/entry-6460.html#chapter-4). The writings of Paul French, as always, have been extremely illuminating (see, for example, his *China rhyming* website, http://www.chinarhyming.com/page/2/). I thank all those concerned for making their findings public.

Readers will almost certainly recognize several characters who appear in *Shanghai Squeeze*: Sir Victor Sassoon, for one; Tu Yue-sheng, for another. And then there is Charlie Chaplin himself, and Inukai father and son. There is also Kenji Doihara, master spy and Japanese military police general, who was carrying out a considerable amount of deception in Manchukuo, not Shanghai, during the period covered in *Shanghai Squeeze*. He is also said to have taken photographs of his 15-year-old cousin in the nude and offered them to one of Japan's imperial princes, who immediately made her his concubine. So far as I am aware, she was not called Miyoko Noguchi.

Hirohito, Crown Prince of Japan and later its Emperor, did pay a state visit to the United Kingdom and Europe in 1921. Soon after his arrival, King George V apparently walked into Hirohito's bedroom and lectured him in his pyjamas on constitutional monarchy—a subject to which the future Emperor of Japan probably should have paid more heed. The King's son, Edward Prince of Wales, looked after the young Japanese prince during his stay and, among other things, took him to play golf one afternoon. So far as I know, nothing untoward, of the kind described by Sir Victor Sassoon and Mikhail Borodin, occurred that same evening.

For the record, however, I should point out that there really was a night club called Frolics, located just off Regent Street in London in the early 1920s, and that it was the favourite nocturnal haunt of female Soviet spies whose job was to attract men of good standing into a honey trap and/or recruit them to the Communist cause.

Edward's younger brother, George, was the fourth son of King George V and Queen Mary. Handsome and glamorous, he had to be weaned off an addiction to morphine and cocaine by Edward. He was also rumoured to have been bisexual and to have had love affairs with, among others, Noel Coward and Anthony Blunt. He died mysteriously in a plane crash in 1941. At the time of events related in *Shanghai Squeeze*, George was touring South America with the Prince of Wales, so could not have made a fleeting appearance in Tokyo in the company of Kiki Montagu-Rose at the end of the book, or hooked up with a fictitious Imperial Prince called Tadahito.

There's something else I should probably clarify for the sake of all royalists. While Nisshō Inoue, the 'Shining One,' was indeed the leader of the so-called Ketsumeidan, or League of Blood, he came from a poor, rural background and was in no way associated with any member of the Japanese Imperial family, fictitious or real. His second-in-command, Lieutenant-Commander Hitoshi Fujii, *was* ordered to the battlefront in Shanghai where he was killed during the hostilities described, but certainly not by the hand of 'Chunky' Pan Chan-ki who is a product of my imagination.

Remarkably, members of the Ketsumeidan *did* intend to assassinate Charlie Chaplin during dinner with the Prime Minister of Japan. Their motive is obscure, but seems to have arisen from a conviction that Chaplin's death would encourage the United States to declare war on, and then be defeated by, Japan—a conviction as deranged as the numerous assertions made by Donald Trump and other attention-seekers on social media. That Chaplin was not assassinated was indeed due to his unanticipated fascination with *sumō* wrestling, which he was watching that fateful afternoon with the Prime Minister's son, Ken Inukai. As a result, he was late for his dinner appointment and the United States had no immediate reason to declare war on Japan—certainly not because of the murder in Tokyo of a London-born Hollywood actor.

Other known and less well-known real-life figures also make an appearance. Percy Finch writes about Gracie Gale and her high-end whorehouse at number 52 The Line, on Kiangse Road, where she really did employ a chef called Fat Lu. Amongst her 'girls' were Singapore Kate, Lotus, and Belle, as well as Big Annie, who enjoyed knitting when not in bed with one or another of Gracie's well-heeled clients.

Then there are the Wiedemeyer sisters, who did nothing more sinister than run the Zeitgeist Bookstore at 130 North Soochow Road; and 'Lolly' Lo Li-kwei who really was a Chinese detective, although all I learned about him was his name. Much more is known about General Jan Antonovich Berzin, chief and virtual founder of the Fourth Department (Intelligence) of the Red Army, and Mikhail Markovich Borodin, who served as an agent of the Comintern in China from 1923 to 1927, and who may, or may not, have been posing as 'Mr Brown' in England in 1921 at the time Crown Prince Hirohito paid his state visit.

The rest of the supporting cast in *Shanghai Squeeze* are, I believe, more or less figments of my imagination, although the story involving pianist Simon Meyer's kidnapping and Freddy Fox's cut-off finger bears a passing (though less tragic) resemblance to that of Simon Kaspé, an accomplished Russian Jewish pianist visiting Harbin, who was kidnapped, ransomed, tortured, and eventually murdered by a gang of fascist criminals a year later in 1933.

I have done my best to portray my real-life characters as they were in their real lives. Sir Victor Sassoon did indeed sport a monocle, have a penchant for trout curry, take photographs of young (and not so young) women wearing few or no clothes, and walk around with the help of sticks because of a flying accident that crippled him for life. He lived in a penthouse at the top of the Cathay (later Peace) Hotel. For his part, Tu Yue-sheng worked out of the Hotel Donghu on Route Doumer, from which he would venture out in a bullet-proof car, protected by gun-toting Russian thugs. His face pockmarked from the ravages of opium, and sporting very long fingernails, he presented Chiang Kai-shek with a Junkers 87 on the latter's birthday, and proceeded to emblazon it with the Board of Opium Suppression Bureau logo.

Kiki Montagu-Rose's account of how she learned to 'make a matchstick feel like a Havana cigar,' as well as other sexual techniques when obliged to accompany her husband to brothels, is based on salacious rumour concerning Mrs Wallis Simpson, later the wife of King Edward VIII. This is the kind of gossip that appeals to a writer of fiction more than it adheres to actual fact.

In general, I have resorted to considerable inventiveness when portraying my real-life characters. So far as I am aware, for example, Irene Wiedemeyer was not a *ninja* assassin in her spare time, although she almost certainly worked in some capacity for the Comintern, and Sir Victor did not take a photograph of the Crown Prince of Japan in *déshabillé*—something his guardians in the Imperial Household would never have tolerated of their future emperor.

The rest, of course, just has to be true.